ISHTAR C(

Mahir Salih

To Jane

Mahir Salih

ISHTAR COMING

ISBN:

CONTENTS

Prologue
1. Rendezvous in Baghdad
2. Abu Nuwas
3. Sunbathing at the Alwiyah Club
4. The garden party
5. A few close friends
6. The reunion
7. Tomorrow's another day
8. The love nest
9. Lost in London
10. Friend to the rescue
11. Girls' night out
12. A twist of fate
13. A very important party
14. Consummation
15. Betrayal
16. Discovered
17. Back to Baghdad
18. A patriotic duty
19. The proposition
20. An unwelcome visitor
21. Honey trap
22. Bilal
23. Breaking point
24. Rashid Street
25. Intelligence HQ
26. Pawns in a game
27. News of an arrest
28. Interrogation
29. Tears at bedtime
30. Abu Ghraib
31. A romantic dinner

32. A prison visit
33. Friends in high places
34. Clutching at straws
35. Condolences
36. Birthday bash
37. Like a bird

Prologue

In a garden in Baghdad's Adhamiyah district, two middle-aged ladies sit chatting over a cold beer. The thermometer has hit 45 degrees Celsius, melting the tarmac on roads across the capital. But here in the garden, a breeze from the nearby River Tigris offers some respite from the summer heat – if not from the heated emotions at play.

The conversation soon escalates to an argument, culminating in open confrontation. Blame and accusations are hurled in both directions. Among the dominant words are 'love', 'betrayal', 'sex', 'infidelity' – and several swear words.

The older of the two women stands up and throws her aluminium garden chair to the ground. The younger woman reciprocates the action, although with some caution. Moments later, they are actually fighting, scratching with their long nails and biting at skin.

These two women have abandoned all reason, falling back on raw emotion. The physical wounds may heal, but the emotional scars will last a lifetime.

This is not the first time two women in their social circle have gone from polite chit-chat to open combat – and it will not be the last.

Rendezvous in Baghdad

The Adhamiyah district of Baghdad was once a rural suburb, comprised of farms providing Baghdad with vegetables and fruit, including dates from the abundant palm trees. Farmers drew their water from the Tigris, which marked the district's western border. During the British occupation of Iraq after World War I, the area became home to affluent Iraqi families who built attractive mansions. By the 1980s, it had been incorporated into the city proper. However, it remained wonderfully peaceful, even as war raged between Iraq and Iran from 1980 to 1988, with the nearest fighting just 70 kilometers away.

Many of those residing in Adhamiyah during the 1980s had made their money during the oil boom of the previous decade. Now they owned fancy foreign-brand cars, including Volkswagens and Chevrolets that had been assembled locally as part of the country's improved relations with the USA. Some of the big businessmen would drive the latest models of Mercedes-Benz, as would those with good positions in Saddam Hussein's entourage. Members of the nation's elite, including Saddam's troubled sons Uday and Qusay, would often drive BMWs.

The oil boom had also brought other riches: people wore designer clothes from French brands like Chanel, Yves Saint Laurent and Cacharel. Many women from affluent backgrounds would shop for dresses in London's Oxford Street, flashing their cash at posh department stores like Selfridges or the more affordable Marks & Spencer. Due to its connection with Israel, however, the latter chain was banned by the Iraqi authorities, so shoppers returning to Baghdad airport would conceal their purchases as they passed through customs.

The less affluent residents were unable to shop in London, but they would find other means of looking chic and modern. Many relied on local designers and tailors, including ladies with the skills to produce copies of dresses featured in Western magazines, such as the highly popular German publication *Burda*.

Middle Eastern women, and particularly those from Iraq, loved to look elegant, dressing immaculately whenever possible. Such sayings as 'appearances are deceptive' meant nothing to them. A young woman could happily spend a whole month's salary on a dress.

In the more traditional areas of Baghdad, during the 1980s, one could see a very obvious distinction between the younger and older generations. Some younger women had started to wear Western clothes. The older women, meanwhile, would often wear the same long, black dresses worn by previous generations; if they wore Western clothes outside of the house, they would be covered by a full-length black *abaya*. The same distinctions could be seen outside of the capital too, even in small villages.

Since the end of World War II, women had increasingly been permitted to do jobs traditionally reserved for men, and this trend increased during the war with Iran, when so many men were needed for military service. Women were allowed to travel abroad, but under Saddam's iron-fist regime, young men were forbidden from leaving the country. The president was determined to ensure there were no obstacles to Iraq's victory over Iran, which he pursued with the aid of the West.

He established a system of oppression designed to ensure that no opposition to his rule could prevail. Paranoia was rife in Iraq, and anyone suspected of political subversion was at risk of imprisonment and torture. On the other hand, the authorities allowed the Baghdadis a huge degree of social freedom; the booze flowed freely at bars, restaurants and house parties. Of course, this was not particularly strange for Baghdad, which was famous for its beer-halls in ancient times.

* * *

Our story begins in the early 1980s, in the grounds of a luxurious mansion in Sabah Street in the Adhamiyah district. It was home to Selma, a tall, slim woman with a confident stride and a personality to match. At six feet tall and endowed with natural beauty, she was an impressive figure. This evening, as she left the house and marched down the garden path, she looked much younger than her 48 years, which was a good thing, because her true age was a closely guarded secret – more closely guarded than the location of Saddam's stores of US-supplied chemical weapons.

Tonight, she would be dining with friends, and she was dressed to kill. Her smart, new outfit had been created by the famous Iraqi designers Suha Al-Bakry and Nuha Al-Razi, big names in haute couture. Consisting of a short skirt and a jacket with padded shoulders, it epitomized the power-dressing style of the period. Her high-heeled shoes were shiny and white, topped off with little lace bows. She wore a false-pearl necklace and colourful wooden earrings. Her hair had been done specially: curled, waved, teased and fluffed up in the 'big hair' fashion.

Nodding at the doorman, she passed through the iron gates and into the street, her hips swaying from side to side like a super-model. There was a swagger in her walk, a sense of pride. She click-clacked along the pavement a short way, stopping by a shiny, blue Volkswagen saloon.

The June sun was still high in the sky, and Selma put on her sunglasses, throwing her green eyes into shade. She was more concerned, though, about her heavy make-up, which had a tendency to melt in the heat and sweat. She heaved a sigh of frustration and looked at her watch.

Lagging slightly behind was her husband, Hassan. He was still putting on his tie as he shuffled down the garden path. He dropped the car keys and had to root around in a flower bed to find them. He was dressed to kill too, but he had somehow forgotten to tuck in his shirt at the back.

Hassan had not always been so dishevelled. He came from a rich old Baghdadi family and was once considered a Prince Charming, a prize catch, complete with wealth, charm and good looks. He and Selma had married following a passionate romance, and she was the envy of many girls in the middle-class neighbourhood of old Baghdad where she had grown up. Selma was the third of four children: one boy and three girls. Her father was a merchant with a modest income, making her origins relatively humble compared to Hassan's. Selma's mother, meanwhile, was a submissive housewife, whose main concern was to look after her family and to obey her husband.

Despite the general improvements in the position of women during the previous decades, Selma had failed to make the most of her opportunities. Due largely to the distractions of love and gossip, she had failed to complete high school, an essential step for any respectable middle-class girl in the 1950s. Educated or not, the adult Selma had convinced herself that she was rather cultured. She was always ready to share the fact that she knew several languages and had travelled abroad.

She was also fearlessly outspoken, always gossiping and undermining both friends and neighbours. Nobody was spared from her icy tongue and wicked sense of humour. In her trademark theatrical manner, she would mock public figures and media personalities – even daring to criticise the regime.

She was an astute observer of human nature, with an impressive ability to interpret other people's states of mind, although she rivalled Freud when it came to sexualising the actions of those around her. She was particularly drawn to social taboos, taking every opportunity to discuss topics such as homosexuality and sex before marriage. By definition, taboos are not to be mentioned, but such rules did not seem to apply to Selma. Indeed, her open comments on the personal lives of others often exceeded the limits of polite society. At times, she would even fabricate the so-called 'facts'.

Selma's own personal life was far from perfect; despite appearances, life had not been particularly kind to her. At the beginning of her marriage, she was madly devoted to Hassan. They had enjoyed a lavish honeymoon in Europe, and the first few years had been very happy. Their relationship was based on love and an amazing sex life. He was the rich playboy who all the girls of Adhamiyah wished either to marry or to date. Endowed with natural beauty, Selma had won the big prize.

Then, after the birth of their second child, things started to go wrong. Under pressure from mounting business responsibilities, Hassan increasingly turned to booze. As a coping strategy, it was a total failure. He became sloppy with figures and paperwork, and missed numerous meetings. Late nights and hangovers became the norm, and pretty soon he was routinely losing out on business opportunities, to the detriment of his bank balance.

Selma felt disappointed and gradually lost respect for Hassan, whose alcoholism made life ever more tedious and complex. Realizing that his marriage was on the rocks, Hassan's desperation grew more intense, and the business finally slid out of control. The couple found themselves living off their savings, dipping ever deeper into the money he'd inherited from his family. What had once been a warm and loving relationship was now cold and distant.

As their children grew to adulthood, Selma found she had more and more time on her hands. She had always enjoyed socialising, but now there seemed to be acres of time to be filled each day. Before long she was expanding her social circle in all directions. Her unhappy marital situation cannot have been entirely a secret, for there was no lack of men ready to lavish her with compliments, and soon she found herself responding in kind.

The first betrayal was the hardest, but the others followed with relative ease. She had no intention of replacing Hassan, but she felt justified in enjoying intimacy wherever it was on offer. In a society where family was considered a sacred institution, with the husband and wife devoted to their children and extended family, there was no question of divorce. Husband and wife were expected at least to maintain the appearance of fidelity. They could have their separate lives – including the occasional affair – so long as it was all done with tact and discretion.

However, Selma soon approached a red line that was shocking even by her own standards. She found herself falling for Hassan's younger brother Ali, a married man with several children. She had had a crush on him when they were much younger, but now it was more serious. She was consumed by intense passion and sexual desire, and it was only her religious beliefs and rather fragile sense of right and wrong that stopped her throwing herself at the man.

One evening, events took a dramatic turn. Selma had been invited to a house party, and she had gladly accepted. She always felt most alive in the midst of a smoking, drinking, gossiping crowd. Indeed, it was her natural element. Added to which, on this particular occasion, she knew that Hassan would be busy elsewhere, leaving her free to dance and flirt as she wished.

All the previous day, she was consumed by the thought that Ali might be attending the party too. She was excited by the prospect of seeing him, but also anxious at the possibility that he might not be there.

Around mid-afternoon, she finally picked up the phone and dialled his number.

'Hello, Ali. It's Selma. How are you?'

'Selma, it's so nice to hear from you. I'm fine, thanks. And you?'

'I'm very well, thanks be to God. I'll be quick Ali, because I'm in a terrible rush. Are you going to the party tonight?'

'Which one?'

'Leila's party. It starts at eight o'clock.'

'Yes, I've been invited. I'll probably go. And you?'

'Yes, I'm going. I'm so glad you'll be there, Ali. You can keep an eye on me. I need a strong man to make sure I don't get into trouble.'

Ali laughed. He'd always enjoyed Selma's sense of humour. Others found her remarks too cutting at times, her sarcasm too thick. But to Ali, she was simply spirited and outspoken. He knew that, deep down, she was a good person.

'I'll be there, Selma. And don't worry. I'll keep you out of trouble.'

'Thank you, darling. I don't know what I'd do without you.'

'Eight o'clock then.'

'Eight o'clock.'

They hung up, and Selma found herself grinning from ear to ear.

She enjoyed herself wonderfully that night. Indeed, she was on top form, telling any number of jokes and spreading countless rumours. Then she spied Ali at the bar, refilling his glass – and she decided to pounce.

'Ali, my darling. I've been looking for you all evening.'

'Selma, wonderful to see you.'

They kissed on the cheeks and clinked glasses.

'How about some fresh air?' she said.

'Yes, some fresh air would be good.'

They were both a little drunk as they stepped onto the balcony. They lit cigarettes and blew the smoke into the night air. As Ali took a sip of his Martini, Selma felt a desperate urge to hug him, kiss him – and perhaps more. She linked her arm through his and leaned her head on his shoulder – a gesture that could be understood to mean any number of things, some of them quite innocent.

Her next gesture, however, could not be mistaken. She took his face in her hands, and looking deep into his eyes, leaned in for a kiss.

Ali looked momentarily shocked, backing away in silence. As he did so, he bumped into an item of balcony furniture, spilling his drink on his trousers.

'Woops!' he said. 'It seems I'm losing my balance – too much Martini. I'll have to slow down a bit. My next one's a lemonade.'

He took out a handkerchief and dabbed at his trousers. Selma took a step forward and thought of grabbing his hand, drawing him close. While she hesitated, Ali folded the handkerchief and returned it to his pocket. There was an awkward silence, and then he drained his glass and returned to the party.

Selma turned and looked into the night air, puffing furiously on her cigarette. On one level, she respected Ali for remaining loyal to his brother. On another level, however, she was hurt and deeply disappointed. Thus far in her life, no man had dared to reject her advances.

Returning home that night, she vowed to get her revenge. If she couldn't have Ali, then she would make sure that no other woman would either. As for the two brothers, she would shatter their treasured sense of loyalty beyond repair.

Abu Nuwas

Abu Nuwas Street followed the course of the Tigris through Baghdad, running down the eastern bank for several miles from Tahrir Square to the University of Baghdad. The street took its name from the great eighth-century poet who lived in the glory days of Baghdad, when it was the capital of a huge empire. Abu Nuwas was famous for his verses on various hedonistic pleasures, particularly wine, women and boys. Over a thousand years later, the street bearing his name was packed with cafes and restaurants – a setting in which the poet might have been quite comfortable.

Many of these venues sold fish caught from the river, including the bonnie, shabout and gattan. Fishermen were fortunate if they caught the bonnie, as it was the most desirable and expensive of the local fish. The Iraqi-Jewish singer Salima Mourad, who was famous in the 1920s, sang passionately about a fisherman who caught her some bonnie. The song had stood the test of time, and it was still drifting from the open-air cafes and restaurants at the height of Saddam's rule.

Abu Nuwas Street was abuzz with life and the clinking of glasses as a blue Volkswagen drew up to the kerb. The front door on the passenger side opened and two fine legs emerged, followed by the rest of an elegant, apparently sophisticated woman. It was Selma, dressed in her tight, white outfit, hair

17

puffed and teased to perfection. She stood on the pavement for a while, fussing over her cuffs and checking her watch as Hassan tried his best to park the car neatly against the kerb, shifting back and forth, apparently at random. He was already drunk, and anything more complex than driving in a straight line was proving difficult. In the end, Selma walked around to the driver's side and yanked him out of the vehicle. Jumping behind the wheel, she completed the parking process in two deft movements. She got out and slammed the door hard, dropping the keys safely into her handbag.

The happy couple headed to a prestigious outdoor restaurant named Al-Hamra (Arabic for 'red'), the décor of which was inspired by the Al-Hamra Palace in Granada, Southern Spain. Diners wishing to enjoy the warm evening air could sit at simple wooden tables on the freshly cut lawn by the river bank. As regular clients, Selma and Hassan never had trouble getting a table. They often gathered here with friends, allowing Selma to catch up on the gossip and show off her latest outfit.

As they passed through the gates, she turned to her husband, who lagged behind, scolding him for moving so slowly. As per usual, she made no effort to hide her bossy, domineering and dismissive attitude toward the father of her children. The waiter greeted them warmly and led them to a table; he smiled in admiration at Selma's glamour and beauty.

The restaurant specialized in fish, brought fresh from the river and grilled by an open fire, as per local tradition. The couple ordered: Selma would have the bonnie, while Hassan went for lamb. While they waited, they indulged in mezes: fattoush salad, cucumber, yoghurt and beans. They ate hummus too, washed down with arak, a potent spirit made from grapes and aniseed. While some people preferred the milder Zahlawi arak, produced in Lebanon, Selma and Hassan always drank the best Iraqi brand: Massaya.

Selma mixed her arak with water, a process that turned it milky white. As a dedicated heavy drinker, Hassan declined the water, settling for a triple measure on the rocks. He was a firm believer in the rule that any arak-related hangover could be evaded by combination with certain foods, such as lamb shank with rice and nuts (*khouzi*) or a boiled sheep's head (*pacha*).

At the other tables, middle-class Iraqis were showing off their cosmopolitan credentials – and their spare cash – by drinking imported wines and whiskeys. They'd picked up such ideas from the movies or while holidaying abroad.

Hassan and Selma consumed the mezes to the sound of traditional Arabic music and the hits of famous singers such as Umm Kulthum. This Egyptian star had mesmerised the Middle East with her soulful renditions from the 1930s to the 1970s.

There really was no better soundtrack to an evening of al-fresco dining by the banks of the Tigris.

The married couple had arrived early, so they weren't too surprised to find themselves alone at the long table in the centre of the lawn. Pretty soon, however, their friends began to arrive in dribs and drabs, exchanging the usual kisses and compliments on attire. They took their seats beside Hassan and Selma, gave their orders to the waiter, and launched into the important business of the evening: gossip.

Selma was once again in her element – exchanging rumours and issuing pronouncements on all manner of sacred, unmentionable topics. She speculated on who was cheating on their spouse, indulging in homosexuality, suffering from mental illness, and showing signs of alcoholism. She even accused others of being cruel and incorrigible gossips.

She knew very well that being implicated in any of the above actions – with the possible exception of being a gossip – could tarnish a family's reputation for generations to come. However, such considerations were no deterrent to Selma, who seemed to feel that the rules of common decency applied to everyone on Earth besides herself.

Of course, she was not alone in exhibiting double standards; such hypocrisy was not unknown in this relatively conservative society. However, these days she was really laying it on thick, racking her brains for slanderous comments worth uttering, disguised as always behind a heavy veil of friendly goodwill. What powered this current wave of loose talk was the disappointment and frustration she still felt from the collapse of her marriage, compounded by Ali's rejection of her advances. Her pain had been channelled along the path of least resistance, a path that promised instant returns.

As she started on a fresh glass of the milky liquid, she glimpsed a strangely familiar face in the crowd of new arrivals. It was a slender lady with light-brown skin, her hair dyed red. She was wearing a blue summer dress of cotton, most likely purchased on a trip to Europe. Selma eyed the garment enviously; if it was a Chanel or YSL design, then it was probably beyond her budget these days.

At such a distance, Selma couldn't quite place the woman, but she guessed that she was a few years younger – perhaps early 40s. She wore just a few accessories: wooden bracelets and gold earrings. There was a sense of elegance and style, and with the pretty, youthful face, it made for a great package.

As the woman approached through the crowd, Selma suddenly realized who she was looking at. It was Loma, a long-time rival – in terms of looks, popularity and much more besides. The new hair colour had been disorienting, as was the straight, shoulder-length bob. Loma's hair had always been chestnut brown, long and rather wavy. This new look must have cost an absolute bomb.

'What a coincidence!' Selma whispered to herself.

The two women had grown up in the same part of Adhamiya, and Loma's parents were now neighbours of Selma and Hassan in Sabah Street. Loma had qualified as a biology teacher, later marrying an ambitious up-and-coming politician who had benefited from joining the Ba'ath Party. The two women might easily have been friends, but Selma was naturally competitive; the more her own wealth leaked away, the more she resented Loma's success.

Moreover, there was an old feud that still smouldered. Selma had always considered Loma to be her main rival in winning Ali's heart. Long before Ali and Loma had married their respective partners, they had been lovers, although the romance had failed. Selma had always wondered whether the passion that had once existed between them lingered on, and whether they were ever tempted to act upon it. For all she knew, they might still be lovers.

Loma greeted some friends at a nearby table and took a seat. In the dim red lighting of the outdoor restaurant, she suddenly recognised Selma. She was not keen to meet her. Indeed, the idea of talking with her made her sick. She was aware of Selma's jealousy and her suspicions, and nothing was more likely to ruin her evening than to rake it all up in public.

She fixed her eyes on the table and unfolded her napkin, and as she did so, her breathing began to quicken. She could feel a wave of panic rising in her brain, spreading through her body. She closed her eyes and focused on her breathing, waiting for the feeling to pass.

Selma felt as if she had found the Holy Grail. She had never missed an opportunity to gather, process and synthesise information for the purposes of spreading gossip about her favourite victim. By now, she had a whole armoury of slanderous comments at her disposal. Tonight, with so many friends and strangers present – including Loma's husband – there was no limit to the harm that might be done.

As the evening drew on, the music became louder and a belly-dancer took to the floor, moving slowly between the tables. With her pink, two-piece chiffon dress and fleshy figure, she churned her belly and gyrated her hips. It was an impressive display, and the men found themselves repeatedly distracted from their conversations. The alcohol worked its magic, the voices became louder and the belly-dancer's ill-coordinated movements resulted in several bumped tables and spilled drinks.

By now, Selma had switched to vodka, downing several measures of liquid courage. She had spent much of the time thinking up a plan of action, and now she had one. She approached Loma's table, which was right by the water's edge, and began talking to Sulaf, a mutual friend from the same neighbourhood.

'Of course, you know Loma,' said Sulaf after a while.

Selma replied in a theatrical tone: 'Oh, my dear, I knew Loma long before I knew you.'

Loma turned and greeted Selma with an artificial smile. She could not hide her agitation. Even so, determined not to be intimidated, she rose from her seat and stepped closer.

'Hello, Selma. So nice to see you,' she said, exchanging kisses with her sworn enemy.

'Me too, darling. I am surprised to see you in Al-Hamra. I didn't know you were used to such places.'

It was an obvious put-down, a reference to Loma's modest family background.

'Things do change,' said Loma in a low voice. 'Actually, we have table permanently reserved for us. Let me know if you are ever desperate for one.'

'So very kind of you.'

'Not at all. I'm only glad to help. We may go on to the Alwiyah Club after dinner. Are you and Hassan members?'

'But of course! We've been members of years and years. But it has become a little shabby recently. They let anyone in these days.'

'Oh, I don't think they've ever been particularly selective, Selma. They let you in, after all.'

'Well, that's because my husband helped them out financially many years ago. They would have gone under if it weren't for Hassan's good advice.'

'How is the business side of things these days?'

'Very well indeed, thank you, Loma. Luckily, Hassan is able to get by without accepting favours from corrupt politicians. It's so important to maintain some sense of dignity, don't you think?'

'Oh, we have plenty of dignity, Selma. But thank you anyway.'

'Well, I'm very happy for you both. Of course, you've had to work for it, Loma. It's not easy to overcome the past, and I know you didn't have it easy before your marriage. Those are the rumours anyway. People can be so unkind. It only takes one vicious rumour to bring the whole thing crashing down.'

To Loma, this last comment was like a bomb going off. Her eyes widened and her jaw dropped. She thought for a moment that she might pounce on Selma and scratch her eyes out there and then. Instead, she stood motionless, tense, struck dumb.

Selma smiled and stood up, showing off her long legs. She said goodbye to Sulaf – who had been engrossed in watching the belly-dancer – and returned to her table.

Loma stood still, silently watching her attacker withdraw. The hurt and anger were so intense that felt she might burst into tears. She returned to her seat and tried to compose herself. She downed a tall glass of beer but felt no less emotional. Indeed, in her current state, drinking hardly seemed to be the solution. In the face of such humiliation, it seemed she had two options: fight or flight. With her reputation on the line, of course, open combat in a crowded restaurant was out of the question.

Loma looked around but couldn't see anyone in her group who might provide her with support. Her husband was busy flirting with the younger women; he didn't even recognize her presence. Then she spotted Madeha, her dearest friend, sitting at the far end of the table. She walked over and explained that she was feeling ill and would be going home early.

The two had been friends since high school and they had shared many a secret. Madeha was recently widowed, her husband killed in the war with Iran. He left her with two children, whom she supported by working as a school teacher, the meagre salary supplementing her war-widow's pension.

'I'm sorry to ask, but would you mind driving me home?'

'What about your husband?' said Madeha. 'Won't he take you?'

'I think he's busy.'

The two women looked over and saw the husband sitting with one arm around a young lady while he regaled his neighbours with yet another hilarious anecdote.

'Okay, let's go,' said Madeha, grabbing her things.

They walked towards Madeha's old Russian Lada with the headlights painted yellow, just one of many precautions required during wartime. Sometimes Loma missed the days of modesty and frugality. She enjoyed her Mercedes but thought at times that it was too flashy. And while it was nice to be chauffeured by her husband's driver, she really preferred the freedom of driving herself.

* * *

As they sped north along Abu Nuwas Street, Loma wound down the window and closed her eyes, savouring the fresh breeze on her face. She sucked in the cool air that blew in from the great river. Suddenly, she burst into tears. At first she cried quietly, but soon she was sobbing uncontrollably, her face cradled in her hands.

Madeha pulled up by the side of the road.

'What's the matter?' she said, handing over a tissue.

'I'm terrified of her.'

'Who do you mean, Selma?'

'Who else? She's a total bitch.'

'So what's new? We all know Selma pretty well.'

'You don't understand, Madeha. She could ruin me if she wanted to.'

'Ruin you how?'

'Regarding Ali.'

'What has she said?'

'Nothing very much, but she's dropping heavy hints. More like threats, actually.'

'Well, I doubt she'd ever say anything very blatant. After all, you know a few of her dirty secrets, I'm sure. You could retaliate if you wanted to. She knows that well enough.'

'Yes, but she's the sort who wouldn't care. She just wants to cause harm, at any cost.'

'Well, I doubt she'd have the guts. And anyway, the past is the past. We can't dwell on it, Loma. If we worried about the skeletons in the closet all the time, nobody would get any sleep.'

'But she could do so much damage with that big mouth of hers.'

'Possibly, Loma, but she hasn't. Not yet. And there's no point in anticipating terrible things that may never happen. You'll just make yourself ill for no reason.'

Loma looked out the window. She blew her nose and watched mournfully as the cars sped past. She wondered briefly where Ali was tonight. What was he up to? Was he alone?

'Let's go to the Sheraton to have a drink,' said Madeha. 'I haven't been there yet, but apparently the architecture is state-of-the art. We used to have a lot of fun in the old days, if you remember. Even the simplest pleasures put a smile on our faces. I think a few drinks in a pleasant environment should boost your spirits.'

'Yeah, okay. Let's do it.'

They took off again, the Lada weaving through traffic at high speed, navigating ever closer to the brand-new concrete structure that towered over its surroundings. They parked by the entrance, drawing a scowl from the doorman, who was used to dealing with more expensive cars. The women passed through the massive doors and climbed the marble stairs within. As they surveyed the expensive décor, the question uppermost in their minds was the location of the restaurant. Two women turning up in a hotel bar might find themselves in all sorts of trouble, but in a restaurant they could happily get drunk free from interference.

As they passed through the lobby, they were stopped in their tracks by a white marble statue on a plinth above a water feature. It was a curvaceous woman in a long dress, arms outstretched as if in welcome.

'Well, I suppose that's why they call it the Ishtar Sheraton,' said Madeha.

'Do they?'

'Yes, didn't you notice? It was in huge letters outside?'

'I must have been thinking of something else.'

Madeha was examining the statue carefully, walking slowly around it in a clockwise direction. Aside from being a biology teacher, she was a keen student of history, particularly the ancient history of the Middle East. If she hadn't majored in biology, she might easily have opted for life as an archaeologist, digging up the desert in search of past civilizations.

'Who is she then?' said Loma at last.

'Ishtar, the Babylonian goddess of love.'

'Well, she looks very friendly.'

'Don't be deceived, Loma. She was also the goddess of sex, fertility, war, chaos and a number of other things. Love was just her opening gambit. What followed was often a fate worse than death.'

'Charming.'

'Yes, quite. She caused all sorts of trouble by way of seduction, combined with her furious temper. She tried to seduce the warrior king Gilgamesh, for example, and got very angry when he turned her down. She unleashed the Bull of Heaven and … well, I forget the details, but it wasn't pretty.'

'Sounds quite a handful then.'

'Just a bit. She once descended into the Underworld, and underwent numerous trials, just so she could wrestle control from her sister, who happened to be the queen of the Underworld at the time.'

'Gosh, what a bitch!'

'Exactly, and she was so determined to succeed that she submitted to being slowly stripped naked, one garment at a time as she passed through the Seven Gates of Hell. To be honest, she was such a whore, so I don't think she really minded being stripped naked. She probably enjoyed it.'

'Well, it shows determination, if nothing else,' said Loma with wry a smile.

'It also reminds me of another, rather aggressive female figure in our close circle – someone with a very high opinion of herself. Although if she visited Hell, I'm quite sure they'd *beg* her to keep her clothes on. I bet she sags all over the place.'

'You're terrible!' exclaimed Loma, laughing.

'You see,' said Madeha, 'you're feeling better already. Let's get that drink.'

They walked briskly past the bar – which was populated mostly by chain-smoking businessmen – and entered the restaurant. The soft lighting and smooth jazz music made for a relaxed atmosphere. They sat down and ordered two glasses of gin fizz, munching on the free snacks. When the waiter handed them the food menus, they set them to one side.

'Perhaps later,' said Madeha.

'As you wish, madam.'

As they took their first gulps of gin fizz, the two friends sank into silence, nurturing their own thoughts.

To the outside world, Madeha seemed fully functional. However, she was still in shock at the sudden death of her beloved husband, Mohamed. Theirs had been a good marriage, one built on genuine love, and they had looked forward to growing old together. Now it was over.

She viewed the war with Iran as quite unnecessary and could find no justification for Mohamed's death. Certainly, she didn't believe that he would ascend to Paradise as a martyr, despite the claims of clerics and state-run propaganda outlets. She generally had no time for propaganda, and the idea of it intruding on her grief made her thoroughly sick.

It was Loma who broke the silence: 'You're looking sad.'

'Yes, well, don't we all?'

'Are you thinking of Mohamed?'

'I'm always thinking of Mohamed, every day. But it's no use. There's nothing to be gained by it.'

'You're very brave.'

'I don't have any choice.'

'You're still very brave.'

They fell silent once more. Loma finished her drink and looked into the bottom of the glass.

'You're going to be okay,' said Madeha.

'Am I? How do you know?'

'Well, your husband's going abroad, isn't he?'

'Yes, to London.'

'What's his new job?'

'He'll be First Secretary at the embassy, dealing with political affairs. But I don't see how that will help.'

'Well, the embassy will pay for your relocation. A few weeks from now, you'll be living in London. All this stuff with Selma will be history.'

'I haven't decided yet whether I'm going.'

'What's keeping you here? Wouldn't you rather be in England?'

'Maybe. I'm not sure. The whole idea seems unappealing.'

'Is it Ali?'

Loma heaved a sigh and sipped at her drink.

'I suppose so. And I'd miss my friends. But, of course, that's silly. I should probably follow my husband. After all, it's expected. People would talk, otherwise.'

'So there you go. You'll go to London and forget all about Selma. And she'll forget all about you.'

'Well, that's a nice thought.'

'Don't forget, if she were ever to mess with you seriously, she'd be in a lot of trouble. Your husband wouldn't take it lying down, and he's very well connected.'

'I'm not sure he'd exactly jump to my defence if he knew my history with Ali.'

'Maybe not, but he would defend *his own* honour – and Selma wouldn't last five minutes. She'd probably wind up in jail.'

'Perhaps you're right.'

'I know I am. And anyway, if you're going to survive someone like Selma, you can't take a defeatist attitude. You have to be strong from the start. If she sees even the slightest sign of weakness she'll strike. So above all, be strong.'

'I'll certainly try.'

Madeha began to browse the food menu, raising her eyebrows at some of the prices.

'If we're going to do some serious drinking,' she said, 'I think we ought to eat something.'

'I thoroughly agree. But it's on me this time. It's the least I can do, after all your help.'

'If you insist, my dear,' said Madeha with the impish smile that was her trademark.

'I do insist.'

'Very well then – I'll have everything!'

They burst out laughing. It was the first of many moments of levity that evening, as they reminisced, gossiped and told well-worn stories. Solidarity combined with booze worked wonders on them both. Indeed, Abu Nuwas would have been proud.

It was 2am before they left the Ishtar Sheraton, rather unsteady on their feet and full of Dutch courage. As they passed back through the lobby, Loma stood defiantly before the goddess of love and war, arms spread wide in imitation.

'Come on, you bitch,' she said, 'give it your best shot!'

Sunbathing at the Alwiyah Club

The swimming pool at the Alwiyah Club was busy. The more serious-minded patrons were swimming up and down, while others floated in the shallows or splashed each other for fun. A red beach ball could be seen sailing back and forth, propelled by a pair of giggling children. More boys and girls – the offspring of club members – could be seen larking about on the neatly-cropped lawn, a few of the girls sporting brightly-coloured bikinis. Around the pool were dozens of tables and chairs, most of them empty. Once the afternoon heat had eased off, more members would drift outside, taking their seats for a drink and perhaps a meal.

The Alwiyah had opened in 1921, providing a comfortable hang-out for the British who ran Iraq, that modern nation recently created by the likes of Gertrude Bell. The club had offered shelter from the sweltering heat of summer, a well-stocked bar, good food and the latest news from home. Outside, there was a lush garden, a pool and tennis courts – ideal for refreshing body and spirit.

The main building had been created in the British Colonial style, and there were very few alterations in the following six decades. The restaurant was still famous for its old-fashioned English etiquette and friendly Iraqi-Assyrian waiters. The menu boasted a

Sunday lunch of roast beef, vegetables and gravy, along with a range of sumptuous Eastern dishes, such as boneless grilled chicken stuffed with rice, almonds and sultanas.

In line with the club's colonial heritage, membership applications from Westerners were still accepted as a matter of routine. Iraqis were also permitted to join, although their social credentials were carefully scrutinized beforehand. The result was a watering hole for the city's social and economic elite. The reception staff checked the membership passes of all who sought entry, or else checked their names against guest lists. A car-park attendant stood ready to identify any vehicles that didn't display the yellow badge with the club logo in the windscreen.

The Alwiyah Club took its name from the modern, residential district in which it was located. Immediately to the west was the Tigris and Abu Nuwas Street, while just north were the Ishtar Sheraton and Midan Firdos – or Paradise Square. Several national monuments had been erected in the square, including the ultra-modern Monument to the Unknown Soldier in honour of the martyrs of the war with Iran. With the passage of time, the square would also see two statues of Saddam – one of which would ultimately be toppled by invading US troops.

On this particular afternoon, however, warfare was far from the mind of Zelfa – Hassan's sister – as she relaxed by the pool. She lay on a sun-lounger, soaking up the strong mid-afternoon rays, a lemonade by her side. Half Greek and half Iraqi-Arab, Zelfa was a stunning amalgamation of genes from East and West. A natural blonde with green eyes and fair skin that tanned well, her feminine allure was highlighted this afternoon by her flesh-coloured bikini, a garment that left little to the imagination. Today, she wore thick Christian Dior sunglasses, without which the dazzling sun would have blasted straight through her eyelids. In a culture where direct exposure to the sunlight was generally avoided, Zelfa was an exception. Indeed, she had perfected the art of tanning, timing her sessions well and turning frequently to obtain just the right shade of bronze.

Zelfa was a divorcee, having been dropped by her husband on the discovery of her extramarital affair with a colleague. She worked as an interpreter, making the most of her fluency in Arabic, Greek and English. On this income and what remained of her father's wealth, she managed to support herself and her only daughter in relative comfort.

Being a divorcee – and a beautiful woman – she had to watch out for the wolves. Men often assumed she was an easy target. This assumption was based largely on the view that, with the husband out of the picture, a divorced woman was in need of sex from some other source, a problem compounded by the difficulties of finding it in such a conservative society.

Zelfa often reflected on her mother's advice: 'Beware of the wolves!' These days, she was surrounded by hungry beasts; there was always someone inviting her out on a date or else flexing his muscles by the pool. As it happened, the wolves were not so wrong about Zelfa's needs, nor her willingness to have them met. It was the mediaeval Iraq poet Al-Mutanabbi who said that only the risk-takers win in the game of leisure, and even as a married woman, Zelfa had been willing to take risks. She had taken a big risk in having an affair with a colleague, and it had led to divorce. She knew very well that any further risk taking might mean the further deterioration of her already-tattered reputation – and yet she was only human.

She opened her eyes and found that she was being watched from across the pool. It was a young diplomat from the US Embassy, which had recently reopened following a long closure sparked by the Arab-Israeli war of 1967. Zelfa knew this young American, though not well. He had made a pass at her on a previous occasion, without success. He was very popular with the women at the club, and yet there were serious obstacles to establishing any sort of intimacy. The authorities were constantly alert to the dangers of foreign interference and espionage, and the intelligence apparatus frowned on friendships between foreigners and Iraqi citizens. They were particularly careful about Americans. An Iraqi woman seeking to date an American man, for example, would find her romantic activities closely monitored, perhaps even terminated.

The man across the pool seemed to realise that he had been noticed. He rose from his sun-lounger and began to stroll around the pool in Zelfa's direction. She checked out his trim, muscular body and his tight swimming trunks. She closed her eyes again, trying to pretend that she hadn't noticed.

'Good afternoon! My name's Jerry,' he said, oozing confidence.

'Good afternoon,' she replied.

'What's your name?' continued Jerry, his tone direct and assertive, as one might expect from a representative of America, a nation so used to projecting its power overseas.

'You Americans are very straightforward and practical,' she smiled. 'Why should I tell you my name?'

She closed her eyes again, having decided to play hard to get on this occasion. When the moment came, she was confident she could turn on the charm. Her role model was Delilah, whose powers of seduction had won over the mighty, long-haired warrior Samson.

'Is there a problem,' ventured Jerry, 'or is it culturally unacceptable in Iraq to ask a woman's name?'

'No, of course not. My name is Zelfa. I am just surprised to find an American man talking to me in that way. Even Iraqi men find it difficult to talk to me.'

'Why? Are you special?' His voice had changed now, becoming more soft and inquisitive.

'No, but I'm different,' she said, 'very different.'

She removed her sun-glasses and turned on her side, resting on one elbow as she smiled up at him. Her movements were graceful and cat-like, the overall impression inviting. Jerry took a seat on the neighbouring sun-lounger.

They launched into a rambling yet superficial discussion, sharing information on their work, family and social status. Much of what they said consisted of exaggeration and half-truth, but that didn't impede their enjoyment. After all, they both had something to boast of, one way or another.

Meanwhile, the couple were being watched from a distance. A middle-aged lady sat in the shade, her dark, beady eyes locked in a hard stare, a mean smile on her lips.

'With the right ingredients, this should make for a nice little dish,' she thought.

The woman's name was Malaka and she happened to live in the same Adhamiyah street as Selma, Zelfa and Loma's parents. She came from an underprivileged background, having started out as a cleaner, working alongside her mother in the city's smart, expensive houses. She had even worked for a while for Zelfa's parents, a fact that both women tried hard to forget. Then she was accused of stealing silver and spent some time in prison. On her release, she met a madam and worked the city streets, renting her body and saving what money she could. Eventually, she went into business for herself, setting up her own brothel and stocking it with fresh young flesh.

Her business had the blessing of the authorities, especially officers of the intelligence apparatus – or *Mukhabarat*. Not only did they make use of the girls themselves, but they incorporated the business into their professional operations. Foreign diplomats were known to frequent such places, and if they could be lured into the beds of certain girls – or boys – they were ripe for blackmail. Few diplomats were keen to see their names in newspaper articles alleging immoral acts. In such ways, Saddam's men obtained no end of diplomatic, political, economic and military information.

Malaka often employed girls from poor families or those who already had problems with the authorities. They were willing to work for next to nothing, and they often went unpaid for some time. However, she also kept a few classy girls on the books. They attracted the high-rollers and the more discerning diplomats who wanted a little cultured conversation with their kiss-and-cuddle. Malaka had always thought that Zelfa would make a good whore, if only she were open to being recruited.

Malaka had not escaped the scorn of Selma, who knew of her employment history and time behind bars. More than once,

Selma had made unkind comments within Malaka's hearing, referring to her as 'that *kawada*' – a slang term for a female pimp. Before long, the term had been adopted as Malaka's nickname among Selma's social clique.

Selma's dislike of Malaka was compounded by jealousy, for the *kawada* had done well for herself, ultimately accruing more wealth than Selma and her husband, who were very much on a downward slope. The final nail in the coffin had been when Malaka had moved to Sabah Street, buying the large house next door, which belonged to Hassan's family. Her generous offer was enough to save the family from the bailiffs; it was an act of generosity that Selma had never forgiven. Indeed, sandwiched between a whore on the one side and Loma's mother on the other, Selma had the distinct feeling that Sabah Street was going rapidly downhill – and with it her own status.

Despite her success, Malaka had never forgotten her humble origins. She had been born in a poor neighbourhood far from Adhamiyah. The house in which she was raised was typical of old Baghdad: grim and crowded, set in a labyrinth of dusty, narrow alleyways that offered shelter from the heat and a fair chance of evading one's enemies.

As a young woman, she had never left the house without first donning her *abaya*, that loose black garment that covered her from head to toe, protecting her from the lustful gazes of passing men. Her head was covered, meanwhile, with a traditional black *hijab*. Only her face and hands were visible, although she often left the front of her *abaya* open, providing a glimpse of the cheap, ankle-length dress that she wore underneath.

In some ways, Malaka's story was similar to that of Baghdad in the 1980s. Her origins were Oriental, but she had been seduced by so much that was Western, abandoning the old, cramped architecture for something more spacious and modern. She had thrown off the *abaya* and *hijab*, preferring fashions and hair styles that originated in London, Paris and New York. She had also thrown off the shackles of traditional thinking on sex and morality, adopting a more laissez-faire attitude all round. Finally, she had been seduced by the Iraqi intelligence apparatus, which had shown her the social, political and financial benefits of cooperation.

Her journey up the social ladder had been slow but sure. She had started by soliciting herself to soldiers and students who were struggling to find a sexual encounter outside of marriage. Aided by her good looks and fine, youthful figure, she had progressed to military officers, successful professionals and politicians. Finally, there were intelligence officers. Now, many years down the line, all she needed was to make a phone call and all her demands would be met. When some posh family found itself in a jam, they would contact Malaka, who had the connections to find government jobs for young men seeking to avoid front-line duty as an army conscript. She also intervened on the behalf of families seeking the release from prison of sons, brothers, or husbands – although she drew the line at political cases. In return, she would often be paid in cash. Just as often, however, people repaid their debts by frequenting her establishment, where they paid over the odds for some fun with a pretty girl. And so, another fly was trapped in her web.

She lit a cigarette and drew on it thoughtfully, eyes still pinned on the flirtatious couple. Jerry had ordered two bottles of Scheherezade beer. He had thought it wise to show his local knowledge; in truth, he would have made a better impression on Zelfa by ordering Heineken. Even so, she was content to sip her drink in the company of this attractive young man, who clearly had trouble keeping his eyes off her suntanned flesh.

Malaka's presence in the garden that day was not entirely accidental. The previous week she had been summoned to a meeting with an intelligence officer. They wanted her to keep tabs on this new American diplomat, a cocky youngster who drove his Chevrolet freely through the streets of Baghdad. But they didn't want Malaka just to monitor his movements; if at all possible, they wanted her to infiltrate the US Embassy, to find out what sort of badness they were up to. At first, she had considered the task horribly difficult, but not anymore.

Malaka was not alone at her table in the shade. She had recently been joined by a middle-aged Iraqi lady of aristocratic bearing. Her father had been prime minister in the early days of Iraqi independence, and now she was trying to win Malaka's heart, seeking to ensure that what remained of her father's land would not be confiscated by the authorities. Assuming such confiscations originated in some ordinary government department, something could perhaps be done to avert it. Of course, if some member of Saddam's family – such as his sons Uday and Qusay – were involved, it was another matter entirely.

'Look at the lovebirds!' said Malaka, her voice dripping with sarcasm.

The aristocratic lady had been in the middle of her plea, but now she stopped and looked over to the pool.

'Well, that's not entirely surprising,' she said. 'That woman is known to be a tart. She has finished with the Iraqis and now she's moved on to the Americans.'

'She'll get herself into trouble if she isn't careful.'

'Of course she will. Her family is considered to be prestigious, but in reality, they're just dirt. Assuming the rumours are correct, that is.'

'What rumours?'

The lady looked around to be sure they were not being overheard. What she was about to say was enough to land a person in jail.

Finally, confident that they were alone, she whispered, 'Have you heard the story of her daughter and Uday?'

Malaka stared back. It was the sort of hard, emotionless stare that might be interpreted in any number of ways, and the lady began to wonder if she had spoken too freely. She looked over her shoulder once again, just in case.

Beneath the poker face, Malaka was elated. If she had prayed to Allah for some leverage with Zelfa, her prayers could not have been answered more fully.

The garden party

Selma had put a lot of time and effort into arranging her summer garden party. She enjoyed throwing parties and used a range of pretexts, such as the several birthdays she had each year, or her daughter's graduation from college. Often there was no reason at all; it was just a party, a chance to maintain her social status by entertaining the elite in style. The summer garden party was something special, however, with an extended guest-list and ample opportunity to show off the beauty of her property, both inside and out. This year, she had to sell a few items of jewellery to fund the enterprise, but she was by now resigned to such ignominies.

The garden was large, consisting of a spacious lawn, flower beds, rockeries, and a central water feature, all surrounded by tall fruit trees that provided some welcome shade. The party proper didn't start until dusk, when the temperatures were more bearable. If they were lucky, a cool breeze would blow in from the Tigris. As darkness fell, colourful lights would twinkle around the garden, adding a touch of fairy magic.

With the help of a little music and lots of booze, the party soon got going. Tonight, the guest-list included family, friends, foreign diplomats and a range of important public figures – from judges and politicians to famous musicians and heart surgeons. By sundown, there was quite a gathering around the long table where the drinks and nibbles were laid out. The volume of the chatter and the occasional peal of laughter suggested that all was going well.

Having spoken at least once with all the more important guests, Selma now found herself at the far end of the garden, checking on a batch of fairy lights that seemed a little dim. She noticed a couple in the shadows, embracing and kissing passionately. As she watched, another couple emerged from the undergrowth, approached the first pair and began to swap partners. Selma stood and watched as they exchanged kisses and caresses. Before long, she was feeling aroused, a sensation aided by the large quantity of vodka-and-orange she had consumed. She reminded herself that she was the hostess of an important party – and that her husband was somewhere nearby. Perhaps, after all, he still had his uses. She wandered casually back up the garden, drink in one hand, cigarette in the other.

'Selma, darling!' said a voice from beside the water feature. It was Mostafa, an old friend, sporting an immaculate white-linen suit. 'Why are you wandering around all alone?'

'I'm looking for my husband, as it happens. You haven't seen him, have you?'

'He's inside. I think he may have fallen asleep. You know – too much drink.'

'Well then, I'll have to go and wake him,' she said, stomping off toward the house.

She was furious. How could Hassan humiliate her in such a way, falling asleep at the most important event of her social calendar? Perhaps their marriage was at an end, but he could at least make an effort to pretend – tonight of all nights. As for her sexual desires, what hope was there if this alcoholic lump was the only option on the menu? Yes, it was all quite unbearable, and Hassan would be made to pay.

Any trained psychologist would have been fascinated by the range of Selma's emotions and the speed with which she could switch from one to the other. In the blink of an eye, the smile would vanish, replaced with a sneer, even the gnashing of teeth. The jolly laughter of a firm friend gave way in an instant to the sharp barbs of sarcasm, even the fierce screeching of a sworn enemy. Any psychologist with the nerve to delve deeper would find a personality ruled by strong emotions: egotism; arrogance; entitlement; a yearning for recognition; resentment; jealousy; malice; hatred; vengefulness; furious anger. Much of the nastier stuff was rooted in a sense of having been denied what was owed her: namely a slavish recognition of her greatness and a continual shower of adoration, not to mention great wealth and a fantastic sex life. In short, she was trapped in a circle of egotism; the more she demanded the raw materials of contentment, the more furiously unhappy she became – and it was always someone else's fault.

As she mounted the stone steps to the patio, she noticed an unexpected guest. She stopped in her tracks, momentarily swerved from the course of revenge. It was the new American diplomat that she'd seen at the Alwiyah Club. She couldn't recall having invited him, and she wondered who might have done so. Perhaps it was Zelfa? According to rumour, she had been flirting outrageously with the man. Most likely she was sleeping with him already, whore that she was.

Jerry had not seen Selma, so engrossed was he in reading the label on a bottle of local beer. Selma stepped to one side, taking cover behind a potted shrub. She watched and waited, and before long Zelfa emerged from the house holding a glass of champagne. She was looking stunning this evening, her blonde hair a mass of waves and curls, her bronze body squeezed into a little black dress. She greeted Jerry with the traditional cheek kisses and the pair launched into animated conversation on the topic of local beer. Selma strained to hear, but there was too much ambient noise.

Selma's relationship with Zelfa had never been great. Zelfa was far too confident for Selma's liking, and as for her good looks and sexy figure – well, it was just unbearable. The final nail in the coffin had been Zelfa's divorce, which had set her free to play the field. And she was apparently quite successful in this department, brushing aside the risks of social exclusion – and even prison – to bed an American diplomat. Selma might easily have felt admiration; instead, she felt malice.

She often wondered at the source of Zelfa's success with men. Perhaps it was magic? When the topic of magic had arisen in the past, Zelfa had admitted to being interested. She had a few books on magic too; Selma knew this, because she had once gone through her book shelves. No doubt such books contained spells for trapping men, and Zelfa was just the sort of person to stoop to such things. She was a Muslim, of course, but hardly devout. And though she would never admit publicly to dabbling in the dark arts, she probably had more faith in magic spells than divine intervention from Allah.

Selma had once asked Zelfa if she possessed a magician's doll, one of those little human-shaped figures that one stuck pins into. Zelfa had blushed and feigned incomprehension – then changed the subject. Yes, thought Selma as she peered through the potted shrub, Zelfa had clearly trapped this American with magic. She looked pretty pleased with herself too. But it would end badly; that much was certain.

Selma began to feel a little cowardly hiding behind a shrub. There were benefits, of course, to snooping unseen, but it was hardly her style to be avoiding confrontation. Just as she was on the point of emerging, a new arrival burst onto the scene. It was Malaka, marching from the house and stopping abruptly on the patio. Her slightly dumpy middle-aged figure had been squeezed into a leopard-pattern dress, a long gold-sequinned shawl draped around her shoulders. Everything else was gold too: long-tasselled earrings; thick chain-link necklaces; rings on every finger. Her face was hidden beneath several layers of make-up, her long, false eyelashes caked in mascara. She regarded the garden much like a general surveying the battlefield before committing his troops. She took a tug on her long menthol cigarette and proceeded down the steps, taking care not to trip on the ends of her shawl. Malaka had never been to one of Selma's parties before. However, tonight she was the guest of honour, and before long she planned to make herself the uncrowned queen of the party. Selma had long resisted making Malaka's acquaintance, preferring to snipe at her from a distance. After all, what sort of person openly consorts with whores and pimps? However, recent events had thrown a new light on things.

Selma and Hassan had been beside themselves with worry over their son, Ahmed, who had been conscripted into the army and sent to the front line, within range of Iran's bullets and bombs. So many young men had been martyred and it seemed only a matter of time before Ahmed followed suit. Selma and Hassan's attempts at pulling strings had come to nothing; even Hassan's uncle, a colonel in the army engineers, had refused to help. At such a moment of national crisis, he'd said, it was unthinkable for any man to fail in his duty.

Then, one day at the club, Selma had swallowed her pride and approached Malaka with the problem. A phone call had been made, and within a few days Ahmed was on a bus back to Baghdad. He would spend the rest of his military service at a headquarters unit in the capital, safe from harm.

Malaka had refused cash payment for her services. All she wanted was friendship, she said, and loyalty. Selma had been alarmed by the suggestion of accepting the *kawada* into her social circle, but there was really little choice. After all, if Malaka could save Ahmed from harm by picking up a telephone, then presumably she could do the opposite. Indeed, Malaka could probably have the entire family shifted to the front line – or somewhere similarly unpleasant – if she so desired.

Selma had long been known for her dismissive comments on the state of modern Iraqi society. 'This country is only fit for prostitutes, pimps, and parasites,' she would say, a bold assertion that sent a ripple of nervous laughter round many a dinner table. She had never imagined that she would find herself so deeply imbedded in the filth. And not just embedded, but enslaved.

By now, Selma had given up on looking for her husband. He could sleep through the whole party, for all she cared. She stepped from behind the shrub and descended into the garden, smiling archly at a bemused Zelfa as she went. Malaka was over by the water feature, waving her arms around as she regaled her audience with an anecdote. There was quite an audience too. It seemed everyone wanted to suck up to the bitch this evening. No doubt some of them were already in her debt, while others were looking to become so. This evening, what irked Selma more than being in the woman's debt was the fact that she had stolen the limelight. Selma saw no option but to assert herself, to show that she was not cowed, that she would not be upstaged. Most important of all, she would show that the current state of things was exactly as she had planned, that everything was unfolding according to her wishes.

'Malaka, darling!' she shouted as she pushed through the crowed, arms outstretched. 'I'm so glad you could make it, my dear. I know how busy you are, what with all your business activities. It's wonderful of you to tear yourself away for my little gathering.' Malaka had, in fact, been in the middle of delivering her punchline, and the annoyance was clear on her face. Even so, she refused to admit to having been up-staged.

'Selma, darling!' she said, embracing her host and delivering three kisses. 'I'm so glad to see you again. This garden of yours is so cosy – such a pretty little corner. I was just telling...'

'But Malaka, you must see the house. Come with me now, and I'll give you the royal tour.'

'Selma, not so fast! I'm still getting to know people. I need to mingle a little first. Here, this is someone you don't know, I'm sure.'

Malaka turned to her right and gestured to a pretty teenager in a mini-skirt and pink top with puff-shoulders. Her belly button was showing, pierced by a little golden ring.

'And this is?' Selma said, eyebrows raised.

'Colette, one of my protégés. Say hello, Colette.'

'Good evening. I'm so happy to be here,' said the girl, smiling sweetly.

Selma was speechless. Malaka had actually had the cheek to bring along one of her prostitutes. The implication was clear; Selma's house and garden were to be treated like any street corner, a suitable venue for the sex trade. If Malaka had slapped her in the face, the insult could not have been more blatant.

Malaka couldn't help smirking. On the one hand, she was sensitive to smears against her reputation. On the other hand, she got a thrill from confronting snobs such as Selma with the harsh realities of her business. She liked to rub their faces in it, particularly when they were in no position to complain.

Yes, there as a great deal of power in being a madam; even common whores had a degree of power, if they knew how to play the game to their advantage. Once, when a teenager had resisted recruitment, she had delivered a brief lecture on just this topic. 'Those men may despise you in the daytime,' she had said, 'but they will kiss your feet at night. You will get not only money but also power, and that is vital for survival these days. It's like having an air conditioner on a hot day. You can work it the way you like; everything is under your control. You just need to know how to play the game.'

Selma was still in shock, the silence growing ever more uncomfortable. If she wasn't careful, the gaggle of guests around her would conclude that she'd lost her nerve. Under pressure, she fell back on her instincts, blanking the young whore and resuming her discussion with Malaka.

'Why, what a lovely dress you're wearing, my dear. I do hope you didn't kill it specially for my party?'

Malaka threw her head back and laughed aloud. There was no greater display of self-confidence than full-bellied laughter.

'Oh, Selma, you tease! No, I had it sent over from Milan. It's the only place to buy clothes these days, don't you think? Tell me, where did you get that wonderful gown of yours? It's not home-made is it? I know you're terribly clever with a needle and thread.'

Selma was worried that the exchange might descend into a cat-fight, which was an outcome she really couldn't afford. At that moment, she spied an escape route. Jerry and Zelfa were standing in a far corner of the garden, chatting with Selma's rather slutty friend Soda. The two women were laughing; apparently, the American was not only handsome but also funny.

'Malaka, I'm afraid you'll have to excuse me,' she said. 'I've just spied my sister-in-law, and I simply must say hello. I do hope you enjoy yourself. It's so lovely to see you again.'

She disappeared before Malaka could summon a reply, striding across the lawn like a soldier advancing on the enemy. As she went, she gulped down the last of her vodka-and-orange, picking up a glass of white wine as she passed the drinks table. It was a very long time since she'd been placed on the back foot, and she was sorely regretting having involved herself with Malaka. For the first time, she wondered if she should have left Ahmed to fight it out with the Iranians. After all, some mothers coped very well with the death of a child.

Malaka resumed her story, delivering her punch-line with good effect. The general chatter resumed, but everyone was aware that she was more interested in events at the far end of the garden. By now, Selma had been welcomed into Jerry's little group, and everyone was busy exchanging kisses. It seemed rather ironic that Selma should seek refuge in the company of an American who already had a large target on his back.

'Look how tall he is!' said Colette. 'Are all Americans like that? And such lovely hair!'

'I'm pretty sure he'll get Soda into the sack tonight,' said a sour-faced woman at Malaka's elbow. This woman had been among the first to greet the American when he first joined the club, but he'd pretty much blanked her, a fact that only added to her sourness.

'No, he's more interested in Zelfa,' said another woman. 'Just look at the way he eyes her.'

'How on earth can you see from such a distance?' said Malaka. 'I think you're all horribly cruel. I'm sure they're simply good friends. Gosh, what a wonderful water feature this is. I should do something similar in my own garden. I have an Italian fountain – Tuscan marble – but it's really too big.'

The conversation turned to fountains, but Malaka was only half listening. For the rest of the night she had Jerry and his little harem under close observation. She was happy to find Zelfa making such rapid progress. Few women in Malaka's social circle could perform the role of honey-trap so effectively – and the American would make such a wonderful fly. Of course, if events could be managed in such a way as to ensure the public humiliation of Selma, then so much the better. After all, there was nothing sweeter than killing two birds with one stone.

A few close friends

Zelfa was on her way to the kitchen to grab another bottle of wine when the telephone rang. As she stepped into the hallway, she was sure it was Jerry. He often called in the evenings to arrange their next rendezvous, normally involving a swim and a spot of lunch at the club. She felt a tingle of excitement as she lifted the receiver and put it to her ear.

'Hello.'

'Hello, my darling. This is Malaka.'

Zelfa was struck dumb. Who on earth was Malaka?

'Are you there?' said the voice again.

It took Zelfa a few more seconds to recall the real name of the woman so often referred to as the *kawada*. When she finally remembered, she was thoroughly confused. Why on earth would this woman call her at home? They had never been friends.

'Hello, Zelfa. Is something wrong? Are you free to talk?'

'Yes, so sorry. I'm free to talk now. How are you, Malaka?

'I'm very well, my darling. And how are you?'

'Fine, thank you.'

There was an awkward silence, and then Malaka continued.

'I know you must be entertaining this evening, so I won't keep you too long. But I wanted to invite you to brunch tomorrow at my house. It will be a very small gathering, just a few close friends. It would make the world of difference to me if you were to join us.

We so rarely get the chance to talk, and I so want to pick your brains about décor.'

'Décor?'

'Yes, I'm having my living room redecorated, and I just can't decide on colours. I know you have a great eye for such things, and it would be wonderful to have your input.'

It seemed a flimsy pretext for a brunch invitation, but Zelfa could hardly refuse, at least not without time to think of an excuse.

'Sure, I'll be happy to attend, but I don't know very much about decorating.'

'You have excellent taste, my dear. That's all that matters. I'll see you at 10 o'clock tomorrow morning. Don't be late.'

'Yes, of course. Thank you.'

'You're welcome.'

Zelfa was in the kitchen when the telephone rang again. She answered once more, certain this time that it must be Jerry.

'Hello.'

'Darling, this is Malaka again.'

'Hello.'

'I just wanted to add that you must feel free to bring a friend or two. Perhaps Crista would like to come along, assuming she's in Baghdad?'

'Yes, she's here right now. How did you know?'

'I didn't know, my darling. I just guessed. I know you two are so close. Tell her I begged her to come.'

'Yes, I will, of course.'

'And if you wanted to bring Jerry, that would also be wonderful.'

'Jerry?'

'Yes, my dear, Jerry, the charming American from the club. I have yet to make his acquaintance, but I'm dying to do so. I have a soft spot for charming Americans. He'll enjoy talking to some of my friends tomorrow. They're all highly cultured.'

'Yes, well – if I see Jerry, I'll certainly mention it.'

'That's wonderful. Tomorrow at 10.'

'Goodbye.'

'Goodbye, my darling.'

Zelfa really was confused now. Why on earth would Malaka be so keen to get everyone together? What on earth could she be up to?

She grabbed the wine and returned to the living room, where Crista was sitting on the floor, looking through a pile of records, everything from Umm Kulthum to Abba. A melancholic song from the Lebanese super-star Fairuz was oozing from the speakers. Zelfa joined her friend on the floor and refilled their glasses.

Crista and Zelfa went back many years. They had attended the same school in Baghdad, entering womanhood together and sharing all their deepest secrets. They had played together, walked to school together, and swam in the Tigris during the summer months. They had even dated the same boys, swapping and sharing whenever the fancy took them.

They also shared a passion for magic. As teenagers, they had both believed fiercely in the power of spells to attract a mate or curse an enemy. More than once they had taken a hair from some boy to an old woman rumoured to have special powers. For a small fee, the woman would cast her spell, and invariably the girls would have success. They would even tinker with the spirit world, visiting cemeteries and calling upon the spirits to lend them their powers. Had university not interrupted their explorations, they might easily have taken up magic as a profession, although they would no doubt have been disowned by their families for doing so.

The girls had differed only in their talents: while Zelfa excelled in languages, Crista had been more of a scientist. She had finally qualified as a dentist, finding a well-paid job in Tikrit, the birthplace of Saddam, some 90 miles north of the capital. Whenever she could, Crista would drive down to Baghdad and spend the weekend with her best friend. They would drink, listen to music and gossip.

The hot topic these days was Zelfa's new love interest. She was fast falling in love with Jerry, and Crista wanted all the details. Sadly, there wasn't much to tell. The love birds would invariably meet at the Alwiyah Club, swim, sunbathe and chat. And then they would part, promising to meet again soon. There was plenty of gazing into each other's eyes, and even some hand-holding — but that was about it. They had kissed on only two occasions, and only furtively, when they were sure nobody was looking. As for spending the night together, such a move involved numerous risks, both social and professional; for now, they had decided on a policy of patience.

To Crista, however, it was all very exciting, not least of all because her own love life was non-existent. Not only was she single, but she hadn't felt the touch of a man's hand for quite some time. It was not that she was a lesbian — despite the rumours — but rather that her heart had been broken many years before, and she'd never quite recovered.

Crista's family were Christian, part of a religious minority provided with certain privileges by Saddam, who saw them as a reliable political force. Indeed, many of Saddam's trusted advisers were Christian, as was his deputy prime minister. The Christian community was a closed one, however, resisting any outside interference. According to Iraqi law, Muslim men were permitted to marry Christian women, but many Christian families opposed such matches. It was Crista's bad luck that she had fallen in love with a Muslim man.

Her mother, an Assyrian, was initially sympathetic, hoping only for her daughter's happiness. However, Crista's father, a jeweller from a proud Christian Arab family, strictly opposed the match. Despite much pleading, he remained utterly intransigent.

'I would rather see you dead than married to a Muslim,' he had said, and from the hardness in his eyes, Crista knew that he wasn't exaggerating.

Eventually, caught in the middle, her mother also begged Crista to forget about the young man and find a nice boy from her own faith. As tensions mounted, the mother threatened suicide, at which point Crista made one last desperate effort. She visited an old lady known for her magical powers, begging her to cast some sort of spell. The lady started by divining the future, serving Crista a coffee and then examining the grounds in the empty cup. The omens were not good, said the old woman; the match would certainly fail.

Crista gave up there and then. Returning to her parent's home, she wrote a long letter filled with heartbreak and regret – and she never saw her lover again. He emigrated to the US, desperate to forget her, but she never forgot him. He was with her every evening at sunset, as she sat in their favourite spot by the banks of the Tigris, dreaming of their life together, their future home and children. Since then, Crista had focussed primarily on her work, resigned to the life of a spinster.

The Fairuz album came to an end, and Zelfa turned to her friend.

'I just had the strangest phone call,' she said.

'Who was it?'

'Malaka.'

'Who?'

'Oh, you may not remember her, but she used to be a house maid. She cleaned our house when I was a kid. Then she got into trouble with the police and wound up … well, as a prostitute.'

'A prostitute?'

'Yes, or rather, as a madam. She's made a lot of money out of it, apparently. Now she lives in the big house at the far end of the street, next to Selma. I often see her at the Alwiyah Club.'

'So, what does she want with you?'

'I'm invited to brunch tomorrow.'

'Brunch?'

'That's right. You're invited too. And Jerry.'

Crista burst out laughing.

'Don't laugh,' said Zelfa. 'She was perfectly serious. I didn't know how to refuse.'

'She's probably lonely.'

'I don't think so. She's got the biggest network in Baghdad.'

'Well, perhaps she's trying to become respectable?'

'Maybe, I don't know. She was at Selma's party last week, making lots of noise. I suppose she wants to be properly accepted into polite society or something. It's all a bit strange.'

'So, are you going?'

'I suppose so.'

'And Jerry?'

'I suppose I'll have to ask him along, the poor thing.'

Crista burst out laughing again. When she had gained control of herself once more, she proposed a toast: 'Here's to our new best friend.'

'To our new best friend.'

They clinked their glasses and drained them dry.

* * *

By the time they arrived the next morning, brunch had already been dished up. The big table on the patio was heaving with food: pita bread; boiled eggs; yoghurt with cucumbers; fattoush salad; hummus; foul beans; broad beans; falafel; peppers stuffed with minced beef and rice; stuffed vine leaves; a selection of cheeses; olives; baskets of croissants and *pain au chocolat*. In addition to the tea, coffee and juice, there was a bottle of arak – for those who preferred to start drinking early. Of the half-dozen guests seated around the table, several had already made that decision.

'Zelfa, darling!' said Malaka, climbing the patio steps from the garden. 'I'm so glad you could make it.'

'Malaka, so nice to see you.'

They exchanged air-kisses, neither of them keen to ruin their make-up.

'And Crista!' said Malaka, standing back with faux shock. 'You're looking quite stunning. It's so long since I've seen you up close. I'd forgotten how pretty you are.'

'That's very kind,' said Crista.

'You look wonderful too, Zelfa. I love the dress.'

'Thank you.'

'And I see you've brought your lovely daughter along,' continued Malaka, kissing Nada, who had been skulking in the background.

'Yes, I thought she could be more help with your decorating,' said Zelfa. 'She's a very talented artist. If she finally decides to go to art school, she'll make a big splash someday.'

Nada was cringing at her mother's praise but managed a polite smile.

'Then she'll want to speak with my friend Zeinab,' said Malaka, indicating an attractive young lady in a floral dress. 'She's a fine sculptress. You may have seen her works on display at the national museum of art. She specialises in horses; modern art, of course.'

'Yes, I think I may have seen some of your work,' said Zelfa. 'Glad to meet you.'

Malaka then introduced the other guests at the table: a professor of economics from the University of Baghdad, sporting a large white moustache; a female news anchor who appeared every night on Zelfa's TV; and an antiques dealer, looking very smart in his dark morning suit.

As they all exchanged kisses, Zelfa wondered at Malaka's selection of friends. They were certainly more cultured than she'd expected – more cultured, in fact, than any gathering she'd encountered in several years. Perhaps, after all, she'd been wrong about the old whore.

'Please excuse the mess,' said Malaka, indicating the garden, which was littered with trestle tables, chairs and boxes in various stages of unpacking. 'I'm throwing a garden party this evening. Nothing too fancy, just a hundred people or so. It's mainly to say thank you to Selma for such a lovely party last week. I had such a wonderful time, and I know that so many other people did.'

'Yes, it was nice,' said Zelfa, although not quite with conviction.

'But to be perfectly frank,' continued Malaka, 'I much prefer intimate gatherings like our little brunch party – just some good food and the right kind of company. It's all so much more relaxed. Don't you think?'

'Oh, absolutely,' said Zelfa, pouring herself a large arak. 'I prefer little gatherings too. I'm honoured that you would think of inviting me.'

'Don't be silly, my dear. You've always been a cut above the rest.'

The conversation switched to the food, which was a relief for both Zelfa and Crista, who felt their powers of small talk rather limited that morning. As the select gathering exchanged opinions on the best in regional cuisines, Zelfa listened quietly, occasionally glancing at her daughter, who had hardly spoken since arriving.

Nada was a continual cause of worry for her mother. At 19 years old, she was a beautiful girl, having inherited her mother's array of attributes, a mix of East and West. From her Greek grandmother she had inherited blonde hair and blue eyes, while her tan-friendly olive skin came from her father. While Zelfa had long hoped Nada would capitalize on her artistic talents, she might easily succeed as a super-model. Today she was wearing tight, white trousers and a hand-embroidered vest bedecked with faux gems. Her jewellery was not fake though: gold earrings studded with diamonds; a chunky gold necklace; gold rings and bangles.

In another context, such beauty might have been a blessing, adding to the girl's enjoyment of life. However, as a member of Iraq's social elite, she was prey to certain wolves in high places. In particular, she had come to the attention of Uday Hussein, the president's eldest son by his first wife. He was known as a bloody and psychopathic character, prone to acts of raw violence, fuelled in part by his taste for hard drugs. He indulged his sexual passions with a continual supply of fresh meat, issuing orders for particular young women to be invited to his various luxury residences. Those girls who would not come willingly were sometimes abducted by Uday's thugs, after which the president's son would invariably have his wicked way.

Many families were convinced to comply with Uday's wishes, offering up their daughters in return for money, expensive gifts and various favours. No one could say no to him. The consequences for such families – and the girls themselves – were mixed, to say the least. On the one hand, they had penetrated the very highest levels of the nation's elite, with access to wealth and favour. Some of Nada's jewellery, for example, had been flown in specially from De Beers in London.

On the other hand, there was the continual risk of violence – including rape, torture and death – along with irreversible harm to a young lady's reputation. Many potential suitors would fear involvement with a woman who had been used by Uday. After all, who could tell when the tyrant's son might want her back?

And then there was the general stain on any girl's reputation resulting from having engaged in extramarital sex, perhaps even orgies. Such a reputation was hard to live down, and few respectable families would want to be tainted by association. Zelfa knew this from her own experience, and it was a constant source of grief that Nada was doomed to face the same obstacles to happiness. Indeed, Zelfa felt immense guilt at having failed to protect her daughter from such a fate.

And yet, every time the Rolls Royce drew up outside their home, she found herself powerless to intervene. A smartly dressed man would ring the doorbell, and Nada would rush outside, climbing into the back seat. By sundown, she would be sipping champagne at one of Uday's palaces or perhaps at the Grand Habbaniya Hotel in the desert to the west of Baghdad. Zelfa would simply be told that her daughter would return in a few days.

Now, as they sat on Malaka's patio, Zelfa watched Nada with sad eyes. From time to time, the girl would check her gold watch, and finally she stood up and made her excuses. She had another appointment that afternoon. Zelfa knew where she was going.

'It's such a shame that you're leaving so soon,' said Malaka.

'I'm very sorry, but I can't be late. Thank you for a lovely breakfast.'

Nada kissed her mother goodbye and was gone.

The light-hearted natter resumed and Zelfa poured herself some more arak. She felt a wave of relief when, half an hour later, the doorbell sounded and Jerry stepped onto the patio, looking trim and delicious in a khaki suit and polo shirt.

'Jerry, darling!' said Malaka, rising from her seat and bestowing two large air-kisses on the American. 'I've so longed to meet you, and now you're in my home. It's really such an honour.'

Until this moment, Zelfa hadn't imagined that Malaka knew much English. But on reflection, it was pretty obvious. After all, she must have been on intimate terms with plenty of English speakers over the years.

'I am honoured to have been invited into your lovely home,' said Jerry, calling on his extensive diplomatic training. He then immediately switched to fluent Arabic: 'And particularly to have been invited to such an intimate gathering of friends. I am very touched by your expression of friendship.'

'Not at all, my dear. Allow me to introduce everyone.'

He dutifully exchanged kisses, complementing everyone on their good looks and fine attire. He seemed to know the economics professor already and praised his paper on agricultural reform. Zelfa thought that he might be overdoing it a bit, but she forgave him when he returned to her side and planted a firm kiss on her mouth. It was a risky move, but then she had never imagined that he was anything but a risk-taker. Indeed, it was one of the things she loved about him.

'Well, you seem to be having a good time, ladies,' he said.

'Very nice, thank you. This is Crista, the best friend who you've heard so much about.'

'Lovely to meet you,' said Jerry. 'Everything she's told me has been good.'

'I'm not so sure of that,' she joked. 'Zelfa knows all my dark secrets.'

Zelfa couldn't help noticing that Jerry's eyes flitted between Crista's pretty face and her breasts, which were displayed to good advantage by her thin cotton dress. A wave of jealously surged through Zelfa's brain, but she told herself to get a grip. It was only normal for men to look at a woman's breasts, and Crista had done nothing wrong by dressing nicely. Even so, Zelfa gripped Jerry's hand tightly under the table – a gesture that he returned.

An hour later, everyone was full. Conversation had been wide ranging, covering food, art, travel, archaeology, sport and even – very briefly – politics, although Jerry refused to be drawn on US foreign policy. Zelfa noticed that he had also refused the arak.

'Zelfa, you must come and see my fountain,' said Malaka suddenly. 'And then I'll show you the living room.'

'Of course, I'd love to.'

They walked through the garden arm-in-arm, stopping at the Tuscan fountain, which formed a most impressive centre-piece. Zelma expected Malaka to launch into a history of the object, but instead she broached quite a different topic.

'It's difficult to conduct a love affair in such a critical environment, isn't it?'

'I'm sorry?' said Zelfa, taken aback.

'Your affair with Jerry; I can see that you're both very much in love.'

'Well, I wouldn't say that we're in love, actually. It's more of a friendship than anything.'

'Zelfa, you needn't be coy with me. I'm an experienced woman. Too experienced, some might say. In any case, I can see when two people are in love, and all I want – all I ever want – is for love to blossom and be given a fair chance.'

'Well, that's nice.'

'Yes, I feel very strongly that nothing should stand in the way of love. And yet, it must be very difficult for you and Jerry under the circumstances. People can be so cruel. And with Jerry's job, there are other obstacles, of course. He must be constantly under surveillance.'

'Oh, I don't know about that. I think such things are exaggerated.'

'Don't be so sure, my dear. There are eyes and ears everywhere.'

'Do you think so?'

'I know so. Which is why you need a friend.'

'What sort of friend?'

'Someone who can provide you with a safe place to meet – a room or apartment where you and Jerry can be entirely alone, with nobody watching or listening; a place that you can arrive at separately and leave separately, with nobody knowing a thing about it; a place where you can be truly yourselves for the first time; a place where love can blossom.'

Zelfa was astounded by such a frank offer – and from such an unlikely source. And yet, she couldn't deny the advantages of such an arrangement. She stood silent for a moment, running her hand back and forth in the cool water of the fountain.

'And you would be able to arrange this?'

'Yes, absolutely I can. And it can be done without the *Mukhabarat*'s knowledge. I know their ways, and that means I know their blind spots also. Your mother was very kind to me when I was young, Zelfa. You might think of this as my way of expressing my gratitude. And I know that she would be looking down on you from Heaven, urging you to say yes.'

Zelfa was silent for a moment longer, and then she spoke, very softy.

'Thank you, Malaka. I'll certainly think about it.'

'That's wonderful, my dear. Here is my business card. You'll find my private number on the back. Call me any time, and we can meet to discuss the details.'

Zelfa slipped the card into her purse. Then the two women began their leisurely stroll back to the house. Zelfa had by now plunged into a daydream, imagining herself naked in Jerry's strong arms, wrapped in cool silk sheets. Malaka was also daydreaming, although her vision had more in common with a pornographic movie – shot on 8mm film through a hole in the wall.

The reunion

Selma had been stressed all day. Not just stressed, but also angry. The very notion of attending a garden party thrown by her neighbour – a former prostitute and house-cleaner – was unpleasant, to say the least. Not just unpleasant, but outrageous. So far as Selma was concerned, Malaka was about as far beneath her on the social scale as it was possible to be. The idea of them mingling happily at a party on Malaka's spacious property seemed to imply that Malaka had finally gained acceptance into polite society, which meant the gap between them was rapidly closing. While Malaka was steadily accruing wealth and status, Selma seemed to be losing it. Malaka was nearing the top of the greasy pole, while Selma was slipping down it. None of which was acceptable, of course.

Added to which, Malaka was clearly seeking to upstage her, throwing a garden party just one week after her own – and just a few metres down the street. Many of the same people would likely be there, with perhaps a few more illustrious guests thrown in for good measure. This was a direct challenge to Selma's self-appointed role of high-class hostess extraordinaire. It was, in fact, a slap in the face.

It was unthinkable, therefore, that she should accept Malaka's invitation. And yet, bearing in mind the happy return of Selma's son from the front line, she could hardly refuse.

By the time she arrived, just after 9pm, the party was well underway. There must have been at least a hundred people present, dressed up to the nines and having a roaring good time. There were a dozen circular tables on the lawn, weighed down with food and booze, including some expensive imported brands that Selma could never have afforded to lay on. There were fairy lights galore, even strung from the overhanging branches, something that Selma had never managed. The music was good too, and several guests had taken to dancing on a low wooden platform erected specially for the occasion. At first glance, this party was indeed better than the previous week's.

Selma was used to making grand entrances and being greeted by a gang of devoted friends and allies. Tonight, however, as she stood on the patio, she struggled to spot anyone she knew intimately. There were quite a few rich-and-famous types: television personalities, politicians, academics, musicians, artists, businessmen, diplomats, and a sprinkling of military officers. There were at least two government ministers and several shady types with 'security' written all over their faces. While Selma could put a name to several of the faces in the crowd, she wasn't on first-name terms with them.

Her heart leapt when she finally spotted a friend: it was her old pal Elham. She lived just a few streets away, and they had spent many an evening gossiping viciously about some mutual acquaintance. Elham always spoke her mind – and loudly – and yet Selma never felt in danger of being upstaged; although Elham was a decade younger, she was rather plain-looking beneath her layers of make-up. Tonight, she wore a long black dress with padded shoulders.

Selma made her way through the crowd to the marble fountain, where Elham was standing.

'Elham, darling!'

'Selma, darling!'

At that precise moment, a waiter passed by with a tray of champagne, and the two friends each took a glass.

'Cheers!'

'Cheers!'

They drank in gulps.

'Elham, my dear, you're looking fabulous. I love the dress.'

'Thank you, darling. I wasn't sure what to wear. One doesn't want to show up one's host. She tends to have rather strange taste. I thought it best not to be too showy.'

'Well, you look ravishing.'

'You look ravishing too, my dear. I just love the shoes.'

'Oh, they're nothing. Just something I slipped on. From Paris, I think. I forget now.'

They drank a little more champagne and looked around, eagerly searching for someone they might consider an ally amid a sea of strangers.

'Oh, look,' said Elham. 'There's Soda. I didn't know she'd been invited.'

'Apparently so. Who's that she's talking to?'

'That's my husband.'

'Oh, yes, of course it is. How silly of me. He looks younger than usual.'

'That's probably because Soda is chatting him up, tart that she is.'

'The woman has no shame. I wouldn't be surprised if she charged by the hour.'

'I don't suppose she charges very much.'

The two friends laughed loudly, grabbing more champagne from another passing waiter.

Soda was a widow. Her husband, an army officer, had been killed in the early days of the Iran–Iraq War. Soda had grieved for a while, and then set about satisfying her sexual appetite with the help of lonely soldiers on leave from the front. In the process, she provided a service for men suffering from the stresses of war and an excess of testosterone. These soldiers would spend a few days in the city, exhaust themselves in Soda's bed, and then disappear. Within the space of an afternoon, they could experience the horror of war and the fun and glamour of city life. Unfortunately for Soda, she had once confided this aspect of her life to Selma. As a result, everyone in Adhamiyah knew about it.

'So, where's our hostess?' asked Selma. 'Is she hiding or something?'

'I think she's inside,' said Elham. 'That's her up there on the balcony, isn't it?'

'Yes, I think so. Who's she talking with?'

'I have no idea. Clearly, she doesn't feel the need to come down and mingle.'

'She might at least say hello.'

'Remember, Selma, the woman has no breeding. She came up from the gutters.'

'That is one thing I never forget.'

Selma's eyes drifted over to the patio, just in time to see her two offspring – Ahmed and Sheza – walking down the steps onto the lawn.

'Oh, my children have arrived. I wasn't sure that they were coming.'

'Well, that's lovely. Gosh, haven't they grown!'

Selma's son, Ahmed, had been back in Baghdad for almost two months now. His new office job at army headquarters suited him well. He was an energetic and outspoken young man, but hardly used to roughing it. In fact, he was more comfortable in his mother's company, shopping for clothes or bossing the domestic staff around. Since his early years, he had followed his mother like a shadow, taking her as his primary role model. In the process, he had acquired the habits of continual gossip and fighting at high volume with anyone who challenged his point of view.

He was, in fact, gay. But since his mother was so violently opposed to homosexuality, the boy had never dared to reveal the true nature of his desires. Indeed, since adolescence, he had worked hard to keep his urges under wraps. This only added to the ferocity of his temper whenever it was unleashed.

If anyone in the family knew of Ahmed's true nature, it was his sister. Sheza had seen the tell-tale signs in his speech and body language. From time to time, she would make some cryptic reference to his 'tendencies' and watch him squirm and sweat as his parents looked on, baffled. As a young woman with sadistic tendencies – no doubt inherited from her mother – Sheza found the whole situation highly amusing. The siblings often argued, but Sheza invariably won. With the nuclear option held in reserve, how could she lose?

This evening, they had set their enmity to one side in order to enjoy the party. Having failed to spot their mother in the crowd, they wandered off in search of booze.

'I don't think they've seen us,' said Elham. 'We should call them over.'

'No, wait a moment,' said Selma, grabbing her friend's arm.

She had spotted two new arrivals on the patio. It was Loma and Madeha; the pair seemed to be inseparable these days. In fact, neither of them would have had the courage to attend tonight's party alone. For one thing, the idea of partying with Malaka seemed rather strange. Added to which, Loma was worried that she might bump into Selma once more. If so, she would certainly need back-up.

'Look at that bitch,' said Selma.

'Which one?'

'Loma, of course. Who does she think she is? If she put her nose in the air any higher, she'd fall over backwards.'

'She thinks too much of herself, that's for sure.'

'They've probably just crawled out of bed.'

'Do you think they're lovers?'

'Of course they are. They can't have the men they want, so they play with each other beneath the sheets.'

'That's disgusting.'

'Of course it is. Just look at them – total degenerates.'

Just then, Malaka emerged from the house, stepping through the French windows. She greeted Loma and Madeha warmly, embracing each in turn. Moments later, she was placing drinks in their hands and ushering them back inside.

'Where's she taking them?' demanded Selma.

'Back inside, apparently.'

A few seconds passed, and Madeha appeared on the patio once more and started waving at Selma. Having gotten her attention, she then beckoned her forward, much like a dog owner calling its dog.

Selma decided on a brash show of confidence, striding headlong toward the house, glass held aloft.

'Malaka, darling!'

'Selma, darling!'

'It's so wonderful to see you again. The party is just fabulous.'

'I know, it's going just as I planned. You're looking divine.'

'And so are you. What interesting earrings!'

'Do come inside, I have something to show you.'

Selma was led into the living room. Loma and Madeha were already there, examining a large oil painting above the fireplace. They turned and saw Selma standing before them. The three women stared at each other, eyes wide, mouths open.

'Now, I've brought you here for a reason,' said Malaka, addressing everyone at once.

'What's that?' said Madeha, a strained note in her voice.

'I'm having my living room redecorated, and I want your advice. I can't decide on the colour. Beige was all very well last year. It went well with the brown furniture. But I'm having a new three-piece suite delivered, and it's purple – dark purple. I thought of having mauve walls to match. But I'm told it will clash. What do you think?'

'Well, I'm not sure, really...' began Loma.

'Purple is such a bold colour,' ventured Selma.

The door bell rang.

'I'll just get that,' said Malaka, marching from the room in her high-heeled leather boots.

In her absence, the three women exchanged greetings.

'I had no idea you'd been invited,' said Selma, eyebrows raised.

'Why shouldn't I be?'

'No reason at all. I just didn't think you knew Malaka.'

'Everyone knows Malaka.'

'Well, I suppose you have certain things in common.'

'Meaning?'

'Nothing at all, my dear. You really mustn't be so sensitive.'

'I'm not being sensitive. I'm just not sure what you're driving at.'

'There you are, being sensitive again. How's your husband?'

'He's fine, thank you. Of course, he's very busy.'

'He's not coming to the party then?'

'No, he has to prepare for London.'

Selma felt a pang of resentment at the mention of London. With the war raging, she had no hope of gaining permission to travel abroad. Meanwhile, this little whore would be living in London for years, thanks to her husband's job. She looked pretty smug about it too, showing off the new dress her husband had brought back from Italy. Not to mention the Ferragamo handbag and shoes by Fendi, a brand famous in Italy since the 1920s but generally unknown in Iraq – except by a very privileged few.

Selma did her best to hide her feelings: 'Yes, I understand he's been promoted. Ambassador, isn't it?'

'Not quite so important, I'm afraid: First Secretary, Political Affairs.'

'Oh, well, it's better than nothing. When do you leave?'

Loma opened her mouth, but no words came out. She was still not entirely sure that she would be going.

'She's probably going to wait until he's settled in first,' said Madeha.

'Very sensible,' said Selma, a wry smile on her lips. She sensed weakness here, and the prospect of exploiting it was suddenly thrilling.

'Yes, I'll probably wait a while,' confirmed Loma.

'You're right,' said Selma. 'And anyway, London can be very melancholic. It's a gloomy place in the winter, very grey and cold. You might want to try it first for a few months, just to see if you can handle it. Not everyone can. I've known people fall into deep a depression after moving to London. They leave behind their friends and family, the culture they know, the people they love – and before they know what's happening, they're in a deep depression. Once you fall so low, it's very hard to recover. Suicide is very common in London, you know.'

'I don't think she's going to fall into a depression,' said Madeha. Just as Selma was on the point of digging the knife deeper, Malaka returned from the hallway, bringing a new guest with her. It was Ali, looking smart in a white linen suit, his moustache neatly trimmed that morning.

Loma held her breath and stared, heart pounding.

'I think you all know Ali,' said Malaka. 'We go back a long way too, of course.'

There was silence, the sort of silence you could cut with a knife.

Malaka continued, apparently oblivious: 'I was just telling the ladies here about my plans for redecorating the room. The colour scheme is the big problem. I was thinking of purple and mauve. What do you think?'

She turned to Ali, expectantly.

'I'm not so sure,' he said. 'I suppose …'

Just as he was on the point of offering an opinion, Malaka threw her hands in the air.

'Oh my God! I've forgotten the caviar! Please chat amongst yourselves until I return.'

She disappeared, her various scarves and robes billowing behind her.

'Well, this *is* cosy,' said Selma, heaving with sarcasm. 'I see you've brought some wine with you, Ali. Is it a gift for someone? An admirer, perhaps?'

'Just something for the hostess.'

'Let me see,' said Selma, stepping forward and taking the bottle. 'Oh, lovely! French wine, a Bordeaux. Is it a good vintage?'

'I think it's pretty good.'

'It's old anyway,' said Selma. 'You should give it to Loma. She likes the older wines, something with a hint of the past. You do prefer something with a good vintage, don't you, Loma?'

'I have no idea what you mean. I like French wine, yes.'

'But you prefer the old to the new, right?'

'What on earth are you talking about?'

'Well, never mind. I suppose any gift from Ali would put a smile on your face, right?'

'I'm quite happy with what I've got, thank you.'

'Or do you save the best wines for your wife?' continued Selma, turning to Ali.

'My wife makes her own decisions when it comes to wine.'

'Yes, of course she does. And where is the lovely lady this evening?'

'She's at home with the children. We couldn't get a baby-sitter.'

'That's a shame. I'm sure Loma would love to meet your wife.'

'I believe they've already met, some time ago.'

Ali glanced at Loma, who was staring into her drink.

Selma paused to assess the situation, which she was enjoying immensely. She was sorely tempted to escalate the tensions. If she could possibly reduce Loma to tears, then so much the better. On the other hand, for some strange reason, she was reluctant to come off as an outright bully in Ali's presence. Like it or not, his opinion still mattered to her.

Ali made the decision for her, stepping forward and taking the bottle from Selma's hands. 'I'll put this outside,' he said, and he left the room.

Loma was looking quite mortified, her face pale. Selma left the room, laughing to herself.

When Malaka returned, she was carrying a tray of caviar. Noting that the room was empty, she smiled and stepped into the garden.

* * *

Selma was now back by the fountain with Elham, who had finally managed to grab hold of Ahmed and Sheza. They were all drinking heavily. Elham had found a large bowl of punch, and she was sharing it around. Selma took a glass and finished it off in seconds, then took another.

'What was that about?' said Elham.

'Oh, just a little reunion.'

'What reunion?'

'Loma and Ali – and me, of course, as an observer. I must say, Loma has definitely missed her Ali. They must have made a wonderful couple. I'm sure they were passionate lovers. It's a shame she couldn't hang on to him. My heart bleeds for her, it really does.'

Selma was talking loudly now, and deliberately so. She broke into a forced, theatrical laugh. Several people turned to look in her direction.

'She's going to miss Ali all the more when she goes to London,' continued Selma. 'She'll have to rely on her husband for affection, and we know how that's likely to work out. Yes, the little bitch will miss her Ali like crazy.'

'Where is her husband, by the way?'

'He's preparing for his big move, apparently. He'll be some sort of secretary at the embassy in London. I suppose he has lots of paperwork to sort out. That's if he's not with one of his girlfriends. And he's got quite a few girlfriends, of course. It must be quite time-consuming to say goodbye to them all – one by one.'

Selma laughed even louder than before, turning yet more heads. People were starting to whisper now, putting the rumours into circulation.

Loma was standing beneath a nearby tree, doing her best to ignore Selma's dramatics. Suddenly, she decided she'd had enough and made to leave, but Madeha grabbed her wrist.

'Don't back down,' she said. 'Remember, be strong. You have to stand up to her.'

'I'll try. But if she says one more thing to me …'

At that very moment, Ali arrived from nowhere. He was still holding the bottle of wine.

'Hi, Loma, how are you?' he said.

'Fine,' she muttered, gazing down at the grass.

She wished the earth would open up and swallow her. Several scenes from her past flashed before her mind's eye: her first date with Ali; their first kiss; the time they got caught in the rain and ran through the streets hand in hand. She recalled the strength of their love, and how she'd felt she was the happiest person in the world. She recalled her plans for a simple white wedding, ideally followed by two children – a boy and a girl. Then she recalled the betrayal, the agony, and the scandal that had left a black spot on her past.

'Are you alright?' said Ali, his voice soft with concern.

'I'm feeling a bit sick, actually.'

Madeha put her hand on Loma's back and began to rub it gently. Loma began to cry.

Ali wanted to pull her to him, to hold her tight, comfort her and shower her with kisses. He wanted to love and protect her, to tell her that he still loved her and that nothing would keep them apart – not even his wife and children. Instead, he simply laid a gentle hand on her shoulder and watched in silence.

This was all too much for Selma. She marched across the lawn, pushing people aside, her face like thunder. She stood before Loma, hands on hips.

'What's the matter now?' she demanded. 'Missing your husband already?'

'Leave her alone, you horrible woman!' said Ali.

Selma ignored him and continued: 'Don't worry, Loma, you've got Ali here to protect you. It'll be just like old times: two love birds, consumed by passion, united in mind and body, standing firm against the world. Of course, you're both married now, but that need not stand in your way. After all ...'

'Stop it!' screamed Loma. 'Just leave me alone! You've ruined my life already. What more do you want?'

Loma's outburst had been heard over the music. Everyone was looking her way now. The entire party was focused on events beneath the tree. As hostess, Malaka really ought to have intervened. However, she continued setting out little dishes of caviar on the tables.

Selma, meanwhile, was momentarily stunned. She hadn't expected the worm to turn like this. Now there was no backing down. She laughed again, louder than ever: 'There's no point in blaming others for your mistakes, my dear. I can hardly help it if you made the wrong choices.'

Loma lifted her glass of vodka, ready to throw it in Selma's face. Madeha grabbed her wrist: 'Don't!'

'You're just a slut!' screamed Loma. 'You're a whore and a slut and an evil bitch!'

She pulled her wrist free and threw the vodka in Selma's face – glass and all.

Selma reciprocated, throwing her drink at Loma, then grabbed her neck with both hands, sinking her highly polished nails deep into the soft skin.

Loma screamed and began raining blows down on Selma's head. Selma backed up for a moment, and then launched herself forward once more, scratching at Loma's face and eyes. Loma grabbed hold of Selma's hair and yanked down hard, so that she was bent double.

Seconds later, they were on the floor, rolling around on the wet grass, screaming at the tops of their voices: 'Bitch! Slut! Whore!' They scratched and slapped, and at one point Selma sunk her teeth into the soft flesh on Loma's upper arm. Loma screamed again and punched Selma square in the face.

Madeha and Ali were desperately trying to separate them now, assisted by several other guests, although without success. Then Ali felt a series of blows against his back and shoulders. Looking round, he saw Ahmed, his face contorted with rage, fists swinging in huge arcs through the air. He was screaming like a woman: 'Leave my mother alone! You whore! You bitch! I'll kill you! I'll fucking kill you!'

Ali wrapped his arms around Ahmed to stop the fists flying. In this way, the two men also fell to the grass and began rolling around, gathering grass stains on their freshly laundered suits.

Finally, Selma seemed to lose her energy. She wasn't as young as she used to be, and she certainly wasn't used to the exercise.

Madeha pulled Loma to her feet and frog-marched her across the lawn. Up the patio steps they went, through the living room, and out the front door.

As they drove back to Madeha's house, Loma wound down the window and watched the passing scenery in silence. If nothing else, she had at least reached an important conclusion: she would be departing for London at the first opportunity.

Tomorrow's another day

The next morning, Loma woke up early. She felt exhausted from the party and its harrowing events. Her sleep had been interrupted alternately by sweet dreams of Ali and nightmares of the witch Selma. She had a terrible hangover: every muscle ached and her head pounded.

She heard noises downstairs and decided that there was no point trying to get back to sleep. She went to the kitchen and found, to her surprise, that Madeha was busy cooking. She had a pan on the hob, with onions and fava beans gently simmering.

'Good morning,' said Loma, her voice just above a whisper.

Madeha turned round, startled: 'Oh, good morning. Did you sleep well?'

'What do you think, after that wild night? I told you before, there's no point trying to mend relations with that bitch.'

'Yes, Selma is Selma. She can't be changed.'

'She's just a vicious and mean old bitch,' said Loma, going to the fridge and pouring herself a glass of milk.

'Cheer up and forget about her. I'm making some *bakela*,' said Madeha cracking two eggs into the pan of beans.

'That's too much for me this morning, I'm afraid. Anyway, I have to watch my figure. I bet the women in London are all slim.'

'I don't think they can compete with you.'

'You're very sweet, as usual.'

Madeha served herself a plate of *bakela*, leaving the rest in the pan. She then poured two glasses of tea and joined Loma at the kitchen table.

'There's some on the hob if you want it.'

'Thank you,' said Loma, 'I'll just have some of yours.'

She tore off a scrap of bread and dipped it into the tasty mess on Madeha's plate, then popped it into her mouth. They were silent for a minute, Loma gazing through the window as Madeha tucked into breakfast. Their friendship was such that long silences were rarely uncomfortable. In any case, it was early, and Loma's eyes were not yet fully open.

'So, what are your plans?' said Madeha, pushing her empty plate to one side.

'Oh, I suppose I'm going to London.'

'I suppose so.'

'Yep, the sooner the better. I really can't go through last night again.'

'No, of course not.'

Loma sipped her tea and looked through the window again.

'Did she hurt you?' asked Madeha?

'I've got a couple of scratches, that's all.'

She pointed to her neck, which still bore the marks of Selma's nails.

'Ouch!' said Madeha.

'Yeah, I should probably put some make-up on it. I don't want Riaz asking questions.'

'Don't you think he'll find out anyway?'

'I suppose he will, but I'd rather delay any confrontation, if at all possible.'

'Of course. So, when are you leaving?'

'Well, he's flying out next week, on Friday. I was going to put it off as long as possible, but now I'll probably try and get on the same flight.'

Madeha suddenly looked very sad, tears welling up in her eyes.

'I'm going to miss you, you know,' she said.

'I'll miss you too, my darling.'

'But we can talk on the phone. Call me when you get to London.

'No,' said Loma. 'Let's write letters. I prefer putting things down on paper. We can write every week.'

'Okay, if you say so. But it takes almost two weeks for a letter to arrive from London. I'll be bothering the postman every day.'

'Me too.'

Their chatter had awoken Madeha's kids, and they now came thumping down the stairs in their pyjamas.

'What's for breakfast?' said the boy, wiping sleep from his eyes.

'I think I'd better go,' said Loma. 'If I can get home before Riaz wakes up, that'll be great.'

The two friends walked to the front door and held each other tight. Loma could feel Madeha's body shaking softly as she cried.

* * *

It was a weekend and pretty early, so the streets were largely empty as Loma drove home. She headed along Abu Nuwas Street, with its grand palm trees, and crossed the 14th July Bridge over the eternal River Tigris. She rounded the corner by the presidential complex and felt herself shaking. She had been inside the place several times, always for official receptions, to which her husband was frequently invited. The idea of encountering Saddam or one of his sons filled her with dread. Meeting with his disturbed wife wasn't much better.

Her husband was one of Saddam's favourites, but that provided little in the way of security. The President was paranoid about those around him. Anyone who was unlucky enough to fall under suspicion was beyond helping. It didn't matter how much you loved them.

Loma sped up, heading further west, away from the river, until she reached the affluent suburb of Mansour. She pulled up at her 1960s house, built on the American model, with a front garden and a large garage to one side. She parked the car and walked through the door connecting garage with house.

The maid rushed to greet her, concern written all over her face.

'Good morning, madam. The children are fine. They've had their breakfast and are watching TV in the lounge.'

'Is my husband up yet?'

'He didn't come home last night, madam.'

Loma sighed deeply.

'My good old husband!' she said, dumping her handbag on the kitchen table.

More than likely, he had spent the night with one of his mistresses, a secretary, or even a prostitute. She had become used to this kind of behaviour on his part. Meanwhile, she was required to perform the role of devoted wife and mother – as expected by society and the extended family. Loyalty was a highly prized value, but it seemed to be all on her side.

It was on the question of a woman's role that Loma felt some gratitude toward Saddam. He had banned polygamy in Iraq, ruling against the tradition that a Muslim man can have up to four wives. Indeed, this move, along with various other acts of modernization, had won him some popularity among many Iraqi women. Of course, none of this stopped Riaz from sleeping around.

Loma called for her maid and explained that she would be leaving for London in a week's time. She would be going with her husband, probably on the same flight, and the children would be coming too. Loma would start making a list of everything that had to be packed, and the maid would have to help. The suitcases would have to be brought into the bedrooms, and boxes would be needed, along with lots of packing tape.

Loma wanted to take all of her personal belongings, everything to which she had a sentimental attachment. Taking it with her would by symbolic: she was going to London with a view to making it work. Yes, she would be leaving a lot behind in Baghdad, but she must take as much as possible with her.

She climbed the stairs to her bedroom and began to sort through the wardrobes, putting the clutter into various piles. Some things she would be taking; others would be remaining behind; while certain other stuff could be dumped or given away. A nice Yves Saint Laurent dress would be given to her niece, for example. Meanwhile, Madeha could have the long, silver earrings of Bedouin design. They didn't seem quite suitable for a diplomat's wife, and there was no point leaving them in an empty house. Even so, she must be sensitive when giving them to Madeha, so that it didn't look like charity. It would be explained as a memento, which was not entirely untrue.

 The week passed very quickly for Loma. When she wasn't packing, she was saying goodbye to a continual stream of friends and family. Some showed their loyalty and affection, seeking to boost her confidence ahead of the big move. However, a greater number emphasised how important it was that she fully support her husband in his new job. Others merely wanted to benefit from Loma's giveaway, hoping for a generous hand-out.

The day before her flight to London, Loma suddenly felt very stressed. She had a terrible sense of suffocation, as if she were being controlled by events, rather than the other way around. For the past week, she had managed to block out all thoughts of the dreadful fight with Selma, and her husband hadn't even mentioned it. If he'd heard any rumours, he wasn't interested in raising the topic. Despite several intimate sessions in bed, he hadn't once mentioned the marks on her neck.

Now, as she sat alone in the kitchen, nursing a vodka and tonic, it all came back to her: the sarcastic comments, the insults, the drinks flying in both directions, the screaming and fighting – rolling around on the grass. She blushed with shame to think of how many people had seen her in that state. It was a wonder that Riaz hadn't scolded her for such an embarrassing display. After all, the very last thing he needed at this point in his career was a public scandal.

There were few more prestigious positions than First Secretary at the embassy in London. The foreign ministry was the jewel of the Iraqi crown, and its employees were appointed only after careful vetting. A posting to London was highly prestigious, a sign that one's skills and loyalty were truly appreciated.

A foreign posting had many advantages. For one thing, one was at some distance from Saddam's entourage. Added to which, the embassy staff had an apparently bottomless expense account at their disposal. Saddam wanted to show the world that his country was both powerful and wealthy, and big spending on the part of Iraqi diplomats was one way of achieving this. Extravagant parties were thrown on a regular basis, and embassy staff could often be seen at the best restaurants.

Loma phoned Madeha, and they arranged to meet at the Alwiyah Club. She drove back across the river and parked in the club car park. As she headed for the club house, she looked up at the Ishtar Sheraton, which loomed over the entire neighbourhood. The doorman held the door open as Loma passed inside. He was a nice man, one of the many Egyptians who had found work in Baghdad, replacing those young Iraqis who were serving at the front. She walked through into the garden and took a seat in the shade of a huge eucalyptus tree. It had been planted, along with all the others, by the British, who brought them from Australia. She ordered a cup of tea and watched the children splashing about in the pool. She was relieved to see that neither Malaka nor Selma were present; if they had been, she would have departed immediately.

A few minutes later, Madeha came in, wearing a simple T-shirt and tight jeans, a large shawl draped around her pelvis, so as not to attract the attention of young men. They kissed and hugged, and this time it was Loma who burst into tears as Madeha held her tight.

'What's the problem?' Madeha asked.

'I don't know. I feel upset and depressed, and I can't talk honestly with anyone.'

'What about me?'

'You know you're the only person I trust.'

'So, what's wrong?'

'It's all building up – leaving my family behind, and my country. Also, I'm worried there'll be some big scandal at some point. That would ruin everything.'

Loma was shaking.

'Do you mean Selma?'

'Who else? After the party, I'm more worried than ever. I used to think she was wicked, but now I realize that she just doesn't care. She's really crazy. She might do anything.'

'Don't worry. It's been a week, and nothing has happened. If she was going to do something, you'd have heard about it already. Anyway, you're leaving for London tomorrow, and people have a very short memory. In a few weeks, it will all seem like a bad dream.'

'Yes, but while I'm in London, Selma will be free to spread rumours about me. She'll put her spin on the fight at the party.

She'll say it was all my fault. And I won't be around to defend myself.'

'Yes, but everyone knows Selma's a troublemaker. They'll take anything she says with a pinch of salt. Anyway, you'll be so busy with your new life in England that it won't matter. I mean, does it really matter what people are saying in Baghdad when you're shopping at Harrods?'

Loma didn't reply. She sipped her tea and looked around the garden, as if Selma or one of her allies might be lurking behind a plant. She tapped her fingers on the table.

'I can't just let her talk trash about me,' she said at last. 'That sort of thing can ruin a reputation. My husband has an important job now, and I can't jeopardize that. I just feel I should try to fix things somehow before I leave.'

'How? What can you possibly do in the next 24 hours?'

'I don't know. Perhaps I could talk with Selma and get things straightened out once and for all. What do you think?'

Madeha shook her head and sighed.

'Listen, Loma, there's nothing you can do now. The more you stir things up, the more the problem will grow. You'll just have to let Selma expend her energy how she chooses and live with the results. Eventually, she'll wear herself out. It might take a while, but eventually that point will come. The important thing is for you to focus on your future. And try to enjoy it.'

Loma smiled: 'Yes, you're probably right. I do forget sometimes that I'm supposed to be enjoying life.'

'Exactly, and this is our last day together, so let's enjoy it while we can.'

'Don't say that, Madeha. This isn't our last day. We'll always be friends. That's the one reliable thing in my life.'

* * *

Several miles north along the river, Selma was standing in her garden, breathing in the fresh air, scented with the perfume of a thousand flowers. She was sipping Turkish coffee from a small cup. Once she had finished, she would read the grounds.

Most woman would prefer to use an expert for such readings, but Selma did her own. She had learned from an old lady, who had been willing to part with her method for a hefty fee. Selma was by no means a professional, but she had often performed readings for others, partly as a way of showing off, but also because it offered such a great opportunity to look into other people's lives, to read their minds and exert influence.

Her victims were often women with troubles but no intention of paying a psychotherapist. In their culture, 'psychotherapy' was obtained from various sources, all free of charge. They would gossip, chatter and complain endlessly, laying their issues bare to some trusted confidant. It was only when such methods failed that they might turn to a magician or sheikh. Such people would tell fortunes, cast out spirits and even put curses on enemies. Selma had often adopted the role of informal 'wise lady' – although she was kind enough never to charge.

She wandered back toward the house and sat in the shade of the colourful canvas awning. Just as she was on the point of reading the coffee grains, her son arrived.

'Hello, mother.'

'Hello, Ahmed.'

They kissed and the boy sat down at the table.

'Are you going to the club?' he asked, largely because he hoped for a lift there himself.

'No, my darling. I'm staying at home today. I have various things to do.'

'Like what?'

'Various things ...'

She was affecting an air of nonchalance, but Ahmed knew is mother well enough to see through it. She had something on her mind. Most likely, it was that bitch Loma.

He wasted no time.

'Have you heard about Loma?' he said, suddenly animated.

'What about her?'

'She's leaving for London tomorrow.'

'Yes, I knew that already, my dear. I think everyone knows that.'

'How can she be allowed to leave the country after what she did to you? Why is her husband allowed to keep his job? He should have been stripped of his position immediately.'

'Well, what have I always said? This country is only fit for three kinds of people: parasites, prostitutes, and pimps. The rest have to get by as best they can.'

'Of course, you're quite right, Mother. But I can assure you of one thing: she will not get away with what she did.'

'I agree with you completely, my dear Ahmed. She will not get away with it. Not at all.'

Selma turned her coffee cup over. She leaned forward and peered at the grains. The omens were clear: revenge!

The love nest

A few blocks from Zelfa's house, Jerry sat in his blue Chevrolet, listening to the radio. A popular Iraqi singer was belting out a tune that had become ubiquitous in recent weeks. Jerry hummed along, occasionally muttering the lyrics – something about undying love, sweet memories and broken hearts. He would much rather be listening to the Rolling Stones, but the cassette player was broken, and he hadn't gotten around to getting it fixed. Such tasks were way down his list of priorities these days. Right now, he was waiting for Zelfa, and she was already 15 minutes late, a fact that made him anxious for a number of reasons.

From a purely professional standpoint, he was concerned that his operation may have been compromised. He'd been tasked with building friendships within Iraq's ruling elite, or at least with people who had access to such circles. By way of friendship – and perhaps even love – he was to obtain information of value to the US government. This might include details on who held power, who made decisions, who was loyal to whom – and who might be convinced to work in secret for a foreign power.

Zelfa had been Jerry's first port of call, and she had proven a promising prospect. After all, it was rumoured that her daughter spent her weekends at parties attended by Uday Hussein. With some tact and discretion – and a certain amount of charm – there was no telling what information he might be able to glean.

Of course, Jerry knew that he was under surveillance by the *Mukhabarat*. His arrival at the US Embassy had been low-key, but his cover as a Foreign Service Reserve Officer was hardly convincing. The Iraqis had worked out which car was his, and he had been tailed more than once. He'd also noticed some rather stiff men in suits sitting at a discrete distance while he chatted with Zelfa at the club. There was a good chance that they'd noticed this burgeoning love affair, and they'd been right to pay close attention.

In which case, perhaps Zelfa wouldn't be coming today. Perhaps their secret meeting had been cancelled without his knowledge by some Iraqi spook. Perhaps Zelfa was already locked in a cell at *Mukhabarat* headquarters, facing a barrage of questions. If so, then Jerry would have to keep his distance; he'd have to walk away and start digging elsewhere.

But his concerns were more than merely professional. After several weeks of intimate discussion with Zelfa, he was starting to fall in love. He had tried to resist the process, but it was clearly futile. As he sat in the car, he felt a dull ache in his chest; he longed to see her, to hold her, to exchange kind words and kisses. The very thought of her being in a jail cell, meanwhile, caused him distress: he felt the hairs stand up on the back of his neck; his feet suddenly felt heavy and cold; beads of sweat gathered on his forehead.

He looked at his watch again; she was 20 minutes late now. It didn't take 20 minutes to walk from Sabah Street to his current location. Perhaps something was wrong. He checked the rear-view mirror, then the wing mirrors. There were several cars parked in the street, but he couldn't see anybody in them. Nobody was loitering in a doorway, nobody stood on a street corner. So far has he could tell, he hadn't been followed from his house that evening. And if he had, the circuitous route he'd taken through the winding streets had been sufficient to lose the tail. Possibly, therefore, it would be safe to walk past Zelfa's house, or at least take a peek from a distance.

He turned off the radio, removed the keys from the ignition and opened the door. As he did so, he saw something through the windscreen. It was Zelfa, rounding the corner, heading toward him with her head down. She was wearing a light chiffon dress with a flowery pattern. She had bought it from Karada, spending a small fortune in the process. The fabric clung to her tanned, toned legs as she marched along the pavement, high heels clacking. Jerry sat back in his seat and closed the door. He waited, wondering if a gang of Iraqi intelligence officers might pounce on her at the very last moment. But they didn't.

'Hello, my darling,' she said, climbing into the passenger seat.

'Hello, sweetheart.'

They exchanged a long and passionate kiss. Jerry started the engine and pulled out from the kerb, shifting through the gears like a racing driver.

* * *

The journey took less than 10 minutes. The flat was less than a mile away, still within Adhamiya, and Jerry had studied the route in some detail the day before. In fact, if it hadn't been for the question of security, they might easily have walked it.

'Aren't we going to park?' said Zelfa as they sped past the apartment block.

'Yes, but not here,' said Jerry, glancing at the entrance, where a sleepy doorman rested on a rickety wooden chair.

They reached the end of the street and Jerry turned a sharp left, barely bothering to reduce speed. Zelfa was thrown gently up against the door as they rounded the corner.

'We're going the wrong way,' complained Zelfa.

'Don't worry, we'll come back.'

Jerry checked his mirrors and turned left again, then parked in the first available spot. He sat motionless, watching for movement in the mirrors. Zelfa was growing impatient now.

'Aren't we getting out?'

'Just a second.'

He turned and pulled a small sports bag from the back seat, then removed the car keys and opened the door. He stood for a while in the street, looking in every direction.

'Jerry?'

'Yes, I'm here. Let's go.'

'At last!'

'Just being cautious. Better safe than sorry.'

The apartment block was modest but well cared for, consisting of six floors, a mix of flats and offices. Washing hung from the balconies, and a bird sat in its cage, singing a tune. Zelfa introduced herself to the doorman, explaining that she was a friend of Malaka. The doorman smiled and nodded. Any friend of Malaka was welcome, he said.

'We've come to see apartment 27,' said Zelfa.

She was shaking a little as she spoke, almost swallowing her words.

'Ah, yes!' said the doorman, disappearing into his little room and returning with a key.

'Fifth floor,' she smiled, holding open the lift door.

'Thank you.'

The apartment was small but more than adequate for their needs: kitchen, bathroom, living room and bedroom. The décor was from the 1960s and hardly attractive, the colour scheme a ghastly mix of orange, purple and brown. But, of course, they hadn't come here for the décor.

'Oh, this is wonderful,' said Zelfa excitedly, as she stood on the balcony. 'I can see the river from here. Come and have a look, Jerry.'

There was no answer.

Jerry was in the kitchen, unpacking his sports bag, which sat on the kitchen table. He took a screwdriver and began to remove the covers on the plug sockets, examining the wires, and then returning them to their former state. This task completed, he did the same with the light switch. He then pulled out the fridge and the stove, checking every nook and cranny – inside, outside, above, below, front and back. He then started on the cupboards, which were thankfully bare. He then stood on a chair and peered at the overhead light. Having checked everything manually, he returned to the bag and retrieved a small electronic device and began scanning for bugs, waving it high and low, watching for the little red light.

'What on earth are you doing?' said Zelfa, standing in the doorway.

'Just making sure that we're not being listened to.'

'Why?'

'Relax, Zelfa. It's just a precaution. I work at the US Embassy, remember?'

'But don't you think this is going a bit too far? Do you really think
Malaka would spy on us?'

'Well, how well do you know Malaka?'

Zelfa was silent. Perhaps he was right: better safe than sorry.

She returned to the lounge and turned on the TV. Collapsing on
the sofa, she grabbed the remote and began flicking through the
channels. The highly cultured presenter was talking to the
camera, introducing a French film. Afterwards, he would settle
down to a discussion on the movie with several intellectual
guests. It was just what Zelfa would be watching tonight if she had
decided to stay home alone. For a brief moment, as her date
rummaged through his bag of tools, she wished she had done
exactly that.

'What's this?' said Jerry, appearing suddenly, screwdriver in hand.

'A French movie. Do you want to watch it?'

Jerry screwed up his face. Action movies were more his thing.

'Maybe later,' he said. 'I have to finish checking the flat.'

'Sure, I'll leave you to it.'

Zelfa turned off the TV and went into the bathroom. She was glad
to find a pile of clean towels and a fresh bar of soap. As she
showered, she couldn't help smiling to herself.

It was another hour before Jerry had finished checking all the
rooms. He took a shower and crept into bed beside Zelfa. He lay
on his back and breathed a big sigh. She put down her book and

turned toward him, spreading one arm across his hairy chest, ensnaring his legs in her own. She closed her eyes and squeezed.

'Wow! At last!' she whispered. 'I've waited so long to do this.'

'Yeah, it feels pretty good, doesn't it?'

They lay there in silence for a while, basking in the joy of romantic union.

'Wait!' said Jerry, suddenly springing from bed.

'What is it?'

'I didn't see that before.'

He placed a chair against the far wall and stood on it, peering closely at an ornate brass light fixture without a bulb.

'So, what is it?' demanded Zelfa, clearly weary.

'It's a light fixture.'

'So, what!'

'So, I'm checking it.'

'This is getting ridiculous!'

Jerry jumped down and wandered into the kitchen, returning moments later with a bulb in his hand. He then hopped up on the chair once more and screwed the bulb into place. He pulled on the little cord that dangled down, but the bulb didn't light up.

'So, it's broken,' said Zelfa.

'Apparently so.'

'Please don't tell me that you want to fix the wiring now.'

'Maybe not tonight.'

'Can you come back to bed at some point?'

Jerry unscrewed the bulb and placed it in a draw, then crept beneath the sheets.

'Honestly, Jerry, don't you think you're going a bit overboard with all this?'

'Well, it's better ...'

'I know: better safe than sorry.'

'Exactly. You're learning.'

Jerry was smiling broadly as he raised himself on one elbow and began to shower Zelfa with kisses. First her mouth, then her eyes, forehead, ears and neck. She closed her eyes, savouring the delicious sensation as he worked his way down her body.

'Jerry, turn out the bedside lamp,' she whispered.

He reached across and flicked the switch.

* * *

In the street outside, two olive-skinned men sat in a black Mercedes, watching as the bedroom went dark. They were there all night, listening to the radio, chatting and smoking incessantly. They took it in turns to sleep, welcoming the dawn with a breakfast of bread and cheese, washed down with lukewarm coffee from a flask. They watched in silence as the two love birds emerged onto the street, Jerry tucking in his shirt and smoothing down his hair. Zelfa was dabbing her face with a powder-puff as she stepped into the bright morning sun.

'She looks exhausted,' commented one of the men.

'I don't suppose she got much sleep,' said the other, chuckling.

Five minutes later, the two men exited the Mercedes and crossed the street. They wore fine greys suits, sunglasses and thick moustaches, and each carried a sports bag, not too different from Jerry's. The men greeted the doorman, who knew them well. There was no need to provide these two gentlemen wIth keys; they always brought their own.

Upstairs, they entered apartment 27 first. As the door swung open, they stopped to listen, in case any guests had arrived unseen. The two men checked each room in turn, and then set to work. Opening their bags, they pulled out numerous tiny microphones, each with its own coil of wire, along with little battery packs, radio transmitters, and various tools. They started in the kitchen, then worked their way through the living-room, bathroom and bedroom, inserting two bugs in each room. They pulled the bed away from the wall and removed the backing from the headboard. After all, if they were to record pillow-talk, they'd have to get in nice and close. The microphone installed, they put the bed back in position, replacing the sheets and pillows exactly as they'd found them. Then they got to work on the two telephones in the bedroom and living-room. The handsets were dismantled, the bugs inserted, and the handsets screwed back together.

Before leaving, they inspected the brass light-fixture on the wall opposite the bed that Jerry had found so fascinating. Standing on a chair, the shorter of the two gentlemen removed one of the four screws that attached the fixture to the wall. This done, he carefully inserted a screwdriver into the hole, then pulled it out. He placed his mouth close to the hole and blew. Finally, he took a little torch and shone it inside.

'That should be fine,' he said.

'Okay, let's go.'

They returned the chair to its former position and then embarked on a final inspection of the apartment, checking that each room was exactly as they had found it.

Their next call was at the flat next door, number 26. Inside, they were greeted by a young man, also in a smart grey suit, but bearing all the signs of a night without sleep. After a muted greeting, he stood back and watched as his colleagues got to work in the bedroom. They set their bags down on the bed and unzipped them. The shorter of the two men climbed onto a box and opened a little wooden cabinet attached to the wall. His partner, meanwhile, removed an 8mm cine-camera from a bag and began cleaning the lens.

'This is going to be a beautiful little movie,' he said.

'Yes, we'll get an Oscar for this one.'

Lost in London

It was a chilly spring morning in Kensington, that up-market London neighbourhood known for its historic sites and abundance of consulates and embassies. Among them was the Iraqi Embassy, located in Queen's Gate, a busy thoroughfare not far from Hyde Park, the largest of central London's green spaces. The embassy was located in a large, five-story terraced house, part of a long row in the Regency style. With its portico, columns and balconies, and a fresh coat of white paint, it reflected the wealth and status of its owners.

Just a few blocks south of the embassy was the Natural History Museum, an imposing Romanesque structure built from hand-carved stone blocks. It took a decade to complete, opening to the public in 1881. To the north was the Royal Albert Hall, an enormous, red-brick concert venue built in honour of the Royal Consort, Prince Albert. Opening some ten years before the museum, its circular shape was inspired by the amphitheatres of Rome. Meanwhile, across the park to the north-west sat the most elite of all local structures: Kensington Palace. This sprawling red-brick building had been a royal residence for several centuries, with various additions by great architects such as Christopher Wren, the genius behind St Paul's Cathedral.

On the south side of Hyde Park, not far from the Royal Albert Hall, was Loma's new home, just one of several buildings accommodating Iraqi officials in London. It was a pleasant terraced house with a modest garden and plenty of room for a small family and their domestic staff. On this particular morning, Loma stood at the living-room window on the second floor, looking down on the park, with its joggers, dog-walkers and office workers scurrying about. The gloomy sky, with its grey clouds, promised yet more rain. She sipped from her cup of tea and reflected – not for the first time – that London wasn't really her thing.

Of course, she was in a very privileged position now. She had two salaries: one in the UK and another in Iraq. She was able to shop in the West End and Knightsbridge, like many other British ladies, and without the need to budget. She could satisfy her own needs and those of her immediate family, and still send gifts to relatives back home. Best of all, she was able to send parcels of goodies – clothes, make-up, jewellery, handbags and shoes – to her mother for sale at a profit in Baghdad. As the nation transitioned from socialism to capitalism, there was a growing spirit of entrepreneurship, accompanied by a yearning for all things Western. Loma didn't particularly need the money, but there was something satisfying about turning a healthy profit from such transactions, and much of it went to keep her mother in comfort. Loma couldn't exactly claim to be bored. London itself was far from dull: there was no end of dinner parties and embassy receptions to keep one busy, not to mention brunch meetings and shopping trips with other women in diplomatic circles. And yet, after nine months in the city, Loma still felt horribly lonely.

For one thing, her husband was always busy, writing reports, holding meetings, attending conferences, and dealing with the media. Often, he would 'work late' at the embassy, which Loma took to mean one of two things: either he was actually working, or else he was on a date with his secretary. Sometimes he would not come home at nights, claiming some important meeting at the Ritz or Claridge's. She had also learned of his visits to Soho, where he presumably made use of the whores.

In the early years of their marriage, she had protested at such behaviour, even dissolving into tears and throwing plates. But after many attempts at reforming Riaz, she had given up. He always promised to mend his ways, but a short while later she would find him at it again. She had found the whole situation both humiliating and depressing – but even these feelings had come to seem 'normal', just part of the burden shouldered by any dutiful wife and mother.

Perhaps she would have been less forgiving if she'd been more interested in sex. Riaz had a high sex drive, but Loma had never felt properly able to reciprocate. She'd felt plenty of passion for Ali, but intimacy with Riaz had always seemed more of a chore than a pleasure.

She had long pondered the option of divorce, concluding every time that it was out of the question. For one thing, she would never subject her mother and children to such shame. Added to which, Riaz would never allow it. His career depended on maintaining the appearance – not matter how thin – of a stable marriage and home life. A divorce, coupled with allegations of infidelity, might mean a block on future promotions, perhaps even unemployment. No, Loma would just have to put up with the situation as best she could.

There were compensations, of course. She loved her two boys, aged ten and twelve. They were her little treasures, providing her with a reason to get out of bed each morning. She had hoped to send them to Eton or Harrow. However, the waiting lists were long, and the fees extortionate. Added to which, Riaz didn't want to be seen as mixing too freely with Britain's social elite. Instead, they opted for King's College School in Wimbledon, a small but respectable private school not far from the famous tennis courts. The boys seemed happy enough there, and with private tuition, their English was coming along very well. They were even becoming good at cricket, which was quite a surprise.

Yes, the boys were a definite compensation, thought Loma, as she finished her tea and wandered into her study, taking a seat behind her desk. She pushed a button and moments later, a Filipino maid knocked and entered.

'Have the boys gone to school?' said Loma.

'Yes, ma'am. They left half an hour ago.'

'Good, thank you. I forgot to kiss them goodbye for some reason. I have my mind on other things today. Will you bring me some breakfast please?'

'Yes, ma'am. What would you like?'

'Toast and marmalade, please, and a fresh pot of tea. I'll have it in here.'

'Yes, ma'am.'

Loma looked around the room, which was tastefully decorated in the Regency style. The curtains, carpets and wallpaper had all been carefully selected, while the furniture and ornaments were all genuine antiques. The rest of the house was the same, each room with its own colour scheme. She could hardly complain, and yet it all seemed so sterile in contrast to her beloved Baghdad. The same could be said for the supposedly great architecture of Kensington. Indeed, London in general seemed to follow the same principle: grand and impressive, but empty at its core.

A few weeks earlier, Loma had complained to her Iraqi housekeeper that London was overrated, and that nothing could compare to the great Gardens of Babylon. The housekeeper had wanted to point out that the Gardens of Babylon were only in history books, whereas London was real. However, she valued her job too much to risk making such a comment. Instead, she agreed with her boss, commenting that England could be a cold and unwelcoming place, particularly for Arabs.

As Loma waited for breakfast, she began to wonder whether Selma had been right about London. Perhaps any Iraqi moving to the city was bound to feel isolated at some point, at risk of falling into a depression? Once one started on the downward spiral, perhaps there would be no recovery?

The maid entered and began setting the breakfast down on Loma's desk. She was followed by Mona, a junior secretary from the embassy, bearing a bundle of files and newspapers. She had been helping Loma to prepare for a meeting with Iraqi students in London. While the wives of diplomats were not technically obliged to engage in such work, Loma hoped that by keeping busy she might stave off the blues.

'Read me the news, will you, Mona?' said Loma, spreading marmalade on her toast. She had studied English at school, but she still struggled at times with the language of newspapers.

Mona began to read through the broadsheets, translating into Arabic as she went. She focussed on the headlines and first paragraphs, selecting only the more important stories. Suddenly, she stopped, open-mouthed.

'What's up?' enquired Loma, sipping her tea.

'Well, this story seems to be false. It can't be true.'

'What is it?'

'Well, this story says that Uday Hussein has been gambling in the south of France and has lost huge amounts of money.'

'Let me see,' said Loma, snatching the newspaper and reading for herself.

The secretary stood in silence, barely daring to breathe. A minute later, Loma folded the newspaper roughly and handed it back.

'Get rid of this now. I don't want such rubbish in my house. You must show it to the press secretary, though. I'm sure he'll have something to say about it.'

'Yes, ma'am.'

'Make sure my husband knows about it too.'

'Yes, ma'am.'

'You can leave me now. I won't need you again today.'

The secretary departed, shaking life a leaf.

As Loma devoured her breakfast, she pondered the consequences of such a scandal for Riaz. It wasn't his fault, of course, if the British newspapers chose to slander Saddam's son, but Riaz would be among those Iraqi diplomats held responsible if the issue wasn't dealt with swiftly. If things escalated, he might be punished, perhaps even thrown in prison.

What would he do? How would he handle it? Would he issue a denial? Would he speak with the newspapers? That really wasn't his specialism, of course. He was more at home making secret arms deals with shady Western suppliers.

Loma had met Uday on several occasions over the years, and each event was burned into her memory. One time at a Foreign Ministry event, he'd started swearing at officials, cursing them openly. Everyone had been terrified, and they were glad when he finally left for a party elsewhere. Another time, at the Presidential Palace, he had been high on drugs. After starting an argument with someone, he'd disappeared upstairs with his bodyguard, and Loma had heard the sounds of gunfire. Uday was just as keen on collecting guns as he was on cars.

Loma phoned the press secretary.

'Has the ambassador read the newspapers this morning?'

'He's in a meeting, ma'am. But if you're referring to the story about Uday Hussein, then I'm aware of the problem. We'll be deciding on a response later today.'

'What do you think can be done?'

'That's up to the ambassador, of course, but I can tell you that he won't be happy. Needless to say, the allegations are completely untrue. It seems the British really can't leave us alone. Not content with having abused us in various ways throughout history, they now want to undermine our leadership. It's a deliberate act of intimidation, probably orchestrated by British intelligence. Margaret Thatcher may well be involved, bearing in mind her personal grudge against the ambassador.'

'Yes, I wouldn't be at all surprised,' said Loma.

'Well, I must get on, I'm afraid. Thank you for your concern.'

'You're very welcome.'

Loma hung up and started going through her papers. She couldn't decide on the topic of her speech to the students. Perhaps it might be something on the power of higher education to open up a world of opportunities. On second thoughts, she wasn't sure how convincing she would be in delivering such a message. After all, she'd gone from school to a failed love affair, and then from university to an unhappy marriage with a cheating husband. Who was she to lecture young people on the value of education?

She threw down her papers and walked back into the living room, standing once more at the window. Down in the park, a young couple was standing beneath a tree, exchanging kind words and gentle kisses. Loma thought of Ali, and the next second she was thinking of Selma.

What was the bitch doing these days? Was she making trouble in Baghdad, spreading rumours? Perhaps the secret was already out?

Loma climbed the stairs to her bedroom, locked the door and picked up the phone. Sitting on the bed, she began to dial Madeha's number. Pretty soon, she realised that she'd forgotten it. She hadn't called her best friend for over a month now. She tried again, getting a wrong number. On the third attempt, she got through, although there was plenty of static on the line.

'Hello, Madeha, is that you?'

'Yes, it's me. Is that Loma?'

'Yes, darling. It's so good to hear your voice at last.'

'Same here, Loma. Good to hear from you.'

'How are you, darling?'

'I'm fine, what about you?'

Loma was simultaneously happy and anxious. There seemed to be a hint of hesitation in Madeha's voice, as if she was hiding something.

'Is something wrong?'

'No, I'm fine.'

'Has something happened? Has Selma been making trouble?'

'Just a bit.'

'What has she been saying?'

'Oh, the usual thing, I'm afraid. But she seems to be more reckless than ever. I wasn't there, but apparently she told Soda that you were in love with ... someone. She said it quite loudly at the club, and I think lots of people must have heard. You know what she's like.'

'What did she say? Did she mention ...?'

Loma stopped short of finishing her sentence, aware that the phones might be bugged.

'No, apparently not. There was no history lesson. But she's telling people that you're in love.'

'So, it's just a matter of time before she spills the beans.'

'Maybe, Loma, maybe not. It's hard to be sure what she'll do next.'

There was a tone of weariness in Madeha's voice, and Loma thought that her life in Baghdad must be less than inspiring.

'Madeha, I want you to come to London,' she said.

Her friend was silent, apparently in shock at the idea.

'When? I'm working.'

'Well, it's spring break soon, isn't it? Don't you teachers get holidays?'

'Yes, of course.'

'Well then, you'll spend your spring vacation in London.'

'But we need special permission to travel abroad.'

'Don't be silly, that's not a problem. I'll speak to the Foreign Ministry and get it organised for you this week. And I'll get them to provide you with air tickets, free of charge: Iraqi Airways, first class.'

'What about my kids?'

'Well, you can send them to your mother's place, can't you? They'll enjoy that. She looks after them half the time anyway, doesn't she?'

'Yes.'

'So, there you go. It's no problem at all. And I really want to see you, so you have to come, Madeha. I'm afraid you have no choice.'

'Okay, I'll come.'

'Thank you, darling. We'll have a wonderful time.'

After the phone call, Loma dialled another number, one that was more permanently etched in her memory.

'Hello, Mum, it's Loma.'

'Loma, my darling! How wonderful! Where are you?'

'I'm still in London, I'm afraid.'

'Are you coming home?'

'Not just yet. I have to stay here for a while. I have lots to do.'

'But are you alright?'

'Yes, I'm fine, Mum. How are you?'

'I'm keeping well, my dear. Nothing to complain about.'

'How are the neighbours doing?'

'They're alright. Wedad finally gave birth. It's a boy, very healthy. Soda's son may go to the front, and she's worried, of course.'

'What about Selma?'

'What about her? She's just the same as usual, gossiping about everything under the sun.'

'It's probably best to steer clear of her then.'

'What do you mean? I'm not afraid of a little gossip.'

'No, but you don't want to get involved, do you?'

'I don't know what you mean, Loma. I'm not a little girl. I don't think there's anything that Selma could say that would be too shocking for me to hear.'

'No, but I'd rather you didn't get involved anyway. Think of my position now, Mother. With Riaz doing his new job, we can't afford any scandal. So, I'd rather you just steered clear of Selma from now on, if you don't mind.'

'It's a bit difficult, my dear. She's my neighbour, after all. I see her in the street.'

'Yes, but don't go to her house, please. Just do this for me, can you?'

There was a short silence, and then her mother spoke.

'Alright, darling, if it makes you happy. I don't want you to be stressed.'

'Thank you, Mother. I love you very much.'

'I love you too, darling.'

They chatted some more, Loma listening to her mother's account of daily life back home, all the while trying to disguise her own growing sense of alienation in the glittering West. When she finally put the receiver down, she felt a wave of relief. Perhaps the whole situation could be managed after all.

She returned downstairs and resumed her position by the living-room window. The romantic couple were now sitting on a park bench. The man had his arm around her shoulders and their heads were touching.

Loma drifted back 15 years, to her affair with Ali. They had been very much in love, two teenagers determined to marry at some future point. In the meantime, they were conducting their affair in secret, meeting for walks by the river or holding hands on park benches. Meeting without a chaperone was considered a disgraceful act, and so they avoided locations where they might be spotted by friends or relatives. Over the course of a year, their love grew: they shared secrets, expressed their admiration, and asserted their life-long devotion. After university, once every other hurdle had been crossed, they would seek their families' permission to marry.

However, Ali couldn't wait so long before satisfying his sexual desires. He wanted them to consummate their love now, giving physical form to their spiritual bond. Loma finally gave in to his begging, and they found themselves in a tacky hotel, a place occupied largely by prostitutes. As Ali started kissing Loma's naked body, she felt herself simultaneously paralyzed with fear and sexually aroused. She wanted him badly, but she knew that they were committing a sin in the eyes of religion, an act that neither family would forgive. Moments later, she felt a sharp pain as her virginity was taken. Within a minute, Ali was finished, lying on top of her, sweating and panting. He kissed her sweetly, speaking of love, but she felt sure they'd made a terrible mistake. In the following weeks, she explained that she wouldn't be sleeping with him again before they were married. He was upset at first, but he finally agreed to be patient. They returned to holding hands on park benches and throwing stones into the Tigris. Not long after, Loma found that she had missed her period. In a panic, she told Ali, tears streaming down her face. If she was really pregnant, it would be a disaster.

Ali reassured her, saying that he would speak with his parents, saying that he'd found the woman of his dreams, and that he intended to marry – with their permission. He wouldn't mention the pregnancy, of course, but he would urge a swift marriage. Loma felt at least a little reassured. Her family was not exactly wealthy, but they were respectable enough, and there was no good reason to reject the match.

A week later, Ali phoned Loma, saying in whispers that his parents had refused. They had been shocked at his sudden declaration of love for a girl they hardly knew. He had begged them to think it over, and they agreed to do so. However, when they eventually returned to the topic, they were more adamant than ever: Ali should finish his engineering studies before even thinking of marriage, and when he did marry, it should be to some nice girl from a better family. Ali argued strongly, even raising his voice against his father – but it was no good. They wouldn't budge.

In desperation, Loma appealed to the only person she thought capable of intervening on her behalf: Ali's sister-in-law, Selma. Loma had already come to think of her as a relative of sorts, perhaps a kind aunty, although they'd never actually spoken. She approached Selma one day at the club and began to tell the story. She avoided mention of the pregnancy, but said they were desperate to married as soon as possible.

'I don't know what you think I can do to help,' said Selma.

'Couldn't you speak with his parents? Tell them that I'm not a bad person.'

'I suppose I could, but I don't think it would make much difference.'

'Why not?'

'They're very stubborn people, and they want the best for their son.'

'But I'm the best for their son. We're in love. Doesn't that count for anything?'

Selma smiled, sipping her drink through a straw. 'Darling, you have to understand how these things work. It's not all about love. It's about making a match that works on every level. They need someone bit more … classy.'

'Classy?'

'Well, from a better family.'

'But Ali loves me, and I love him. That's all that counts!'

'And how long is it since you've actually seen Ali?'

'About three weeks, I think.'

'So, he's avoiding you?'

'No ... he's just being cautious.'

'Darling, if I know men at all, they'll talk about love all night long, but the moment things get a little difficult, they'll disappear like a puff of smoke.'

'Not Ali.'

'Perhaps he's had time to think things over? Maybe he's wondering what sort of woman you really are? I mean, if you'd give your virginity to him out of wedlock, who's to say that you wouldn't give yourself to another man in future, once you're married?'

'What on earth are you talking about?'

'After all, a good man like Ali really deserves to marry a virgin. You're not a virgin any more, are you?'

Loma hadn't mentioned sex, but apparently Selma had guessed anyway. The wicked smile on her lips seemed to point in that direction.

'He loves me. I know that much,' said Loma, almost in a whisper.

'Every dog needs a lamp post to piss on.'

Loma was shocked at this crude and callous comment. She had apparently misjudged Selma entirely. Stunned into silence, she rose to her feet and walked slowly away, leaving the 'kind aunt' chuckling to herself.

That evening, she phoned Ali's house, but the servant who answered the phone said that Ali was away. She tried again the next night, with the same response.

Her next visit was to her best friend, Madeha. She confided the whole story, and before long they'd arrived at a dreadful conclusion: an abortion was the only way forward. Madeha knew a female gynaecologist who would do it cheaply, and nobody would find out. The following week, they walked into a run-down clinic in the Bab Al-Sharqi neighbourhood.

The grumpy old receptionist, who made no eye contact, asked for the patient's name. Loma's mind had gone blank, quite forgetting the false name she'd rehearsed. Madeha came to the rescue, spelling it out clearly. The receptionist was used to such scenarios, and she accepted the cash payment with little ceremony.

A young nurse led Loma into a small operating theatre smelling strongly of antiseptic. There was an operating table and some surgical instruments: scalpels, needles, syringes, various plastic tubes and some vaginal dilators. The nurse told Loma to remove her clothes and change into a blue medical gown. Soon, an elegant, middle-aged woman, entered. In addition to the white coat, she was wearing heavy make-up and gold jewellery, as if she was going to a party. With no explanation, she told Loma to lay back on the operating table while the nurse placed her feet in the stirrups, ready for the procedure. The doctor put on some gloves and began checking her instruments.

'Aren't you going to give me some sort of anaesthetic?' asked Loma, her voice shaking.

'Are you sure you need it?' said the nurse. 'This procedure is no more painful than intercourse.'

Loma was silent, but she felt the tears rolling down her cheeks as the doctor placed the dilator inside her. The pain was real, but nobody seemed to care. Perhaps she deserved it?

Loma closed her eyes as the doctor began extracting the foetus, piece by piece. The nurse stood by with a series of swabs, wiping away the blood as it poured out. Finally, there was the sharp pain of a needle, and the doctor began to apply stitches, repairing the hymen – as she'd never even had intercourse.

Two porters transferred Loma to a trolley and she was given some tablets to swallow.

'They'll take the edge off the pain,' said the doctor, smiling weakly.

Loma was wheeled into the recovery room and covered with a blanket. Madeha was waiting impatiently for her friend, who was suddenly feeling very drowsy.

'Are you alright, Loma?'

'What have I done?'

'Darling, you'll be alright. Just hold on.'

'God forgive me,' said Loma, drifting off to sleep.

In the following weeks, Loma wrote a letter to Ali, explaining what she'd done, and why. But she never received a reply. Nor did he ever call.

A year later, she learned that Ali had married a nice girl of his parents' choosing. Loma spent an entire weekend crying, only pulling herself together because her mother was growing so worried – and asking too many questions.

Several years later, when Loma was pregnant with her second son, she got a call from Madeha. She'd heard something through the grapevine, and it required a chat in private. They met at Madeha's house, sitting in the shade of two large palm trees. Madeha had been speaking with one of her cousins who had known Ali's family for many years, and she'd recently been invited to a party at their house. After a few drinks, tongues had been loosened, and various episodes of family history had been raked up.

Apparently, it was Selma who had dissuaded Ali's parents from agreeing to the marriage. She had told them that Loma's family were quite broke, and Loma was a gold-digger, seeking to rebuild the family fortune. Added to which, Ali wasn't Loma's first target;

she'd tried the same thing with several other men. Shocked at the idea of their son being used in such a way, the parents had put their foot down once and for all, and the young couple's dreams were in tatters.

Loma awoke from her daydream. She looked down at the park bench, but found it empty. The young couple had moved on.

* * *

Next morning, Loma got up early. Riaz had not returned from his 'meeting' at the Ritz. Strangely, she didn't mind. In fact, there was something quite liberating about having a husband who spent his energies on other women.

She showered, dressed and went down to her office, taking a seat by the large window overlooking the back garden. She called the maid and ordered a strong black tea, brewed in the Iraqi style. She sipped it from a small glass with gold trim, resting on its own dainty saucer. She watched the birds in the garden, wondering how long it would take them to fly to Baghdad. How wonderful it would be to fly away like that – to take wing and disappear! She phoned the senior administrator at the embassy, a young man named Adil. She was sure that he had a thing for her. At one embassy party around Christmas time, she'd caught him taking a close interest in her tight-fitting dress. He was single, so there wasn't much harm in it. And the situation provided her with a certain power.

'Hello, Adil. How are you this morning?'

'Very well, ma'am. And you?'

'Wonderful, Adil. Thanks for asking. Listen, I need your help.'

'Anything to be of service, madam.'

'Well, my best friend is hoping to visit London. I want her to get here ASAP and with as little complication as possible. Do you think you can arrange the travel permission?'

'Yes, of course. It's no problem at all. I'll get on to it today.'

'Oh, that's wonderful, Adil. You really are a star.'

'Not at all. Anything for you, madam.'

'You're so sweet.'

For the rest of the day, Loma felt like she was floating on air. She put on one of her favourite cassette tapes: the love songs of Egyptian star Abdel Halim Hafez. It brought back happy memories: of home, the heat of Baghdad, of love ... Reclining on the sofa with a glass of wine in her hand, she allowed herself to imagine that life might turn out fine after all.

When Riaz returned home at dinner time, he was puzzled by his wife's good mood.

'I suppose you're happy that your friend is visiting?'

'Oh, you've heard about it, have you?'

'Of course I have.'

'Maybe I'm just happy to be married to such a wonderful husband.'

There was no trace of sarcasm in her voice, but they both knew it was a lie.

Friend to the rescue

The next two weeks passed slowly for Loma, as she anxiously awaited the arrival of her good friend. However, she also had a new spring in her step, a new brightness of mind, a sense of hope in the future that had been very much missing in recent months. Finally, the big day arrived, and she was up long before anyone else. It was a Saturday, and so the kids were still lazing in bed. Riaz had a series of meetings that day, but the first didn't start for another few hours. As Loma pulled on her dressing gown, he was still snoring away, oblivious to his wife's growing excitement. Today, she felt she could pretty much glide through her Jane Fonda workout video, perhaps twice. Normally, she struggled to keep up for thirty minutes, but this morning she had the strength of ten women. Of course, there was no time for exercise today; there were much more important things afoot.

She showered and dressed, then carefully applied her Clarins face-mask, which she had purchased at Selfridge's. She wanted to look young again, as she had in the early days of her friendship with Madeha. She then carefully applied her make-up, using the YSL products that had come as a boxed gift from Riaz following one of his trips to Paris. She had often wondered whether the gift had, in fact, been picked out by one of his whores. Today, she really didn't care.

She warmed up the curling tongs and gave her hair some body, then set the whole thing in place with a liberal dose of hair spray. The weather was chilly, but she was determined to dress for spring, picking out a short-sleeved, white dress with a pattern of pink roses. She donned a pink cardigan to match, red Charles Jordan shoes, and her white Louis Vuitton handbag.

Standing before the mirror by the front door, she gave herself a final inspection. Yes, she looked just as young and attractive as she could ever hope for. Nobody would ever imagine that she was the mother of two boys, locked in a desperately unhappy marriage. She tried a smile, and it didn't seem entirely false.

She picked up the phone and informed the chauffeur, Tony, that she would be leaving in ten minutes. He said he would be there in five. Originally from the East End, Tony was among a handful of English staff employed by the embassy. Now in his early thirties, he had formerly served in the army, then worked as a limo driver, doing the Heathrow Airport run. He seemed more than happy in his current job, which was by far the best paid. Of course, the embassy was always aware of the dangers involved in hiring such people. There was no telling what information they might be passing to British intelligence. However, after a thorough background check, the embassy's security staff had concluded that he was no more of a risk than any other British citizen.

Loma liked Tony very much, and they'd often discussed his working-class upbringing, with its distinctive Cockney accent. She didn't particularly understand the nuances, but she knew that it was quite different from the Queen's English.

'The Queen speaks very nicely,' Loma had once said.

'She can afford to, ma'am,' Tony had replied, laughing.

Meeting the Queen had really been the highlight of Loma's time in London thus far. Riaz had been invited to a garden party at Buckingham Palace, and Loma had spent the whole afternoon by his side, watching wide-eyed as ambassadors, generals, aristocrats and captains of industry mingled. She was particularly impressed with the handful of actual royals present, including Queen Elizabeth II herself.

'I really admire that woman,' Loma had whispered.

'Don't say such stupid things,' Riaz had snapped, clearly alarmed. The only person Riaz and Loma should be admiring was the Iraqi ambassador – and Saddam Hussein, of course, although he wasn't present at the party. Admiring the Queen of England could get them into a great deal of trouble.

Here was another avenue of self-expression cut off, thought Loma, another opinion that she could not express openly within her husband's circles. It was only to Madeha that she could safely make such comments, and only when they were alone, with no chance of being recorded.

Loma heard the Mercedes pull up outside. With a final glance in the mirror, she grabbed her keys and stepped outside. Tony was looking very smart in his black suit, peaked cap and shiny shoes. He held the car door open.

'Thank you, Tony.'

'Pleasure, ma'am.'

Tony knew that Loma would not want to be late for Madeha's arrival, and bearing in mind the warnings of heavy traffic that he'd heard on the radio, he put his foot down. They zoomed down Exhibition Road, between the Science Museum and the Victoria and Albert Museum with its sooty façade. As they turned into Cromwell Road and picked up speed, Loma could not help gazing at the Natural History Museum. She loved this grand old building, and she couldn't wait to show Madeha. They would spend an entire day here, peering at the exhibits.

The car passed down Gloucester Road, through Earl's Court and onto the A4. Loma noticed the buildings getting gradually scruffier. They raced through Chiswick and Hounslow, and along the M4, finally navigating a series of roundabouts to Heathrow Airport.

'Tony, make sure to go to Terminal 3, please.'

'Yes, ma'am. That's where we're heading.'

Finally, they stopped in the multi-story car park. Before Tony could open the door, Loma had rushed out, striding off to the arrivals building.

'Wait here, Tony,' she said, not bothering to look back.

She wanted to meet her good friend alone. No strangers, no matter how well-intentioned, were going to intrude on this particular reunion.

Loma entered the enormous, high-ceilinged hall, swarming with travellers, friends and relatives from every corner of the world. She stood before a bulky arrivals monitor, scanning the list for Iraqi Airlines flights. Madeha's plane had landed twenty minutes ago; she would be collecting her baggage by now. Loma's heart leapt with joy. She was so excited that she almost squealed.

Suddenly, there was a familiar voice behind her. She turned quickly to find the embassy's public relations officer standing there, a polite smile on his face. He was carrying a sign with Madeha's name on it.

'What you doing here, Ahmed?'

'Good morning, madam. I'm here to welcome your friend from Baghdad.'

Loma was crushed. Was the embassy to intrude on every aspect of her life?

'There's really no need. I'm greeting her. It's all taken care of.'

'We have a car for her, madam. The ambassador asked me to arrange it.'

'But this is ridiculous. I have a car already. Tony is here with me.'

Ahmed suddenly looked perturbed. The last thing he needed was confusion about the correct interpretation of embassy protocol.

'I am here to interpret for her, madam, in case she requires any assistance.'

'Don't be ridiculous, Ahmed. Her English is better than yours. She excelled in English at university. What does she need an interpreter for?'

Ahmed opened his mouth to speak, but no words came out. His face was now bright red. He really didn't want to get into an argument with the wife of the First Secretary, Political Affairs.

'Alright, we'll greet her together,' said Loma, though she was clearly unhappy.

'This way, madam.'

As they walked to the arrivals gate, Loma was fuming. Men were pigs, all of them, without exception. If only the men could all die off, the world might be just about bearable.

By now, Madeha was passing through customs, her trolley loaded with baggage, more than enough for a two-week stay. Her main suitcase contained several boxes of Iraqi dates and packets of spices from Loma's mother. Even so, she opted for 'nothing to declare'.

She'd had a wonderful flight. First-class air travel certainly lived up to its reputation, with its luxurious seats, *haute cuisine* menu and fine wines. The Iraqi Airlines hostesses were a sight to behold, like moving works of art, meticulously presented. They were selected for the job based on strict rules concerning beauty, height, waist size and language skills. It was well known that even Saddam Hussein could not succeed in appointing a woman to the staff if she didn't meet the standard.

Before boarding the flight that morning, Madeha had been anxious. She hadn't flown for seven years, and passing through the airport checks at both ends seemed fraught with danger. Once in the air, however, all the tension drained away. And she was encouraged by the importance of her mission: to provide much-needed moral support to a good friend.

Loma was waiting eagerly, like a mother on the verge of reunion with a lost child. Ahmed was standing next to her, holding the sign bearing Madeha's name. The first wave of Iraqi travellers began to emerge, pushing their trolleys and looking around anxiously. They were carrying the usual range of presents, including the traditional baklava sweets: delicate layers of pastry with a stuffing of walnuts or pistachios, held together with honey or syrup. There were cries of joy as families saw their loved ones, followed by hugging, kissing and tears.

Loma's heart was beating fast. All of a sudden, a familiar face appeared around the corner, smiling broadly. It was Madeha, with the same olive skin, hazel eyes, and big Roman nose. She seemed to have put on a bit of weight, and she was wearing a jumper in anticipation of the cold British weather. But it was still the same old Madeha.

The women threw their arms around each other, squeezing tight, while Ahmed looked on, slightly embarrassed. His presence suddenly seemed rather pointless. The women were crying now, kissing each other repeatedly on the cheeks.

'How are you?' Loma said, standing back to get a better look.

'I'm fine, darling. I'm a bit tired, but that's okay. First class was great, just wonderful.'

'I know. It's one of the few perks of the job.'

'And visiting places like London, of course. I'm desperate to start walking the streets.'

'We'll start right away, Madeha. Don't worry about that, there will be plenty of walking.'

'Good morning, madam,' said Ahmed, cutting in.

'Good morning,' said Madeha, shaking hands.

'This is Ahmed from the embassy,' said Loma. 'We won't be needing you any more, Ahmed. Thank you for coming, but I'll take it from here.'

'As you wish, madam,' said the official, making a discrete exit.

As they walked back to the car park, Loma explained about Tony.

'I trust him completely, but I don't think anybody else does. He's English, so we have to be careful what we say in front of him.'

'Of course, I'll be discrete.'

'We can have a proper chat once we get to café or something.'

'No problem.'

As they sped back to the embassy, Loma felt her surroundings looked slightly less ugly. Madeha, however, was feeling a little disappointed. She'd always imagined London to be beautiful in every respect, but the suburban and industrial scenes passing her window were far from inspiring.

Picking up on Madeha's disappointment, Loma began to describe the historical buildings in Kensington, including the Natural History Museum, which they would certainly visit.

'And then, of course, there's Kew Gardens.'

'What's Kew Gardens?'

'Haven't you heard of it?'

'Never.'

'It's a very famous botanical garden. They have huge greenhouses, filled with warm, steamy air and plants from all around the world. It's like a jungle inside. They have palm trees and everything, just like back home. I go there sometimes when the weather gets too cold and miserable, just to remember what a warm country feels like.'

'It sounds wonderful.'

'It's one of my favourite spots. Let's go there now, if you have the energy?'

'Now? Are you sure?'

'Yes, let's do it. That's if you're not too tired?'

'No, I'm fine. Let's do it.'

Loma leaned forward and give instructions to Tony, who changed course, heading for Brentford. They crossed the elegant Kew Bridge, and Madeha got her first glimpse of the River Thames. It looked rather cold and grey, but the brightly coloured houseboats gave it a bit of life.

Tony dropped the two women by the main gate. They purchased tickets from the little office and started walking. Madeha was impressed by the greenery, the lush lawns and enormous trees. She was also taken aback by the freshness of the air, which seemed to be blowing like a hyperactive air-conditioner.

'Well, I never knew you were so much into gardening,' she said, teasing her friend.

'For your information, I am. Or rather, I love nature. Anyway, be patient.'

'I'm entirely at your service.'

'Good, then we can stop here for a while.'

The entered a café, which was heaving with customers. They two women sat down and examined the menu.

'I'll have to try the breakfast tea, with scones, jam and cream,' said Madeha.

'I can see you're going to gain some weight while you're here.'

'I don't think anyone will notice. I'll just put on another jumper.'

'Good idea,' said Loma. 'In that case, I'll have some too.'

As they tucked into their tea and scones, Loma shared every scrap of information she had on Kew Gardens, before starting on a long list of the sights they would be visiting in the next few days. She seemed so excited by it all, but eventually she ran out of steam, and sat gazing out of the window.

'Is there something on your mind?' said Madeha.

'Well, isn't there always?'

'Is it Selma?'

'Yes, as always. I can't seem to get it out of my head.'

Loma looked around the café, as if someone might be lurking, listening to their conversation. Madeha did likewise, wondering whether Loma was just being paranoid.

'Is it safe to talk here?' she said.

'Yes, I think so. That's partly why we stopped her. I wanted a chance to talk to you before we got home. I'm afraid we can't talk at my house. You never know who's listening.'

'I understand.'

Loma was playing with an empty packet of sugar, looking very glum.

'So, what has Selma being saying about me?'

'Like I said, she's just been spreading the idea that you're in love with Ali.'

'Is that all?'

'Well, it's all I can be sure of. But apparently, her son has been talking too, and he's not so delicate. He knows some of Malaka's girls, and apparently he told one of them all about you and Ali ...'

'What?!'

Loma had raised her voice, causing several customers to turn and look.

'Keep your voice down, Loma,' said her friend. 'We came here to be discrete. It doesn't help if you start shouting.'

'I'm sorry, but this is quite upsetting. What did the little prick say?'

'I don't know what he said, but this girl – I don't know her name – she then went and told Malaka, apparently. And now Malaka is talking quite openly about some sort of on-going love affair between you and Ali.'

'But that's insane! I never even see Ali. We haven't had a proper conversation for years. The last time I spoke with him was at Malaka's party, and that was all Malaka's fault. And anyway, I'm living in London. How on earth could I be having an affair with him?'

'I know, darling. It's all bullshit, but that's what people are saying.'

'Oh, my God!'

Loma had raised her voice again, causing more people to look over. She was crying now.

'Listen, please calm down. Everyone is looking at the two hysterical women from the Middle East. It's hardly discrete.'

'Well, I'm sorry, but my life is falling apart. What am I supposed to do?'

Loma placed her handbag heavily on the table, spilling the milk and rattling the cutlery. She pulled out a packet of tissues and blew her nose.

'Listen,' said Madeha, 'let's pay the bill and go for a walk. Maybe some fresh air will help.'

They paid and left, wandering down the winding paths between the enormous trees, past flower beds bearing their first tentative spring blooms. Loma seemed lost in a dark dream, unwilling to speak, and Madeha didn't want to disturb her. Finally, they arrived at a quaint house built of timber and red bricks.

'Where are we?' asked Madeha.

'Oh, this must be Queen Charlotte's cottage.'

'It's very nice.'

'Look, there must be something I can do to stop Selma, isn't there?'

'I don't know. Like what?'

'I mean, it must be possible to persuade her that she's not going to get anything out of this whole situation. I mean, what is she trying to accomplish?'

'I suppose she's jealous?'

'But my love affair with Ali finished 15 years ago, for God's sake!'

'I know, but I suppose she thinks that Ali still love you.'

'Do you think he does?'

'I wouldn't be surprised. I don't think he loves his wife. They don't spend much time together, so far as I know.'

Loma was silent for a while, gazing up at the charming old cottage. She blew her nose, then started talking once more, this time with more confidence.

'Well, perhaps she just needs to realise that I don't have any intention of getting back together with Ali, and then she doesn't need to feel jealous anymore?'

'Maybe, but I think she'd have to hear it from you. Otherwise she wouldn't believe it.'

'You mean talk to her on the phone?'

'Yes, how else?'

'All the phones in my house are bugged. I'm pretty sure of that.'

'What about writing a letter?'

'What, and give her physical evidence of my involvement with Ali? You must be crazy!'

'Well, I don't know then,' said Madeha, growing annoyed.

They started walking again, and pretty soon they found themselves by an exit.

'Look,' said Madeha, pointing. 'There's a pay-phone. Why not call her now?'

'Are you serious?'

'Yes, of course I am. Just phone her and tell her what you just told me. Say you're not interested in Ali anymore, and so she has no reason to be jealous. Tell her that if she wants Ali, she's welcome to have him. See what she says.'

'Do you think she'll accept that? She's a lunatic, you know.'

'Okay, but it's worth a try. Do you have a better solution?'

Loma stood in silence, looking at the phone booth. Suddenly, Madeha grabbed her arm and pulled her through the exit. They squeezed into the phone booth together, Madeha lifting the receiver.

'We need coins,' she said.

Loma reached into her purse and pulled out a handful of silver, feeding it into the slot. Then she began to dial, first the country code for Baghdad, then the city code and then Selma's number. She knew it by heart because it was the same number she had dialled many years ago in order to speak to Ali; when his parents died, Hassan and Selma took over the house, along with the old phone number.

As Loma waited for Selma to pick up, she recalled those late nights when she would call Ali in secret and he would pick up after just one ring. They would talk in whispers, and she would play music down the phone to him: all the Iraqi and Egyptian love songs.

Suddenly, Selma answered, her voice surprisingly loud and clear. In fact, she sounded like a diva rehearsing her big scene at La Scala.

'Hello? Hello?'

Loma was gobsmacked. Her tongue was paralysed, as if she'd totally forgotten Arabic.

'Hello, who's there?' insisted Selma.

Loma looked at Madeha, who was silently urging her on. But it was no good, she just couldn't find the right words.

Selma lost patience and started swearing. From the crude names she was using, she seemed to imagine that the mystery caller was a man, perhaps one of her many admirers. She was simultaneously furious and exalted – glad to show her husband and offspring how desired she was by the opposite sex.

Loma hung up. She turned to Madeha, who wrapped her arms around her. They stood together for a while, like mother and child.

Then they walked back to their starting point, not bothering to enter the greenhouses. Somehow the promise of warm air and palm trees didn't seem so appealing any more.

Tony noticed that Loma had been crying, but he didn't say a word. He just drove them back by the quickest route. As they crossed the river, the grey clouds finally burst open, and rain poured down onto the city streets.

As they neared home, Loma pointed out the Natural History Museum.

'Wow! That's wonderful,' said Madeha, truly impressed by the intricate stonework.

She had inherited her love of all things historical and cultural from her late father. As a young girl, they had gone to the Iraqi Museum together. Gazing at artefacts that dated back six thousand years, she felt intimately connected with the kings and queens of Babylonia. She would also join her family on visits to important archaeological sites. Bumping along in their old Volkswagen, they would explore the ruins of Babylon, then drive south to the remains of Ur, and to Nineveh in the north. There were so many sites, in fact, that they had all become jumbled in her memory, but the experience started a life-long obsession with history.

They drove passed the Iranian embassy, where a group of Iranian students had taken hostages just three years earlier. Soldiers from the Special Air Service had famously broken the siege in a bloody rescue operation that was televised worldwide.

The car stopped, and Tony opened the door, holding an umbrella overhead. The rain was still falling heavily, and Loma's Filipino maid hurried forward with an umbrella of her own, offering to help with Madeha's luggage.

'*Hamdela al-salama*,' she said, thanking God for the visitor's safe arrival.

Madeha thanked her and scurried into the house, a bag in each hand.

'You're in the big guest bedroom,' said Loma. 'Come with me.'

Madeha followed her upstairs and into a bright, finely decorated room. The maid had already put the fire on, and there was a pile of fresh towels on the bed, along with a freshly laundered dressing gown.

'Come down when you're ready, and I'll show you the house.'

'Sure, I won't be long. I may have a quick shower.'

'Of course, take your time.'

Madeha was happy to find the bathroom equipped with an old enamel bath. She set the taps running and poured in some bubble-bath, then undressed and slipped into the warm water. Somehow, she'd gotten pretty wet and muddy on the circuitous journey from the airport. She was also feeling rather tired. A bath was just exactly what she needed. She closed her eyes and began to drift away.

She was awoken by knocking and a loud voice beyond the door:

'Are you okay in there?'

'Yes, sorry. I must have fallen asleep in the bath. I'll be down in a minute.'

'Okay, see you soon.'

Madeha, dragged herself from the warm water and towelled herself dry. Standing before the long mirror, she examined her figure, which wasn't as young-looking as it used to be. There were a few stretch marks, the signs of child-birth. Also some love handles, which seemed to be growing, perhaps due to age, but also because food was one of her few pleasures in life.

She wondered if she was still attractive to the opposite sex. Her husband had been dead for several years now. She should perhaps move on and find a new husband. But was she really ready? And if she was ready, would anybody want her?

She shook herself out of her daydream and dressed quickly, throwing on some comfortable trousers and another warm sweater. Then she padded downstairs and into the living room. Loma was standing by the window, a glass of wine in her hand.

'At last, the princess arrives!'

'I'm so sorry. I just fell asleep.'

'That's quite alright, darling. I'm only teasing. Here, have some wine. We'll be eating dinner in a while. The cook's preparing something now. I don't know if you're hungry, but I'm famished. Those scones have disappeared to nothing.'

She handed Madeha a glass of dry white, and they sank into the sofa, side by side.

'So, what do you think of the house?'

'Oh, it's wonderful. I love the décor. Did you do it yourself?'

'You must be joking! This isn't really my style. I mean, it's not bad, but it's all a bit too English for me. I miss my old ornaments.'

'Yes, I know what you mean.'

Madeha looked around the room, inspecting the expensive paintings and antique vases.

'What's that?' she said at last, getting to her feet.

'Oh, that's a statue I bought soon after I arrived. I got it from a little shop next to the British Museum. They sell ancient objects at very reasonable prices. I was a bit surprised to find it actually, but I just had to have it.'

Madeha stepped over to the bookcase where the object was positioned. It was a little bronze statue, about 12 inches tall and clearly very old.

'It's the goddess Ishtar, isn't it?'

'Yes, it is.'

'How odd!'

'What do you mean?' said Loma, joining her friend.

'Well, we were looking at a statue of Ishtar only last summer, if you remember, at the Sheraton Hotel in Baghdad?'

'Of course I remember. That's why I bought it. I remembered everything you said about love and war, temptation and revenge. I thought perhaps I could do with some of her power.'

'And has it worked so far?'

'I think you've seen how powerful I am, Madeha. Remember my performance earlier today? You can judge for yourself.'

'Well, maybe she's just getting warmed up?'

'Let's hope so.'

Madeha gazed at the statue a while longer, recalling the myths she'd learned about how the goddess was worshipped, with women prostituting themselves at her feet by the banks of the Euphrates. She pondered life in those ancient times, wondering at the strange and exotic lives those women must have lived. She wondered whether her own life had the power to become strange and exotic – or if it would to be dull to the very end.

'Hello,' whispered Loma. 'Are you still with us?'

Madeha emerged from her dream.

'I'm so sorry. I seem to have drifted back in time.'

The maid knocked and entered, setting down a plate of *kletcha* pastries that Madeha's mother had sent to Loma. The two women returned to the sofa and started on the pastries, chewing the delicious mix of nuts and dates, occasionally uttering groans of pleasure. Madeha was glad to see that something had the power to bring a smile to her friend's face.

They drank more wine and began to unwind at last. Loma gave an extensive account of her daily life in London, making sure to steer clear of any controversial subjects. She then turned to their favourite of all topics: shopping. She was just in the process of comparing and contrasting Harrods and Harvey Nichols, when Riaz walked in. His day of meetings was finally over, so he would be joining them for dinner.

'It's so wonderful to see you,' he said, exchanging kisses with Madeha.

'Yes, it's lovely to see you too, Riaz. Thank you for allowing me to stay in your wonderful home. It's quite beautiful.'

Riaz looked around, as if he hadn't taken much notice of it before now.

'Yes, I suppose it is quite nice, isn't it?' he said, chuckling gently.

Loma smiled to herself. She knew exactly why Riaz was so glad to see Madeha. While the two friends were busy entertaining each other, he would have more time to himself. Or rather, he would have more time to spend on his other women.

A gong sounded in the hallway, and the maid appeared.

'Dinner is served,' she said.

'Wonderful!' said Riaz. 'Bring your wine, Madeha, and we'll go through to the dining room.'

Madeha heaved a heavy sigh. 'I'm afraid I might have to go to bed. I'm so sorry. But if I were to sit down for dinner now, I think I might fall asleep.'

'Are you unwell?' enquired Riaz, apparently concerned.

'Not at all, it's just been a very long day, what with the flight and everything. I'm also not very hungry. I think I had too much to eat earlier … on the plane.'

Loma was grateful to Madeha for not mentioning their improvised lunch at Kew Gardens. Any unscheduled events of that sort might provoke suspicion.

'That's alright,' she said. 'You go to bed, and we'll see you in the morning.'

On reaching her bedroom Madeha, stood before the big window overlooking Hyde Park. The rain was still pouring down, and the sky was dark. Somewhere in the distance lightning flashed, followed by a long rumble of thunder. A storm was heading their way.

Girls' night out

In the following days, the two women spent their time chatting, shopping, eating, drinking, lounging in various cafés, and ticking touristic sites off Madeha's must-see list. The much-anticipated museums were visited, as were Big Ben and St Paul's Cathedral. Tony would drive them to their destination and wait patiently in the car, then take them to the next stop. In the evenings, they would return home, dining together and watching films with a bottle of wine, glad that Riaz was busy elsewhere.

They both felt suddenly much younger, as if they'd stepped through some portal into a previous time, or perhaps drunk from a magical elixir that wipes away the years. They hadn't had so much fun since their university days, and all their usual concerns melted into nothing. Loma seemed to have quite forgotten the Selma saga, which had prompted her to invite Madeha in the first place, and Madeha was content to say no more about it. They were, in fact, happy to indulge in denial – with a capital D.

It was on the fourth day, over a late breakfast, that Loma put a new proposal to her guest.

'Let's see a bit of the London nightlife.'

'Alone?'

'No, let's go out with our boyfriends,' said Loma, giggling. 'Of course, alone. Tony's busy this afternoon, taking Riaz to various meetings, but we can use public transport. I want to show you the

Tube. I mean the London Underground. We can do a little shopping locally, and then jump on the Tube. And if we stay out very late, we can just get a cab home.'

'Oh, that sounds wonderful,' said Madeha.

She had long been aware of London's underground railway network, the oldest in the world. Baghdad's own metro system was still under construction, the project on hold for the duration of the war.

They walked east a few blocks, through Knightsbridge to Harrods, where they browsed the various departments, ogling the luxury goods on sale. Madeha was proud to think that the new owner, Egyptian tycoon Mohamed Al-Fayed, was a fellow Arabic speaker. Since 1967, when Israel had triumphed in the Six-Day War, many Arabs had felt a deep sense of humiliation, an inferiority complex in relation to the entire Western world. And here was an Arab – or at least an Egyptian – running England's most prestigious retail outlet.

They quickly found the clothes department, with its rows of outfits by glamorous designers: Lanvin, Christian Dior, Cacharel and Elizabeth Arden. Madeha tried on a dress by Armani and instantly felt like Joan Collins on the set of *Dynasty*. She quickly changed back into her own dress – the product of an Iraqi designer – when she saw the £300 price tag. She was used to the more affordable products of Soha Al-Bakri and Noha Al-Razi.

Loma had no such concerns, picking out a fine summer dress without checking the price. She charged it to her account, asking for it to be delivered to her address, along with a bottle of Dior perfume. Madeha watched, open-mouthed.

Exhausted by their shopping, they stopped at the Harrods bar for an afternoon snack and a bottle of champagne, again charged to Loma's account. Madeha hadn't drunk such an expensive beverage since her wedding, and after two glasses she was feeling a little tipsy.

As they headed through the exit, they exchanged pleasantries with the porters, who looked fine in their long, green coats and peaked caps. They had been carefully selected for their good looks and social skills, and the two ladies felt like princesses leaving their palace, having bid farewell to their thrones.

Arriving at Knightsbridge metro station, Loma attempted to walk through the barrier and found it unyielding. A member of staff explained that she should buy a ticket first. She felt rather stupid, but reflected that she'd only used the Tube twice before, and never under the influence of champagne. They purchased tickets to Piccadilly Circus and tried again, and as they descended the escalator, Loma raised her fist into the air, letting out a cry of triumph: 'Freedom!'

'Long live freedom!' replied Madeha, likewise punching the air.

She was thrilled at the novelty of the experience, descending ever deeper into the earth, walking along echoing tunnels, like some high-class mole navigating its subterranean home. The train itself was even more thrilling, ratting and swaying through the tunnels, the passengers pressed together, crammed into little seats or hanging from straps. The breeze that blew through the carriage seemed to hint at danger. Loma noticed her friend's excitement and smiled.

The two human moles emerged at Piccadilly Circus, and Madeha was dazzled by the illuminated advertisements fixed to the buildings, blinking in every colour of the rainbow. As Loma consulted her guidebook, Madeha watched the couples gathered around the Eros statue, chatting, kissing and posing for photographs.

She remembered her husband Mohamed, whose protective attitude had been so reassuring. He hadn't been particularly romantic, but he was kind and strong. She recalled his smell, his smile and the comforting sensation of being held in his arms. Also, the moment she'd received news of his death on the frontline, and how she'd collapsed in tears on the kitchen floor. It had taken her months to pull herself together.

Suddenly, another image flashed into her mind. It came from deeper within her memory banks, from a compartment that she rarely allowed herself to access. It was the smiling face of another man, much younger and slimmer. This was Munir, her boyfriend for the first year of university. They had been deeply in love, speaking often of their future plans, sharing their deepest secrets. He was a keen student of politics, always debating the ins and outs of mankind's various ideological struggles.

Then, one day, she had received a frantic phone call from a pay-phone somewhere in Baghdad. The *Mukhabarat* had raided his apartment while he was out, apparently suspecting him of subversive political activities. She had agreed to meet him at the international railway station, which had featured in several Agatha Christie tales, including *Murder on the Orient Express*. Their farewell was like something from a novel: the dark platform, whistles blowing as the train started to move, the desperate final kisses, and the hot tears running down their cheeks.

She had never seen Munir again, nor heard from him. For all she knew he was in prison, or perhaps dead. There was a slim chance that he'd made it to another country, but if so, he never sent a postcard. Mohamed had been a good husband, but her feelings for Munir could never be matched.

'Hello, are you still in London?' said Loma, looking up from her guidebook.

'Yes, I was looking at those couples.'

'Do you have anyone in mind?'

'No, I'm a widow and a mother. That's all. I won't be bothering with love again.'

'But you're not dead yet. There's no harm in a bit of window-shopping.'

Loma had vocalized a thought that had been dormant in Madeha's mind: perhaps she would never marry again, but that didn't mean she must necessarily deny herself some intimacy.

'Yes, I'm only human,' she said, as if to herself. 'I have emotional and physical needs, just like anybody else.'

'Let's see if we can find a nice bar,' said Loma, looking back at her book.

'Excuse me? Surely you mean a café? After all, we're respectable girls, not sluts.'

Madeha struck an exaggerated super-model pose, flicking her hair back out of her eyes.

Loma grabbed her friend's arm, laughing, and dragged her off down the street.

'Voila! This is Café de Paris. According to my book, it opened in 1924, and has enticed some rich and famous patrons, like Princess Margaret and the Prince of Wales. Aside from a period of closure during World War II, it's been serving horribly expensive cocktails every day without fail. This would seem the perfect place to revive some historical practices of our own.'

'Yes, let's do it.'

As they entered the dark interior, Loma observed that high-society prostitutes were rumoured to sit at the bar. It would be safer sitting at a table, she said.

'Shame!' said Madeha.

They found a table, and moments later a waiter handed them cocktail menus bound in brown leather. Loma was reminded of their trip to the Al-Rashid Hotel in Baghdad just a few years earlier. This hotel had been built to accommodate Arab leaders during the famous summit in Baghdad, an act of retaliation against Egyptian President Anwar El-Sadat's visit to Israel in 1977. There were few hotels to top the Al-Rashid in terms of opulence. Back in London, the girls found themselves somewhat dazzled by the cocktail options, plumping finally for two bloody Marys, complete with Worcestershire sauce. It was a new experience for Madeha, but she persevered. Before long, they had trained her glasses dry and ordered two more. They tucked into the nibbles – olives, crackers and nuts – and began to feel that life really couldn't get any better.

Two middle-aged men were sitting at the bar, chatting and smoking. They were smartly dressed and not at all bad looking. The older of the two was grey-haired, but this just added to his distinguished, aristocratic look. His dark-grey suit was probably from Saville Row, and Selma was sure she'd caught a whiff of Brut aftershave. The men were looking over at their table now, making discrete comments on their female company and occasionally laughing.

Loma offered them a very obvious wink.

'Behave yourself,' said Madeha. 'There's no need to be vulgar. I think you're a bit drunk.'

'Well, I learned it from you, if you remember,' said Loma, raising her glass to the men.

To Madeha's horror, they rose from their bar stools, grabbed their drinks and wandered over to the table.

'Good evening, ladies,' said the older of the two. 'My name is Michael. This is Tom. Do you mind if we join you?'

Loma suddenly realised the impact of her impetuous behaviour, and she began to blush. She forgave herself instantly, however, on the basis that she was doing her friend a favour.

'It would be our pleasure,' she said, and the gentlemen took their seats.

Tom was clearly several years younger. He was blonde and slim, and his suit seemed more likely to have originated from Marks & Spencer. Loma supposed that they occupied different professional ranks, perhaps within the same organization. Whether they were doctors or lawyers or businessmen, she didn't know, but they were clearly not among life's losers.

Loma did all the talking, introducing herself and her friend as PhD students at University College London. They were experts in art history, she said, and their research had demonstrated that the English were a very cold people – at least compared to the Italians, who had produced such hotheads as Caravaggio and Michelangelo. She was clearly teasing, a fact accentuated by her huge smile.

'Well, we soon warm up once you get to know us,' said Michael.

'Yes, that's what I've heard,' replied Loma, laughing.

'Tom's particularly warm once he gets going, aren't you, Tom?'

'Oh, one of the warmest around, no doubt about it.'

'Well, I'll take care not to get burned,' Loma replied.

She was enjoying herself enormously now. Indeed, as her banter grew ever more reckless, she found years of stress escaping from her system. Madeha was still feeling slightly alarmed, but with the aid of another bloody Mary, she relaxed into the flirtatious vibe. The booze also helped demolish her inhibitions regarding the language, and before long she was trotting out long and complicated sentences without stopping to think. They were riddled with grammatical errors, of course, but nobody seemed to mind, least of all the two men.

They talked about everything and anything, and the girls found themselves captivated by their companions' dry English humour. They seemed to be working almost as a comedy double-act, a sign of their close partnership in life. Neither Loma nor Madeha could recall laughing so much in years.

Then it came to crunch time. Michael looked at his watch and pulled a humorous face of disapproval.

'Oh, it's getting horribly late. I feel we really should be moving on. I don't suppose you ladies would be interested in continuing this conversation in my hotel suit? It has a nice sofa and a well-stocked bar – and room-service, of course.'

Madeha was by this time seething with desire for Michael, and yet her automatic response to was to feign shock at such an indent proposal.

'How dare you! We're respectable ladies, not easy girls who go to a strange man's hotel room. We've only just met you.'

'Well, I do apologise. I meant nothing by it, I can assure you, beyond a chance to continue our delightful conversation in more comfortable surroundings.'

Madeha was simultaneously reassured by Michael's polite apology and aroused by the fact that his leg was now touching hers underneath the table. She didn't know if their legs had been touching for some time, or whether this was a new development. But if it was intended to lure her into more intimate contact, then it was certainly working.

Beneath it all, however, was a lingering sense of shame: both the sexual shame that religion generally imposes on women, and the shame felt by a widow as she contemplates her first sexual experience since the passing of her husband.

During Mohamed's service on the front-line, he had only managed to visit home once every few months. Unlike many married women, she had welcomed her husband's outpouring of sexual desire on these occasions, rising to the challenge several times each night. He made her feel like a corpse that had been suddenly resurrected. Now, after several years, she had the very same feeling again – although now it was a white-haired Englishman performing the magic.

Loma, who had taken the lead in events thus far, was suddenly struck by the risks involved in this little escapade. If they went back to Micheal's hotel suite, he would probably expect to take Madeha to bed, which meant that Tom would perhaps want Loma for himself. And while Loma wasn't at all averse to spending the night with this handsome young man, she knew that she would be risking her life. If the embassy security staff suspected that either woman had spent the night with a British citizen in London, they would be put on the first plane back to Baghdad. British intelligence was well-known for its use of honey-traps, and men were just as willing to perform such roles as women. Loma didn't even want to think about the consequences of being caught up in such a scandal.

She looked around the bar, wondering for the very first time whether they were being watched. She kicked herself for not having thought about it before. Her eyes danced from table to table, person to person, eliminating each face in turn. None of them seemed very obviously to be Iraqi intelligence operatives, but of course, the best spies were never obvious.

'I think we should leave,' said Loma, picking up her handbag and getting to her feet.

'Why? We're having a nice time, aren't we?' said Madeha, clearly disappointed.

'Well, it's been very nice chatting, but I think we really must be going home. Come on, I'll pay the bill at the bar, and we can get a cab.'

Madeha struggled reluctantly to her feet, shrugging her shoulders to Michael, who was doing his best to be philosophical.

'It's sad that you have to go, ladies,' he said, 'but I wouldn't wish to impose. Allow me at least to get the bill for you.'

'No, don't be silly,' said Loma, doing her best to squeeze past Madeha as she pulled on her coat and scarf.

But it was too late; Michael was already at the bar, handing over his credit card. Tom was helping Maheha with her coat, complimenting her on the fine quality of the material.

Loma heaved a sigh. How nice it would be to have the freedom to take advantage of such situations, to allow oneself to be seduced by a real gentleman from time to time. Such was not her fate, obviously.

They shook hands politely with Tom and Michael, thanking them for a wonderful evening. Before they could depart, however, the two men reached into their wallets and pulled out their business cards.

'Take this,' said Michael, 'and call me any time you want to meet again. I find you quite fascinating, and I'm sure we have plenty more to talk about.'

'Thank you very much,' said Madeha, her words slightly slurred. 'I'll call you some time.'

Loma hoped to God that she wouldn't.

Outside, the girls found that it was raining again. They strolled down the street, arm-in-arm, their coats over their heads for protection. They were both a little unsteady on their feet, and before long they realized that they were wandering aimlessly, heading north-east into Soho. Loma hailed a cab and they collapsed onto the backseat, giggling like two school girls.

Loma retrieved Tom's card from her pocket and read it, squinting in the dim light.

'Tom Redcliff, Investment Analyst. Well, that's an interesting job title. I think I prefer the man to the job,' she said.

Madeha was doing her best to inspect Michael's card, but she had trouble focusing. In the end, she gave up and tucked it into her bra. Leaning back in the seat, she closed her eyes and imagined his strong hands massaging her breasts. She realised for the first time just how drunk she was. Everything was spinning, as if she were in a small aeroplane, falling to earth in a tight circle. She opened her eyes and found that the inside of the cab seemed to be spinning too. She gripped the door handle and hoped the ride home wouldn't take too long.

Loma wasn't in such a bad way, perhaps because she was more used to drinking. That said, she was certainly a little drunk. She looked out of the window as they passed through Soho, and she wondered what the chances were of bumping into Riaz tonight. How would she feel if she discovered him here, entertaining a prostitute? Would she care? She was pretty sure that she wouldn't. In fact, she almost wished she could stumble across him in such circumstances, just so that she could laugh in his face and tell him that he meant nothing to her any more – absolutely nothing.

'What are you thinking?' said Madeha, suddenly clutching Loma's hand.

'I was thinking about Riaz.'

'You don't care about that old fool, do you?'

'No, not at all – I don't care at all.'

'Me neither. I don't care about anything!'

'Yeah, who cares!'

'Who cares!'

They were laughing again, but this time like older women who had seen it all and concluded that nothing in life was really of any consequence.

The taxi driver looked in the rear-view mirror.

'Are you ladies alright?' he said.

'We're more than alright,' said Madeha. 'We're wonderful!'

'Yes, we're wonderful!'

They were still laughing when the cab reached its destination. However, they took great care to calm down before stepping onto the street. It wouldn't do for anyone to see them so happy.

A twist of fate

When she awoke the next morning, Madeha had a terrible hangover. Her body was heavy, and her eyelids seemed to be sewn shut. She had a sharp pain in her head, as if she'd been hit with a rock. As she rolled gently onto her back, she felt a slight wave of nausea. Thinking back to the night before, she recalled at least three different types of booze: champagne, bloody Mary, and a large bottle of English bitter that Michael has urged her to try. She was no expert, but she was pretty sure it was the mixing of drinks that had given this hangover its nasty edge. She would have to make a note of that for the future – assuming Loma was willing to trust her again with London's nightlife.

She dragged herself from bed, showered, dressed and applied some simple make-up. She checked her Omega watch: 11:30am. This was an embarrassingly late hour to be coming down for breakfast. She crept downstairs, half expecting Loma to be angry. But the house was quiet, the living-room empty. The eerie silence reminded her of the evacuation of her neighbourhood in the early days of the war with Iran. She moved to the window and looked into the street.

'Can I help you, ma'am?'

Madeha turned to find the Filipino maid standing in the centre of the room.

'Oh, no, I was looking for Loma.'

'Madam has had an emergency. She had to go out.'

'What happened?'

'Not to worry. There are always emergencies in the embassy when someone comes suddenly from abroad.'

Madeha was bewildered. She opened her mouth to ask a question, but decided against it.

'Would madam like some breakfast?'

'Just some tea, please. And some toast, if that's okay.'

The maid turned and left the room, and Madeha sank into one of the plush armchairs.

What on earth was this emergency, and who was the sudden visitor from abroad? Perhaps some Iraqi minister was in London? Perhaps it wasn't an 'emergency' exactly, but a busy day that required all hands to the pumps?

Even so, she was a little put out that Loma had not left a note. After all, Madeha had come to England on a rescue mission, giving up her holiday time to provide moral support. The least Loma could do was stick around for the duration of her visit.

The maid came in with a tray of tea and toast, setting it down on the coffee table. Madeha turned on the television, just in time for the midday news. Like so many people in Iraq, she admired the BBC for its impartial coverage of world events, including the war with Iran. Residents of Baghdad often tuned into BBC Radio, rather than relying on Iraqi state media. Today, however, there was no coverage of the Iran-Iraq war; perhaps the British were growing bored with it.

She ordered another pot of tea and was just settling into the next programme – something about antiques – when she sensed someone behind her. It was Tony, the driver. He was combing back his blonde hair.

'Sorry to startle you, ma'am.'

'Where's Loma?'

'She had to go to the embassy, I'm afraid.'

'Is she alright?'

'No need to worry. She's fine.'

Just like the Filipino maid, Tony's expression seemed to say: 'I'm sorry I can't say more.'

'Will you be heading into town today, ma'am?'

'Alone?'

'I only ask because I'm likely to be busy with the car all day. There's quite a lot going on at the embassy, and they need all the drivers they can get.'

'Not to worry, Tony. Just point me in the directly of the Albert Memorial, please. I haven't seen it yet.'

'Yes, of course. It's just a short walk from here.'

As Madeha started along the pavement, she felt a sudden thrill at being alone in London, free to wander at will. She crossed Kensington Road and entered the park, a vast expanse of lawn, criss-crossed by paths and adorned with sturdy trees. Turning east, she soon arrived at the Albert Memorial. She had read in detail about this ornate stone edifice, featuring a statue of Prince Albert, the beloved husband of Queen Victoria. It was a symbol of her deep love for a man who had been loyal and loving from start to end.

As Madeha gazed at the prince, her thoughts turned to Munir. She recalled a strange rumour from several years back: a friend returning from London reported seeing him in Hyde Park. He had been at a spot known as Speaker's Corner, apparently, standing on a box and delivering a speech – like so many other enthusiasts, rebels, prophets and lunatics. He had been ranting about the Middle East, scolding the leadership of Iraq for various crimes. At the time, Loma had dismissed the claims, assuming that her friend had allowed her imagination to run wild. After all, it was well known that Iraqi intelligence operated freely in London, under the watchful gaze of MI5, tracking dissidents and bringing them to justice – one way or another. The idea that Munir would be delivering subversive speeches 500 metres from the Iraqi embassy was ludicrous.

Even so, she turned and began walking slowly across the grass toward Speaker's Corner. On arrival, she found several speakers standing on little boxes, each setting forth some bold vision or other, each with their own little gaggle of listeners. She was shocked to find one young man openly insulting the British leader, Prime Minister Margaret Thatcher. Anyone who attempted to publically insult the Iraqi leader in Baghdad would be hauled off to jail within minutes. Torture and death would no doubt follow. Nearby, other speakers were promoting their own faiths: Islam, Protestantism, Mormonism. There was also a devoted member of the Communist Party of Great Britain, and another demanding the re-introduction of capital punishment. One rather energetic young man was arguing against the detention of mentally ill patients, who he said were forced to take medicines that only made them worse. Just metres away, two men argued over the Arab-Israeli issue, each on their own box, each trying to shout louder than the other.

She approached the proponent of the Arab cause and stood watching him, impressed by the passion with which he delivered his sermon. He sported a scruffy, grey beard, a Palestinian scarf and glasses with thick, black plastic frames. He seemed to have a heavy Arab accent of some sort, and Madeha struggled at first to understand his English. She closed her eyes in an effort to identify the words more clearly. She was transported back a dozen years to the train station in Baghdad, on that fateful night when she'd kissed Munir for the last time.

Her heart skipped a beat and she opened her eyes wide, staring at the man before her. She could see it clearly now. The man on the box was Munir. The beard and the glasses had provided a degree of disguise, and he had clearly aged, putting on a bit of weight. But there was no doubt that this man was her former lover, the man with whom she planned to spend eternity. Now, apparently, Fate had thrown them together once more.

She was terrified. Her heart was beating like a steam train. The nausea she had felt when she first awoke came back, but stronger than ever. She thought her legs might give way beneath her. Taking a deep breath, she walked to a nearby bench and took a seat, watching and listening as Munir railed against Zionism and Western Imperialism.

Half an hour passed, and the crowd began to thin out. Perhaps Munir was repeating himself by this point, or perhaps the spectators were hungry for their lunch. Apparently, Munir was also getting hungry, for he stepped down off his box – an upturned milk-crate – and picked up his shoulder bag.

Madeha was horrified at the thought of a re-union after all these years. What should she say? Was she supposed to scold him for not getting in touch? Did he still love her, despite the long silence? Or perhaps he was happily married now? And what if Madeha was being watched by someone from the Iraqi embassy? Any contact between herself and Munir was bound to bring them both disaster

She started walking quickly toward the street, head down, woolly scarf across her nose and mouth. This was the only option: run and don't look back. After all, if he could do it, then so could she.

'Madoha!' came a voice from behind.

It was clearly Munir's voice; she would recognize it anywhere. And he was calling her by his pet name for her – a playful mispronunciation that nobody else had ever used.

She stopped in her tracks, turned and walked slowly back. As she grew closer, the familiar face came more clearly into view. He removed the glasses and stuffed them into a pocket. Apparently, they were just part of his disguise.

'Madoha, it's me, Munir,' he said, a broad smile revealing his bright, white teeth.

'Yes, I know,' she said. 'I recognised you.'

'So, you were just going to walk away?'

'Well, it was quite a surprise to see you, to be honest. And you walked away from me, if you remember, many years ago. I thought you were dead.'

Munir stood looking at her, eyes sparkling, beaming with joy. Madeha couldn't help responding with a smile of her own. Yes, she had often felt angry that he'd never been in touch, but now she was happy to see him alive. So happy, in fact, that it felt like a dream. She wanted to pinch herself, to be sure that it was all real.

'What are you doing here?' he asked at last.

'I'm visiting Loma. Do you remember her?'

'Of course I do. I heard her husband works at the embassy.'

'Yes, he's First Secretary for Political Affairs. It's a big promotion.'

'So, are you on holiday?'

'Yes, I'm ...'

She didn't have time to finish her sentence before he spoke again: 'You're so beautiful. You're just as beautiful as you always were. I can't believe my eyes. It's so amazing to see you!'

'Thanks, Munir. You haven't changed either,' she said quietly.

'Well, I'm a bit older, and a bit fatter. And I feel my age too. It's hard living in exile. I haven't seen my family for over a decade, and I probably never will.'

'Well, that's the path you've chosen, so I suppose you have to pay the price.'

She regretted making this last comment, which reeked of resentment. It wasn't fair to resent Munir for being passionate about politics. She only regretted that she had never learned his fate until now. She continued, making every effort to sound more sympathetic than judgemental.

'So why didn't you write to me after you left?'

'Are you serious? If I'd written to you, the *Mukhabarat* would have been round your house within the hour. They monitor all the mail, you know. They knew you were my girlfriend, of course. You were lucky they didn't send you to jail just for knowing me. If we had started exchanging letters, you'd still be in jail today.'

'How do you know that I didn't spend time in jail?'

'Well, I have ways of keeping tabs on people. There's a big network, and people travel back and forth all the time. I asked people to report back to me whenever possible. I learned about your wedding, for example. That was hard news to bear at the time. But what could I do?'

It was Madeha's turn to remain silent, shocked to think that he'd been aware of the various twists and turns of her life, but unable to intervene. He must have suffered a lot.

He continued, his tone soft: 'I'm sorry to hear about your husband, by the way. That must have been a terrible blow.'

'Yes, it was hard.'

'I'm sure.'

'But I'm getting over it now. I have a new lease of life these days. Visiting London helps.'

'Well, it certainly is good from my point of view. I thought we'd never meet again. And now here you are, standing before me. It must be Destiny!'

'I suppose it must. I've seen you again and again in my dreams … and now it's real.'

They couldn't help laughing, and he gently squeezed her arm. The physical contact sent a warm tingle through her entire body. In an instant, they were locked in a firm embrace, squeezing hard, rocking from side to side. Madeha closed her eyes and felt the warmth of his body. She felt the tears rolling down her cheeks, just as they had done at the railway station so many years before.

'Come on,' he said at last, 'let's get a coffee.'

'Alright.'

They walked back toward the centre of the park, holding hands all the way. They skirted the Serpentine, with its ducks and pedal boats, stopping finally at an outdoor café.

She sipped her cappuccino and listened as Munir told his story, including his daring escape across the border into Syria, then through Turkey and into Greece. He was a British citizen now, having gained official status as a political dissident. He was writing for an opposition newspaper in London, always under a false name. Madeha was glad to discover that he was still single. There had been several women, he said, but somehow it never felt right. She knew exactly what he meant.

They ordered sandwiches and more coffee, followed by numerous snacks. Madeha had quite forgotten about seeing the sights of London. Her whole world had been reduced to one table in a public park, and she would happily spend the rest of her holiday right there, so long as she could keep talking with Munir.

Noticing that the sky was growing dark, she checked her watch.

'Oh my God!' she said. 'It's six o'clock. I've been out for hours, and I didn't leave a note for Loma. She'll be worried. She might think I've been kidnapped or something.'

'Don't worry. Loma will understand. I'll walk you back.'

'No, don't walk me back, Munir. They'll see us together and there will be hell to pay.'

'Okay, but let me walk you just a little way.'

'Alright, just to the park gates. No further.'

They stopped by the Albert Memorial, looking up at this monument to undying love.

'Wonderful, isn't it?' she said.

'It's a symbol of imperial power as much as anything. But I admit that it's beautiful.'

'Loma will be so glad to hear that you're alive and well. I can't wait to tell her.'

'Are you mad? You can't tell Loma about me.'

'Why not? She's my best friend. I can tell her anything. Don't you like her?'

'Of course I like her, but you can't risk it. What if someone starts to ask her difficult questions? It would be safer for her – and for us – if she could answer those questions honestly. The less she knows, the safer it will be for everyone.'

'Okay, if you say so,' whispered Madeha.

'Will I see you again?' he asked.

'Yes, tomorrow. I'll be at the same café at 2pm. Will you be there?'

'Yes, of course I will.'

They held each other once more, indulging in a long and passionate kiss. It was as if they'd never been apart.

It was the maid who opened the door, but Loma was in the hallway behind her, an expression of extreme stress on her face.

'Where on earth have you been?' she demanded.

'Out for a walk.'

'I thought something terrible had happened to you.'

'Well, it hasn't. I just went for a nice stroll and had some lunch and watched the ducks. I read my book for a while, and then I came back. What's the big problem?'

'I just had no idea where you were. I was about to call the police.'

'I'm sorry, it won't happen again.'

'You didn't meet up with Michael did you?'

'No, I didn't. Don't be so ridiculous. And please to make such suggestions again.'

Loma realised she'd touched a raw nerve, and she instantly regretted it.

They stepped through to the dining-room, where Loma poured them each a glass of wine.

'So, tell me more about your day,' she said.

'Oh, it was nothing special. I saw the Prince Albert Memorial, and I wandered around Hyde Park, and met some interesting people.'

'Who did you meet?'

Madeha was not used to telling lies, least of all to her best friend. But she had no choice, inventing several strangers and telling of the fascinating conversations they'd had about this and that. She made no mention of Speaker's Corner; indeed, if she were asked about it, she was prepared to say that it didn't particularly interest her. Finally, she decided to change tack.

'What was this emergency at the embassy then?'

'Oh, it wasn't really an emergency. The ambassador's wife Nora asked me to help her. They suspect a VIP will be visiting soon.'

'Who is it?'

Loma lowered her voice to a whisper: 'It's one of Saddam's offspring, probably Uday. There are rumours that he's been gambling in Monte Carlo. Another rumour is that he's purchased a mansion in Nice for the singer Raja. Apparently, after so much hard work, he's ready for a holiday in London. He has a very nice house here, of course, near Windsor. We have to make sure that everything runs smoothly and the press is kept under control.'

'Gosh, it all sounds a bit nerve-wracking. I don't know how you cope.'

'Oh, it's not so hard. I just feel bad about leaving you alone. I'll be busy for the next few days, I'm afraid. Will you be alright?'

'Yes, of course. I'll find some way of entertaining myself.'

* * *

Madeha found plenty to keep her occupied in the following days. She and Munir met once more in Hyde Park, and then dined in Edgware Road, Soho and Hampstead Heath. They visited the British Museum, where he stole a long kiss in front of the huge Assyrian bulls. In the National Gallery, he fondled her breasts beneath her jacket as she stood looking at the works of Van Dyke. He chased her around a tank at the Imperial War Museum, and a security guard ordered them to leave. It was in the café at the Tate Gallery that the mood suddenly became more serious.

'Will you marry me?' he said, holding her hand across the table.

'What did you say?'

Madeha was incredulous. What he was suggesting seemed an impossibility.

'I asked if you'd marry me. I'm quite serious.'

'But my life is in Iraq. I have two children there. I can hardly leave them with my mother and move to England.'

'I'm sure we could find a way to organize things.'

'How?'

'Well, we could be married here, in England, and you could visit from time to time. Eventually, when the children are grown up, you could seek British citizenship and move here permanently. By that time, they'd have forgotten all about me.'

Madeha was silent. His suggestion seemed simultaneously reasonable and utterly insane, fraught with all sorts of danger for them both.

'I'll think about it,' she said at last. 'In the meantime, let's take it one day at a time.'

'Alright,' said Munir.

He was smiling, but there was sadness in his eyes.

A very important party

Vehicles had been arriving all day, dropping people off and picking them up: designers, florists, security staff, cleaners, musicians and caterers. Among the inanimate deliveries were boxes of fresh flowers, some freshly laundered table linen, plates and glasses by the crate-load, and a hundred gold Rolex watches decorated with Saddam's photo. Additional police officers had been deployed in the surrounding streets, and two diplomatic-protection officers from Scotland Yard had stopped by to check on arrangements. This evening, a VIP guest would be visiting, and everything must be perfect.

Normally, the only decoration on the white facade of the Iraqi embassy was the national flag. Today, however, it was adorned with strings of lights, like an enormous Christmas tree. So too was the ambassador's residence next door, which was sufficiently spacious to host high-class parties with live music and dancing. It was here that the reception would be held.

The entire embassy staff was hard at work, checking lists and making phone calls, liaising with British officials and printing name tags. Loma had been helping Nora since early morning, tasked, among other things, with ordering the booze. The finest wines and champagnes were coming from Harrods and Fortnum & Mason, as were vintage whiskies, the preferred tipple of the illustrious guest.

Nora, meanwhile, had been focussed on the flowers, which she'd ordered from various florists across Kensington and Chelsea. As they arrived, she supervised their distribution about the residence, ensuring that the most beautiful were most prominent. The final batch was delivered around mid-afternoon, and she sniffed the bouquets one by one.

'They hardly smell at all,' she said. 'Flowers in Iraq smell much stronger.'

'It's the lack of sunshine, madam,' said an embassy aide by her elbow.

The delivery man raised his eyebrows in astonishment. The flowers seemed quite fragrant enough to him. He wanted to say something about foreigners always complaining, but he bit his tongue.

Moments later, a string quartet arrived, along with their instruments. Nora greeted them one by one and instructed the aide to show them the venue. The music had been a particular headache to arrange. After much debate, it had been decided to provide a variety of options: classical music for the early evening, then traditional Iraqi music, followed by pop music for the late-night disco. With a little more warning, they might have been able to hire a celebrity performer, but not at short notice.

Just as she thought she might get a break, several white vans arrived from Heathrow Airport, loaded with food. Maxim's restaurant in Paris, that most revered of establishments, was doing the catering. According to rumour, the restaurant was closed to diners until the Iraqi Embassy contract had been completed. Luckily, there were several chefs and a catering manager on hand to transfer everything safely to the kitchen. Nora thought about helping but made an executive decision to leave well alone.

She returned to the embassy, looking rather stressed, and invited Loma into the garden for a cigarette break. As she did so, a telephone rang on the ambassador's desk. Nora stood in the doorway as her husband answered. He listened carefully to the voice at the other end, thanked the caller politely and replaced the receiver. His face was rather pale – or lemon-yellow, as is often said in Iraq.

'He'll be here at 8pm. Let everybody know, will you?'

He was trying to appear calm in front of his wife, but he was shaking like a leaf.

* * *

Loma walked briskly home and jumped into the shower. Her husband had already dressed for the party and was now searching for his gold Cartier cufflinks. He was shouting and swearing at the servants, who he accused of either losing or stealing them.

Emerging from the bathroom, Loma began searching the draws, finally spotting the cufflinks on the floor by the bed. She handed them over, receiving not a word of thanks.

Madeha sat in the living room, trying to focus on her novel, not sure whether she should be doing something more productive. She was perplexed by the atmosphere of mild panic. It reminded her of the early years of the war, when the Iranian air force launched raids that sent civilians scurrying in search of shelter.

'I'm sorry we can't invite you,' said Loma, appearing in the doorway, draped in a dressing gown. 'It's just a question of security, apparently. You haven't been properly vetted, so we can't issue an invitation.'

'Oh, that's quite alright. I'm actually glad to be staying at home. You all seem horribly stressed about this party.'

'Well, it's still a big secret. Everyone knows a VIP is coming, but only a select handful knows who it is. You're very privileged in that respect.'

'I suppose I am.'

'Of course, one never knows what might ...' Loma stopped herself mid-sentence and changed tack. 'Would you help me pick out some clothes?'

'Yes, of course.'

They stood before the wardrobe while Loma held up dress after dress, none of them particularly impressing Madeha.

'What about that little black number you bought at Harrods the other day?'

'Yes, of course. Here it is. What do you think?'

Loma pressed it against her body. It was very stylish, cut just above the knees, with a low front and no sleeves.

Madeha stood back: 'Wonderful, just perfect.'

'Well, it should be perfect. It's an Emanuel. They designed the wedding dress for Princess Diana. I think hers might have been more expensive – but only just.'

Loma slipped into the garment and Madeha zipped her up at the back.

'Oh, you look magnificent, Loma. You're showing quite a bit of flesh though.'

For the sake of modesty, Loma reached into the wardrobe and pulled out a black-and-silver shawl, which she draped across her shoulders.

'That's just perfect. You'll knock them dead," said Madeha.

Loma had been hoping to visit the hairdresser before the party, but all such plans had been shoved to one side. She made do instead with curling tongs and heaps of hairspray, assisted by Madeha, who was skilled in such operations. She slapped on some Elizabeth Arden make-up and a liberal dose of Chanel No. 5. Finally, Loma kissed her friend goodbye and dashed out the front door.

Madeha went to her room and collapsed on the bed, looking at the ceiling. She was indeed glad to have been left off the invitation list. The last thing she wanted was to be in a room with Uday Hussein, particularly not as a single woman. She thought of her husband, then of her children, and finally of Munir. She had been pondering his offer of marriage; the more she thought about it, the less crazy it seemed to be. There was no doubt that she wanted to be with him, tied to him forever, and perhaps a way could be found.

She reached into her handbag and pulled out her little pink address book, turning to Munir's number. There was no name, just the letter M, followed by a number with a north-London code. Her heart skipped a beat at the idea of hearing his loving voice. Was it safe to phone from the house, she wondered? Were the phones really bugged? Or was that just paranoia? After a moment's reflection, she skipped downstairs to the living room, lifted the receiver and began to dial.

* * *

Guests were arriving at the ambassador's residence now, lining up in the entrance hall to be searched by the security men, with their dark suits and moustaches. In addition to the various officials, there were some esteemed members of the Iraqi expatriate community, several wealthy businessmen, and a smattering of academics and creative types. Among the academics were several Iraqi-government spies posing as PhD candidates; they were tasked with mingling, their ears tuned to any expressions of dissent.

The wives of the Iraqi officials had made a special effort to look their best, hair piled high, the make-up inch-thick. One lady seemed to have overdone it, with a clear difference in tone between her dark hands and her pale face. Another lady had managed to squeeze into her most expensive dress, purchased several years before, but her belly was making every effort to escape through the seams.

The younger generations looked more impressive. The girls, who had begged to be allowed to wear jeans, had been forced into dresses that were simultaneously respectable and flattering. After all, they might meet their future husband at such an event. One girl, just 15 years old, looked particularly dazzling, with her green eyes, beauty-queen looks and womanly figure. Her parents were immensely proud of her, confident that she'd make a fine match someday.

The ambassador and his wife were standing in the entrance hall, greeting guests as they arrived. He was very anxious, not least of all because, despite being continually asked, he was not yet allowed to reveal the identity of the guest of honour.

Suddenly, his personal assistant arrived, whispering in his ear: the convoy was three minutes away. The ambassador checked his watch and found that Uday was well ahead of schedule. He just had time to rush to the bathroom and return to his position before a convoy of cars – black Mercedes and limousines – turned into Queen's Gate and drew up outside. Doors were thrown open and body-guards rushed to the limousine, forming a protective cordon. One pulled the rear passenger door open, and a tall, slim man stepped onto the red carpet. He sported his usual dark moustache, but now it was balanced by a week of beard growth. He looked smart enough, though, in his Saville Row suit. He enjoyed looking the part whenever he visited England. After all, he had purchased the Windsor mansion of Wallis Simpson, the American divorcee who had married King Edward VIII, prompting his abdication. Uday liked to think that he was also something of a rebel, although he had no plans to relinquish his power.

He strolled into the building and shook hands with the ambassador and his wife, who bowed and curtsied respectfully.

'Hello,' said Uday, his face the very picture of boredom.

'Your Excellency, we are honoured. We hope to ...'

Before the ambassador could finish his well-rehearsed opening remarks, Uday started shouting instructions to his security team, then demanded directions to the bar. A body-guard indicated the way and the president's son followed, as did everyone else.

The bar was situated at one end of a long room fringed with tables and chairs. At the far end was a small stage, in front of which was the dance-floor. Taking their cue from the ambassador, the string quartet launched into a lively piece by Mozart. Uday didn't notice the music; he was busy shouting at the barman, demanding a particular brand of whiskey that was proving hard to locate. The barman was frantically opening boxes and rummaging under the counter. Finally, a waiter arrived from the kitchen and handed over the correct bottle. Uday grabbed it and poured himself a double measure, helping himself to a handful of ice. He was joined by a small group of intimates, including his personal-security chief, and they began to chat amongst themselves.

The ambassador attempted to establish a degree of normality, instructing the waiters to hand out champagne and nibbles, while he did his best to mingle. Nora was likewise putting a brave face on things, frantically meeting and greeting, smiling and dishing out compliments left and right. She was wondering whether it might be best to move the schedule forward a bit, dishing up the buffet before the whiskey had a chance to take effect.

Uday and his gang started to circulate, speaking only amongst themselves. Somewhere near the stage, the VIP spotted the charming 15-year-old girl, with her beauty-queen looks and womanly figure. He whispered into his personal assistant's ear, and the man whispered back. Uday logged the young lady for future reference. The girl's parents, meanwhile, were looking deathly pale, deeply regretting their decision to bring her along. While Nora was in the kitchen, issuing orders to speed things up, Uday turned his attention to the music.

'What's this rubbish?' he said.

'A string quartet, Your Excellency, comprised of members of the London Philharmonic Orchestra. They are among the best performers available. They specialise in Baroque and Classical music, including ...'

Uday shouted at the musicians, telling them to get off stage, demanding instead some music that he could dance to. In particular, he wanted *I Shot the Sheriff* by Bob Marley. The ambassador whispered in the ear of his personal assistant, who rushed into another room, returning moments later with a four-piece pop band. Hastily setting up their equipment, they launched into the Bob Marley tune, but it was far from perfect. Uday was furious, throwing his whiskey glass at the drummer, who ducked just in time. The president's son turned to the ambassador, his face red with fury.

'Why didn't you hire someone famous, like George Michael?' he shouted.

'Your Excellency, we did try, I assure you. However, he's fully booked. We also inquired about Phil Collins and Elton John, but they also have engagements elsewhere. We had very short notice of your arrival. I can only apologise.'

'What do you mean? There was plenty of time. If you'd offered them enough money, they would have been glad to play for me. You clearly didn't try hard enough.'

'I apologize, Your Excellency,' said the ambassador, bowing his head.

He knew that there was no point in offering further excuses. Only a grovelling apology would do, and he was well trained in such things. Even so, he knew that he might not be the Iraqi ambassador to London for much longer.

The band finished their tune and launched into a George Michael song. Fortunately, they knew all his songs and played them well. It was less fortunate for the young girl that Uday was in the mood to dance. He walked over to her, grabbed her wrist and dragged her onto the dance floor. She looked terrified, glancing over her shoulder at her parents, who were passionately urging her on. Before long, she found her rhythm, and Uday smiled for the first time. The ambassador urged his other guests to join His Excellency on the dance-floor, and they dutifully obliged. Before long, the party began to take on the appearance of normality.

In the adjoining room, Nora was supervising the buffet. The long table was weighed down with countless delicacies, most of them French. During a suitable pause in the dancing, Nora told the catering manager to bang the dinner gong, and guests were invited to feed. Uday was the first in the queue, and for once he seemed to have little to complain about, ravenously munching on chicken legs and eating caviar from the pot. Half an hour later, there was a collective sigh of relief when he informed the ambassador – through his head of security – that he was heading to the nearby Mint Casino for a spot of gambling. His excellency would not be returning that night. The teenage girl's parents were particularly relieved.

* * *

Loma returned home early on the pretext of a headache, leaving her husband to smoke cigars with his colleagues. She staggered upstairs and soaked in the bath, eyes closed. It was over, thank God. There might be repercussions, of course, including a swift return to Baghdad. But at least the party was over.

Slipping into a tracksuit and slippers, she went to Madeha's room but found it empty, the light off. Just then, she heard a door slamming downstairs. She went down to the kitchen, then through to the living room, and finally into the study. She was quite puzzled, and stood in the hallway, wondering whether someone had just come in or gone out. She was on the point of calling the maid, when Madeha came out of the downstairs toilet, looking rather surprised.

'Gosh, you gave me a shock!' she said.

'So did you, Madeha. Where have you been?'

'In the toilet.'

'No, I mean … Oh, never mind.'

Madeha wandered through to the living room, clutching her handbag. She was glad she'd decided to remove her coat the moment she stepped through the front door.

'So how was the party?'

'Horrible, of course. But thankfully it's over.'

'I hope nothing bad happened?'

'Nothing out of the ordinary. No guns were fired, if that's what you mean.'

'Well, that's something.'

Loma collapsed into the sofa and closed her eyes.

'Gosh, you really do look exhausted,' Madeha said, sitting down by her side.

'I just don't know how long I can go on. I mean, with the marriage. How can I stay with a man I no longer love? And why should I have to put up with all this stress just for the sake of his career?'

'It doesn't help to be thinking of Ali so much.'

'You're right, it doesn't help at all.'

'You poor thing.'

'Well, you know what it's like, Madeha. You were happily married, so it's a bit different, but I do recall you were once heartbroken over … what was his name?'

'Munir.'

'That's right, Munir. He just up a left, didn't he?'

'He had his reasons. He was facing prison for his political beliefs. I can hardly blame him.'

'No, of course not. But you do still miss him, right?'

'Yes, sometimes.'

'Did you ever learn what happened to him?'

Madeha was suddenly alarmed by Loma's line of questioning. What was she driving at? Had she found out about their secret meetings? Was Munir in danger?

'No, I never found out,' she said, walking to the drinks cabinet. She poured two glasses of red wine and resumed her seat.

'It's all very said,' said Loma, draining her glass in one go.

Madeha put her arm around her friend's shoulders, and Loma leaned in close.

'Yes,' said Madeha, 'it's all very sad. But at least we've got each other.'

'Yes, we have.'

Consummation

The next morning, Madeha woke up early, padding downstairs to the kitchen while everyone was still fast asleep. She made herself a cup of Twinings tea, using a teabag, something she would never have considered back in Iraq. Rummaging through the fridge, she pondered her options, settling finally on a feta-cheese sandwich. She consumed her unconventional breakfast by the window overlooking the back garden. As she gazed at the neatly cropped lawn, there was one thing on her mind: Munir's proposal of marriage. Was she right to be so hesitant? Could she ever be happy alone?

She suddenly felt an urge to call him. Swallowing the last of her sandwich, she sneaked into Loma's office and began to dial the number that was seared into her brain. The phone rang a dozen times, and she was on the point of hanging up when someone answered.

'Hello?' said a man, his croaky voice suggesting that he'd just crawled from bed.

'Good morning. Is that Munir?'

'No, he's in his room.'

'Can I speak to him please?'

'I'll get him.'

The man wandered off. Madeha listened to doors opening and shutting, and muffled voices in the distance. Her heart was pounding now, butterflies in her stomach.

Just as Munir seemed to be approaching the phone, Madeha became aware of movement upstairs; someone was awake in the house. It might be Loma, or even Riaz. She gently replaced the receiver and slipped back into the kitchen, resuming her position by the window.

'Good morning,' said a voice behind her.

It was Loma's elder son Walid, standing in the doorway in his pyjamas, hair sticking up at all angles. He was still rubbing the sleep from his eyes.

'Good morning,' said Maheda. 'You look sleepy.'

'Yes, I am a bit.'

'Can I get you some breakfast?'

'Sugar Puffs, please.'

'Coming right up.'

Walid had come to view Madeha as a sort of aunty, more like a sister to his mother than a mere friend. He had gone to school with Madeha's son in Baghdad, playing on the same football team.

Madeha prepared the cereals while the boy looked on, sipping occasionally from a glass of juice. She ran through the usual range of questions relating to school and plans for the weekend, Walid answering with the skill of a child used to inquisitive adults. Finally, he took his breakfast cereals and disappeared into the living room, tuning the TV to a cartoon.

Moments later, Loma walked into the kitchen, fully dressed, hair and make-up done. She had on a smart, blue skirt-suit with padded shoulders and gold trim.

'Good morning,' she said, opening the fridge and pouring a glass of milk. 'You're up nice and early.'

'Yes, I couldn't stay in bed for some reason.'

'You're feeling alright, are you?'

'Absolutely fine. I just didn't want to rot in bed when it was such a nice day out.'

'Well, I've got to dash out, I'm afraid.'

'Going somewhere nice?'

'I've got to go shopping with Nora. We've got a list of things to buy for the First Lady and her daughters. We'll be trawling the shelves at Harrods and Harvey Nichols. It'll take most of the day, I suspect.'

'Nice work if you can get it.'

'It sounds more glamorous that it actually is, believe me.'

'Do you need any help?'

'I'm afraid I can't ask you along, Madeha. The shopping list is a closely guarded secret. You'd need security clearance, which is more trouble than it's worth.'

'That's fine.'

'I'm sorry, but I'm going to have to leave you alone until this evening. What will you do?'

'Oh, I'll be fine. I'll probably go for a walk in the park and then wander up Oxford Street. There are all sorts of shops I want to check out. I'll have lunch in a café somewhere.'

'Sounds lovely. I'll see you tonight then. Enjoy yourself.'

'You too.'

They exchanged kisses and Loma departed for the day. Moments later, Madeha was back in the office, quietly dialling Munir's number. The call was answered instantly.

'Hello.'

'Munir, it's me.'

'Where are you?'

'I'm at Loma's place.'

'You shouldn't call me from there. It's not safe. I've told you before.'

'I'm sorry. I just had to speak to you.'

Despite the ticking-off, Munir's voice was soft and warm, like a spring breeze in Baghdad.

'Loma has left me alone today. She's gone shopping. Can we meet up?'

'Yes, I think I can get away.'

'Where shall we meet?'

'Let's say 10 o'clock at Marble Arch. I'll be waiting outside the tube station.'

'Is that where you live?'

'Not far away.'

'Okay, see you there.'

They blew kisses down the phone and hung up.

Madeha raced upstairs, showered and set about choosing a dress. She stood before the long mirror, holding up three options: white, dark red, and a flowery pattern. She draped each one over her naked body, wondering which would be more suitable for a romantic tryst. Eventually, she plumped for the flowers. Anyway, all that mattered was that it should hide the cellulite that she'd accumulated in the course of two pregnancies – aided by too much baklava.

She slipped into the dress, pulled on some warm stockings and began the search for shoes and a jacket. Finding nothing suitable among her own wardrobe, she was on the point of heading to Loma's room when she remembered that Riaz might be home. She considered the options spread over the floor and finally picked out a pair of sensible walking shoes and a thick cream-coloured jumper. What did it matter anyway? Munir was the last person to bother with such things; what mattered was being together.

Grabbing her bag and coat, she stepped outside. Soon she was on a bus bound for Oxford Street, taking a seat upstairs. As the bus crept around the edge of the park, she gazed through the steamy window, turning her options over and over.

Was she doing the right thing? Was it madness? There seemed little chance of his marriage plan working; and yet, she could hardly imagine life without Munir now. The thought of spending a year or more in Iraq without seeing him was unbearable. She could never tell her family, and even telling Loma seemed an impossibility. After all, she might feel compelled to share the information with her husband. One way or the other, Loma would be exposed to danger. How long could a long-distance relationship last? Everyone said such arrangements were doomed to failure. Perhaps she could get a job in London? If Loma could move to London, why couldn't she? She could bring the children too. It would be a wrench for them, but it was perhaps workable. British schools weren't so bad, were they?

She was jolted from her thoughts by the realisation that she was already in Oxford Street. She pressed the red button and raced downstairs. She got off at the next stop and walked back toward Marble Arch. She was a good half-hour early.

Passing the Tube station, she turned right into Edgeware Road, with its fine array of Middle Eastern shops and cafés. She instantly felt the change in atmosphere; it was like walking down Al-Rashid

Street in Baghdad. Despite the cold weather, Arab men sat at tables on the pavement, sipping Turkish coffee and smoking *sheeshas*. Men from the Gulf walked along in their long white *dishdashas,* their heads draped in cotton *keffiyehs*. There were women in traditional dress too, sporting full-length black *abayas*, their faces hidden behind *niqabs* – just as their mothers and grandmothers had done, going back through the centuries.

The smell of kebab, cooked the traditional way on charcoal grills, wafted from a nearby restaurant, and Madeha began to feel horribly homesick. She missed the heat of the sun, the smells of her garden, and the breeze from the Tigris. She missed her family too – particularly her mother and her boys. London was alright, but it wasn't home. Could it ever be home? How on earth did Munir manage?

She stopped to look through the window of a café. Inside, several Arab men sat around a table, sucking on their *sheeshas* and playing backgammon. They had recreated their Middle Eastern culture here in England, a little bubble in which they felt secure. Was that the way it had to be? Living in a bubble for the rest of one's life?

She checked her watch and found that she only had five minutes to retrace her steps to Marble Arch. She turned to walk back the way she had come. As she did so, she noticed a young Arab man on the other side of the street watching her. He was lighting a cigarette and staring at her intently. He was expensively dressed: a nice grey suit and a black woollen coat. Madeha remembered what Loma had said about the prostitutes who made a living from the wealthy Arabs in the area. Madeha suddenly felt embarrassed; she looked down and walked fast.

Suddenly, she felt a hand on her shoulder. She spun around, ready to defend herself.

It was Munir, smiling his usual warm smile.

'Munir! You frightened the life out of me!'

'I'm sorry, my darling. I didn't mean to.'

'Where did you come from?'

'I live a few streets away. I was en route to our rendezvous.'

'Well, give me a hug anyway.'

He folded her into his arms, and they stood on the pavement for a while, wallowing in each other's warmth as they rocked gently from side to side. Madeha looked across the street and saw the smartly-dressed Arab walking away, collar up against the cold.

'Where are we going?' she said at last.

'I know a great little Syrian café near here. You'll love it.'

They set off up the street, hand-in-hand.

Munir was right; Madeha did love the café, particularly the baklava, which she washed down with the best coffee she'd tasted for ages. However, she was not entirely at ease. She kept scanning the other tables, wondering whether any of the customers might be Iraqi. If so, did they recognize her as Loma's friend? Did they know Munir? Would their little meeting get back to the embassy somehow?

Munir managed to guess her thoughts. He called the waiter and paid the cheque.

'Let's go to my place. We'll have more privacy there.'

'Are you sure? Is it safe?'

'Well, I've been living there for the past eight years, and I've never had any trouble.'

'No, I mean … Oh, never mind.'

'We'll be quite safe. Don't worry.'

'What about your flat-mate?'

'That wasn't my flat-mate. That was just a friend who slept on the sofa last night. I've given him his marching orders. It'll be just you and me.'

* * *

Two minutes later, Madeha was standing in the living-room of a cramped one-bedroom apartment. The place was damp and musty, and there was a definite chill in the air. Munir put his hand on the ancient radiator and fiddled with the knob.

'It's a bit temperamental, I'm afraid. It will get going in a while. Take a seat.'

Madeha looked around at the dated furniture: a little kitchen table with a plastic cover; two rickety wooden chairs; an old armchair with the stuffing falling out; and a tiny sofa-bed, draped in a worn woollen blanket. Not wishing to seem too picky, she took the nearest seat, which happened to be the sofa. She felt a spring sticking up through the cushions and moved to one side. Munir was already in the tiny kitchen, which was no more than a corner of the living room separated by a folding screen. He was preparing Iraqi tea on an open flame.

'It's not exactly luxurious,' he said, 'but I find it comfortable enough. It's all I can afford on my wages anyway.'

'Who owns it?'

'The landlord's a man from Saudi Arabia. I've never met him. I think he owns the whole building. I just pay my rent to the guy on the ground floor and he takes care of everything.'

Madeha felt suddenly depressed by the squalid surroundings. Hoping to distract herself, she picked up a handful of glossy magazines from the coffee table: *Al-Mawed* and *Al-Shabaka* for lifestyle and gossip, and *Alif Beh* for politics. She flicked through them one by one, stopping finally at an article in *Alif Beh* on the topic of Iraq's economic reforms.

'So, is this how you maintain your link with home?'

Mounir entered the room carrying two glasses of tea on a little tin tray. He set them down gently on the coffee table and took a seat on the sofa.

'Partly, yes. I try to keep up with all the major developments. It's part of my job anyway. A journalist who falls behind with events isn't much use to anyone.'

'No, I mean, how do you stop yourself feeling homesick? Does reading really help?'

'I don't think anything can really make up for losing one's homeland,' he said, dropping sprigs of mint into the tea. 'It's just a matter of getting used to living in exile.'

'I'm not sure I could cope. London's fine to visit, but I'm not sure I could live here.'

'There are ways of coping.'

'Like what?'

Madeha was looking into his eyes now, searching for clues as to his mood.

'Do you know the old Iraqi saying about a woman being a man's home in a foreign land?' he said, running a hand gently through her hair.

'Yes, I seem to remember hearing that.'

'Well, your being here means I'm never without a home. You're my home, Madeha. So long as you're with me, I'll never have reason to feel homesick. I could be on the moon, but you'd make me feel right at home.'

His eyes were glistening with love. Madeha heaved a deep sigh. She knew exactly what he meant; she felt it too. And yet, somehow, it didn't make her feel any better. If anything, it simply piled on the pressure to make a decision.

Munir leaned in and planted a kiss on her mouth. She returned the kiss, and before long, she was laying back against the cushions, with Munir kissing her eyes, mouth and neck. She felt she'd swallowed some powerful drug that sent soft waves of pleasure through her body, from top to toe.

'Can you take this off?' he said, pulling at her woollen jumper.

'Maybe we could get off this sofa?' she replied. 'It's not exactly comfortable.'

'No problem. Follow me.'

Taking Madeha's hand, he led her into his bedroom. It was tiny, just big enough for the double bed and a narrow wardrobe. The thick curtains kept it shrouded in darkness. He turned on the bedside lamp. Draped in a red scarf, it provided no more than a dim glow. Munir pulled off her jumper and dropped it onto the floor. As Madeha fell backwards onto the bed, she felt for a moment that she was in a Chinese opium den. The sensations that followed could hardly have been more delicious if she were.

* * *

When she awoke, the room was quite dark. She rolled onto her back and stared at the ceiling, trying to make out some sort of detail. There was nothing but vague shadows; she might be in any room, in any corner of the world. She was completely naked, but not in the least bit cold. Perhaps the radiator was working at last. She recalled their love-making, which had been passionate and fully-committed, powered by love and longing. They had held nothing back, nor had they lacked energy. She could still feel him inside of her and the motions of his body, rocking back and forth. She could feel his mouth on hers and his fingers in her hair. She recalled her orgasms, and his. And how they'd held each other tight after each climax. She remembered that she had cried, and that he had comforted her. And then, apparently, they had both fallen asleep.

 Life had come full circle. She had loved this man and longed to marry him, longed to consummate their marriage in a big double bed. And now this had come to pass, although not quite as planned. There had been no white wedding, nor gifts and congratulations from friends and family. There had been no honeymoon, no new home in need of decoration, no children to name and raise together. Instead, their love had been consummated many years down the line, in a gloomy, damp bedroom in London's bedsit-land. And it had been consummated out of wedlock, a fact that could never be made public.

Even so, a decision had been made, an irrevocable step taken. For now, Madeha had finally committed herself to this man. She had hesitated to accept his offer of marriage. And yet, by dint of having lain with him, she had affirmed their bond, committed herself as surely as if she had said 'I do'. Of course, religious conservatives would have scolded her for such behaviour, but Madeha felt sure that God was smiling on the couple, for He alone knew what was in their hearts.

A motorbike sped past the window and she was reminded of the passage of time. She leaned over to peek through the curtains. The sky was growing dark, the first street lights flickering into life. It must be late afternoon at least. She peered at her watch, but couldn't make out the hands. Loma would be wondering where she was.

'What's up?' said Munir.

He was stretched out naked on the bed, the sheets piled on the floor.

'I'm just checking the time,' she said. 'I have to get back at some point.'

'Well, don't go just yet. I want to spend a bit more time with you.'

'I can't stay too long. Loma will miss me. And I haven't even done any shopping.'

'Well, at least have a cup of coffee before you go.'

'Alright.'

Munir planted a big, soft kiss on her mouth and wandered into the bathroom. She watched his naked body moving through the shadows. She heard the toilet flush, and then saw him return to the bedroom. He flicked on the overhead light, a bare bulb that dazzled Madeha's eyes.

'So, you do have a light in here?'

'Yes, of course. What did you think?'

She shielded her eyes with her hand. Then sitting up, she grabbed the sheets from the floor and covered herself, suddenly shy of her middle-aged body. Munir was rummaging in the wardrobe.

'What are you looking for?'

'This,' he said, turning with a Polaroid instamatic camera in his hands.

'What's that for?'

'I want something to remember you by.'

'What are you talking about?'

'Well, we're not married yet, and you're going back to Iraq in a week. So, I'll need some way of remembering what you look like. I may never see you again.'

'I can give you a passport photo, if you like.'

'No, I want something more ... natural.'

He inserted a new film and held the camera up to his eye, snapping a picture. The flash went off, blinding Madeha.

'Stop! Munir, stop it! I don't want my photo taken like this, sitting in bed.'

He was laughing now, his usual, gentle laugh that she found so disarming. He sat on the bed, pulled out the photo and wafted it back and forth until it was dry. As the image appeared, a broad smile grew on his face.

'Wow, that's lovely!' he said.

'Let me see,' she said, trying to grab at it.

He held it out of reach, saying, 'No, it's mine. You can see it later. I want one more anyway.'

He then stood at the end of the bed and loaded another film into the camera. Before Madeha knew what was happening, he had yanked the bed sheets to the floor, leaving her naked and exposed. She curled up in a foetal position, desperately covering her private parts.

'Smile!' he said, holding the camera up to his eye.

'No!' said Madeha, 'Not naked!'

'Just relax, will you? It's only for me. Nobody else will see it. Just relax.'

Madeha uncurled herself slightly and sat up in bed, though she kept one hand over her groin and an arm across her breasts. In fact, she was on the point of running from the room, but a voice in her head was saying, 'Trust him, just trust him!'

Laughing to himself, Munir leaned forward and gently pulled Madeha's arms down by her sides. She resisted at first, but finally gave way, exposing herself fully to view. She smiled, just as she would for a family photo.

The flash went off again, and once more she was dazzled. When her vision cleared, Munir had left the room, camera and all.

Clanking sounds were coming from the kitchen.

'What are you doing?' she shouted.

'Making coffee. What do you think I'm doing?'

Madeha checked her watch again. She was shocked to discover that it was nearly six o'clock. She was horribly late. She jumped from bed and began frantically dressing. Within a couple of minutes, she was in the kitchen, her arms around Munir, giving him a heartfelt goodbye kiss.

'I'll come back tomorrow, if I can. I'll call in the morning to let you know.'

'No, don't call me. Just come straight here. I'll wait for you until noon.'

'Okay, my love. Take care.'

'I love you.'

'I love you too.'

Madeha skipped down the stairs like she was floating on air. After so many years, her heart's deepest wish had been fulfilled. At last, she knew what true happiness felt like. With love like this on one's heart, anything was possible.

Betrayal

Madeha walked the few blocks to Oxford Street and ducked into
Selfridges, with its huge stone columns and acres of shopping
space. She looked at the list of designer names on offer – Louis
Vuitton, Chanel, Aramis – wondering whether she could actually
afford to buy anything. She settled on Yves Saint Laurent, picking
out a dark lipstick and a foundation pack. Rushing to the counter,
she paid with traveller's cheques, cursing herself silently for such
a waste of hard-earned money. She would much rather have
spent it on books for her kids.

Leaving the shop, she crossed Oxford Street and headed south
down a side street. She stopped in a little clothes shop, the
windows promising warm winter woollens at reasonable prices.
Within five minutes, she had purchased a new cardigan and a
thick scarf, two items that might actually come in useful.

By the time she had walked the half-mile back to Loma's place,
night had truly settled on the city. A fine rain was falling, the wet
streets reflecting the car headlights. For the first time, she felt
cold, and she wrapped the new scarf tightly around her neck.

It was Loma who answered the door – and she was not happy.

'Where on earth have you been? It's nearly eight o'clock.'

'Is it really? I'm so sorry. I must have lost track of time.'

'Where were you?'

'I was just shopping. I went to Selfridges and … well, all sorts of other places.'

She held up her shopping bags.

'Get that wet coat off,' said Loma, sounding like a concerned nanny fussing over a naughty child. 'You're soaking wet. Come into the lounge by the fire.'

Madeha did as she was told, standing by the fire and accepting the glass of wine that was thrust into her hand.

'That's a lovely scarf,' said Loma, apparently willing to de-escalate the mood.

'I'm sorry for worrying you,' said Madeha.

'No, don't worry. It's my fault. I shouldn't leave you alone all day. I'm being a terrible hostess.'

'That's hardly your fault. After all, you are the wife of an important diplomat.'

'Yes, apparently I am. And I have lots more to do in the next few days. I'm supposed to go down to Windsor for lunch tomorrow.'

'To Uday's house?'

'I'm not supposed to say anything about it. Let's just say that I'm not going to be around tomorrow. Or the next day, in all probability. So, I'm afraid, you're going to have to spend more time in Selfridges.'

'If I absolutely must,' said Madeha, with a big smile.

* * *

When she arrived at Munir's apartment the next morning, he was still in his dressing gown. The air was thick with smoke, and there was a young man sitting on the sofa.

'This is Khaled,' he said.

'Hello,' said Madeha, offering her hand.

The young man shook hands but remained seated. He seemed more interested in packing his little rucksack, stuffing it with various files that were spread out on the coffee table.

'Khaled's just leaving,' said Munir from the kitchen as he set about making fresh tea.

Madeha sat on a wooden chair and watched the young man as he tied his laces and pulled on his jacket. He wasn't all that young, she decided, possibly in his early thirties. And yet, his face was lined with worry, his movements somehow cramped by pain. In addition to his blue track-suit, he wore a tatty old leather jacket and a woollen hat, which he pulled down over his ears. He could do with a good shave too.

Khaled shuffled over to the door and let himself out, not bothering with a final farewell.

Munir entered and placed the tea on the kitchen table.

'He's not very friendly,' said Madeha.

'Oh, he's alright. He just has a lot on his mind. He tends to take things a bit seriously, but his heart's in the right place.'

'Who is he then? Does he work at the newspaper?'

'No, not at the newspaper.'

Munir seemed intent on pouring the tea, sharing out the mint leaves with perfect equality.

'So where does he work?' insisted Madeha. 'Is he a friend or a colleague?'

'Does it matter where he works?'

'I don't know. I didn't think so, but you're making me wonder now. I mean, is there some secret here?'

'Of course not. He's got a computer business. He buys and sells old computers.'

'Okay. So how do you know him?'

'Listen, Madeha, I'll tell you everything in good time. There's lots you don't know about me and my friends, and it will take some time to get around to everything. Patience is a virtue.'

Madeha stirred a spoon of sugar into her tea and took a sip. It was delicious, just like home. She didn't mind burning her lips a bit if the tea was good enough. She watched Munir as he stirred in a third and a fourth sugar, apparently lost in thought.

'Alright, I'll tell you about Khaled,' he said. 'But you've got to keep it to yourself.'

'Okay.'

'No, you've got to promise.'

'Okay, I promise.'

'Khaled was politically active at Baghdad University. I never knew him in Iraq, because he's much younger. About seven years ago, he was arrested and tortured. Finally, they released him, and he escaped through Syria, just like I did.'

'So, is he a political refugee here?'

'He's got official leave to remain in the UK, yes. And that means he can work here. But he still has to be careful about the Iraqi *Mukhabarat*. And he makes it a policy not to trust anyone.'

'Is he politically active here?'

'Madeha, you can't repeat this to anyone, okay?'

'Okay, I said I would keep it a secret.'

Munir sipped his tea, pondering how much to say, and how to go about saying it.

'He's very active. He maintains links with Iraqis here and abroad. He has contacts all across Europe and even in the States and Canada. He has links with British intelligence too.'

'British intelligence? Oh my God!'

'Madeha, I'm warning you. If you say one word about this to anyone ...'

'Munir, trust me,' she said, leaning in and gently touching her forehead against his. 'You can trust me. Totally.'

'Okay, I trust you.'

'So, what exactly is he up to? I mean, is he planning some sort of revolution?'

Madeha was smiling, partly because she wanted to lighten the mood. Munir, meanwhile, was looking deadly serious – more so than she'd ever seen him.

'He has lots of plans, yes. And some of them may happen sooner than you imagine.'

'Like what, exactly?'

'Can we stop talking about this, please? I'm really not comfortable with this topic. It's between me and Khaled, and it's better if you don't get involved. I mean, it's safer for you.'

'Okay,' said Madeha, squeezing his hand.

She hadn't come here to upset Munir. If they only had a few days together, she wanted to make sure they were filled with love, the source of happy memories.

'Let's take the tea in your bedroom,' she said, standing up.

'Good idea,' he said.

* * *

The afternoon passed much as the previous one, although Madeha took care to leave much sooner. She purchased some thick socks and some Scottish shortbread biscuits on the way home. That evening she described to Loma the wonderful day she'd had, hopping from shop to shop, café to café.

When she arrived outside Munir's flat again the following day, she heard raised voices within. She stopped and listened. One of the voices was clearly Munir's. They were in strong disagreement about something. She thought of knocking on the door, but decided it was a bad moment. She was just on the point of walking downstairs when the door was yanked open.

Khaled was standing in the doorway, wrapped up warm and ready to depart. He was in the process of pulling his rucksack onto his shoulders. He glared at Madeha, and she noticed that his eyes were bloodshot, as if from too little sleep. Without saying a word, he squeezed past and headed downstairs.

Madeha entered and closed the door behind her. Munir was in the kitchen, apparently content to let the rituals of welcome slide on this occasion.

'You're early,' he said.

'I'm not early,' said Madeha. 'Well, not by much. Anyway, does it matter? I thought you'd be glad to see me.'

She sat on the sofa and looked around the room. It seemed messier than before, the ashtray overflowing with cigarette buts. There were empty beer cans in the rubbish bin and dirty glasses on the table.

'It seems you had a little party while I was away.'

'Just a few friends,' he said, emerging with the traditional two cups of tea. 'Let's go straight into the bedroom.'

'There's nothing like getting to the point,' she said.

They made love just as passionately as ever, but afterwards she found it impossible to sleep. She just lay on her back and stared at the ceiling, running through the same old thoughts. To add to the mix, she was now wondering whether she could really fit into Munir's life in London. Could she see herself hanging out with Khaled and others like him? Would she want her children to be exposed to such people?

Finally, bored with her own mental habits, she decided to throw caution to the wind and light up a cigarette. She hadn't had one for nearly a year, but extraordinary problems called or extraordinary solutions. She leaned across the bed, reaching over her sleeping lover, and grabbed the packet of Marlboros from the bedside table.

The first drag was wonderful, bringing on a delicious light-headedness. She closed her eyes and savoured the sensation. There was a certain thrill in doing something that she knew for certain was bad for her. Just like falling in love.

'Give me one,' said Munir, sitting up in bed beside her.

She handed over the packet and he lit up.

They smoked together in silence for some time. Madeha wasn't sure if the lack of conversation was due to their being so comfortable with each other, or rather because there was some subject hanging in the air that neither of them wanted to broach. Perhaps it was a bit of both.

'So, are you actually staying in the embassy?' said Munir.

'No, I'm around the corner, in Loma's house.'

'Is that where Riaz has his office?'

'Well, they both have private offices in the house, but his official office is in the embassy.'

'I see.'

'Why do you ask?'

Munir grabbed the ashtray from the bedside table, placing it on the sheets between them. They tipped their ash simultaneously.

'Do you think you could get hold of Uday's travel schedule?'

'What?'

'His itinerary. The places he'll be visiting in the next few months, where he'll be staying, what he's doing on each day. That sort of thing.'

'I know what an itinerary is, Munir. I'm just not sure if I heard you right. Did you ask if I could get hold of it for you?'

'Yes. What's so strange about that?'

'What's so strange? Well, it's highly illegal and very dangerous. If I was caught, I'd be flown home and then thrown in jail. I'd then be tortured and probably murdered. And I can promise you that if they tortured me, I'd give up all my secrets in about five seconds.'

'You're being dramatic.'

'I'm not being dramatic, Munir. I'm being serious. And I'm shocked that you would even ask me to consider such a thing. I mean, I'm really shocked ...'

'I only asked if you would be able to do it, hypothetically speaking.'

'Hypothetically speaking, Munir, it may be possible. But I'm not going to try it, obviously. I value my safety too much. You must be crazy. I've got children too, don't forget. What would happen to them if I were put in prison?'

Munir was silent, sucking on his cigarette. He blew smoke rings into the gloom.

'Why do you want it anyway?' said Madeha.

'It's not for me. Khaled asked for it.'

'Khaled? That scruffy, smelly little man? You'd risk my safety to please him?'

'I just told him I'd ask you. That's all.'

'And what does he want it for? Is he going to assassinate Uday Hussein? Please tell me he's not so stupid as to try something like that.'

'I have no idea what he plans to do with it. He just said it would be useful. Presumably, it's for the cause.'

'The cause? What cause? I thought I was your cause? Or perhaps politics is more important to you than our relationship?'

'What relationship? You're going home in a few days, Madeha. I'll probably never see you again.'

'What are you talking about? Of course you will!'

'Well, I asked you to marry me, and you still haven't answered.'

'That doesn't mean I'm rejecting your offer. It just means I'm thinking about it. I'm thinking about how to make it work. But right at this moment, I have to say, I'm not feeling very much like marrying you. I mean, why should I marry a man who would put me in danger for the sake of keeping his lunatic friends happy?'

'You're being dramatic,' said Munir, throwing off the sheets and getting out of bed.

'No, you're being dramatic. Where are you going?'

'I'm going to make coffee.'

And he left the room.

Madeha puffed furiously on her cigarette and glared at the ceiling. She was in shock. Munir's suggestion was idiotic. Even if she could get hold of Uday's itinerary, there was the danger that the leak would be discovered at some point. And she would be among the prime suspects. Was he really willing to put her in danger for the sake of politics?

Suddenly overcome with anger, she jumped from bed and pulled on her clothes. Grabbing her bag and coat, she walked from the apartment, slamming the door behind her. As she reached the bottom of the stairs, three flights down, she heard Munir call her name, but she didn't answer.

* * *

She barely slept a wink that night. Every half an hour, she got out of bed and went to the bathroom. Then she stood by the window and looked out at the park, steeped in darkness; she gazed at the yellow street lights, and the rain that seemed to have been falling all week. There was lightening somewhere in the distance, but no thunder. She tried to read her novel, but found herself just staring at the page, taking nothing in. At 4am, she took a shower, hoping that it might cleanse her mind, but after drying herself off and climbing back into bed, she was just as anxious as ever.

How could he suggest such a thing? Was her safety really so unimportant to him? Was his loyalty to 'the cause' so very important that he'd risk having the love of his life tortured to death for it? Or perhaps she'd over-estimated her importance? Maybe it was people like Khaled that really had value in Munir's eyes? They were fighting for a nation's freedom, whereas Madeha was only fighting for her own happiness, and that of her children. It occurred to her for the first time that Munir had taken practically no interest in her children. What sort of father would he make? On the evidence thus far, not a very good one.

The next day, she arrived at Munir's flat a little later than usual, allowing time for Khaled to depart. Munir let her in. He was looking tired and sullen, and he disappeared instantly into the kitchen, as if to hide from her searching eyes.

'No kisses for your girlfriend, then?' she said.

'I'm making the tea.'

She sat on the sofa and mentally reviewed what she'd come here to say. She wished for a moment that she'd written it down, but that would have been against the 'security' rules.

As soon as he set the tea down on the coffee table, she started on her speech.

'Munir.'

'Yes.'

'I've got something to say, and I want you to listen very carefully.'

'Okay.'

'I love you very much. That's the first thing, and it's important.'

'I love you too.'

'I know you do. Or at least, I think you do. And I'm seriously considering your offer of marriage. I have no idea how it would work in practical terms, but I'm considering it, because I love you so much, and I really can't think of spending my life without you. At some point, if we stay together, we will have to make it official. So that means marriage. For me, it's partly a question of when, but also of how, because there are various difficulties.'

'I know,' he said, 'but I'm sure we can overcome those difficulties. Every problem has a solution.'

'I agree. But there's something else, and it's important. It has to do with trust.'

'I trust you.'

'I know you do, and I trust you. Or rather, I mostly trust you. But what you asked me to do yesterday, stealing Uday Hussain's itinerary from the embassy … that's just insane. It would put me in great danger, and I'm just shocked that you'd be willing to risk my safety. And that makes me wonder if I should really be trusting you so much. Do you see what I mean?'

'Well, it's not for me. It's for Khaled. He asked me to ask you, so I did.'

'Right, but why? I mean, if he asked you to shoot me in the head, would you do it?'

'You're so dramatic!'

'Maybe I am, but I've got a point to make. Because you seem to be putting him before me at the moment, to the point of being willing to risk my life for the sake of his political goals.'

'It's not just politics, Madeha, it's our country. It's freedom. It's about overthrowing a dictator and winning freedom for our people. That's important.'

'Yes, I agree. It's my country too. I'm also a patriot, Munir, and I agree that it's important. But are you willing to risk having me tortured and killed in order to achieve it?'

Munir was silent, looking into his glass.

His silence was the straw that broke the camel's back.

'Right,' said Madeha, suddenly standing up. 'If you're not able to answer a simple question like that, then I think there's not much more to talk about. I think I should go now, and we should leave things for a while. I may visit again before I go back to Iraq, just to say goodbye. And I'll think some more about your marriage proposal. But you also need to think about your priorities. You should also think about whether you deserve my trust.'

Munir sipped his tea, apparently unable to summon any comeback. For a brief moment, Madeha felt sorry for him, but then she reminded herself that she had vowed to be strong. Whatever else happened today, she must be strong.

As she got to the door, she suddenly remembered the photographs.

'Munir, the photographs you took. I need them back, please.'

'What photographs?'

'The ones you took the other day, when I was in bed. I need them back, please.'

'Khaled has them,' said Munir.

He was looking her in the eyes now, his face entirely expressionless.

Madeha suddenly felt sick. Her head began to spin. She reached out and grabbed the door frame.

'What the fuck to you mean? Why does Khaled have them?'

'He said it wasn't safe to keep them here.'

'Wasn't safe? Why? What are you talking about? Did you show them to him? Did he see them? Why did you let him have them? What's wrong with you? Those are pictures of me naked in bed. Naked! Why would you tell anyone about them? What's wrong with you?'

She was shouting now, on the verge of a screaming.

Munir stood up and stepped closer, his face still entirely devoid of expression.

'He said you could have them back after the operation.'

'What operation? What the fuck are you talking about?'

'The intelligence-gathering operation. To get the itinerary. He said if you get the itinerary and hand it over, he'll give the photos back.'

'Why? What the fuck are you talking about?'

'It's just for security. He has to have some security. That's what he said. Otherwise, you might talk.'

'And you agreed to that?'

Munir shrugged his shoulders.

Madeha punched him square in the face, then again, raining blow after blow on his head. She was screaming as she did so: 'You fucking bastard! You bastard! You bastard!'

Munir covered himself with his hands and curled up on the sofa, waiting for the assault to end. Apparently, he didn't feel himself in any great danger.

Finally, Madeha turned and left the apartment, running downstairs faster than ever. She ran down the street, her face a flood of tears, great sobs catching in her throat as she gasped for air. She ran down Edgeware Road, across Marble Arch, through Speakers' Corner, and right across Hyde Park. She didn't stop running until she reached the Albert Memorial, that monument to deep and undying love. Here, she collapsed on a bench and cried for a full ten minutes, winning looks of concern from joggers and dog-walkers. Being very English – and this being London – nobody stopped to ask what was wrong.

* * *

The house was empty when she arrived home, and she went straight to her room. She wanted to collapse on the bed and cry some more. But she knew that her eyes must already be puffy, and more crying would only make them worse. Instead, she stepped into the bath and took a long shower, washing several times from head to foot. She wanted to wash away the filth of this horrible man, a man who had suckered her in and then betrayed her trust. In the end, she sat in the bath and dissolved into tears.

An hour later, she was downstairs in the living room, curled up on the sofa in her jogging suit. She had her novel and a large glass of arak. She was still sitting there, gazing into the flames, when Loma returned home at lunch time.

'Hello, you look nice and cosy,' said Loma.

'Yes, I thought I'd have a quiet day indoors. I also need to stop spending for 24 hours.'

'I know exactly what you mean. London is horrendously expensive. We must have spent millions in Harrods this week. You'd be shocked if you knew the truth of it.'

'I think I can guess.'

Loma poured herself a glass and topped up her friend's, then joined her on the sofa.

'Are you sure you're alright? You seem a bit subdued.'

'Yes, I'm fine. I'm just ready to go home, I think.'

'I'm sorry. I've been a terrible hostess.'

'Not at all. You've been wonderful. I'm just missing my children.'

Loma looked more closely at her friend's face.

'Have you been crying?'

'Crying?'

'Yes, you look puffy round the eyes. You look like you've been crying for an hour.'

Madeha was silent. She wanted desperately to spill the beans – but so much had happened, so many lies been told, so much done that might have serious consequences. There was no way she could tell the truth, no way at all. She'd come too far to turn back. And yet – if one person in the world could get the truth out of her, it was Loma.

'Madeha, I know something's wrong. Why don't you tell me?'

There were tears now in Madeha's eyes, and the first had started its meandering journey down her left cheek. It was useless now to pretend. She had to open up.

'Well, do you remember Munir?'

'Your boyfriend from university?'

'Yes, that's the one.'

'What about him?'

'Well, I met him in London, and we had an affair.'

'What are you talking about?'

'I met him two weeks ago, soon after I arrived. I bumped into him purely by chance. And we've been seeing each other ever since. It's a full-blown love affair. I've seen him most days. I've been hanging out in his apartment while you were working.'

Loma was speechless, her mouth hanging open, eyes wide.

'I'm sorry I didn't say anything at the time,' continued Madeha. 'I didn't know where it was going. And I didn't want to worry you if it was just a fling.'

'So, was it just a fling?'

'No, not really. He asked me to marry him.'

'My god! What? He's an exile.'

'Yes, I know.'

'He's a political activist. He's on the terrorism watch-list. He's known at the embassy. You can't hang around with people like that. You'll get arrested. They'll throw you in jail, Madeha. Are you crazy?'

'I know, I know … but I love him.'

'You've lost your mind. You've completely lost your mind. What were you thinking?'

'I know it's stupid, but it's love. We can't help who we fall in love with. Of all people, you should know that. What about Ali?'

'We were teenagers. That was different. You're a grown woman. You've got children. How will you manage to marry a dangerous fugitive and still look after your children? Did you think about that? Or are you going to give up your children?'

'Loma, don't shout.'

'I'm not shouting. I'm just shocked.'

'Well, don't be so shocked. It's over. I'm not marrying him. I told him today that it's over. That's why I've been crying.'

Loma breathed a sigh of relief. She put down her glass and put an arm around her friend. Madeha rested her head on Loma's shoulder and began to cry all over again, her body shaking.

'It's okay, it's okay,' said Loma, stroking her hair.

They remained like that for some time, like mother and daughter, rocking gently from side to side. Finally, Madeha straightened up, pulled out a tissue and blew her nose.

'So why did you break it off?'

'He asked me to do something that I wouldn't do.'

'What was that?'

'Go onto your husband's computer and get Uday's itinerary.'

Loma shot to her feet, dropping her glass of arak on the coffee table, where it smashed to pieces. There was a look of horror on her face, as if she'd seen a child decapitated before her eyes. She tried to speak, but no words would come out. She looked around the room, wondering how many microphones might have picked up their conversation and committed it to magnetic tape.

Madeha decided that she might has well be hung for a sheep as for a lamb.

'He took photographs of me naked in bed, just to remember me by. But when I asked for them back, he said I can't have them until I've given him Uday's itinerary. But it isn't really Munir doing all this. It's his friend, Khaled.'

Loma closed her eyes and grasped her hair with both hands.

'Please listen …' said Madeha.

'I can't deal with this. I just can't …' said Loma, running upstairs.

As she did so, the maid appeared with a brush and dustpan, ready to clean up whatever mess had been made.

Discovered

Loma sat in the conservatory, a new cigarette on the go, gazing into the garden. It was a beautiful morning. Spring had finally arrived, with its blue skies and sunshine. The flowers were opening, bringing bright colours – red, blue and yellow – to the garden borders. The birds were celebrating, hopping from branch to branch and tweeting with joy. They had no inkling of the gloom in Loma's heart.

Of all the quandaries she'd faced in her life, none was more perplexing than this. Having learned of Madeha's situation, she was now required to choose between supporting her or betraying her. Loma could never support her to the extent of facilitating an act of espionage; that would be suicide. But she might help her to escape the situation somehow, either by retrieving the photographs or calling Munir's bluff.

She had spent most of the night staring at the ceiling and pondering ways to get the photos back, but she could think of nothing. She knew of nobody in London whom she might trust with such a job. Everyone she knew with a security background happened to work for the Iraqi government. Aside, that is, from Tony. Perhaps, for the right price, he could summon some of his old army friends and do some digging around. But there was no guarantee that he wasn't involved with British intelligence, and that carried its own dangers.

No, she had concluded, if Madeha couldn't get the photographs back herself, there was no way it would happen. Perhaps, then, that was the solution: Madeha would simply have to visit Munir once more, appealing to his sentimental nature. If he loved her at all, he might relent.

But there was still the option of calling his bluff. Perhaps if Madeha were to return to Iraq immediately, refusing point-blank to complete 'the project', she would find that the threats had been empty. After all, sending out incriminating photos of people close to the Iraqi Foreign Ministry – as Madeha now was – would only provoke the wrath of the *Mukhabarat*, who would not stop until Munir had been hunted down and clamped in irons. In which case, perhaps the whole blackmail scheme was just a bluff – and perhaps Madeha was willing to take the gamble.

Then again, if the gamble failed, and if the photos did indeed start to circulate, then Madeha would be among those hunted by the *Mukhabarat*. And it would take them about five minutes to come bursting through her door. At which point, of course, Loma might also be implicated, along with her husband. After all, how could Madeha have conducted an affair with a dangerous subversive right before Loma's eyes without her being aware of it? Weren't they supposed to be the best of friends?

The irony of the whole thing, of course, was that Madeha had come to London to provide moral support to Loma. She had indeed lifted Loma's spirits in the early days, but this had been swiftly followed by an act of deception that had brought potential disaster to Loma's door. As it turned out, any plan that rested on the reliability of good friends was inherently flawed.

Loma returned to the possibility of ratting on her friend. It was her least favourite option, but it had to be given fair consideration. After all, if Madeha had been stupid enough to bring disaster down on her own head, was this any reason why Loma should suffer? Madeha may have condemned her own children to life without a mother, but why should Loma's children suffer such a fate?

Alternatively, perhaps Madeha might be convinced to turn herself in? If she explained that it had been a misunderstanding, that she had been tricked and had never intended to go through with it, perhaps the authorities might be lenient? But what exactly did 'leniency' mean in such cases? Life in prison, as opposed to execution? Months of torture, rather than years of it? All such outcomes were unthinkable.

Finally, having come to no useful conclusions, Loma wondered if it might be best to do nothing at all, to ignore the problem and allow it to resolve itself. After all, it seemed quite possible that Madeha was doomed – and any attempt to save her was futile.

Loma stubbed out her cigarette. As she did so, she reflected that, if nothing else, her friendship with Madeha had taken a knock from which it might never recover. She had never imagined how much it might hurt to be deceived by a friend. She had always assumed that such feelings were confined to the arenas of romance and marriage. But apparently not, because this cut like a knife.

As she got up from the wicker chair, she found Madeha standing behind her, motionless, in the middle of the conservatory. She was fully dressed, coat on, handbag at the ready.

'Good morning, Madeha. I didn't know you were up.'

'I'm going out to change my ticket.'

'What ticket?'

'My flight. I'm going to the travel agent to see if I can change it to tomorrow. I just want to go home as soon as possible.'

'But what about …? Don't you have anything else to do in London?'

'I've decided that London isn't good for me. If I stay here, I'll only get myself in trouble. The only option is to leave. So that's what I'm doing.'

Loma was on the point of expanding the discussion when she stopped herself, mindful of the ever-present danger of microphones.

'I'll be back in the afternoon some time,' continued Madeha. 'I'll change my flight, grab some lunch and do some last-minute shopping. I want to get some books for my children.'

She turned and left before Loma could find anything useful to say. The front door banged shut and the house was in silence once more. Loma slumped back into her wicker chair.

So, there it was: the decision had been made. And Madeha had been kind enough to make it all on her own, without troubling her friend with further discussion. She had taken the whole burden upon herself, gambling on the blackmail being a bluff. She had been a fool, but having seen the cold light of day, her courage was showing through. Hopefully, if she lost her gamble, and if she was subsequently arrested, her courage would extend to not implicating anyone else.

Deciding that further cogitation was pointless, Loma went into her study and launched into some work. Nora didn't require her help that day, and so she was free to focus on her Iraqi students. There was another presentation to be prepared, another speech on the value of education and the importance of patriotism, of helping one's nation. Loma wasn't sure how much of it she believed, but she knew what was required of her.

She was still in her office in the mid-afternoon when the telephone rang on her desk.

'Loma Mostafa speaking. Hello.'

There was silence.

'Hello,' she repeated, heart pounding.

The line was crackling and traffic could be heard passing by. Perhaps the call was coming from a phone box?

'Listen, whoever this is, you'd better stop wasting my time. Either say something or hang up.'

'Is Madeha there?' said a man, speaking Arabic with a Baghdad accent.

'Who?'

'Madeha. I know she's staying with you.'

'Who is this? What do you want?'

'I want to speak with Madeha.'

'Well, she's not here, so you'd better explain what you want, and I'll pass on the message.'

'Tell her to meet me at the same café tomorrow at noon. Tell her to come alone.'

'I'm afraid I can't do that. She's flying back to Iraq tomorrow. You'll have to write to her there. Who is this, by the way?'

The man was breathing heavily down the line. Loma grew suddenly angry.

'Look, I don't know who you are, but whatever you want, it seems you won't be getting it. So, stop bothering my friend and go away. That's my advice to you.'

She slammed down the phone. Her head was spinning and she thought for a moment that she might scream. Instead, she lit another cigarette and got back to writing her speech.

* * *

She was still in her office at 6pm when Riaz burst in the door, waving a manila envelope in the air.

'Look at this! Look at this! Look at what your idiot friend has done!'

'What has she done? I can't see what you're waving around.'

'This!' he shouted, slamming the envelope down on the desk.

Loma opened the envelope and removed the contents: two Polaroid photos showing Madeha naked in bed, and two more photographs showing her walking through Soho with an unidentified man. They were holding hands, but the man's face had been blacked out with a marker pen.

There was also a fax message in Arabic reading: 'You may like to know that Madeha is both a traitor and a whore.' The message was signed, 'A Patriot'.

Loma read the fax message and frowned.

'But what does it mean,' she said, feigning ignorance and confusion.

'It means that your friend has been sleeping with the enemy.'

'But where did they come from? Who sent them?'

'I have no idea who sent them, but they were delivered through the door of the embassy, addressed to me. Luckily, nobody else has seen the contents yet. But your friend has placed us in an impossible position.'

'I don't understand.'

'Don't play the fool, Loma. I know you're not stupid. Madeha has been having an affair in London, and she's obviously been doing it with your knowledge. And according to this, she's been involved in treasonous activities, mixing with the enemy. And you're up to your neck in it.'

'What activities? What enemy? I have no idea what you're talking about, Riaz.'

'Didn't she have a boyfriend at university?'

'Yes. So what?'

'Well, he's here in London, and my guess is that he's the man in the photograph. He's a subversive, and someone has apparently found them out. Where is Madeha?'

Riaz turned and stood in the doorway, shouting up the stairs:

'Madeha! Madeha! Come down here right now! I want to speak with you!'

'She's gone to book a new ticket to Baghdad. She's leaving tomorrow.'

Riaz laughed out loud; it was a vicious laugh, one of triumph.

'She's running away. So, she knew about this in advance. We'll, she won't be going anywhere alone, I can tell you that.'

He reached for the phone, but Loma grabbed his wrist.

'What are you doing? Who are you calling?'

'The chief of security. We must inform him without delay. If we do so, we will not be tainted. I will say that you informed me of the situation this morning, and my fears were confirmed this afternoon when the photographs arrived. We will inform them of the situation, and it will be understood that we did the right thing.'

'I can't possibly do that. I love Madeha. She's my best friend. I couldn't possibly ...'

'Loma, you have to choose: either you accuse her or you will be accused of conspiring with a traitor. And you have to make up your mind quickly, because I'm phoning the office now. Make up your mind. Do you want to spend the rest of your life in prison? And bear in mind that this is partly your fault. You should have been watching your friend, rather than letting her wander around London sleeping with revolutionaries. She's a whore! She's a whore and a traitor!'

Riaz was furious, leaning across the desk, his face close to his wife's. His eyes were bulging with rage and his jaw was clamped tight.

Loma was paralyzed; she couldn't move; her head seemed to be buzzing.

Finally, she found the strength to speak: 'But Riaz, listen ...'

Riaz yanked his hand free and dialled an internal number.

'Give me the head of security.'

* * *

It was just gone 8pm when Madeha returned. She called to Loma, her voice bright and cheerful, as if she'd just received good news.

'Hello! Loma!' she said. 'I've found some wonderful books.'

She stepped into the living room, weighed down with shopping bags.

Loma was sitting on the sofa, a double whiskey in one hand, a cigarette in the other. She was deathly pale. By the fire was Riaz, hands behind his back, looking terse. Two men grey suits stood by the book-case, hands folding in front of them.

'What's wrong?' said Madeha quietly. 'Has something happened?'

'We've been informed of your activities, Loma. I'm afraid you'll be returning to Baghdad.'

'What are you talking about?' she said, looking at her friend on the sofa.

Loma looked away. She simply couldn't bear to watch. She still loved her friend, but there was nothing that could be done to save her. It was all too horrible.

'We've received some photographs of you, Madeha, implicating you in subversive activities. You will need to leave London immediately and explain yourself once you're back in Iraq.'

'Explain what? I haven't done anything. Loma, tell them. I haven't done anything.'

Loma looked into her friend's eyes.

'I think you'll just have to explain everything,' she said.

'Explain what? I've done nothing wrong!'

'You can explain that once you're back in Iraq.'

Riaz nodded to the two gentlemen in suits, and they grabbed Madeha by the arms.

She started shouting: 'But I'm flying back tomorrow anyway. I've booked a flight for the morning. I'm going home anyway. Let me go!'

'You're taking a different flight, I'm afraid,' said Riaz. 'You leave at midnight. Take her upstairs to pack.'

As the men whisked Madeha out of the room, Riaz took her bags of shopping.

'Perhaps you can make sure her children get the books?' he said, handing them to his wife.

Loma took the bags and remained on the sofa, staring into the log fire. All she could do was light another cigarette and smoke it; then another; and another.

Half an hour later, Madeha came downstairs with her luggage. Loma walked into the hallway as her friend was ushered out the front door.

'Madeha,' she said.

Madeha turned to look, but she didn't reply. Her eyes were red from crying, and she already looked like death.

Moments later, the car pulled away from the kerb and sped off toward Heathrow. Loma could only guess at Madeha's destiny, but she knew it wasn't good. In all probability, they would never meet again.

* * *

In the following days, Loma was interviewed several times, first by the head of embassy security, then by a succession of *Mukhabarat* officers, including some who were travelling with Uday Hussein. Out of respect for Riaz's position, all the interviews took place in the living room, with tea and biscuits served by the maid.

Loma stuck to the story she had told Riaz. Madeha had spent a lot of time on her own, largely because Loma had been so busy helping Nora. She spent much of her holiday shopping, as well as visiting historic sights and tourist attractions. Aside from this, Loma could not account for her movements. Loma had thought nothing was wrong until near the end, when Madeha returned one day looking very tired and emotional. She confronted Madeha about it, but she explained it away, saying that she'd become lost in the back streets. Loma had thought that perhaps Madeha was hiding something. Perhaps she had met some unsavoury characters in the course of exploring London? She had informed Riaz, who had agreed to have Madeha followed. However, that same afternoon, the photographs had been delivered to Riaz. Loma had been totally shocked. She had suspected that something was wrong – but nothing of this sort. Finally, she and Riaz had agreed to inform the chief of security. And the rest was history.

Apparently, Loma put on a convincing performance each time, because the interviews finally ended, and she was thanked for her cooperation. She asked whether she would need to give testimony in court, but she was told that there was no need for a trial. In such matters, decisions were taken 'internally'.

So that was it. Loma and Riaz were cleared of any suspicion of wrong-doing. Indeed, Riaz came home at the weekend with a smile on his face, reporting that he'd been commended on his work in rooting out a spy. Loma was thanked once more for her cooperation.

'So, you see, we did the right thing. And now it's all over,' said Riaz, pouring himself a large glass of Chardonnay.

'Yes, but what will happen to Madeha?'

'That's not our problem. She has dug her own grave. Now she will lie in it.'

'I can't just throw away a friend like that. I care about her.'

'So maybe you want to go to prison too? Is that it?'

'No, of course not. But I care about my friends, Riaz. It's called loyalty. It's called having a heart.'

'It's called being an idiot, Loma. And just for the record, if I'd known what an idiot you were, I'd never have married you. If you must know, I'm this close to divorcing you.'

He held up his hand, measuring an inch between finger and thumb.

This was too much for Loma. She began laughing.

'Oh, if only you would! If only you would just go ahead and fucking divorce me! Nothing could make me happier than to be finally free of you, Riaz. You've done nothing but lie to me, cheat on me, betray and humiliate me from day one. If only you had the guts to divorce me, I might finally be free. And then I could be happy. I could start living my life at last!'

Riaz strode across the room and loomed over his wife, who recoiled on the sofa. He raised his hand, as if to slap her round the head.

'I ought to beat you,' he shouted. 'I ought to beat you to death for saying that. I'm your husband, and you will obey me! You will never say such things again, Loma! If you do, so help me God, I'll kill you with my bare hands! I'll fucking kill you!'

'Go ahead, kill me! I would be happy to be finally finished with this life, and with this shitty marriage. You're a curse, Riaz. You're nothing but a curse. Kill me, then! Kill me if you're going to, you fucking coward!'

Riaz lowered his hand and swallowed the rest of his wine. He then stalked from the room and disappeared upstairs.

Moments later, Loma rang for her maid.

'Would you please make sure all my laundry is done, Maria? I'll be travelling to Baghdad in the next few days. I may be away for quite a while.'

Back to Baghdad

Loma woke to find a smiling air stewardess offering her a cup of strong black tea. She sipped the hot beverage slowly, glad of its reviving powers. Through the window she could see a layer of cloud like fluffy cotton wool, illuminated by the first rays of the morning sun. Between the gaps were glimpses of her homeland, scraps of desert and occasional patches of green. Pretty soon, Baghdad would no doubt come into view.

She had been drifting in and out of sleep the whole night, her thoughts consumed with Madeha's situation. What had happened to her since her departure from London? Was she dead or alive? Most likely she had been taken to prison, but what had they done to her there? She might be better off dead.

She had overheard Riaz discussing the case with the security staff at the embassy. They had mentioned Madeha's interrogation and further detention, but without giving any clues as to location. From her secretary, however, she had learned that Madeha's family had been horrified at the turn of events, relocating to the mother's hometown of Baqubah, a city 50 kilometres north-east Baghdad. Madeha's children had gone with them.

Loma and Riaz, meanwhile, had received official letters of thanks from the office of the President. Loma had been given a delicate gold watch and a huge bouquet of flowers, with a hand-written note from Uday's personal secretary. Riaz got a pay-rise, and there was even talk of him becoming deputy ambassador at his next posting. What had started out as a terrible threat had been turned into a great victory.

Loma felt disgusted with herself. How could she have fallen so low? She hadn't meant to betray Madeha, but neither had she stood up for her. At first, she had defended her, of course, but only weakly – and her efforts had collapsed under the slightest pressure from Riaz. If any further evidence was needed of how her marriage to Riaz had constrained and corrupted her, this was it. She felt suffocated, and now more than ever, divorce seemed her only route to happiness.

She shook her head and opened her book, *In Search of Walid Masoud* by Jabra Ibrahim Jabra. An Iraqi novelist of Palestinian descent, Jabra was deft at portraying the lifestyles, values and intrigues of Iraq's middle-classes during the 1960s. Normally, Loma would have found his writing engrossing. Today, however, it was too close to reality; every twist and turn of the plot reminded her of the dreadful maze through which she was passing.

Just when she managed to convince herself that Madeha might indeed be shown some leniency, she was reminded of the unresolved business with Selma. It was not just unresolved, apparently, but unresolvable. For the woman seemed hell-bent on destruction, motivated by malice and fury. Short of murder, there seemed little to be done. It was all horribly worrying. Without

Selma, none of this would have happened. Both Loma and Madeha might have lived normal, happy lives. There would have been ups and downs, of course – but not calamity.

The pilot's voice came over the intercom system, announcing the plane's imminent arrival at Saddam International Airport. Loma did up her seatbelt and put away her book. As the aircraft began its descent, she felt her heart pounding. There below were the outlying towns, and there on the western outskirts of the city was the airport. Just two years old, it had cost hundreds of millions of dollars and was the envy of the neighbouring nations. Architects from Iraq, France and the USA had contributed to its design and construction. However, due to the war with Iran, the grand opening had been delayed, and the restrictions on foreign travel meant it was running far below capacity.

The Iraqi Airways jumbo jet touched down with a screech of rubber on tarmac. Loma was reminded of the airline's record of zero flight accidents so far, a fact that had won it the nickname 'Lucky Airways'. Of course, if they had crashed in a ball of flames, she would finally have been free of her problems.

At customs, she was directed through a special channel, where her diplomatic passport was barely glanced at. Her passage was further eased by a slim, young woman from the ministry, who had been sent to welcome the returning hero. Loma felt like a fraud, although it was certainly nice to avoid the queues and prying questions.

She was met in the arrivals hall by her brother and nephew.

'Thank God you're safe!' said the brother.

'Yes, I'm glad to be back.'

'We've got the car,' said the nephew.

Loma thanked the ministry official for her help, saying the official transport would not be needed on this occasion. Her two relatives were keen to help, and she could hardly say no.

Loma sat up front, leaving her seat belt undone, despite the risk of a hefty fine. Through the open window, she eyed the new housing developments that were springing up on the edge of the city. There were advertising hoardings too, and huge portraits of Saddam Hussein, smiling benevolently at his people. Yes, she really was home now.

'Could you take me to Mum's house, actually? I want to see her before anything else.'

'Of course,' said her brother. 'She's pretty keen to see you. She's been cooking for two days.'

'So, what did you bring me from London?' said the nephew from the back seat.

'Oh, plenty. Don't you worry. It's all in my cases.'

'Did you bring any aftershave?'

'Of course, I did. I brought six different kinds. And as you're the first to ask, you get to choose which one you want.'

As Loma got out of the car, she saw her mother stepping from the house and hurrying down the garden path. Dressed in her black *abaya* and headscarf, she looked identical to thousands of other grandmothers in villages across the country. She burst through the gate and wrapped her arms around her daughter, showering her in kisses.

Loma began to cry, her make-up running down her cheeks. Next to join the huddle were her two sisters, whose familial affection was mingled with excitement at the prospect of high-class gifts. They were also keen to remain close to the one family member who really seemed to be going places.

The dinner table was groaning under the weight of food, and as more relatives arrived, more dishes were produced. Suitcases were unpacked and gifts handed out, and Loma was called upon several times to describe the sights and sounds of London. By mid-afternoon, feeling like an overworked shop-assistant at Harrods, she made her excuses and disappeared to her childhood bedroom. Laying on the bed, she closed her eyes and waited for her mind to stop spinning.

'Darling, are you asleep?' said her mother, peeking round the door.

'No, Mum, I'm wide awake. Come in.'

Loma adored her mother for her kindness and affection, which hadn't diminished a bit over the years. As the old woman sat on the edge of the bed, Loma burst into tears once more. She curled up and allowed herself to be comforted like a child. Before long, she reached into a pocket and pulled out a tissue, blowing her nose.

'My dear, are you having problems with Riaz?'

'No, we're okay. I'm just upset about Madeha.'

'Well, she brought it upon herself, my dear.'

'It wasn't her fault. You haven't heard the whole story.'

'No, but she's a traitor all the same. You can't betray your country and expect to get off with a slap on the wrist.'

'She didn't betray her country. It was just a misunderstanding. She's done nothing wrong. She's actually innocent.'

'I don't understand. They said that she had collaborated with the president's enemies. Either she did or she didn't.'

'No, she didn't. They were trying to blackmail her into it, but she refused. But, of course, the authorities would never believe that. And I didn't have the guts to stand up for her.'

'Even so, it's not your fault, my dear. You shouldn't torture yourself over it.'

'Mum, you don't understand. She would never have been in this mess if it wasn't for me. She didn't come to London just for the tourism. She came to save me – my marriage, my reputation, and the honour of my family.'

'What do you mean?'

'Come on, surely you know what's been going on? Selma has been slandering me at every opportunity, spreading rumours about me and Ali.'

'But that's an old story, it's history. Nobody cares about that.'

'Well, maybe you think so, but Selma doesn't. She's telling everyone I'm still in love with Ali. So far as I understand, she's telling people we're having an affair.'

'Well, are you?'

'Mum! How could you ask that? Of course not! I'd never cheat on Riaz. I'd never cheat on anyone. And anyway, Ali is married with children.'

'So, what's the problem?'

'The problem is that people don't know the truth. If Selma throws enough mud, some of it will stick. And Riaz obviously doesn't need those sorts of rumours circulating when he's trying to get ahead in his career.'

'But people don't always believe such rumours, my dear. Certainly not from the likes of Selma.'

'It's not just about the rumours, Mum. She physically attacked me, if you remember, at that garden party last summer. I still have the scars from where she dug her nails into my neck. I'm willing to put up with rude words, but I draw the line at being strangled.'

'Yes, I remember. That was very naughty. I never thought she would go that far.'

'I don't think she has any idea of limits. There's no knowing what she's capable of.'

'So, what are you going to do?'

'I don't know what I'm going to do. Probably there's nothing I can do about Selma, but I have to find out what's happened to Madeha. If nothing else, I need to check that she's alive. I don't even know where they're keeping her.'

'Can't you ask Riaz?'

'Are you serious? If Riaz knew I was trying to help Madeha, he'd go crazy. Whatever happens, Riaz can't know about this. He thinks I'm just taking a holiday.'

'Well, you do need a holiday, my darling. Perhaps you should just rest for a while. You need to relax and regain your strength.'

'Of course, I do. But I can't just sit around doing nothing. My best friend is in trouble, and I need to help her if I can.'

'Well, you should be very careful. Very careful indeed. It would only take one small mistake, and you might be implicated too.'

'But I can't just sit here doing nothing. I just can't.'

'I know, my dear. I know.'

The mother rocked her child gently, kissing her hair and calling for the blessings of Allah.

A patriotic duty

Next door, Selma was lying on her recliner in her garden, soaking up the spring sunshine. At that precise moment, she was listening to the tinkling of the water feature. She had put great energy into supervising the gardener in recent weeks, ensuring that the weeding had been done, the lawn properly mowed and the borders coaxed into bloom. Now she was enjoying the fruits of her labours – or rather the gardener's labours.

She opened her eyes and reached for the cold beer that stood on the little folding table. As she did so, she heard the sound of high-heels on the patio.

'Hello! Selma, darling! It's me!'

Selma sat up, covering her bikini-clad top with a silk blouse.

'Malaka! How wonderful to see you!'

She got to her feet, and the two women – who felt nothing but disdain for each other – embraced like old friends.

'I'll get you a drink. What would you like?'

'I've already asked your maid for a gin-and-tonic. She's bringing it now.'

'Well, you've made yourself at home. That's nice.'

'My home is your home, Selma. And I'm sure the feeling is mutual.'

'Naturally.'

'Oh, I do love your garden. It's so … intimate.'

'I was just thinking of having a swimming pool put in. But I think it might detract from the natural feel.'

'Yes, and they're horribly expensive.'

'Oh, I don't bother about expenses. That's for Hassan to worry about.'

'As you say, my dear. I'm sure he knows what he's doing.'

Selma was not keen to get stuck on the topic of finances. The last thing she wanted was for Malaka to start offering hand-outs. Luckily, at that moment, the gin-and-tonic was delivered.

'It's Gordon's, of course,' said Selma. 'I get it flown in from London.'

'Gordon's is fine, my dear.'

They sipped their booze and watched the birds fluttering down to drink from the sparkling water and then flutter off again.

'Have you heard the latest gossip?' said Malaka.

'About what?'

'Your dear friend Loma has returned to Baghdad, and she's visiting her mother next door.'

'So I heard. What's she up to?' said Selma, pretending to be only half-interested.

'It's this scandal with Madeha, of course. The stupid woman has been thrown into prison, and Loma has the idea that she can rescue her. The President himself – may God preserve him – has written to thank Loma for her part in Madeha's capture, but now the stupid bitch is having second thoughts.

'Was it really Loma who turned Madeha in? I thought they were best friends.'

'Maybe so. But my sources inform me that they were sleeping around in London, going to seedy bars to pick up businessmen, and then taking them to hotels. At some point, Loma got cold feet, fearing that Riaz would find out, and so she had Madeha set up.'

'Set up how?'

'Well, I don't know the details my dear, but I can tell you that Madeha would not have been arrested if it weren't for the sordid details provided by Loma. Apparently, there were naked photographs involved.'

'Good God!'

'Yes, and she did it just to ensure that Madeha would never talk.'

'So much for friendship!'

'Indeed.'

The pair sipped their drinks, basking in the sense of superiority that resulted from the disgrace and destruction of others.

'Of course,' continued Malaka, 'Loma has a long history of deceit and betrayal. She lost her virginity before marriage, as you know. What can one expect from such a woman?'

'Well, nobody listens, but I'm always insisting that she and Ali are still at it. If Riaz learned of their secret meetings, Loma would very quickly find herself in big trouble. I think most people would understand if he were to kill her on the spot.'

'Do you have any evidence?' said Malaka, her eyes sparkling with excitement.

'I'm not in the business of prying into the private lives of others, Malaka. Of course, if such evidence came to light, I feel it only right that people should know about it.'

'Quite right.'

'Would you like a cigarette?'

'Very kind, thank you.'

They lit up and blew their first clouds of smoke into the fresh air. Perhaps they weren't real friends, exactly, but they had a great deal in common. It was almost as if they were gods in their garden paradise, passing judgement on mere mortals.

Malaka tipped her ash and turned on her sunbed, looking rather serious.

'Selma, I have a delicate topic that I'd like to raise with you.'

'Of course, go ahead. You can always trust me with a secret. You know that.'

'Yes, I do, and that's partly why I've come to you. But also because you're in a particularly powerful position where this case is concerned.'

'Powerful?'

'Yes, you see, it concerns Hassan's sister.'

'Zelfa? What has she done now?'

'Oh, I can't say I know the details of the whole thing. I'm merely a messenger.'

'A messenger for whom, exactly?'

'Well, there are certain people in public service who value my discretion. And from time to time, I go out of my way to help. I see it as my patriotic duty.'

Selma looked around cautiously.

'The *Mukhabarat*?'

'I don't like to use such terms so openly, my dear. But if you insist on doing so, then I won't argue the point.'

'So, what do they want?'

'I've been asked simply to pass on a message that will be of interest to Zelfa. You may also find it interesting, assuming you're willing to play your part.'

'I'm certainly keen to learn more.'

'Well, you presumably know that Zelfa is dating this American man from the US Embassy? What's his name?'

'Jerry.'

'That right. He's quite good looking, so you can't blame her really.'

'I suppose he has a sort of animal attraction about him, but he's not exactly my type.'

'No, nor mine. Even so, Zelfa is apparently smitten, and that's the problem.'

'How so?'

'Well, he's working for the embassy, and some people are convinced that he's CIA.'

'How would they know? He might be a computer technician for all we know.'

'Some people have looked into it, apparently, and they have ways of knowing these things.'

'And if he is CIA ...?'

'If he is CIA, then there's a danger that Zelfa is being used for intelligence gathering. And even if she isn't, then she might still be accused of it, which is just as bad.'

'So, do you think she's in danger?'

'Well, possibly. And I'm informed that she's already under heavy surveillance.'

'Surveillance by ...?'

'Yes, that's right. By the same people you mentioned earlier.'

'Right.'

'And in the process of conducting their surveillance ... Oh, this is rather horrible to have to say, but I have to say it.'

'Go ahead.'

'Well, in the process of conducting their surveillance, they've apparently obtained cine film of Jerry and Zelfa in bed.'

'In bed? Having sex?'

'Keep your voice down please, Selma. We don't want the neighbours to hear.'

'Of course, I'm sorry. But this is rather shocking. She's my sister-in-law.'

'Yes, and she might be in great danger if this ever got out. If certain people in our government don't take offence, then there's always the chance that the Americans might.'

'So, she might be in danger from both sides?'

'If she isn't murdered, then she might be thrown in jail for sleeping with a foreign agent. At the very least, she would be publicly humiliated.'

'Good God!'

'Yes, exactly. So, to get to the point, it would be in Zelfa's best interests if she would co-operate with certain people in obtaining information from Jerry – secretly, of course.'

'What information?'

'Well, Zelfa would be supplied with a list of things that she has to find out, and it's up to her how she finds them out. She needs to slip her questions into the general conversation, and see what information she can glean from Jerry. Apparently, the best time is in bed. That's when people are most open.'

'And if she doesn't agree?'

'If she doesn't agree, there are people higher up who may lose their faith in her and throw her to the wolves. There's enough in the film footage to convict her of treason, or so I'm told.'

'Treason?'

'Yes, and that carries the death penalty.'

Selma was shaking her head, looking suddenly very stressed. However, as she puffed on her cigarette, the stress began to recede, and a new cocktail of sensations bubbled to the top. It was the thrill of danger, combined with her inborn love of intrigue, overlaid with a sense of pride at having been entrusted with an important patriotic duty.

'She's my sister-in-law, you know. We've had our differences, but I'm very fond of her.'

'Yes, me too. I've always liked Zelfa, and her mother was always very kind to me. That's why it's so important that we handle this right. I'm sure you're the best person for the job.'

'Well, I'll certainly do my best. Give me all the details.'

The proposition

Selma stood before the long mirror and turned sideways. The white trousers were perhaps a little tight, but if anything, they accentuated her womanly curves. The low-cut t-shirt was likewise figure-hugging, but there were no visible love-handles and the reinforced bra was working wonders. She did a twirl in her high-heels and examined the overall effect.

She wanted to look her best – but at the same time casual. She needed to feel sexy and powerful, but she also hoped to put Zelfa at her ease. Kicking off the high-heels, she slipped into a pair of white-leather flip-flops. Yes, that was the effect she wanted: effortless style, a princess at a beach party.

She teased her hair into shape once more and then slipped downstairs to the kitchen, mentally rehearsing her performance. In essence, she was to play the role of pimp: urging a young woman to put her sexual powers to professional use. It was not money, of course, that was required, but information. And yet many of the principles were the same, and like many of the more successful pimps, Selma had the weapon of fear on her side. It would only take one phone call to put Zelfa behind bars for a very long time.

Selma couldn't help smirking at the thought of her new-found powers. She had never imagined that such an opportunity would fall into her lap, much less courtesy of Malaka. But she had never been one to look a gift-horse in the mouth. Working for the *Mukhabarat* on such an important project might win her new allies in official circles, which might in turn help Ahmed to avoid being shunted back to the front-line. Indeed, if the right strings were pulled, he might find himself embarking on a long and successful career in public service, with all the attendant wealth and status.

It had been a long time since the family could boast a general, government minister or senior civil servant among its ranks. That was before the events of 1958, in which King Faisal II was slain along with his family, making way for the Republic. Yes, in the old days, Selma's grandfather had been an important man; there was no reason why she shouldn't bring some of the glory back to her lineage. Added to which, if her new-found powers helped her to get even with Loma, that would be a very nice cherry on the cake. She grabbed the plate of *kletcha* from the fridge and headed through the front gate. Arriving at Zelfa's house, she knocked on the door. She wiggled her toes as she waited for some response, but there was none. She knocked again. Growing increasingly impatient, she rang the bell. From deep within, there were sounds of bumping and shuffling.

The door opened slowly, revealing a sleepy-looking Zelfa, hair all messy. She was wearing a pink silk robe and fluffy slippers. Selma noted with some irritation that she looked young and beautiful even without make-up.

'Zelfa, my dear, you look so tired.'

'What time is it?'

'It's nearly midday. I've brought you some *kletcha*.'

Zelfa yawned, showing her pearl-white teeth. She then stepped back and held the door open, struggling to think of a reason why her sister-in-law might be calling round with a plate of pastries. Drawing a blank, she shuffled into the kitchen, where Selma was already busy making a pot of tea.

'Is something wrong?' said Zelfa.

'Can't a woman visit her sister-in-law from time to time?'

'Of course. It's nice to see you.'

'Well then, just put some clothes on and let me provide you with breakfast. You look like you need it.'

Zelfa went to her bedroom and pulled on a track-suit. On her return, she found Selma seated on the patio, pouring tea into glasses.

'Take a seat. You need to eat something. You look horribly pale.'

Zelfa sat down and stirred sugar into her tea.

'Where's Nada?' said Selma, looking around.

'She went to the Alwiyah Club for a swim with a friend.'

'Is she staying out all afternoon?'

'Yes, she's staying at her friend's house tonight. She's going straight there.'

'Is that so?'

Selma allowed herself a knowing smile as she took her first sip of tea. Zelfa ignored the taunt; she was used to such insinuations from Selma. In the silence that followed the two ladies helped themselves to pastries.

Selma broke the silence: 'Malaka came to see me yesterday.'

'Really? What did she want?'

'She was full of gossip, as usual.'

'I'm not surprised. She seems to take a keen interest in other people's business.'

'Well, it's all part of her profession, I suppose.'

'I suppose so, yes.'

Zelfa was suddenly concerned; could this be the reason for Selma's visit? What had Malaka been saying?

'Unfortunately,' continued Selma, her mouth full of pastry, 'she had something to say about you.'

'Me?'

'Yes, you and that American chap … What's his name?'

'Jerry.'

'That's right. Will you have another *kletcha*?'

'No, I'm fine thanks.'

Zelfa was blushing now, and the more she tried to stop, the more she blushed. Selma made a point of taking her time in choosing another pastry and laying it on her plate. She cut off a sizeable chunk and stuffed it into her mouth.

'What did she want then?' said Zelfa, lighting a cigarette with shaky hands.

'She's heard some nasty rumours, I'm afraid.'

'What rumours?'

'Well, it's a bit unpleasant, I'm sorry to say. I feel pretty bad about having to be the one who breaks it to you.'

'What? Breaks what?'

Selma took a long sip of her tea.

'Well, Malaka has her connections, as you know, and they go pretty high up. Apparently, she heard through the grape-vine that the *Mukhabarat* have Jerry under surveillance.'

'Whatever for?'

'Well, he works for the US Embassy, doesn't he?'

'Yes, of course. But so do a lot of people. Why are they spying on Jerry in particular?'

'They suspect that he's with the CIA.'

Zelfa broke into a coughing fit, tipping ash all over herself. When she recovered, she was blushing more than ever. She was also looking frightened and defensive.

'Don't be ridiculous! Jerry works on trade negotiations. He told me so himself.'

'Well, I suppose he would say that, wouldn't he?'

Zelfa was silent, looking down the long garden. She had a horrible feeling that her wonderful love affair was about to turn sour.

'So why did she tell you all this? What does it have to do with you?'

'She thought that you might want to be kept informed, and she thought that, as your sister-in-law, I might be the best person to break the bad news. And, of course, I agreed.'

'Well, I suppose I should thank you then.'

'You're very welcome.'

'Anyway, nothing's happened between us. We're not even dating really. It's more of a friendship.'

'Well, that's the other thing that Malaka wanted me to pass on.'

'What?'

'This is very difficult, Zelfa, and I hope you won't shoot the messenger.'

'Go on, go on!'

'Apparently, they've been recording your visits to your little love nest.'

'Recording what? What on earth are you talking about?'

Selma sighed deeply and leaned forward, looking Zelfa in the eyes.

'The flat where you spend your nights with Jerry. The flat that Malaka leant to you. Sadly, the *Mukhabarat* broke in and planted cameras and microphones all over the place. They've got you on film, darling. They've got the whole show on film – everything.'

Zelfa sat bolt upright, eyes wide with shock. She looked down the garden, hoping to God that she wouldn't start to cry. Then the first tears welled up and ran down her face. Feigning concern, Selma walked round the table and put her arms around her sister-in-law.

'There, there! Don't be upset. It's not the end of the world.'

Zelfa was rigid. She'd never imagined herself being hugged by Selma, and now that it was happening, she didn't like it one bit.

'I don't understand,' she sniffed. 'How did they get into the flat?'

'I have no idea, Zelfa. But Malaka assures me that she had nothing to do with it. She would never have leant you the flat if she'd know this would happen.'

'Oh my God!' said Zelfa, burying her face in her hands. 'This is terrible! What does it mean? What are they going to do?'

Selma calmly returned to her seat and lit a cigarette of her own. As she did so, she mentally rehearsed her next step. She had no idea about the inner workings of the *Mukhabarat*, but Malaka had coached her on the correct line to take. It wasn't entirely true, but that hardly mattered, so long as it had the desired effect.

'You're asking all the right questions, Zelfa. Because that's the next thing that Malaka said. Apparently, there is some disagreement within the *Mukhabarat*. Some people feel that your sleeping with a CIA officer implicates you in treasonous activities. Other people feel that you're quite innocent.'

'I am innocent, of course. I don't even think Jerry works for the CIA. It's all made up.'

'Well, it may seem that way to you, Zelfa, but that's not how the *Mukhabarat* see it. They're quite serious, apparently. And some people feel that you should be put behind bars. Unless, of course, you can prove your loyalty to your country.'

'Prove my loyalty? How?'

Selma tipped her ash. She had to be very careful about this next step.

'This is a horrible thing to have to say, particularly to you, Zelfa, as I've always loved and respected you.'

'What do they want?'

'Well, it's been suggested that if you were to obtain a few scraps of information from Jerry, then this would show that you're willing to cooperate with the authorities, and they might look upon your case with more leniency. You might even be viewed as a sort of hero.'

'They want me to get information out of Jerry? Are you serious?'

Zelfa was on her feet now, clutching her hair tightly in one hand, cigarette in the other.

'Calm down, Zelfa. It's not such a big deal. They'll give you the questions, and you simply find some why of asking them. Ideally while you're lying in bed. Nothing could be simpler.'

'I couldn't possibly do that. What are you thinking? That would mean betraying Jerry. I could never betray him. I love him!'

'Darling, I didn't want to have to do this, but I think I should perhaps point out that you have no choice in the matter. For one thing, there is sufficient evidence of your collaboration to put you behind bars for 50 years. You might even be shot. And even if you managed to avoid arrest, the film could be made public. It would be in all the newspapers. You'd be ruined. And just think what it would mean for Nada. How could she ever go to college or find a husband after it's revealed that her mother had been fucking a CIA officer, possibly for money?'

'For money? What are you talking about?'

'Well, I'm sure you don't charge Jerry for your services. But other people don't know that. It all depends on what sort of story the *Mukhabarat* want to feed to the newspapers. They have very active imaginations, you know.'

Zelma sat down again and began furiously lighting another cigarette. She clicked away with the lighter a dozen times before it finally worked.

'Calm down,' said Selma. 'You've been presented with a problem, but you've also been provided with the solution. I know you're very much in love with Jerry – that much is plain – but you needn't feel that you're betraying him by seeking a little information. That sort of thing goes on all the time in romance. It's nothing new to engage in a little trickery in the course of a love affair. And you might pull through it very well. You two might even end up getting married at some future point. You just need to pull yourself together and do this little favour for your country – if only to show that you're a true patriot.'

'Would you do it to Hassan? Would you deceive him in such a way?'

'Well, of course I would, my dear. I'm always weeding information out of him. He's my husband, after all. There's nothing that husbands and wives won't do to each other.'

'Yes, but you don't pass the information on to the *Mukhabarat*, do you?'

'Well, I've never been asked.'

'And if you were?'

'Then I suppose I'd obey. After all, these people don't take no for an answer.'

Zelfa knew that further discussion was useless. She looked down the garden at the dappled sunlight on the lawn beneath the palm trees. She could imagine Jerry there, standing naked and smiling at her – that cheeky, playful smile of his. Even now, he was looking like a thing of the past, like a flickering home-movie from years gone by.

Selma interrupted her reverie: 'It could be that you ask your questions, and Jerry turns out to be just an innocent trade representative, as you say. Then the whole business will be forgotten, and you two can get on with your romance as if nothing had happened. It doesn't need to be all doom and gloom.'

'I'll think about it,' said Zelfa.

'That's a good girl.'

An unwelcome visitor

Loma's mother was putting the finishing touches to a flower arrangement in the kitchen. She enjoyed such tasks, finding a certain relaxation in them. And anyway, nobody else was going to make the house look nice. Unlike her neighbours, she couldn't afford full-time servants. If she wanted an extra little touch to cheer the place up, she had to do it herself.

Just as she was adding some water to the vase, she heard the doorbell ring.

'Answer that, will you, Huda?'

'Okay,' shouted a young woman on the sofa.

Loma's little sister had been engrossed most of the afternoon in glossy magazines, imagining what she might do with her wardrobe in the case of unlimited funds. As it was, today she was sporting a pair or tight jeans, a purple T-shirt, and some cheap plastic flip-flops. She was hardly ready for the catwalk.

She opened the front door and found – to her great surprise – Selma standing on the doorstep, looking dazzling in a white silk dress and dangly gold earrings. Huda was well aware of her sister's wrestling match with Selma the previous summer, and she had assumed that they would be steering clear of each other from now on. This unannounced visit, therefore, left her speechless. Selma filled the void: 'Huda, darling! It's so lovely to see you. Is your sister at home?'

Huda turned and shouted into the cool interior: 'Mum! It's Selma!'

She then turned back to Selma and gave her a blank look, an act of solidarity with her sister. Moments later, Selma's mother came into view, covering her hair with a scarf.

'Selma, my dear! What a lovely surprise! Come in, come in!'

In the living room, Selma coolly surveyed her surroundings. Aside from a new coat of paint, the place had changed little in the past two decades. The large rugs were a little worn; the mahogany coffee table bore a few scratches; the gilt frame around the large mirror was a little patchy; there were cushions on the floor, along with several of Huda's magazines. Selma noticed that the sofas and armchairs – handmade in Cairo in the Louis XIV style – were sagging, the dust gathering in the various nooks and crannies.

'Take a seat, my dear,' said the mother, 'I'll bring you some tea. Loma will be with us soon.'

'She's here, is she?'

'Yes, she's resting in her room. Huda, go and bring your sister.'

Huda said nothing and stomped off upstairs, a look of deep disapproval on her face.

'I'm so sorry about the mess,' said the mother, picking up cushions and magazines.

'Oh, you mustn't mind me,' objected Selma. 'I'm used to mess. My house is a rubbish tip at the moment. It's so hard to find the staff these days.'

'Yes, I suppose it is.'

In reality, Selma was delighted to find the room not quite ship-shape. Indeed, it was one of the great benefits of making surprise visits: one instantly put the enemy on the back foot.

As Loma's mother was setting out the tea and pastries on the coffee table, Selma could hear raised voices upstairs.

'Is that children playing in the street?' mused Selma, feigning innocence.

'No, I think that might be the girls upstairs,' said the mother, rushing from the room.

She found Loma in her bedroom, looking quite furious. She was dressing hurriedly after a long sleep, her eyes puffy, hair messed up.

'What is that bloody woman doing here?' demanded Loma.

'She's come to see you. She's brought you a box of chocolates. Perhaps she wants to apologise?'

'Ha! The day that Selma apologizes for something will be the day that Hell freezes over.'

'Well, I can't very well tell her to go now. She's a guest. It's wrong to turn guests away.'

'She's a viper, more like. She's a snake, and you've let her into your house. And now I have to go and deal with her.'

'Well, try not to be too confrontational, my dear. She may be seeking to mend fences. You never know.'

Huda watched in silence, biting her nails. Loma finished dressing, brushed her hair quickly and rushed downstairs. Standing in the corridor, she attempted to compose herself. Recalling some advice she'd once received on stress management, she breathed in deeply, held it for a count of three, and then exhaled. She closed her eyes in the process, but all she saw was her beloved Ali, exactly as he'd looked in his youth – then the inside of the abortion clinic. She felt a wrench in her stomach and a wave of nausea.

She suddenly recalled the Arabic proverb advising that one should deal with danger by singing to it. If this was the case, she must open her mouth and start singing. With one more deep breath, she pushed open the living-room door and stepped inside.

'Selma! This *is* a lovely surprise!'

'Yes, I thought I'd just pop over to welcome you back home.'

'Oh, you really needn't have bothered.'

'Well, it's my duty to be neighbourly at least.'

'Yes, of course.'

'I brought you some chocolates. They're Belgian, I believe.'

She handed over a large, flat box, tied with a red ribbon. Loma set it to one side.

The four women sat around the coffee table, the mother passing out tea and pastries.

'So, how was London?' said Selma. 'The winters can be a bit depressing, I believe. I've only ever been there in spring and summer, of course.'

'No, I didn't find it depressing at all. I love the cool weather.'

'Really? I always thought you were a sun-worshipper.'

'Well, it's different in London. They have so many wonderful ways of dealing with the cold.'

'I just love Regent Street and the area around St James's Palace. It's so authentic, I find. The shops are genuinely English. I bought some wonderful riding boots there once. I forget where, exactly. And Hassan bought himself a shaving set made from wale-bone and Spanish leather. We spent a fortune the last time we visited.'

'I know how it is. I can spend all day in Oxford Street, popping in and out of shops.'

'Oh, I find Oxford Street a little bit drab. The shops are somewhat common. But if you're looking for a bargain, I suppose it makes sense.'

'I don't think I'd be living in London if I were looking for bargains, Selma.'

Loma was singing as hard as she could, but it was exhausting, and there was little sign of the danger receding. More to the point, she fully expected Selma to drop a bombshell at any moment. If she hadn't come to cause trouble, why on earth had she come?

'Huda, come and help me in the kitchen,' said her mother.

Selma and Loma were left alone, and a cold silence descended on the room.

It was Selma who spoke first: 'So, I understand you had a little trouble while you were away.'

'What trouble?'

'Well, I don't know the details, but people talk.'

'Do they? What have they been saying?'

'Something to do with ... what's her name?'

'I have no idea.'

'That's right. Trouble with Madeha, the silly girl.'

Selma lit a cigarette and blew a cloud of smoke thoughtfully into the air.

'You don't mind if I smoke, do you?' she said.

Loma was silent; singing clearly wasn't working. Perhaps she should just let the bitch get everything off her chest – and decide on a response later. At least she would conserve some energy.

Selma continued: 'I'm told that she had an affair with that horrible man from her youth. What was his name?'

Loma said nothing.

'That's right, I remember now. Munir, wasn't it? Such a ghastly little man. They say he's an agitator, plotting some sort of revolution. Probably makes bombs in his spare time. How on earth Madeha could get herself mixed up with someone like that, I just don't know. I mean, what sort of woman spends her nights in bed with a bomb-making lunatic? It's not a question of being naïve. It's a question of moral character – and brains, of course. Surely, any decent, sensible, intelligent woman could see from a hundred yards that the man was trouble? Or perhaps that's what she wanted? Perhaps she has secret revolutionary tendencies? Perhaps she's one of those closet extremists who want to blow us all up? And of course, anyone close to Madeha is inevitably going to suffer too, purely by association. After all ...'

Loma felt herself going dizzy. The room suddenly went dim, then black. She fell sideways off the sofa onto the floor, her plate of pastries smashing on the marble tiles.

Selma stood up, a look of genuine surprise on her face.

Moments later, the mother and Huda were bent over Loma, placing cushions under her head and fanning her with magazines. To everyone's great surprise, Loma sat bolt upright and started waving her arms about.

'Stop fussing!' she shouted. 'I'm alright, stop fussing!'

She then stood up and regained her seat on the sofa. She looked dreadfully pale, perhaps a little green, but there was fire in her eyes.

Selma was smiling now, clearly enjoying the sight of her enemy in disarray.

'You seem to be under the weather. Perhaps it's jet-lag?'

'It's not jet-lag, Selma, it's the stench of your presence in the room. It makes me sick.'

'Oh, I see! I've come here to extend the hand of friendship, and you slap me in the face. Now you're showing your true colours. You're insane, just like your terrorist friend Madeha. She's brought shame upon her family, and so have you. You're two peas in a pod.'

'Well, it's not as if you're helping anyone, Selma. It's you that's spreading the rumours all the time. And it's you who ruined my life.'

'Ruined your life? What on earth are you talking about?'

'You know exactly what I'm talking about, you bitch. I know everything. I know what you did all those years ago. You disgust me.'

'So, you're just the innocent little sheep, are you? What a load of bullshit! You should take responsibility for your actions, you stupid little girl.'

'What actions? Is it my fault that I fell in love with the wrong person? It is my fault that his family turned against me? Whose fault was that, Selma? Can you tell me that?'

'I have absolutely no idea what you're talking about. You must have gone mad. Somebody should call you a doctor.'

'And now, not content with ruining my love life, you're doing your best to harm my reputation and my husband's career, all the while bad-mouthing my best friend. You're just evil. There's no other word for it.'

Selma had grabbed her handbag and risen to her feet. She was either planning another physical assault or getting ready to leave.

'You can call me whatever you like,' she said, 'but I wasn't the one screwing businessmen behind my husband's back in London.'

'What on earth are you talking about now?'

'You know exactly what I'm talking about, you whore.'

'Get out!' screamed Loma, lurching forward. 'Get out of this house now! Get out!'

Selma turned coolly and walked into the hallway. Opening the door, she stood on the threshold.

'You should be very careful, Loma. I'm pretty well connected, you know.'

'What on earth does that mean?'

'It means that I have connections who could cause you a lot of harm. I only have to dial a phone number these days, and your life would be changed forever.'

'Are you threatening me?'

Selma smiled and walked out into the bright sunlight. Loma slammed the door behind her. Returning to the living room, she found her mother and sister standing in silence, their mouths hanging open, too shocked to speak.

'I'm going to my room,' said Loma. 'Don't disturb me please.'

Upstairs, she sat on the bed and closed her eyes. What on earth had just happened? What would the consequences be? She half expected Selma to return with a gun and shoot her dead. Nothing was impossible. And what did she mean about 'connections' and phone calls?

If ever Selma represented a clear and tangible danger, it was now. She was a viper ready to strike, and Loma was the mongoose. It was just a question of who struck first.

Loma grabbed her little black phone book and began leafing through it. She was looking for a member of the diplomatic security team in London who had returned to Baghdad in December. He had been some sort of supervisor, responsible for counter-intelligence. He had been a little creepy, always looking her up and down; now, perhaps, Loma could use that to her advantage.

She leafed through the phone book, trying to recall his name.

There it was: Bilal Mohamed.

She dialled the number, not quite sure what she was going to say.

'Hello,' came the answer, the voice instantly recognizable.

'Hello, Bilal. This is Loma.'

'Madam Loma. What a lovely surprise! I understand you're back in Baghdad.'

'Yes, I am, and I have a favour to ask.'

'Anything for you, madam. Your wish is my command.'

Honey trap

Jerry slowed down as he approached the rear entrance of the US Embassy. He shifted the blue Chevrolet into second gear and nodded to the Iraqi policemen marking the outer perimeter, also to the plain-clothes security officers, with their dark glasses, suits and ties. He wound down his window and rolled up to the gates, manned by US Marines in their immaculate uniforms. A corporal, who had been standing to attention like a wax-work model at Madame Tussaud's, relaxed his posture and broke into a smile.

'Good morning, sir.'

'Morning, Tom.'

The marine checked Jerry's ID card: 'That's fine, sir.'

'How'd you do last night?'

'Sir?'

'The Cubs against the Giants.'

'Oh, we won: 12 to 11.'

'Sounds like a close game.'

'It was close. Keith Moreland hit a flyball at the end. It was beautiful.'

'You must be pretty stoked.'

'Would have been more stoked if the satellite didn't keep cutting out. I suspect the Iraqis.'

'Well, no comment on that.'

'Ever the diplomat, sir.'

Jerry parked in the shade, leaving his window open a few inches; a May afternoon in Baghdad could quickly turn a car into an oven. Exiting the vehicle, he pulled on his jacket and grabbed his briefcase, somehow adopting the air of Clint Eastwood dismounting from a horse with his saddle-bags. It was an attitude that put many people's backs up, but it won him just as many fans among the embassy staff, particularly the young women. Margaret Moore, however, was not among them. Reporting directly to the CIA Chief of Station, this tough New Yorker took her work seriously and had no time for cowboys of any sort. She tolerated Jerry's bravado to a degree, but only so long as he produced results. She watched him from an open doorway, making a show of checking her watch as he stopped to light a cigarette.

'Good morning, Maggie.'

'Good morning, Jerry. Glad you could join us. We're running 30 minutes late, so let's get going. I have a meeting with the ambassador at noon.'

'It's the damned traffic, Maggie. It's murder getting into Al-Mesbah on a Thursday.'

'And yet, it's the same every Thursday.'

'Point taken.'

They walked through the air-conditioned corridors of the embassy, stopping by Maggie's office to collect some paperwork.

Then they headed upstairs, taking their seats in a small, windowless room. Maggie sat behind a desk and began browsing through her files. Jerry lit another cigarette.

'Did you catch the game last night?' he ventured.

'The game?'

'Chicago Cubs against the San Francisco Giants. I thought you'd be watching.'

'I don't follow football, Jerry.'

'It's baseball.'

'I don't follow baseball either.'

'I always thought you were the sporty type, Maggie. You've got the body for it.'

'I played La Crosse at Yale.'

'Of course, La Crosse. I should have guessed.'

Maggie put down her papers and gave Jerry a long, hard look. Jerry tipped his ash.

'So, Jerry,' she began, 'I'm scouring my records for any signs of progress on your infiltration operation with this woman Zelfa. There doesn't seem to have been any update since September last year.'

'August.'

Maggie checked again.

'Ah, yes. September's update was the same as August's. I see you reported that you had "initiated intimate relations" with the target. Are you past the stage of initiating intimacy yet?'

'Some women like a lot of foreplay.'

'Jerry, I hope you don't imagine that I came here to engage in banter?'

'Not at all, ma'am.'

'Unfortunately, I have been appointed to keep tabs on your progress, and that's exactly what I intend to do. I also intend to assess whether this "intimacy" of yours is likely to bear fruit.'

'I don't think she's pregnant, if that's what you're implying.'

'Jerry, I promise you that joking will get you nowhere. This operation is on the point of being canned unless you can provide solid results very quickly.'

'Believe me, I'm pumping her for information at every opportunity.'

'Don't test my patience.'

He held up his hands in surrender.

'Okay, listen, the operation's going smoothly, so far as I can tell. Zelfa, bless her little heart, is deeply in love with me. She's putty in my hands – warm putty. She also happens to have a delightful teenage daughter called Nada who spends her weekends with Uday Hussein and his intimate circle. I'm in the process of finding ways to deepen the relationship with Nada, because she seems to be the best option for top-level gossip.'

'Have you actually met Nada?'

'Only in passing, at the Alwiyah Club. We chatted for a few minutes by the pool. I'm not sure how she views me yet. You know: mother's new boyfriend and all that.'

'So, have you asked Nada if she's willing to supply information?'

'Are you kidding? Whatever I say to Nada might be passed directly to Uday and his merry men. I'd be compromised in a second. No, I need to build trust first, take is slowly.'

'So, if I've understood correctly, your plan is to continue your intimacy with Zelfa for the next several years until her daughter finally – magically – takes a shine to you and starts divulging state secrets. Is that it?'

'When you put it like that, it sounds like a pretty dumb plan. I prefer to think that I'm using my CIA training and my finely tuned appreciation of human nature to put these people fully at their ease, at which point, they will share their concerns with me, along with whatever information they might have access to. This is all by the book, Maggie. It's a slow-burn operation; there's nothing unorthodox about that.'

'And what are the chances of Nada taking a shine to you in the next twelve months.'

'I was thinking that I'd give it another six months. If I'm still getting nowhere, I might perhaps consider introducing an intermediary – some handsome Iraqi boy who's already on our books, someone that Nada might take a shine to. There are one or two at the club that I have in mind.'

'It sounds like you're groping in the dark, Jerry.'

'Some women like that sort of thing.'

'Okay, I've had enough of this bullshit. The US Government is not paying you a good salary – with pension and health insurance – to spend your afternoons perfecting the female orgasm.'

'You could have fooled me.'

Maggie checked her watch and started gathering her papers together.

'Either you present me with some results by the end of the month, or I'm going to have to call time on this operation.'

Jerry leaned back in his chair, nonchalantly crossing his legs.

'So, are you saying that you want me to *rush* a delicate infiltration operation? I don't recall reading that in the training manual at Langley. This could pay off big time, providing access to the inner circles of government, and all we need is a little patience.'

'From where I'm standing, patience needs to be balanced with evidence of progress.'

'I'm not God.'

'I'm glad you realise that, Jerry. I wasn't quite sure. Perhaps if you were omniscient you might be aware of the dangers that a slow-burn operation of this sort exposes you to.'

'Meaning?'

'The longer you drag this out, the more chance there is of this woman …'

'Zelfa.'

'… Zelfa turning the tables and tapping you for information. Has it occurred to you that she might be a honey trap?'

'Impossible.'

'How so?'

'I made the first move. She resisted my attentions. I had to press the point, and finally I seduced her into compliance. She's not the sort of girl to hang around bars picking up off-duty diplomats.'

'No, but she does hang around swimming pools in her bikini, doesn't she?'

'Maggie, she's not a honey trap.'

'How can you be so sure?'

'I'm a pretty good judge of character, and Zelfa's honest from tip to toe.'

'And what about the place where you … conduct your intimacies? How secure is it?'

'Totally secure. I checked every inch of it. No bugs, no cameras. Clean as a whistle.'

Maggie opened the door. Jerry got to his feet and followed her down the corridor.

'You've got until the end of the month.'

'If you say so.'

* * *

Just a few blocks north, Zelfa sat in a fancy Parisian-style café nursing a filter coffee with a dash of milk, no sugar. She had tried to eat her croissant but could manage no more than half. She was too nervous, full of butterflies and light-headed.

Why on earth had she agreed to meet Jerry in this place, so close to the US Embassy? He seemed to be reckless at times, as if he wanted to be caught. Perhaps he didn't fully appreciate the risks that an Iraqi woman was taking when she dated a US diplomat? No, that didn't make sense; *of course* he appreciated the dangers. He was simply a risk-taker, and that meant he was willing to take risks with other people's safety just as much as his own. It was one aspect of his personality that troubled her.

She checked her watch and adjusted her Chanel sunglasses. There were plenty of cars parked nearby, but none of them was Jerry's. She'd give it another ten minutes and then leave. She tried another bite of croissant and chewed it slowly, mechanically.

'Zelfa, sweetheart,' came a voice from nowhere.

She jumped in her seat, spilling her coffee.

Jerry was standing before her, a big smile on his face.

'Oh, don't creep up on me! Where did you come from?'

'From the sky, of course. Where do you think I came from?'

'Where's your car?'

'Around the corner.'

'Well, don't creep up like that. I'm all nerves today. You have no idea how anxious I am.'

'What are you anxious about?'

'Getting caught, of course. There are spies everywhere. And I don't like meeting here. It's too close to the embassy.'

He laughed again and planted a kiss on her lips.

'Okay, you frightened little bunny, let's get out of here.'

'Where to?'

'Somewhere nice and private with a big double bed.'

'Sounds better.'

They paid the bill and drove north to Adhamiya, parking two blocks from the apartment. The doorman smiled and nodded as they got into the lift, closing the concertina doors behind them. Two hours later, they lay in the gloom of the bedroom, the shutters closed, the sheets damp with sweat. Jerry lay on his back, one hand behind his head, the other holding a cigarette. Zelfa lay by his side, head resting on his shoulder. She was twirling his chest hairs around his fingers, desperately pondering her information-gathering mission and how on earth to get started. She knew the list of questions, of course; Selma had been quite clear on that front. But there was no indication of how to raise such topics without sounding false. How did one broach such things? After all, Jerry wasn't an idiot. If Selma was right, he was a trained spy, which made it all the more important to tread carefully.

Selma had explained about the microphones in the headboard, about the man next door listening through headphones, about the tape-recorder that started recording at the push of a button. These were sensitive microphones, Selma had said; they picked up every word that was said – every little moan and groan.

It was all too horrible to contemplate. Zelfa closed her eyes and wondered whether she might just do nothing – and allow the whole situation to disappear of its own accord. After all, there was no guarantee that Selma was telling the truth. Maybe there was no cine film of them having sex, no camera hidden in the light fixtures, no microphones in the headboard. Maybe it was all a wicked hoax.

'Zelfa,' said Jerry, 'I think we need to talk about a few things.' Her heart bounded. What did he want to talk about? Had he guessed her thoughts?

'What about?'

'About you and me, about our future.'

'What do you mean? What future?'

He stubbed out his cigarette and started running his fingers gently through her hair.

'Well, I'm pretty serious about you. I love you, and I think you feel the same about me.'

'Yes, I do.'

'So, it makes sense for us to consider the future.'

'Do you mean marriage?'

She got up on one elbow and looked into his eyes. Was he about to propose?

He smiled a gentle smile.

'Well, maybe, in time. Right now, it's difficult, of course. I'm working at the embassy, and the political climate is tough. But if I were to move back to Washington at some point, and if you were willing to follow me, we might get married in the States.'

'And then?'

'And then we would take it from there. I could get a desk job in DC, and we could buy a house there. Eventually, we could move out West.'

'Where exactly?'

'My dad has a farm in California. We could move nearby. I've always wanted to breed horses. You might enjoy the life. There's lots of sunshine and fresh air.'

'Is it close to Los Angeles?'

'Not really. My dad lives about 200 miles south.'

'Anywhere near Hollywood?'

'Not at all. Hollywood's in LA.'

'I don't know too much about American geography.'

'Apparently not. Don't worry, you'll pick it up.'

'Would you really give up your career for me?'

'Yes, when the time's right. You're very precious to me, and I don't want to lose you. It's just a matter of planning ahead. There's more to life than working in embassies.'

Zelfa rolled onto her back and looked at the ceiling.

'Wow!' she said. 'I never imagined you'd say that.'

'What?'

'Getting married. It's ... wonderful.'

'It makes perfect sense. So long as you feel the same way.'

'Of course I do.'

They lay in silence for a while. Zelfa had quite forgotten the microphones; if she had tried to recall her list of questions, she'd have drawn a blank. Jerry reached down and took her hand, their fingers interlocking like they were made to measure. The clock ticked gently on the bedside table.

'What about Nada?' she said at last.

'Well, she could come too, of course, if she wanted to.'

'I wouldn't leave Iraq without her, so she'd have to come with me.'

'That could be arranged. There are some very good fine-art programmes in the States. If she's as talented as you say, she could get a place with a scholarship. After she graduates, she could move in with us and start thinking about her career. She could work at a gallery. I know people in that field, so it wouldn't be too hard to arrange.'

'But what about the Iraqi authorities? They're not keen on people fleeing the country.'

'Maybe not, so you'd have to decide on your loyalties. If you and Nada were to move to the States with me, it would be for good. No going back.'

'That's a big step. It would be a big step for Nada. She has all her friends here.'

'Does she really have so many friends? I got the impression she was a loner.'

'Well, she goes out at weekends, as you know. She goes to those private parties.'

'With Uday Hussein?'

'Yes, and some other people. They're not real friends, I suppose. It's more her friends from school I'm thinking of.'

'But she'll make new friends in the States, especially if she goes to college.'

'I suppose she will.'

There was another silence. Jerry preferred to let Zelfa lead the discussion, if at all possible. He listened to the clock ticking, lit another cigarette. Finally, he decided to take the initiative.

'It would probably be good for Nada to get to know me. I mean, the whole plan depends on her feeling I'm someone she can trust, if you see what I mean.'

'Of course, yes, she should meet you. I've always wanted that.'

'But it hasn't happened so far.'

'Well, you know the difficulties. Where would we meet? You can't come to my house; it's probably being watched. And I can't exactly bring her here.'

'Why not?'

'Are you serious? You want me to bring my daughter to our little love nest? Do you want her to see the bed where her mummy fucks foreigners?'

'Woah! Hold your horses! There's nothing wrong with fucking foreigners. We love each other. I appreciate that we're not married, but there's no shame in what we're doing.'

'I know that, Jerry, but I'm not sure Nada would see it that way. She still misses her father, you know. The divorce was hard on her. I'm not sure she's ready to be exposed to the full truth of her mother's private life.'

'Okay then, how about we just meet for a meal sometime, maybe next week. I can invite you both to lunch at the Ishtar Sheraton. We can have a civilized meal – fully clothed – and we can just get to know each other. You can just say we're friends or something. I'm sure she'll like me. Most women do.'

'Oh, I'm sure she'll find you very charming.'

Zelfa got to her knees and started tickling Jerry's hairy belly.

'You charm all the girls,' she said, 'and now you're starting on my daughter. I'm going to have to keep a close eye on you.'

Jerry grabbed her wrists and wrestled her onto her back, laying his full weight on her. He looked into her eyes, a big smile on his face. Zelfa smiled back at him, her eyes sparkling.

'I said I wanted to meet your daughter, not fuck her.'

'Well, you have to start somewhere, I suppose.'

Still grasping her wrists, he manipulated her more fully into the missionary position.

'Yes,' he said, 'and I'm going to start right here.'

Bilal

Loma was brushing her thick auburn hair before the bedroom mirror when the maid entered with breakfast on a tray.

'Your tea and toast, my daughter,' said the old woman.

'Thank you, Sadah. Put it by the window, will you?'

Sadah was in her late sixties now, with five grown-up daughters. However, she viewed Loma as the sixth, having helped raise her from infancy. A native of the Shia south, she had few relatives in Baghdad, and Loma was her main source of affection, the object of her motherly pride.

'You're looking very lovely today,' she said.

'Thank you, Sadah.'

'You seem to be happier.'

'I suppose it's nice to be back in my own home.'

'Yes, I always think that's very important,' said the maid as she made the bed.

Loma applied a heavy dose of hair-spray and wandered over to the window. The tea tasted wonderful: just strong enough and no more. And it was a beautiful day outside, with just a few fluffy clouds drifting across a wide, blue sky. There seemed to be more birds in the trees than usual – or perhaps they were just more vocal.

'Yes, I think things might work out for the best,' she said, largely to herself.

'I'm sure they will, my dear, I'm sure they will.'

Loma sped through the streets in her Toyota Supra sportscar, the windows down and the radio playing full-blast. She had spent many years in the shadow of Selma, and it felt wonderful to finally have a plan for dealing with the witch. Well, she didn't have a plan exactly, but she had an ally, and a powerful one. Bilal was not someone to be messed with. He had sworn an oath to protect Iraq and its constitution, which implied protecting those who served the country, including diplomats and their wives.

She couldn't help smiling at the thought that, finally, after so much dithering and heart-ache, she had stumbled upon a workable solution. She was an important person now, and that meant she was entitled to protection. Not just the protection of loyal friends, but of the State and its agents, some of whom were very serious people. If Bilal could not take care of Selma, then nobody could.

Of course, the whole thing would have to be kept confidential, including from Riaz. But if there was one thing that Bilal exuded, it was a desire to be trusted with secrets. And if he wanted to remain in Loma's good books – which he undoubtedly did – then he would certainly respect her wishes in this regard. Perhaps Loma would have to turn on the charm a bit, but there was no harm in a little flirtation.

She zoomed past the palm trees and fashionable boutiques, pulling up by the Mansour Club, a popular hangout of the district's wealthy middle-class. It was also a great alternative to the Alwiyah Club, because Selma almost never visited. From time to time, Uday would drop by, causing a stir with his assistants and bodyguards. This morning, however, the club was largely empty, with not a VIP in sight.

Walking confidently through the gates, Loma headed for the garden café, collapsing in a large wicker chair. She checked her lipstick, ordered a coffee and waited.

There were butterflies in her belly now. For a brief moment, she wondered whether she was doing the right thing. She had no experience in hiring intelligence agents to fix her personal problems, and she could only guess at the potential repercussions. What if Riaz discovered what she was up to? What if Selma were killed, resulting in a murder investigation? What if Bilal demanded more for his services than Loma was willing to give? The list of potentially disastrous outcomes was apparently long. Perhaps she should leave while she had the chance?

Her thoughts were cut short by the arrival of Bilal. He spotted her from the gate and waved, then walked casually through the garden furniture, one hand in his trouser pocket, the other holding his sunglasses. He was wearing a well-tailored blue suit, a white shirt and no tie. With his trim physique and chiselled features, he looked like a fashion model. Only his moustache, speckled with grey, marked him out as an agent of the state in mid-career.

Loma wondered how it was that she'd never noticed his masculine charms. Back in London, he'd seemed sleezy, his wandering eyes inappropriate. Now they were in Iraq – far from Riaz and the embassy – he looked quite different. For a brief moment, she imagined herself as a single woman on a first date. She glanced at his hands and noticed that he wore no rings.

'Madam Loma,' he said, smiling broadly, 'it's truly an honour to meet you again.'

'Likewise, Bilal. Thanks for coming.'

They shook hands and he took a seat.

She noticed his firm chest muscles, the military watch on his wrist, the dark tone of his skin, no doubt from all that rigorous outdoor exercise. His face was lined with experience, but the eyes were youthful. She detected playfulness, also generosity. If there was a killer instinct in there – which presumably there was – he kept it well hidden.

'So, how can I help you?' he said.

'Oh, well …'

She was shocked by his directness. She really ought to have practiced her lines in advance.

'Take your time,' he said, stirring a single sugar into his black tea.

'It's nothing really. More of an ongoing argument that I'm having with an old friend.'

'A friend? From what you said on the phone, she didn't sound very friendly.'

'No, she's not. She makes a big show of being friends, but there's all ways a dagger hidden up her sleeve.'

'I assume you're speaking metaphorically?'

'Yes, of course. She's never threatened me with violence.'

Loma realized suddenly that this wasn't quite true. They'd had a huge and very public fight the previous summer, witnessed by numerous party guests. How had she forgotten?

Bilal sipped his tea in silence.

'Well, we did have a fight once – last year.'

'Was anybody hurt?'

'Just a few scratches.'

'And who started it?'

'Oh, she did. She always starts it.'

Bilal leaned back in his chair and lit a cigarette. Apparently, Loma was expected to do most of the talking.

'Okay, so here's the problem. This woman likes to spread rumours, and she has a particular hatred of me for some reason, so she spreads rumours about me more than anyone else.'

She paused. How much was she going to reveal? Was she expected to tell him about Ali? After all, if she was trying to stop the flow or rumours, why would she go blabbing to strangers?

'You needn't tell me all the details,' said Bilal, apparently reading her mind.

'Well, I don't mind, really. It's just a little … sensitive.'

'It usually is,' he said, smiling.

Loma thought how wonderful it would be if she really had someone in whom she could trust completely – a strong, capable man, with only her best interests at heart. Was it really so much to ask? Surely such people existed in this rotten world?

'Okay, this is the basic story. This horrible woman has been spreading rumours about me. They're quite dreadful. She says I'm having an affair with an old boyfriend.'

'Are you?'

Loma blushed.

'Of course not! I'm a married woman!'

'It happens.'

'Yes, but not to me. I'm faithful to my husband. I'd never do something like that.'

'Okay, so this woman is spreading vicious rumours with no basis in fact.'

'Yes, and it's been going on for years now. It's very annoying to me, and it's also potentially harmful to my husband's career. He can't afford any sort of scandal.'

'Of course, I quite understand.'

'You do?'

'Of course. This is a very common occurrence, and it's normally very easy to fix.'

'How?'

'There are various options. But, if you don't mind, before we go further, I wonder if you could give me some factual details?' He took a little notepad from his jacket pocket, along with a pen. 'Can you tell me the woman's name?'

'Oh, well ...'

Loma felt suddenly very anxious. Once Bilal had Selma's name, the wheels would be in motion. Even if she had second thoughts, there would be no way to call a halt. What if Selma were arrested and thrown in jail? What if she were shot dead while resisting arrest? Of course, it was possible that Bilal already knew about Selma – and this was all just a performance, part of the 'routine' of his business.

Bilal put down his notepad and pen.

'It's okay, we can take this slowly,' he said, still smiling. 'I'm at your service, Madam Loma, not the other way around.'

'Of course, I forgot.'

She laughed with relief, and he joined her. She noticed the whiteness of his teeth, the laughter lines around his eyes, the distinguished bump on his long nose.

Bilal caught the waiter's attention and asked for the menu. And hour later, Loma was feeling more relaxed. The slice of chocolate cake had helped enormously, as had the two beers. Bilal had also been very charming, insisting that they drop 'the serious talk' for the time being and get to know each other.

He had given a rambling account of his childhood in Tikrit, his brief army career and his transfer to the *Mukhabarat.* He peppered his talk with anecdotes, many of them quite funny. Loma was shocked to discover that her new protector held the rank of major. She had assumed for some reason that he was no more than a sergeant. She was flattered that someone so important should bother to help her.

Before long, she had quite forgotten her troubles. It seemed that she was floating in the clouds now, protected by gods, and that Selma was some shabby little insect far below.

During a lull in the conversation, Loma checked her lipstick again, while Bilal lit another cigarette. Blowing a large smoke ring, he returned to the serious business.

'So, do you feel comfortable yet with telling me your friend's name?'

Loma look up at the big blue sky. She heaved a sigh.

'You know, I'm not sure it's really necessary.'

'No?'

'Well, I thought it was, but now that I've had a chance to talk with you, I feel more at ease.'

'That's good.'

'In fact, I'd rather we forgot about the whole thing for the time being.'

'As you wish.'

'And there's no need to bother my husband with any of this. He has plenty on his mind that's far more important.'

'I quite understand. I will say nothing. But please be assured that I am at your service.'

'Yes, I know.'

'If this woman ever threatened you, I would be duty-bound to act.'

Loma reflected. Selma had made a sort of threat, saying she was 'well connected' and could ruin Loma's life just by picking up a phone. But was that really a threat, or just bravado?

'Madam Loma?'

'I'm sorry, I'm just thinking. No, I don't believe she's made any actual threats against me.'

'And you're quite sure you don't want to tell me who this woman is?'

'Not for the moment, but I feel reassured to know that I can call on you.'

'Well, that's what I'm here for.'

Bilal smiled another of his charming smiles and put his notebook away. He then reached into his wallet and took out a business card. He scribbled something on the back and handed it over.

'Now you have my office number, my home number and my car-phone number.'

'Car-phone? Do you really have one of those things?'

'It's very useful in my line of work.'

'Yes, I suppose it must be.'

There was a pregnant silence while Loma dropped the card into her purse.

'Would you like another beer?' said Bilal.

'Well, perhaps just one more.'

Breaking point

It was another hour before Loma left the Mansour Club, and as she climbed behind the wheel, she was feeling rather light-headed. After three beers, she really shouldn't be driving, but she felt invulnerable now. She could go anywhere, do anything, drive at full speed in her sleek silver car – and nothing could touch her. She even had Bilal's card in her purse, which might be very useful if she were stopped by the police.

The meeting had been a great success. Not because it resulted in any firm action, but because she'd made an important new ally – a powerful ally who was willing to spring to her defence at the drop of a hat. Yes, this was a wonderful turn of events, and she felt a celebration was in order.

As it happened, she did have a party to go to. She'd been invited to attend the opening of a show by the famous artist Layla Al-Attar. Loma had been invited largely due to her status as the wife of an important diplomat, and she had no particular reason to decline. She would mingle with the wives of ministers, diplomats, and party members, with critics and artists, chatting about fashion and food, art and jewellery, and any number of frivolous topics. Just possibly, Saddam's wife Sajida would be there too. She was more powerful than most people realized, offering advice in the highest circles, particularly to her husband and sons. Just one word from Sajida could see one's husband promoted to ambassador or minister.

She parked a few blocks from the gallery, hoping the walk might clear her head a little. Mounting the stone steps, she noted that the party was in full swing, with a pianist playing soft jazz on a baby grand, and numerous slender women sipping Champagne in their glittering dresses. Loma slipped into the bathroom and emptied her bladder of that third beer, then stood before the big mirror. She straightened her expensive Chanel dress, checking the pink silk for beer stains or specks of chocolate cake. She applied more lipstick and teased her hair into place. Taking a deep breath, she joined the party.

She grabbed a glass of Champagne from a passing waiter and slipped through the crowd to the buffet table. The pictures were the main event, of course, but they could wait. She was on the point of deciding between the baklava and a chocolate éclair when someone tapped her on the shoulder.

It was the renowned socialite Nadia Salem, looking very expensive in diamond earrings and silver sequins. Nadia was proud of her prominent Baghdadi family and never tired of reminding people that her grandfather had been an important minister during the reign of King Faisal. Such declarations were made quietly, of course, strictly in confidence, for fear that some official of the current regime might take offence. It was with this confidential air that she spoke to Loma now, as they stood before the chocolate éclairs.

'Congratulations on moving up, my dear!'

'Oh, Nadia, it's you. Thank you so much, but what are you congratulating me for?'

'Your husband's appointment to London, of course. I haven't had a chance to speak to you since it was announced. I'm sure he's doing very well. He has a good brain, your husband.'

'Yes, he's doing very well, thank you. It's hard work, of course, but he's used to that.'

'Working all hours, is he?'

Loma wondered for a moment whether Nadia was seeking to imply something improper. Was she referring to Riaz staying out all night with his whores? Was it really such public knowledge?

'Oh, yes, he's working quite hard. He has to, really. It's not an easy job.'

'Well,' said Nadia, taking hold of Loma's hand, 'he has the best wife in the world to back him up. I'm sure you're a great help to him. Will you be returning to London soon?'

'Oh, I'm not sure. I have a few things to do in Baghdad.'

Nadia looked surprised.

'But your children? They're still in London, aren't they?'

'Yes, they're still there. They go to a very nice school in Wimbledon.'

'But how can you bear to be parted from them for so long?'

'Oh, it's not so easy, but ...'

Loma was suddenly desperate to get away. She had come to his party for a drink and some shallow chit-chat, and now she found herself explaining her unorthodox parenting decisions. She looked around for some excuse to leave.

'I must take a look at some of these paintings,' she said. 'I've always liked Layla's work. I haven't seen these yet.'

'Well, don't let me keep you, my dear,' said Nadia, a cryptic smile on her lips.

'I'll catch up with you later.'

'Yes, I look forward to it. Do take care.'

'You too.'

The woman stepped aside, allowing Loma to pass. Once she had gone, Nadia turned to an old friend and commented: 'If Loma Mostafa's dress could speak, it would be saying: "Take me off!" I suppose she eats to cope with depression.'

Pushing through the crush, Loma finally arrived before a large oil painting illuminated by a spotlight. It was modern art, impressionistic, but with some classical skills in evidence. A woman sat on the forest floor, naked, her back to the viewer, and around her were tall, dark trees, denuded of leaves. The forest was bare, the sky a fiery orange, somehow suggesting a distant inferno. The whole situation seemed to represent a nightmare – perhaps a nightmare come true.

Loma frowned. Why was this woman alone in the forest, and why was she naked? Who had taken her there, and what had she been through? What on earth would happen next?

There seemed to be a spooky correspondence between this woman's fate and her own. Both were in danger, exposed to attack at any moment, their lives denuded of hope and joy. She felt a deep pity for this naked woman. She felt like telling her to get up and run, to keep running and never look back.

Loma finished her Champagne in one go, wondering whether it had been such a good idea to come to this show. It seemed she wasn't really up to socialising just yet.

As she looked around for a waiter, she noted two women moving through the crowd, heading in her direction. Her eyes widened in horror as she realised that the taller of the two women was her own personal nightmare: Selma.

'Loma, darling!' she said. 'I thought I might find you here. I've been so looking forward to catching up.'

She bent forward and planted kisses on Loma's cheeks. Loma stood perfectly still, mouth tightly shut. She had never imagined that Selma would have the cheek to speak to her again as a friend, particularly in public. And yet, here she was, putting on her usual show of rank hypocrisy. The woman really was a psychopath.

'I'd like you to meet a good friend of mine,' said Selma, turning to the short, elderly woman by her side. 'This is Dr Fatiha. She's a famous gynaecologist. I'm sure you've heard of her. She helps ladies out when … Well, she's very kind and helpful, and highly skilled.'

The elderly woman shook Loma's hand and offered a weak smile. Apparently, she wasn't entirely happy at being paraded around the place by Selma, but her sense of good manners prevented her from open rebellion.

'Nice to meet you,' said Loma.

'Nice to meet you,' replied the doctor.

Loma examined the woman's face more closely, wondering where she'd seen her before. She was rather wrinkled, perhaps in her 70s, with several layers of make-up over her dark skin. She had applied her lipstick rather clumsily, and her eyelashes seemed to be false. Her eyes seemed shifty, darting in all directions, as if she were looking for some way out.

'Dr Fatiha has been very kind to numerous young ladies over the years, Loma. Always in the strictest confidence, of course.'

The old woman made a move to depart, but Selma had one arm around her shoulders, and she hadn't finished speaking yet.

'You had a wonderful doctor, Loma, didn't you? Many, many years ago … Now what was her name?'

Suddenly, a light went on in Loma's head. She knew where she recognised this withered old woman from. This was the bitch who had removed the foetus from her womb, chopping up the tiny creature that would have grown into Ali's baby. She had performed the procedure with neither anaesthetic nor words of comfort. She had stitched up her hymen, too, like she was mending an old sock.

Loma's empty glass fell to the floor, smashing. Dozens of heads turned her way. The wrinkled doctor stepped back in shock. Selma was smiling.

'My dear, you don't look at all well,' she said.

Seized by panic, Loma turned and ran from the room, knocking several guests aside in the process. Down the stone steps she went, then along the street as fast as she could manage in her high-heels, gasping for air and desperately trying to recall where she'd parked the car.

Eventually, she found it, and fumbling with the keys, she climbed behind the wheel. She pulled out into the traffic, clipping the bumper of a parked car, and raced through the streets, tyres squealing as she took the corners at speed. Within minutes she was parked outside her house, gripping the steering wheel, eyes closed.

Breathe, she told herself. *Breathe deeply. Focus on the breath: in and out, in and out ...*

But it was no good; she just couldn't keep it together. She dissolved into tears, leaning her head against the steering wheel and sobbing like she'd never sobbed before. She clung on tightly, mouth open wide, as the grief poured out.

It was grief for her unborn child, for her beloved Ali, for the life she might have had.

Rashid Street

The following afternoon, Loma found herself in a reclining chair at her favourite hair salon. Joseph was known across Baghdad for his expert hair styling, attracting a continuous flow of well-heeled ladies in search of the latest fashions. Along with his wife, Joseph had built a flourishing business over the past two decades, and Loma was among their most valued customers. It didn't hurt, of course, that she had recently returned from London; it was great for business to have such jet-setting clients on the books.

Joseph was chatty, keen to learn the details of Loma's new life abroad, particularly the new trends in London. However, she was far from talkative. For one thing, she'd been crying intermittently since the previous afternoon, and her voice was now rather croaky. In any case, she had more pressing concerns.

'To be honest, Joseph, I didn't have a great deal of time for such things. I was mainly helping my husband. It's a very busy posting.'

'Yes, of course. I quiet understand.'

Finally, Joseph's work was done, and he held up a mirror for Loma to inspect the new style from every angle. It was certainly shorter than before, the ends curling up just above the collar, with a centre parting and a long fringe that swept away to the right and left. Joseph said she looked just like Linda Evans, the glamorous star of the American soap-opera Dynasty.

'Yes, that's fine,' said Loma, rising from her seat.

Joseph had hoped for a little more appreciation, but he kept his thoughts to himself.

Loma paid and walked back to her car. From her purse, she retrieved a scrap of paper, on which was scribbled an address. The place was not far from Rashid Street, on the eastern bank of the Tigris. Rashid Street was built by the Ottomans in 1916 and was specifically designed for motor vehicles, making it the first of its kind in the city. It was a work of art, lined with colonnades and ornate balconies, the shops selling high-class goods. In 1917, the British took control of Baghdad, and the street continued to thrive, boasting several cinemas and a wealth of cafés where shoppers rubbed shoulders with writers, socialites and politicians. By the 1980s, however, the place had become somewhat shabby, the luxury business drifting to more modern districts.

Loma hadn't been to Rashid Street for several years, largely because she didn't like the hustle and bustle. Today, of course, she had no choice.

She cruised through Mansour, then past Zawra Park and the statue of Maruf Al-Rusafy, the famous anti-imperialist poet. Crossing the river, she slipped into a multi-storey carpark, leaving her Toyota Supra in a dark corner. Before stepping outside, she put on her big Chanel sunglasses and a plain blue headscarf. Still several blocks from her destination, she jumped into a yellow taxi. Two minutes later, she was standing in Rashid Street, trying

to get her bearings. The shops were even more shabby than she'd
remembered. She stood amid the crowds and traffic fumes,
looking left and right in search of the side-street that would lead
her to Bilal. Two men in a shop doorway were looking at her, and
she felt suddenly unsafe. She continued walking, doing her best
impression of a confident women who knew her way around.
There it was: the little side-street that lead into a maze of low-
rent housing. She walked fast, past the kids playing catch with a
ball, past the old scrap-iron trader with his donkey and cart, past
the teenagers loading boxes of cooking oil onto a trolley. She was
glad of the shade offered by the narrow street, and the drop in
volume. But she was also aware of men in doorways watching her
movements, running their eyes up and down her body, from
headscarf to high-heels.

Occasionally she stopped to check the numbers on the houses,
hoping to God that she'd find the place soon. The street took a
sharp bend to the left, and then to the right again – and suddenly
she had arrived. There before her was number 27, a traditional
courtyard house, with dusty old bricks and double doors of
cracked wood. Overhead, a balcony jutted into the street,
complete with intricately carved latticework.

Loma removed her sunglasses for a moment, pushing her hair
back under the headscarf and wiping away the sweat with a

handkerchief. She assumed that Bilal was inside, but she had no idea who might answer the door.

She rang the bell and waited. After a while, she rang again, then knocked loudly. She tried the handle, but it wouldn't budge. She was on the point of checking her scrap of paper when she heard a voice behind her.

'Hello, Loma,' said Bilal.

'Good God! You gave me a fright!' she said, holding her forehead.

'I'm sorry. I've been watching you, just to be sure that you weren't followed.'

'Followed? Who would follow me?'

'One never knows.'

He took a large key from his trousers and unlocked the door. Inside, the house was wonderfully peaceful, if a little dusty. The central courtyard was open to the sun, with several pot plants and an old fountain that had long run dry. There was also a rusty bicycle with a buckled wheel, and some rickety chairs around a low table. Wooden pillars supported the floor above, and stone arches lead into numerous darkened rooms. The place had apparently been built for a large family, and a wealthy one at that.

'I see you're well protected,' said Bilal.

'What? Oh, the headscarf. I forgot all about it.'

She removed the scarf and set to work quickly with a hair brush.

'That's a new style, isn't it?'

'Yes, I had it done just now.'

'Well, you look very glamorous.'

'Thank you.'

'Come upstairs,' said Bilal.

Soon Loma was sitting on a dusty sofa in a large living room. The place was furnished with aging antiques, many in desperate need of repair. On the walls were several yellowing photographs, illuminated by the bare bulb that hung from the ceiling. The shutters were closed, keeping the daylight at bay.

Bilal left the room and returned with a plate of white cheese, some olives, a stack of bread and a bowl of peanuts. He also brought a jug of iced water, some arak and two glasses. Loma hadn't been expecting a party, and she began to wonder what else Bilal had in mind.

'So, here we are,' he said, taking a seat opposite and pouring two stiff drinks.

'Here we are,' said Loma. She took a large sip and looked around the room: 'It's a lovely old place. It certainly has lots of character.'

'Yes, it belongs to an old friend of mine. He inherited it from his family but never had any use for it. He keeps it for sentimental reasons, I think.'

'So why do you have the key?'

'Well, he lives in a village far away, so I keep an eye on the place, just to check that nobody has broken in. That sort of thing.'

Loma wondered how many other women had sat on the same sofa and listened to the same spiel while being plied with arak.

'So, you sounded quite upset on the telephone,' ventured Bilal.

'Yes, I'm sorry for all the drama. I had a horrible experience yesterday after our meeting.'

'Was it due to this person who has been bothering you?'

'Yes, I'm afraid so.'

'Did she threaten you?'

'Not exactly.'

'So, what's the problem?'

'I went to a party – well, an art exhibition – and this woman was there. I was pretty shocked to see her, so that was bad enough. But then I noticed that she had brought someone with her.'

Loma reached into her bag and took out a packet of cigarettes. With shaking hands, she lit one and took a long drag. 'This person was someone from my past, someone I had hoped never to see again.'

'Your alleged boyfriend?'

'No, not at all. I never see him these days. No, it was … well, it was a doctor.'

'What sort of doctor?'

'A gynaecologist. I had seen her in my youth, and I honestly never imagined she'd pop back into my life again. But there she was, being thrust into my face.'

'And why was that upsetting to you?'

'Well, because … because …'

'Loma, you needn't tell me the precise details. Allow me to make some assumptions, if I may? Perhaps in your youth, when you were young and inexperienced, you required some treatment from a gynaecologist? And perhaps you required that treatment because of some romantic relationship in which you were involved at the time? And perhaps you would rather that this troubling aspect of your past life be kept from public view?'

'Yes, that would be a reasonable set of assumptions,' she said.

'And perhaps the person with whom you were romantically involved is the same person with whom you are currently being linked by way of unfounded gossip?'

'That's exactly right. How on earth did you guess?'

'Well, it's part of my job to put two and two together. I have long experience in such things.'

'I suppose it all sounds rather sordid. You must think me a real tramp.'

'Not at all, my dear. Everyone makes mistakes in their youth. We live and learn.'

'I made some horrible mistakes, that's for sure.'

'But now you are a woman of the highest moral character. You are a kind and cultured woman, highly regarded by society and deserving of peace and happiness.'

'You really are too kind, Bilal.'

'Nonsense. I'm only speaking truthfully. If anyone deserves to be happy, it's you – and I will do my utmost to make that happen.'

Loma felt a lump in her throat. It was a long time since anyone had expressed sympathy for her suffering. Indeed, aside from Madeha, she had not confided properly in anyone for many years. Now a relative stranger was offering her kind words, and she felt her defences crumbling. If she wasn't very careful, she might start crying again.

'Have another drink,' said Bilal, leaning forward and pouring more arak.

'Thank you very much.'

'What this woman is doing could be interpreted as an attempt at blackmail.'

'Do you think so?'

'Oh, certainly. Has she demanded any money or favours from you?'

'No, not at all. I think she just enjoys causing me pain.'

'Even so, you're the wife of a diplomat, and it's not uncommon for blackmailers to target the families of political figures and state employees. In this way, they might apply political pressure or even obtain state secrets.'

'I hadn't thought of it like that.'

'Well, sadly, it's quite common. And we take such things very seriously. Based on your testimony so far, I believe there's good reason to investigate this woman on suspicion of attempted blackmail, perhaps even espionage.'

'And what would happen then?'

'If we found sufficient evidence, she would be arrested and charged.'

'And then?'

'And then the law would take its course. Such cases are tried in secret, so your involvement would never be made public.'

'But what would happen to … to the woman who has been giving me trouble?'

'It's hard to say, but I suspect she'd spend some time behind bars. If nothing else, it would give her an opportunity to reflect on her actions. She may come out a reformed character.'

'I suppose it's the only way forward,' said Loma, finishing her second glass of arak and pouring a third. 'I've tried everything else. She just won't give up.'

She gulped down the booze and looked into the empty glass. Tears welled up in her eyes, then ran down her cheeks. She clasped a hand over her face and began to cry.

Bilal rose from his chair and joined her on the sofa, placing a comforting arm around her shoulders. Loma leaned against him, eyes closed, melting in his strong arms. She inhaled his manly scent and wallowed in the warmth of his body.

'So, do I have your permission to proceed?' he said.

'With what?' she replied, looking into his eyes.

'With the investigation.'

'Yes, please. If you don't mind.'

'In that case, I'll start in the morning. If you can give me all the details, it shouldn't be too difficult to get some results.'

'I'll tell you everything I know.'

She closed her eyes again and buried her face in his muscular chest. He held her tight, kissing the top of her head, caressing her back with his strong hands.

'Perhaps you would like to lie down?' he said. 'You seem to be very tired.'

'Lie down? Where?'

'In the bedroom, of course.'

Loma paused, wondering if there were any good reason why she should decline the offer. She reflected on the arid desert that was her personal life, the years of heartache that she had endured. She thought of Riaz, to whom she had always been loyal, but who had repaid her with blatant infidelity. Finally, she reflected that Bilal was right in what he said: she did indeed have the right to be happy.

'Yes, alright,' she said.

Bilal stood up, and with a strength that took Loma's breath away, he gathered her into his arms and carried her from the room.

Intelligence HQ

It was 8am on a fine June morning, and Iraq's intelligence headquarters complex in Mansour was gearing up for another day at the grindstone. The first of several hundred personnel were trickling in through the main entrance. They showed their ID passes, then stood patiently while their bags were opened and their bodies scanned with metal detectors. Before long, the complex would be a hive of activity, with analysts, technicians, administrators and spies taking their seats, shuffling papers, answering phones and discussing secret operations behind closed doors. With a major war raging and threats of subversion on every front, there was no end of work to be done.

Today, one particular staff member was feeling the pressure, watching with rising annoyance as his briefcase was checked for bombs. Now in his mid-forties, Captain Omar Al-Ramadi had worked hard to prove himself over the years. His specialism was surveillance, with a particular focus on counter-intelligence, seeking to root out foreign spies and trouble-makers. He compiled his findings into dossiers that often formed the basis of corrective action. He had several scalps to his name, and there was every chance of his being promoted to major before his 50th birthday. The events of recent days, however, had caused him some alarm. Amid the miles of tape and the stacks of transcripts from numerous operations, he had missed a crucial item of information, something that should have been flagged up immediately. Instead, it had been sitting in his in-tray for weeks. Since Monday, he had been playing catch-up, seeking to produce an impressive report for his chief of section. This morning, he would present his findings – and he prayed to God that he would not be grilled on dates.

Omar's anxiety was compounded by the fact that he was late for work. He should really be at his desk by now, but instead he was standing in the entrance hall waiting while a security guard checked his briefcase.

'Is it really necessary to go through the papers?'

'I'm sorry, sir,' said the guard, closing the briefcase and handing it back.

Omar crossed the spacious entrance hall, with its large portrait of the beloved President, and took the lift to the third floor. His secretary was waiting in his office.

'Good morning, sir. The meeting has started.'

'Already?'

'They went in five minutes ago.'

'What about the film projector?'

'It's all set up.'

Omar grabbed some files and walked down the corridor to the big meeting room. He knocked and entered, taking his seat at a long table. The blinds were closed and the lights off, a silent movie flickering down the front.

The image was somewhat grainy, but there was no mistaking the nature of the action. A man and a woman lay naked in bed, exchanging kisses and caresses. At some point, the woman climbed on top and began to ride her partner, slowly at first, then gradually gaining in speed. She leaned forward and kissed him for a while, then sat bolt upright and continued rocking back and forth. Eventually, she stopped, kissed the man again, and dismounted. The pair lay motionless for a while, gazing at the ceiling.

The man took a pack of cigarettes from the bedside table and lit one, passing it to the woman. He then lit one for himself. They seemed to be talking now, but it was impossible to tell what they were saying without a soundtrack. There were microphone recordings too, of course, but they would have to be played on a different contraption.

Finally, the woman leaned on one elbow and continued talking while casually playing with her partner's penis. The man lay still and blew smoke rings into the air.

There was some sniggering around the table as people exchanged private jokes. Someone whispered that she should be careful with her cigarette. Omar clenched his teeth. The last thing he needed

was for one of his subordinates to start behaving
unprofessionally.

'Lights!' said a voice, and the lights went on.

Omar's boss was seated opposite – a gaunt, grey-haired man with
a reputation for cruelty. If anyone was going to end Omar's
career, it was this man. However, judging by his expression, the
major had enjoyed the film enormously.

'Captain Al-Ramadi, I'm glad you could join us,' said the major.

'I'm sorry I was late, sir.'

'Not at all, not at all. Your cine film is most entertaining.'

'Thank you, sir. I believe it shows ...'

'She's quite a sexy little thing, isn't she?'

'I believe she's very fond of her American lover, yes.'

'Would she like an Iraqi lover, do you think? Someone a bit older,
perhaps?'

There was more sniggering around the table.

'Well, sir, her name and address are in my report,' said Omar,
pushing the dossier across the table. 'If you wished to explore the
possibilities ...'

'I may well do that,' said the major, chuckling to himself and
beginning to browse the file.

Omar knew from harsh experience that it was unwise to speak to
the major when he was reading. Instead, he sat and waited,

wondering if he should wipe the sweat from his brow or leave it there to dry.

'This transcript,' said the major at last, 'the one in which Mr Uday Hussein is mentioned – do you have it in full?'

'Yes, sir. It has been typed in full, and I have a copy here for your information. The exchange you mention is on page 48.'

Omar slid another file across the table. The major began reading, a cruel smile on his lips.

'Well, well, well,' he said, 'this poor young woman does seem to have gotten herself mixed up with some bad company, doesn't she?'

'Indeed, sir. The American is keen to nurture a relationship with Nada – the daughter – who is personally acquainted with Mr Uday. This seems to suggest an attempt at infiltration. That's pure speculation on my part, of course.'

'And has this meeting taken place?'

'Which meeting, sir?'

'The lunch meeting with the daughter at … the Ishtar Sheraton?'

'Not yet, sir. According to the most recent tape recording, from Saturday afternoon, the meeting is to take place on Thursday.'

'What time, exactly?'

'No time has been set, sir, but we are monitoring the home telephones in the hope of intercepting something.'

'I'll have a team deployed to the hotel on Thursday.'

'Yes, sir.'

'You've been a little bit slow with this, but I don't think we've missed the boat entirely.'

'No, sir.'

The major continued reading, while the six other men around the table played with their cufflinks and stroked their moustaches. Finally, he set the documents to one side.

'Aside from the one mention of Mr Hussein, is there anything else you'd like to highlight?'

'Nothing of any great importance, sir. Zelfa has been instructed by her handler to draw certain information out of the American, but so far she's been a bit slow.'

'What information exactly?'

'If you look on page 10 of the report, sir, you'll see ...'

'Ah, yes, I see.'

The major read quietly to himself, his lips moving ever-so slightly.

'And there's no luck on that front yet?' he continued, pinning Omar with his hard eyes.

'Nothing that I can detect, sir, based on the microphone recordings.'

'I see.'

'There is one interesting development. The American has suggested that they might move to the United States and marry there, and she has agreed in principle. However, she said she would not leave without her daughter. Aside from that, everything seems fairly normal, so far as illicit love affairs go.'

'Yes, it's all perfectly normal, aside from the exceptional way that she rides cock,' said the major, and the room erupted in laughter. Omar allowed himself a smile.

The major gathered the documents and rose to his feet, followed swiftly by everyone else. At the door, he turned to Omar and spoke quietly: 'Have a copy of that film sent to my office, will you?'

'Yes, sir, of course.'

* * *

Just as Omar was returning to his office, another man was speaking with his immediate superior about an urgent matter of nation security. It was Bilal, up on the fourth floor, and he was taking a more laid-back approach to his troubles.

He sat in a comfortable swivel chair, while his boss – a full colonel – poured him a whiskey. Technically speaking, they should not be boozing on the job, but the colonel had taken the precaution of locking the door and closing the blinds. He returned the bottle to its draw, locked it, then sat down behind his mahogany desk.

'Cigar?' he said, lifting the lid on a wooden box.

'Thanks very much.'

They fell silent, wallowing in the ritual of biting and lighting,

sucking and blowing, until thick clouds of smoke filled the air.

'So, Bilal, tell me some more about this woman of yours.'

'Well, she's in a bit of a state, it must be said.'

'Nervous?'

'Very nervous, and understandably so.'

'Has she been very open with you?'

'Oh, totally open. She trusts me completely.'

'And you've become quite ... close to her?'

'Yes, I have. Purely in the interests of intelligence gathering.'

'Of course,' said the colonel, smiling.

'She was reticent at first, refusing to share any details of the

suspect. However, after several drinks and some expressions of

sympathy on my part, she gave me the full details.'

'She revealed all, did she?'

'Yes, she did, and I can see her doing so on a regular basis.'

They laughed, the colonel leaning forward to clink glasses with his

subordinate.

'And this other woman, what's her name again?'

'Selma.'

'Yes, Selma.'

'Does she seem the sort to give trouble?'

'She's not particularly political. Neither she nor her husband have any party affiliations. He's a businessman, though not very successful.'

'Bankrupt?'

'Not quite, but almost. They seem to be living on loans much of the time.'

'Any political views that we know of?'

'Nothing very coherent, although she has a big mouth. Apparently, she likes to say that Iraq is a dump and that it's only fit for pigs and criminals.'

The colonel raised his eyebrows. He had very little time for Iraqis who bad-mouthed their own country.

'What sort of threats has she made, exactly?'

'Well, I would describe them as guarded threats that may form the basis of a future blackmail attempt. Whether she wants money or classified information isn't quite clear at the moment, but I certainly think there's cause for concern.'

'Well, if you really think she could be a security threat, then I suppose she should be put under surveillance. Is there any sign that she's being directed by some foreign entity?'

'Not as yet, although she has a very large social circle.'

'Then close surveillance seems the way forward.'

'That's one option, of course, sir. However, I suspect we might have to move a little more quickly on this one.'

'Why is that?'

'Loma's husband, Riaz Mostafa, is in line for a promotion. Since uncovering a spy ring in London, he has been tipped for a senior position within the executive. In which case, we can't risk any sort of controversy. I would suggest some swift pre-emptive action: remove the threat and then conduct investigations at leisure.'

'Yes, I see that's the recommendation in your memo.'

The colonel took a sip of whiskey and leaned back in his chair. He puffed on his cigar and closed his eyes.

'I do think my office would be nicer with music,' he said at last.

'I'm a big fan of Italian opera. Do you like the opera?'

'Opera, sir? Yes, I like some of it. To be honest, I prefer something in my own language.'

'Such as?'

'Fairuz, of course.'

'Of course.'

'Mohamed Abdel-Wahab.'

'Ah, now, there's a man with a soul,' said the colonel, sitting up in his chair. 'I can honestly say, that if one were to compare his voice with …'

There was a knock at that door and the handle moved.

'Just a moment!' shouted the colonel.

He gathered the glasses and locked them in the draw along with the bottle. Rising from his seat, he walked to the door and unlocked it.

'Yes,' he said, adopting his most abrupt, professional manner.

'Sorry, sir,' said the young secretary. 'Some more papers to sign.'

'Very well, bring them in.'

Bilal rose to his feet.

'I'll be off then, sir, if there's nothing else.'

'No, nothing else. You have my permission to go ahead. Take whatever steps you consider necessary under the circumstances. Just keep me updated.'

'Thank you, sir.'

'And good luck with your future intelligence-gathering operations,' added the colonel, offering a sly wink.

'Anything for my country, sir,' said Bilal.

Pawns in a game

Zelfa had everything ready: the bottle of white wine in a bucket of ice, the pastries still in their box, the freshly-ground coffee, a pack of Marlboros – just waiting for the cellophane wrapping to be torn off. She had spent an hour on her hair and adorned herself with several items of gold jewellery. She'd put on her best linen suit and a cream blouse. Originally, she'd tried on some sandals, but in the end, she went for deck shoes, as if she were on the point of jumping onto her million-dollar yacht. Anyone looking at her right now, as she sat on the patio waiting for Selma, might think she was on top of the world.

And that's exactly what she was hoping for: she wanted to keep it together this time, to maintain her cool and exude strength. There was no reason to give Selma the satisfaction of seeing her in tears. People like Selma got their energy from the suffering of others, and so the only response was to act fine – or rather, to *be* fine. Zelfa turned the pages of a glossy magazine. She was looking at pictures of America: fashion models striking poses on the streets of New York, and in some leafy park, surrounded by dogs as the autumn leaves fell around them. Yes, she might be happy in America; she might start a new life and leave her woes behind. Nada would be safer too, away from the influence of evil people – those demonic forces with their roaming hands and dark desires. She jumped at the sound of the doorbell. Selma was right on time.

Loma stood up, ripped the cellophane off the Marlboros and lit one. She inhaled, closing her eyes as the nicotine began to circulate, swimming through her brain. The doorbell rang again; she exhaled and went to greet her guest.

'Selma, darling! Come in!'

'Zelfa, my dear! I've bought some baklava. I didn't know if you'd have anything in. Your cupboards are so often bear.'

'Thank you, but you needn't have bothered. I have plenty in.'

They took their seats and Zelfa poured the wine. The afternoon sun was still strong, but they were protected by a large canvas canopy overhead. It was one of the last investments of Zelfa's husband before the divorce.

'Pastry?' said Zelfa, opening the box of freshly-baked French delights.

'No, my dear. I'm trying to remain slim. But you go ahead.'

Zelfa helped herself.

'I won't be staying long,' said Selma.

'No? That's a shame. I've been looking forward to seeing you.'

'That's very kind of you, darling. But we both have busy lives. I only wanted to give you an update on things at our end.'

Zelfa felt a shock of fear running through her body, a tingle on the back of her neck as the little hairs stood on end. She put on her poker face and sipped her wine.

'I'm sure you'll want to hear the latest,' persisted Selma, hungry for some reaction.

'Oh, do you mean about Jerry?'

Zelfa hoped that she sounded like someone discussing a distant acquaintance.

'Yes, my dear, Jerry. If you recall, he's the man you're madly in love with. The man you're spying on for the *Mukhabarat*.'

Zelfa laughed.

'Oh, Selma. You're so dramatic. I'm hardly spying on him.'

'What would you call it, then?'

'Well, as you said yourself, husbands and wives often weed information out of each other. There's nothing particularly deceitful about that. Heavens, even buying a birthday present for one's husband requires some digging around to find out what they want. And as you said before, Jerry is undoubtedly innocent of these ridiculous allegations, so there's nothing to worry about. I'm sure it will all blow over, given time. Are you sure you don't want some *pain au chocolat*?'

'No, thank you,' said Selma. 'My dear sister, you're putting on a very brave performance, and that's very much to your credit. I admire a woman with courage. But you should remember that there are dimensions of this situation that are not entirely under your control.'

'Such as?'

'Such as the way in which your approach to all this is being interpreted by the *Mukhabarat*. They're keen to get some results, and that's the basis on which you'll be judged.'

'Well, I don't have any results yet, I'm afraid. So, they'll just have to be patient.'

Zelfa stubbed out her cigarette and lit another. Selma smiled, having scented blood.

'Well, that's what I'm here about, as it happens. Malaka tells me that the rumour at *Mukhabarat* HQ is that you don't seem to have been playing the game. You were supposed to ask certain questions, but you haven't even started. You've met with Jerry three times in the past two weeks, and not once have you pressed him on his job, the details of his career, his training, his education, or his political views. It's not like you haven't had the opportunity, either, because you seem to spend more time in bed than anywhere else.'

'What does that mean, exactly?'

'It means exactly what it sounds like. You've scored 10 out of 10 for sexual stamina, my dear, but zero points for grubbing up useful information. And Malaka informs me that if you don't start doing your job very soon, you will find yourself in hot water.'

Zelfa threw her head back and laughed. She had intended to sound unconcerned, even amused. Instead, she sounded highly anxious, on the point of hysteria.

'Hot water? What do they expect from me? Blood? I'm doing my best, but it's not easy, you know, to spring probing questions on a man who has been trained by the biggest, most sophisticated intelligence agency in human history.'

'You mean the CIA, of course?'

'Yes, of course.'

'So, you admit that Jerry works for the CIA?'

'Admit what? No, of course I don't admit that he works for the CIA. How on earth would I know that?'

'But you just admitted to it, my dear. It came out of your mouth just now. You said he works for the biggest, most sophisticated ...'

'I know what I said, Selma. You don't have to tell me what I bloody said.'

'Well, that's reassuring.'

'I'm only repeating that you've told me. I had no idea about it until you started this nonsense. It's you who said he was a spy, not me.'

'Except that you've just admitted to it.'

'Fucking hell, you're unbelievable! I didn't admit to anything!'

Zelfa realized in a flash that she should probably shut up. They had only been talking for two minutes, and already she had made a statement that could land her in serious trouble. After all, if she *did* have knowledge of Jerry's links to the CIA, how had she come by this information? And why hadn't she passed it to the authorities already?

'I think I will have one of those pastries,' said Selma, affecting an aura of deep relaxation, as if she really didn't have a care in the world. Zelfa passed the box and puffed on her cigarette.

'The point is, your attitude is not winning you any friends within the *Mukhabarat*. Malaka tells me that they want to see results – and fast. If you don't start asking Jerry some questions pretty soon, they'll assume you're not willing to cooperate. And then it's just one small step to being charged with treason.'

'Ha! Treason? You must be mad!'

'My darling, don't get hysterical. I'm only the messenger. Don't shoot the messenger.'

'Messenger? You're not a messenger, you're a fucking witch!'

'Do mind your language, Zelfa. It's not lady-like to use such terms. These pastries are wonderful, by the way, where did you buy them?'

'Never mind where I bought the fucking pastries, you evil woman! You come to my house and start ...'

Selma held up a finger and interrupted.

'There was one more thing that Malaka said. Apparently, if you're thinking of leaving the country – for example, to the USA – then you should inform the *Mukhabarat* ahead of time. That goes for

Nada too, of course. They've pretty much made this a rule, so I suggest you comply. You don't want to give them the wrong idea.'

Zelfa was on the point of throwing her wine in Selma's face, but she knew that a fight would ensue, and Selma would certainly win. If anyone was going to get the better of Selma, they'd have to shut her up for good. A bullet through the heart would do the trick. As with werewolves, a silver bullet might be best.

Selma took a large bite of her pastry and offered a philosophical reflection: 'I'm afraid, my darling sister, that you and I are just pawns in a game.'

Zelfa took long drag on her cigarette and closed her eyes. She couldn't see it at the moment, but there was bound to be a way out of this horrible situation. Just a little patience and a little courage, and very soon the solution would turn up. Things often had a way of fixing themselves.

'Oh, is that New York?' said Selma, picking up the glossy magazine. 'I do love New York. I went there years ago with Hassan. Have you been?'

'No, I've never been to America.'

'Of course, I was forgetting. Such a shame. So near and yet so far away.'

Zelfa had had enough. She stubbed out her cigarette and stood up.

'Get out.'

'I'm sorry, darling, what?'

'I told you to get out. Leave now before I throw you out.'

Selma smiled and rose to her feet. She leaned across and picked up two pastries.

'I'll just take a couple back for my dogs. They just *adore* croissants.'

After Selma was gone, Zelfa stomped upstairs and collapsed on the bed. Face down in the pillows, she began to cry.

If only I had a silver bullet, she thought, *I'd kill that witch myself.*

* * *

An hour later, Selma was in her front garden, rearranging the pot plants. The gardener had done well enough with the flower beds, but he was a complete idiot where pot plants were concerned. They needed to be in neat rows, not untidy clumps.

Selma had changed into Levi jeans and a white t-shirt, tidying her hair with an old scarf. Her hands were protected by gardening gloves, but she was worried about her nails. She also loathed sweating, and for these two reasons, she was taking the work very slowly, pausing occasionally to sip from her iced lemonade.

She was on the point of going inside for more ice, when two saloon cars and a GMC van pulled up in the street. Moments later, three men in suits and sunglasses came bursting through the garden gate, followed by several commandos in balaclavas, toting rifles.

'Selma Al-Hashemi?' said the tallest of the suited gentlemen.

Selma froze; she instinctively knew what was happening, but she had no idea why.

Within seconds she was surrounded, the same tall man taking hold of her left wrist and forcing it behind her back.

'Are you Selma Al-Hashemi?'

'Yes,' said Selma, laughing. 'I am Selma Al-Hashemi, but I have no idea why you're in my garden. Would you mind identifying yourself?'

She was doing her best to be light-hearted, hoping she might be able to sweet-talk her way out of this.

'Selma Al-Hashemi, I have a warrant for your arrest. Please come with me to the vehicle.'

'My arrest? What for? There must be some mistake. What are the charges?'

'You'll be informed of that later.'

'What do you mean by "later"? Where are you taking me?'

She tried to wiggled free, but the man pushed her arm further up her back. Another man came and took her other wrist. Moments later, she was being frog-marched toward the street.

'Wait! Wait! Can't I make a phone call first? I have children to look after. I need to call my husband and tell him what's happening. I can't just abandon my children.'

The smallest of the three men, who had been standing in the background, stepped forward.

'Okay,' he said, 'you can make one phone call. But that's it. Then we go.'

Selma was marched into her house, where her maid was standing with her mouth wide open while a commando pointed a rifle at her.

'The telephone is in the kitchen,' said Selma.

They entered the kitchen, and the men let go of her arms. She picked up her address book, which was on the counter, and began to flick through it. Who should she call? A lawyer? A friend? Maybe Malaka? Her husband would be useless in an emergency, of course, so that wasn't an option. Certainly, Malaka was the one with connections.

'Hurry up,' said the tall man. 'Don't take all day over this.'

Selma glanced at the door onto the garden. It had been left open to allow a breeze to blow through the house. She wondered what her chances were of making a dash to the end of the garden and over the fence. It seemed possible. But what then? She'd just be in another garden, and these men were bound to follow. They looked pretty fit, certainly fitter than her. They also had guns.

'Make your call, or we're leaving now,' said the big man, slamming the phone down on the kitchen counter.

She picked up the receiver and began to dial Malaka's number.

The phone was answered by a young woman.

'Hello. Velvet Modelling. How may I help you?'

'I want to speak to Malaka. It's very urgent.'

'I'm sorry, but she's not here at the moment.'

'Well, where is she? This is an emergency. I must speak to her immediately.'

'She's not here, madam. She's in a meeting somewhere else.'

'I need to get a message to her. Tell her that Selma has been arrested.'

'Selma who?'

'Selma Al-Hashemi. That's me. Just tell her that I've been arrested, and that I need her help. Do you think you can do that?'

'Yes, of course.'

The tall man grabbed the receiver and slammed it down.

'Phone call over. Time to go.'

Selma wanted to go upstairs and change, but they wouldn't allow any further delays. Instead, they marched her out of the house and into the back of the van. The maid followed as far as the front gate. Selma just had time to shout 'Tell Hassan to call Malaka!' before the doors of the van were slammed shut.

She was shoved into a seat and hand-cuffed, a hood placed over her head. Two men sat either side, their bodies pressed up against hers. She could smell their body-odour and their cheap aftershave. One of them placed a hand on her thigh, and she began to panic.

'Let me go!' she shouted, trying to stand.

She was slapped round the head and pushed back into her seat.

'You're not going anywhere,' said a voice in her ear. 'Not for a very long time.'

She burst into tears.

'Where are you taking me? Please tell me where you're taking me? What have I done? At least tell me what I've done. Maybe this is a mistake, a misunderstanding. If you tell me what this is about, we can clear it up.'

Her captors sat in silence as the vehicle raced through the streets, turning tight corners that forced the men to lean hard against Selma.

'I have connections,' she said. 'I'm well connected with the *Mukhabarat*, you know. I just need to speak with one person, and this will all be sorted out. If you help me know, I'll make sure there are no repercussions for you when I'm released. Say something! Answer me!'

Still the men were silent, and she felt the same large hand on her thigh once more.

She heard car horns outside and smelt the river. She was trying to guess where they were heading. If they turned right soon, then they were probably crossing the river. Moments later, the vehicle turned right. She timed the next stretch of road and noted a left-hand turn. Most likely, they were in Karkh now, heading for Mansour or even further west.

It seemed she was bound for one of two places: either a *Mukhabarat* interrogation centre, or to Abu Ghraib Prison. If the journey ended soon, it would be the former, while a longer ride would mean the latter.

She began to wonder what Malaka might do to secure her release, and how long that might take. Suddenly, it occurred to her that Malaka might, in fact, be behind all this. Perhaps it was her revenge for all those years of humiliation and name-calling? Just as this horrific thought was unfolding in Selma's brain, the van came to a halt.

So, the Mukhabarat interrogators want to have a go at me first, she thought.

She could stand being executed, but the thought of torture made her feel horribly sick. She'd much rather be finished off quickly. As she was dragged from the vehicle, she began to pray that someone would just put a bullet through her brain.

'Get moving, woman!' came a harsh male voice. 'We don't have all day to wait for Your Ladyship.'

She was grabbed by the arms and marched across an open area, then through a doorway. She tried to peer through the hood, but she could see no more than changes in lighting. There were men talking all around her, but she was so afraid of being struck again that she couldn't focus on what anyone was saying. Suddenly, she needed to pee very badly.

Next, she was marched down two flights of stairs. Round and round, she went, down and down, then through a door and along a corridor. She heard a bunch of keys jangling and a door being unlocked. The guards thrust her into a room, where she fell in a heap. The heavy metal door clanged shut. She lay on the bare concrete floor – sweating, breathless, and utterly terrified.

We're just pawns in a game, she thought.

News of an arrest

Loma picked up a newspaper as she walked through the lobby of the Alwiyah Club. Heading into the garden, she sat down at a table by the pool. She examined the front page, which was filled with news of the nation's numerous victories in the war with Iran. President Saddam Hussein was prominent, as ever, leading the fight, reassuring the people that victory was certain and that the personal sacrifices were worthwhile; the martyrs would get their rewards in Heaven.

She turned the pages, scanning the headlines in search of any item of news worth reading. However, she knew this to be a futile effort, because the only news of genuine interest to her these days was the fate of Selma. And that was the one topic on which she had absolutely no information – nor was she likely to find it in the newspapers.

When the *Mukhabarat* wanted someone to disappear entirely without comment, that's exactly what happened. The arrest was made – often in broad daylight – with little or no explanation, no press release from the authorities, and no details of an upcoming trial. The accused were simply whisked away, and that was that. Any newspaper editor that even thought of spilling the beans would be risking their own sudden disappearance.

When news of such events came to light, it invariably did so by way of gossip. Someone would see a person bundled into a vehicle, or they'd get a phone call from a distraught relative, and the story would begin to circulate. By way of whispers and mumbles, the news would spread: such and such a person had disappeared, and most likely they would not return.

These days, of course, Loma was keeping herself to herself, and so the chances of getting updates through the grapevine were practically zero. If she really wanted to learn of Selma's fate, she would have to hear it from Bilal – and he had made her promise to maintain radio silence for the time being. She was willing to do so, of course, but it was horribly hard.

She continued turning the pages, half expecting to stumble across news of a middle-aged housewife from Adhamiya who'd been murdered in her bed. Or perhaps it would be an overdose of sleeping pills, or else a naked corpse in the desert, half-eaten by wild dogs.

But no, she thought, *I mustn't let my imagination run wild. That won't help at all.*

She hurried through the foreign news, the arts reviews and the recipes, through the sports news and cartoons. Finally, she closed the newspaper and set it to one side.

She looked at the kids splashing about in the pool. They were enjoying themselves enormously, not a care in the world. They should enjoy it while it lasted, before love and marriage and gossip took over. Before politics and violence and everything else.

Beneath her flowery summer dress, Loma was wearing her swimming costume. She had also brought a towel. But she hesitated to take a dip or to spread out on a sun-lounger, as she'd done so many times in her youth. These days, after marriage and motherhood and so much else, she was more cautious. At the very least, she wanted to be fully dressed in case of another impromptu catfight.

Mikhaeel, an old waiter who had trained under the British, walked slowly across the lawn in Loma's direction. He was thin and white-haired now, but he knew all the club members, greeting them each time with genuine affection. Even in his seventies, he was not averse to turning on the charm.

'Madam Loma. It's is so lovely to see you back at the club.'

'Thank you, Mikhaeel. Good to see you too.'

'I was wondering why the garden looked so beautiful today, and now I see that it is due to your presence.'

'You really are too kind.'

'Not at all, madam. There are few flowers in the garden so beautiful as yourself. Iraq is honoured to have you return after so long an absence.'

'I'm glad to be back,' she said, wondering when he would offer to take her order.

'I was in London many years ago, of course,' he continued. 'I trained with IPC, the British oil company. That was in the 1950s, when I was a young man. London was wonderful back then; we had such a good time. I have no idea what it's like now.'

'It's still very nice, Mikhaeel, although a little expensive.'

'Oh, yes, very expensive. But worth every penny.'

He looked into the far distance, apparently lost in a happy memory.

'I think I'll order a drink, Mihkaeel.'

'Of course, madam.'

'I'll have a Turkish coffee please, no sugar.'

'Ah, you have become a Londoner.'

'Well, yes, perhaps. I'm also trying to watch my weight.'

'You have nothing to worry about on that front, madam. You are a jewel among pebbles.'

'Mikhaeel, you're as oily as ever,' she laughed.

He bowed deeply and wandered off.

Loma continued watching the children in the pool, taking turns to show off their diving technique. She missed her boys dreadfully. It had been almost two months since she'd departed, and she longed to hold them. They had spoken on the telephone every week, of course, but it wasn't the same. She wanted to put her arms around them and smother their faces with motherly kisses. But that would mean living once more with her husband, and she wasn't sure she could manage that. The idea of spending the night in bed with him made her flesh creep. She felt sick at the thought of making love with the man. He was so selfish, almost brutal. And on the odd occasion that he made an effort at romance, he came across as deeply insincere, as if he was seeking to charm some idiot young secretary into bed. Perhaps that's how he viewed his wife: some sort of idiot.

Bilal was different. He was smarmy too, perhaps, but at least he had genuine sex appeal. He was trim and muscular, like a soldier, and endowed with a watchful intelligence. He knew how to listen, and he never said more than was absolutely necessary. He had charisma and enough courage for the both of them. Between the sheets, he was obviously very experienced, playing her body like a maestro at his instrument.

She wondered whether she would have the chance to spend another evening with him. Or perhaps it was a one-time deal, payment for the disappearance of Selma? If she did see him again, it would perhaps qualify as an affair. She had never imagined herself possible of betraying her husband, and yet here she was, fondly remembering a recent sexual encounter with another man. She wondered whether she ought to be ashamed of herself, but she concluded that such self-recriminations could wait for some future date. Right now, she intended to relax.

A girl jumped into the pool, sending water splashing in all directions. Loma thought of Madeha, and what she might be up to. No doubt she was in prison. She would be lucky to ever see a swimming pool again. She would be lucky if she saw the sky.

Poor girl, thought Loma, *she followed her heart, and now she's paying the price.*

Tears welled up in her eyes and rolled down her cheeks.

'Loma, my dear, why all the tears?'

Loma looked up to find Malaka staring down at her. She was wearing an expression of concern, but from Loma's experience, it was probably skin deep. Malaka laid a hand on Loma's shoulder and bent forward to exchange kisses before taking a seat at the table.

'You mustn't cry too much, my dear,' she continued. 'You'll ruin your good looks.'

'Oh, I think my good looks are long gone anyway.'

'Nonsense, you're still very attractive, even after two children. Riaz doesn't know how lucky he is. Here, dry your eyes.'

She handed Loma a clean handkerchief.

'Thank you. I'm just missing my children, that's all. Watching those kids enjoying themselves in the pool reminded me.'

'Yes, I quite understand. And you've had a stressful year too.'

'Well, yes, I suppose I have. It's quite exhausting to move house, and London isn't so relaxing as everyone thinks.'

'You have my full sympathy, my dear. I could never be an ambassador's wife.'

As Malaka looked around for a waiter, Loma wondered just how much she knew about her personal life. Did know, for example, that her marriage was a failure? If there was any gossip going around, this queen of whores was bound to have picked it up.

'So, tell me,' said Malaka, lighting a cigarette, 'how long are you staying in Baghdad?'

'I'm not sure. I have a few important things to do here. My husband seems to be coping alright without me.'

'Well, there's plenty to keep your interest here.'

'Yes, there's the club, of course. I don't have too much time for socialising, but I don't think I'll get bored.'

'I was thinking more of the recent developments.'

'What developments?'

'Oh, well, if you don't know about it, then I won't say anything. I don't want to drag you into the whole sordid business. You've always remained above such things.'

'I'm lost. What sort of sordid business are you talking about?'

'Well, have you heard about our lovely neighbour Selma?'

Loma's heart skipped a beat. She did her best to remain composed.

'What about her?'

'You'll never guess.'

'No, I probably won't guess. So why don't you just tell me?'

Malaka looked around again, as if to check that nobody was listening. The gesture struck Loma as entirely fake, a show intended to heighten the sense of drama.

'Don't repeat this,' whispered Malaka, leaning across the table, 'but she was detained last week by the *Mukhabarat*.'

She sat back in her chair, a faint smile on her lips. Loma knew that her reaction was being watched closely, and by a woman well skilled in the arts of deception and interrogation.

'That's dreadful,' said Loma at last, rummaging through her handbag.

'Yes, it is dreadful, isn't it? The poor woman! One can only imagine what she's going through.'

'Is she still in detention?'

'I'm only repeating what I heard, of course, but my sources tell me that she's locked up very tightly and isn't likely to be released any time soon. She might be away for years.'

Loma was still rummaging through her handbag. She had no idea what she was supposed to be looking for. Anything to avoid eye-contact with the woman across the table.

'Have you lost something?' offered Malaka.

'No, I'm fine. I just thought I had another lipstick with me.'

'Your lipstick looks fine, my dear. I shouldn't worry yourself about it.'

Loma leaned back in her chair and gazed at the pool. So, it really had happened: Selma really had been arrested. Bilal wasn't kidding when he said he would take action. And if Malaka's sources were correct, she was still under lock and key.

Loma didn't know whether to be happy or horrified. This was what she'd wanted. But now that it had happened, she felt dreadful. For the first time in her life, she had deliberately plotted against another human being and brought about their ruin. It didn't feel good. In fact, she felt sick.

'My dear,' said Malaka, 'are you sure you're alright? You look a little pale.'

'No, I'm fine. I'm fine, really. I think should probably have had some lunch.'

In fact, Loma was thinking of getting up and leaving, but she thought she might incriminate herself by fleeing the scene.

Just then, Mikhaeel arrived with her Turkish coffee. He placed a little white porcelain cup on the table, pouring the coffee with a skilled hand.

'Bring me a Nescafé,' said Malaka, using the abrupt tone that she reserved for serving staff. 'Leave the milk on the side.'

'Of course, madam,' said the waiter, departing with a bow.

Alone once more, the two women lapsed into silence, Malaka watching closely as Loma stirred three sugars into her coffee.

'So, what was she arrested for?' ventured Loma at last.

'I have no idea. I can't imagine that she's actually broken the law. My best guess is that someone has stitched her up – someone she has offended in the past. Heaven knows, Selma has offended a great many people.'

'Yes, I suppose she has.'

'She was never particularly kind to you, if I remember rightly.'

'Oh, I wouldn't say that. She was just a bit jealous ...'

Loma stopped herself. She had never been too good at this sort of talk. She was too honest, for one thing. She only had to open her mouth and all her secrets started pouring out.

'Jealous of what, my dear?'

'Oh, I don't know. She's just that type.'

Loma sipped her coffee, leaving lipstick on the cup. She decided that she absolutely must change the subject. But what on earth could she talk about with this dreadful woman?

'You're quite right, my dear,' said Malaka. 'You've hit the nail on the head. It was jealousy that did her in. A woman can't go through her whole life like that without someone setting her straight. Jealousy is a sin. She was bound to get her punishment at some point. If not from you, then from God.'

'Why would I punish her?'

'If it was you that had her arrested, I wouldn't blame you one little bit.'

'Me? What on earth are you talking about? I never lifted a finger.'

'Well, you wouldn't need to, would you? With your husband's connections, it would only take a quiet word in somebody's ear, and the job would be taken care of. I must say, Loma, I admire you.'

'Admire me?'

'Butter wouldn't melt in your mouth. That's what everyone thinks. And yet, when the chips are down, you're really quite deadly. I honestly admire you, my dear. You're a strong woman.'

'I'm sorry, but you've got it all wrong. I really had nothing to do with it.'

Loma was getting quite agitated now, and in objecting to Loma's veiled accusations, she jerked her arm suddenly, spilling coffee down her front. Great globs of it began soaking into the white cotton.

'Oh, no!' she said, getting to her feet and dabbing at it with the handkerchief.

Malaka remained in her chair, smiling gently to herself. It was a smile of satisfaction, because until this moment, she hadn't been entirely sure that Loma was to blame. Now, of course, it was as plain as day.

'Don't worry, my dear,' she said. 'Your secret is safe with me.'

Loma looked her in the eyes and knew there was no point in issuing a denial.

'I'll have to go home and put this dress in to soak,' she said.

'Don't worry, I'll pay for the coffee. You run along home.'

'Thank you.'

'My pleasure.'

Loma jumped into her car and sped away from the club. She had no idea where she was going. She should, of course, be going home to soak her coffee-stained dress, but that hardly seemed important now. What was actually important was the news of Selma's arrest, and the fact that Loma was responsible for it. She felt as if she'd just killed someone, and it was quite sickening. Everyone knew that once the *Mukhabarat* bundled you into a car and took you off to prison, you might never see the light of day again. You might face many forms of torture and finally death. Right now, Selma might be undergoing interrogation or worse, and all because Loma had decided to rat on her.

What made it worse was that a pattern seemed to be emerging. First, she had ratted on Madeha, and now on Selma. So, two women were locked up for good, shut up in some dungeon on false charges, without the chance of a fair trial. And all due to Loma's weakness and selfishness. Never in her life had she imagined herself capable of such things. How could she ever look herself in the mirror again after this?

She drove aimlessly around the neighbourhood, turning left and right at random. Twice she passed by Paradise Square, then headed north toward Adhamiya. She was apparently intending to speak to her mother. But what would she say? Was she going to spill the beans and admit to turning Selma in? Was she going to tell her about Bilal?

No, it was impossible. And anyway, there was always the danger that she'd run into Hassan or one of Selma's offspring. She couldn't possibly look them in the eye. If Malaka suspected her involvement, then they certainly would too. They might kill her. She turned around and headed south again, driving along by the river. She crossed a bridge, heading west toward Mansour. If she was going to collapse in a heap – which she probably was – then she should do so in the privacy of her own home.

Perhaps, when she was calmer, she could phone London and speak with her boys. Just hearing their voices would remind her of the goodness of life. Being the mother of two beautiful children made life meaningful. But what if she started to cry down the phone? She wouldn't want her boys to hear her in such a state. And what if it was Riaz who answered the phone? She really couldn't speak to him right now.

Suddenly, she felt horribly alone. There was, in fact, nobody that she could talk to, nobody to confide in. Right now, at this advanced stage in her life, she was totally isolated.

She sped through the streets, wiping the tears away as she went, half wishing that she would crash and put an end to the whole sad story.

But, of course, there was always Bilal – strong, reliable, kind Bilal, with his masculine charm and oceans of official power at his fingertips. She turned into a side street and parked. Grabbing her purse, she walked half a block to a payphone. She took out Bilal's card and tried his office number.

'Hello,' said a female voice.

Loma hung up.

She dialled the car-phone and got an instant reply. This time it was Bilal.

'Hello.'

'Hello, Bilal. It's Loma.'

'Loma, what a nice surprise. How are you?'

'Not great, actually.'

'No? What's wrong?'

'I'm … well, I heard some news today.'

'What news?'

'Is it true?'

Bilal didn't answer. In the background, Loma could hear a car horn and someone shouting.

'Listen,' he said at last, 'let's discuss this in person. It's better.'

'Okay.'

'How about tomorrow night at 7pm?'

'Okay, where?'

'Same place as last time.'

Loma knew what that meant. There would be conversation, of course, but lots more besides. But she wasn't afraid of it. In fact, it's what she wanted, what she needed more than anything.

'Sure,' she said. 'I'll see you there.'

'See you there.'

She blew her nose and continued driving home, this time within the speed limit, obeying all the rules of the road. That one phone call seemed to have fixed everything, like a shot of heroin entering the vein. She felt so much calmer, totally reassured. In fact, she felt like two big, strong arms were wrapped around her, holding her safe in a warm embrace.

Interrogation

Selma spent the first ten minutes of her detention laying completely still, just listening. She was convinced that at any moment a team of guards might burst in and start to beat her. She had heard countless stories about the brutality of such places, and she fully expected that it was just a matter of time before someone started breaking her bones. Her plan was to play dead, and perhaps the beating would be finished sooner.

Finally, she shuffled into a corner and removed the hood from her head. The handcuffs were cutting into her wrists. She did her best to place them in a comfortable position, but without much success. She sat with her back to the wall, knees to her chest, staring into the gloom.

So far as she could tell, there was no light fixture in the room. However, some light from the corridor was filtering in through a grill high on the wall. Once her eyes had adjusted, she was able to see some details of her new accommodation.

The room was three metres wide by four metres long, built entirely of concrete. There was no furniture in the place: no table, no chairs, no shelves, not even a bed. In one corner was a hole in the floor, and she soon discovered that this was the toilet. The stench emanating from this hole suggested that it had rarely, if ever, been cleaned. She pulled down her jeans and squatted over it, emptying her bladder, which had been full to bursting.

Then she resumed her position in the other corner, watching and listening, wondering what on earth would happen next. Aside from the immediate fear of violence, what troubled her most was not knowing why she was there. She had no doubt that her big mouth was legendary, and she had slandered the authorities on numerous occasions. But this had never led to her arrest before. Of course, it could be that the authorities had finally gotten around to dealing with her case, after all these years of trying to ignore her. But that seemed unlikely somehow.

No, this must be the work of a particular enemy, and she began to compile a list of possible suspects – people she had mortally wounded by way of slander, gossip or outright abuse. The list was long, and just when she thought she'd been through everyone, another possibility from the past would loom into view.

She pondered each particular case, each fake friendship, each false accusation, each public spat and malicious rumour. She racked her brains in search of any incident or event that stood out as being more serious, more deserving of revenge on this scale. The obvious choice, of course, was Loma. The woman was, after all, her arch enemy. But this possibility she dismissed for one simple reason: Loma didn't have the guts to pull a stunt like this. She was too weak, too nice, too cowardly by far.

Of course, it might have been Malaka, but why on earth would she turn on her number-one secret agent, just when they seemed to be getting results out of Zelfa and Jerry? No, that didn't make sense. Unless, of course, Malaka had concluded that Selma had already served her purposes and could now be discarded?

Yes, that was a possibility. After all, if anyone had influence with the *Mukhabarat*, it was Malaka. She had been dealing with them for years. The bitch only had to pick up a phone …

Her thoughts were interrupted by the sound of the heavy metal door being opened. She instinctively got to her feet, and two male guards rushed in and started to beat her with batons, yelling at her to sit down.

She resumed her position in the corner, and they stopped beating her. Another guard came in, throwing two blankets on the floor. This, presumably, was to be her bed. Next, a bucket of cold water was brought in, apparently representing her bathroom. And finally, a pile of clothing was dropped on the floor.

'Change into your prison clothes,' said the guard, a chubby man with a thick moustache.

Everyone left, and the door closed behind them, the key rattling in the lock.

Selma went to the bucket and splashed water on her face. She was on the point of drinking some, but then decided against it. There was no knowing what germs it might contain.

She inspected the prison clothing and found it to consist of a blue dress of rough cotton and a pair of flip-flops. She stripped off, splashing more water on her body to wash away the sweat, and then dressed in her prison uniform. She folded her own clothes into the shape of a pillow, and set about making a bed from the two blankets.

She had no idea of the time, and no way of telling day from night in the windowless room. She cursed herself for having removed her watch to do the gardening. That little object might have made all the difference.

As she sat on her rock-hard bed, she noticed the cockroaches for the first time. They ran across the floor, heading down into the toilet hole, then back to the door, where they slipped into the corridor, or scampered up the wall to the grill where the light came in. Normally, she would have smashed them with a shoe or sprayed them with insecticide. But there was no insect spray handy, and she wasn't going to get her flip-flops filthy on day one. And anyway, there was nothing else to see or do in this little concrete box. If nothing else, cockroaches provided some sort of entertainment.

A while later, she was awoken by a metallic scraping sound. Looking round, she saw a tray of food being passed through a hole near the bottom of the door. Selma realised how hungry she was, and the plate of brown bread and lentils disappeared in no time, washed down with a cup of cold water.

She lay on her blankets once again and watched as the cockroaches crawled over her empty bowl, eating up the crumbs. She felt like a giant a cockroach. To the authorities, of course, that's all she was. And pretty soon, they might smash her.

* * *

She dreamed that she was running naked through a dark, deserted city. She was being chased by people with knives, but every time she tried to see their faces, they would slip into the shadows. And then she would start running again: along streets, down alleyways, through houses, jumping from windows, climbing over garden fences. She was terrified that they might catch her, because if they did, she would be cut to ribbons. She was sweating and thirsty, desperately thirsty.

'Get up!' shouted the chubby guard. 'Get up, you stupid woman! Stand up or I'll beat you!'

Selma sat up, bleary eyed. At first, she didn't know where she was. Then it all came flooding back: the arrest, the prison cell, the cockroaches.

The guard grabbed Selma by the hair and yanked her upwards. She staggered to her feet, her body aching from yesterday's beating and a night on a concrete floor. As she was slipping into her flip-flops, she noticed the guard staring at her legs. She tried to pull her dress down to cover them, but it barely reached to her knees.

The guard smiled a greedy smile and grabbed her by the arm, yanking her toward the door. She resisted at first, worried at what might be waiting in the corridor.

'Where are you taking me?' she demanded.

'You'll find out soon enough.'

She pulled her arm free and stepped back against the far wall.

'I'm not leaving this room until you tell me where I'm going.'

The guard was furious. He grabbed the handcuffs, which were still on Selma's wrists, and yanked hard. She screamed as the metal cut deeper into her skin, gnawing at the bruised bones.

'Ow!' she yelled. 'Stop it! Stop it, please!'

The guard yanked harder, dragging her into the corridor. With the help of another guard, she was escorted up one flight of stairs, along several winding corridors, and finally pushed into a yet another small room.

This room was different, though, being much smarter. It was painted pale green, and there were white tiles on the floor. Overhead was a light bulb, and in the centre of the room was a metal table. There were three metal chairs too, and a pad of paper on the desk, along with two ballpoint pens.

'Sit down!' shouted the guard, and Selma sat down.

The door closed behind her, and for a while she was alone. On the far side of the room, was another door, perhaps leading to another office, and on the wall was a small mirror. There was a grey filing cabinet in one corner too, and an electric power socket. There were no windows.

Selma realised that she was shaking with fear. She was also sweating. Normally, she dealt with danger by talking, by cursing and striking postures. And if all else failed, she was ready to fight: to pull hair and dig her nails in.

But here, she had no defences, none at all. She was quite powerless. It was a new sensation, and she didn't like it one little bit.

The door behind her swung open, and someone stepped inside. 'Thank you,' said a voice. 'You can leave us now. I'll ring when I'm finished.'

'Yes, sir,' said the guard.

And the door closed.

A young man in a blue suit came into view, carrying a briefcase. He took off his jacket and hung it on the back of a chair, then he sat down on the far side of table. He opened the briefcase and took out various papers, reading through them slowly. As he did so, he lit a cigar and began to puff, filling the room with smoke.

Selma thought the man couldn't be more than 30 years old. He was trim, fit-looking, with very short hair, like a soldier. He wore a neat little moustache, and she noticed a small scar above his right eye. He was quite handsome, and under different circumstances, she would probably have flirted with him. They might even have taken it further.

She realised suddenly that her hair must be a complete mess, and she ran her fingers through it, trying desperately to give it some shape.

'So, how are you being treated so far?' said the man at last, leaning back in his chair.

'Not too badly, I suppose. I could do with upgrading my accommodation. A bed would be nice, for a start.'

Selma had tried to inject some humour into her voice, but she realised that she had failed. Instead, she just sounded resentful, grumbling.

'Well, it's not a hotel,' said the young man.

'May I ask who you are?'

'No, you may not. I'm asking the questions.'

'Are you my lawyer?'

The man laughed, throwing his head back, as if Selma had made a fantastic joke.

'No, I'm not your lawyer. You don't have a lawyer. I'm here to ask you questions.'

'But I should know your name, if you're to ask me questions in an official capacity.'

'You may call me Mr Saif, if you wish.'

'Is that your real name?'

'No, of course not.'

'Why am I here?'

The man laughed again, apparently amused by Selma's question.

'I suppose you have no idea?'

'That's right.'

'And you're just shocked to find yourself being treated this way, because you've never done anything wrong in your life. Is that right?'

'I won't say I've never done anything wrong in my life. But if something I did has landed me in this place, then I'd like to know what it is.'

'Well, Madam Selma, I'm afraid I'm not at liberty to provide you with any information on that front. All information concerning your case is subject to a code of secrecy, as with all cases relating to nation security.'

'National security?'

'Yes, as in the security of the nation.'

'What are you talking about? How on earth have I threatened the security of the nation?'

'As I said, it's my job to ask the questions. Your job is to answer them.'

'Well, I'll answer as best I can. But it would help if you'd at least give me some idea of what this is all about. Maybe I can explain. It's possible that there's been a mix-up. I mean, obviously there's been a mix-up. So, if you just tell me ...'

The young man slammed his hand down on the table. He was on his feet now, leaning forward, his face close to Selma's. His face was red, and Selma could see suddenly see that he had the cruel eyes of a torturer. The handsome young man was gone, and in his place was a man who got his kicks from causing fear and pain.

At the very least, she thought, *I should avoid making him angry.*

Mr Saif straightened up and removed his tie, undoing his top shirt button. He then removed a key from his trouser pocket and unlocked the door on the far wall. Throwing the door open, he leaned in and switched on a light.

He then sat on the table in front of Selma. He sat so close that his legs brushed up against hers. Little beads of sweat had appeared on his forehead, and Selma wondered whether it was from nerves or exertion – or perhaps excitement.

'Let me see your hands,' he said.

Selma held up her hands, ready to pull them back at a moment's notice.

'Those hand-cuffs look very painful, Madam Selma.'

'Yes, they are.'

'I suppose you'd like them removed?'

'If you don't mind.'

'For every problem there is a solution. That's assuming, of course, that you know who your friends are.'

Selma watched his face for clues as to where this might be going. Whatever he had in mind, she felt sure that it would involve her stepping through the door into the other room.

'Do you know who your friends are?' continued Mr Saif.

'I don't seem to have many friends at the moment.'

'Well, let's see. I could be your friend, if you really wanted.'

'I see. So, does that mean you'd be kind enough to remove my hand-cuffs?'

He reached down, and very gently took hold of her wrists. Then, leaning closer, he looked into Selma's eyes and said: 'The key is in the other room.'

He got off the table, and walked to the open doorway, pulling Selma behind him. She followed, her body shaking with fear.

As she stepped through the doorway, she glanced around the room. There was just one item of furniture: an iron-framed bed of the sort used in army barracks. There was an old mattress on it, but no sheet and no pillow. On the floor was a large metal box, presumably full of tools.

Selma decided that she'd had enough. Whatever this sick young man had in mind, whether it was sex or torture – or a bit of both – she really didn't want any part of it.

Mr Saif yanked hard on the hand-cuffs and Selma screamed at the top of her lungs. He looked in her eyes, his face red with fury. He clenched his fist, apparently preparing to punch her in the guts. Before he could strike, she launched herself forward, taking him by surprise. He staggered back, tripping over the metal box. She jumped on top and began scratching at his face with both hands. The long nails drew blood, just as they had many times before. Mr Saif covered his face and wriggled to one side, then scrambled to his feet and darted from the room. Selma lurched after him, bursting into the other room, only to find him on the other side of the table, holding a pistol. He had it pointed in her direction, his finger on the trigger.

For a brief moment, she contemplated running at him. He'd be forced to fire, and her ordeal would be over before it really got started. While she hesitated, two guards burst in from the corridor, brandishing batons.

'Beat her,' said Mr Saif.

The guards beat Selma for a full minute as she lay on the floor screaming and pleading for them to stop. Just as they seemed to have run out of energy, Mr Saif stepped up, took one of the batons and continued the job, landing blow after blow on her back and shoulders. She raised her hands to stop him, and he cracked two of her fingers with the next blow. She curled up in a tight ball of agony, hoping to God that it would end soon.

When at last it did end, Mr Saif leant over her and said very softly:

'We seem to have gotten off to a bad start, Madam Selma. Perhaps next time you'll be more cooperative? I really do advise it, because you're going to be locked up for a very, very long time.'

He then handed the baton back to the guard.

'Take her away,' he said, and Selma was dragged back to her cell, broken fingers and all.

* * *

In the days that followed, Selma's priorities changed dramatically. First of all, she no longer wasted time on trying to work out why she had been detained. Clearly, she wasn't going to get any straight answers on that front. Perhaps if she had a visitor at some future date, she might make another attempt at gaining some information. But for the time being, there really was no point. Second, she needed to decide on a policy for dealing with the staff here, a policy that would minimize her chances of getting badly mistreated. Presumably, if she hadn't fought against Mr Saif, he would have raped her. So, in this respect, there was something to be said for putting up a fight. On the other hand, if she'd allowed him to have his filthy way, she might have avoided a beating – and she wouldn't be nursing two broken fingers.

Of course, she had always been found flirtation to be an effective means of manipulating men, but in this environment, there were no half-measures. If she wasn't careful, she'd end up being screwed by every man in the building. What she needed was another approach entirely, but she had no idea what that might be.

Finally, she was in great pain. She had bound her broken fingers together using a strip of cloth torn from a blanket. But while this immobilized them, it didn't stop the pain. Between her sore wrists and her broken fingers, and the bruises all over her body, she felt like a giant toothache. In fact, she was so sore that she could hardly move, and she rarely got more than half an hour's sleep before being woken by a throbbing limb. She would shift position on the hard floor, finally dropping off to sleep, only to wake soon after.

Sometimes, she would close her eyes and try to recall the faces of those she loved – which basically meant her two offspring, Ahmed and Sheza. This was a comfort at first, but the more she tried to recall them, the more difficult it became. Finally, she had trouble remembering what they looked like, beyond the vaguest of outlines. Then she felt truly alone.

Every day, she was woken by shouting guards, yanked to her feet and told to stand still while a new bucket of water was brought in. Every day, three times a day, a meal was pushed through the hole in the door. And every day, she would watch the cockroaches – her only friends – scurrying back and forth, exploring her toilet and eating her crumbs.

She had traded her Nina Ricci perfume for the smell of urine. All the comforts of home were gone, as were her beautiful clothes, her jewellery and make-up, also her large house and splendid garden. Now she was in the very gutter of life, being treated like human garbage. She had heard endless stories about *Mukhabarat* detention centres, but she had never imagined that she'd see the inside of one. Soon, perhaps, she would see Hell itself.

She often recalled the Baghdadi saying: 'Hearing about something is not the same as experiencing it for yourself.'

Then, one day, after what she presumed was the evening meal, she began to feel a little dizzy. Her limbs felt heavy too, as if she'd had some sort of stroke – or been drugged. She tried to sit up straight, but she only slumped over on her side. Before long, she was drifting into a strange dream.

In that dream, a door opened and light flooded the room. Several men were standing over her, talking, but she couldn't make out what they were saying. Soon, there was just one man, and the room went dark again. The man lay on top of her, pulling down her underwear, forcing himself inside. She knew it should hurt, but it didn't, because she was numb from head to toe, as if she were made of cotton wool.

Through the mist, she could hear a deep sound, like thunder. She focused all her energies and managed to make out the voice of a man. He was speaking in her ear, and his voice seemed strangely familiar.

'Do you like it like that?' he said. 'Can we be friends now?'

Tears at bedtime

Loma had slept deeply, aided by two sleeping tablets and a bottle of white wine. It took a long while for the sound of the telephone to register, and even longer for her eyes to open. In the end, it was Sadah who handed her the receiver.

'It's your husband,' whispered the old woman.

'Yes?' croaked Loma.

'What on earth is going on?' demanded Riaz. 'I've been calling for hours. Why aren't you answering?'

'I'm sorry, I was sleeping.'

'Why are you so tired? Have you been out partying?'

'What? No, I just took some sleeping pills.'

'If I find that you've been out to all hours with your stupid friends, I'll have something to say about it. I won't have you shaming me with your loose behaviour.'

'Loose behaviour? What on earth are you talking about?'

Loma was sitting up in bed now, straining to open her eyes. What was Riaz referring to? Had someone been talking? Had Selma's gossip finally reached his ears?

'Anyway,' continued the husband, 'I don't have time for that. I have more important things to consider. I'm coming to Iraq in five weeks' time. I need you to come back to London immediately and help bring the children.'

'You're coming home? Why?'

'I've been promoted to the Ba'ath Party National Command. It's a big step up. I have to wrap up in London and start my new job next month. You need to collect the children. I don't have time to take care of all that.'

Loma was speechless, stunned at the prospect of living with Riaz once more.

'You might congratulate me,' he said, clearly annoyed.

'Yes, I'm sorry, darling. Congratulations! It's wonderful news!'

'I need you here next week. The children will have to be taken out of school early. I'll leave that to you.'

'But can't they stay until the end of term at least? What about their school work?'

'Loma, I don't have time to argue. Just be here next week.'

'Alright, I'll start making arrangements. Can I speak with the boys?'

'They go to their friends' houses on Saturdays now. I can't have them hanging around the house while I'm so busy. I'll tell them you're coming next week.'

'Alright.'

'Goodbye.'

'Goodbye.'

Loma put down the phone and stared straight ahead. She was in a daze, as if she'd been hit round the head. How was she supposed to cope with such changes? She wanted to see her boys, of course, but how could she go back to playing the role of dutiful wife? After so much had changed – after the arrests of Madeha and Selma, and after Bilal – how could she play that part again? She had no idea if it was even possible. She might go mad.

At the very least, she needed time to think. If Riaz didn't start his job for five weeks, she could perhaps delay her return to London, find some excuse and remain in Baghdad until she'd decided on a plan. For one thing, she needed to make progress on finding Madeha. She'd come back specifically for that purpose, and yet she'd achieved nothing.

She checked the bedside clock and found, to her horror, that it was already 2pm. She had slept right through lunchtime. She got out of bed and stomped off into the bathroom, indulging in a long, warm shower while she pondered her options. She had meant to identify someone who might be able to help locate Madeha, but so far, she'd drawn a blank. She knew all sorts of people connected with the law courts and the police – but nobody she could trust with this sort of enquiry.

Of course, Selma was now personally acquainted with the prison system, but Loma could hardly call on her for assistance. Selma would rather see her dead. Indeed, if they were ever to meet again, it might easily become a fight to the death. No, Selma wasn't an option.

Bilal was the obvious choice, and yet he was a loyal member of the *Mukhabarat*, an institution dedicated to tracking down and punishing the likes of Madeha. Indeed, so far as Loma knew, Bilal may have been among those who interrogated Madeha before locking her up. How would he react to an enquiry after the traitor's wellbeing? Probably not well.

Having drawn a blank once more, Loma dressed and headed downstairs to the kitchen. Sadah had prepared a delicious lunch, setting it out on the patio, and Loma soon found that she was ravenous. As she munched her way through the salad and beans, washed down with coffee and juice, she reflected that life would be so much easier if she could just go with the flow: forget about Madeha, let Selma rot in jail, satisfy Riaz like a dutiful wife, and raise her beloved children.

Isn't that what any sensible woman would do? she thought. *Isn't the path of least resistance also the path to contentment?*

* * *

It was nearly 6pm by the time she left home. She drove to Joseph's salon, where she sat and listened passively to his gossip, emerging a while later with her hair full and wavy. She drove once more to the multi-storey car park, donned her scarf and shades, and took a cab to Rashid Street. Minutes later, she was sitting on the old sofa in the quaint little room, with its rickety furniture and yellowing photographs.

Bilal was quiet, focussed on setting out the usual delights: cigarettes, nuts, bread, cheese, olives, and arak. Loma had gone to the trouble of bringing a box of klecha, fresh from the bakery. She lit a cigarette, closed her eyes and blew a cloud of smoke.

'You seem tired, my dear,' said Bilal, finally taking a seat on a kitchen chair opposite her.

'Oh, tired doesn't even begin to describe it.'

'Are you not sleeping?'

'I'm sleeping fine, but only with the aid of pills. I slept until 2pm today. Riaz phoned, and he was furious. He said I was a loose woman.'

Bilal smiled and poured the arak, dropping in some ice.

'I'm sure it's just talk. Your husband has no idea about us. You can relax on that front.'

Loma was shocked to hear Bilal talk about 'us', as if confirming that this really was a love affair, not just some seedy transaction. She sipped her drink and suddenly felt at ease. This room was the one corner of the world in which she could be herself – or at least a bearable version of herself.

'So why did you want to meet?' said Bilal.

'Oh, well … I was shocked about Selma. An acquaintance of mine told me that she'd been arrested, and I just couldn't believe it. Is it really true?'

'Yes, it's true. She's being processed right now.'

'Processed?'

'Questioned.'

'And the trial?'

'No trial is needed. She's guilty. We know that.'

'So, what will happen to her.'

'I can't say for sure. But she will serve some time in prison.'

'How long?'

'I don't know. Several years, for sure.'

'My God!'

'You knew it would happen, right?'

'Well, I knew something would happen, but I never imagined how I'd feel about it.'

'So how do you feel?'

'Well, I'm relieved, of course, because she was ruining my life. But I'm also …'

'What?'

'I'm feeling guilty, I suppose.'

'Don't worry. That feeling will pass. I used to feel guilty about a lot of things. But you learn to deal with it. Time passes, and then you move on. Feeling guilty helps nobody.'

'But I've never done anything like this before. You're used to it. I'm not.'

'Listen, you asked me to eliminate a risk, and I've done what you asked. What more do you want from me?'

'Oh, no, don't get me wrong, Bilal. I'm very grateful. Really, I am. You've been wonderful. I don't know what I would have done without you. You're my guardian angel. It's just … it's taking me some time to get used to. I feel dreadful about having someone arrested.'

'That's quite natural. But like I said, the feeling will pass.'

Loma finished her drink and poured another. She knew she was drinking too fast, but she couldn't help it. She needed some Dutch courage before broaching the next topic. She looked around the room, squinting at the old photographs, trying to recall who was in them.

'Congratulations on your husband's promotion, by the way.'

'My God! You know about that already?'

'Of course, I know everything,' he smiled.

'I don't doubt it for a second.'

'Well, not everything, perhaps. But I do take an interest in your situation.'

'You probably know more about my life than I do.'

'I'm not sure about that. But I do know that your husband's job will be an important one. He'd going to be very busy.'

'Yes, I know. And he's going to be in Baghdad very soon.'

Loma wondered if they were going to have a conversation about the future of their relationship, if indeed that's what it was. She thought that Bilal might suggest that they 'take a break' once Riaz was back in Baghdad. But he didn't. Instead, he just picked up a handful of peanuts and started eating them slowly, dropping the shells into a little bowl.

Loma decided it was now or never.

'I still feel terrible about Madeha, you know.'

Bilal laughed, tossing his head back as he did so. Loma could see the fillings in his teeth.

'You feel guilty about Madeha too?' he said. 'You feel guilty about everything!'

'Particularly about Madeha.'

'She got what she deserved.'

'Do you really think so?'

'Well, she was found having an affair with a revolutionary, planning to steal state secrets that might endanger the life of the president's son. She was caught red-handed. That's treason. She's lucky to be alive.'

Loma looked into her drink. This was the first time she'd had confirmation that her dear friend was still alive. She needed to hear more.

'Yes, but do you think that she knew what she was doing? Don't you think that she was manipulated?'

'It doesn't work like that, I'm afraid. In cases like this, there are two sides: you're either with the State or you're against the State. In Madeha's case, if she had informed on this terrorist cell immediately, offering assistance in their capture, it might have been different. But she didn't. Instead, she went along with the whole thing, allowing herself to be blackmailed. She was very stupid. She came down on the wrong side of the situation. That's all there is to it.'

'I think she was naïve. She fell in love and lost her perspective. They manipulated her. She didn't know what she was doing.'

'That's not what you said in your testimony.'

'What I said in my testimony and what I really think are not necessarily the same thing.'

Loma realized she was possibly on thin ice. For the second time in two days, she told herself to shut up. Bilal was quiet. He crossed his legs and looked at his finger nails. He seemed to be waiting for something. Loma took a deep breath and continued.

'The thing is, Bilal, that regardless of what Madeha did or didn't do, I'm concerned about her welfare. Maybe she was stupid, but that doesn't mean I should abandon her as a friend.'

'You should do if you want a long and happy life.'

'Meaning?'

'Meaning that any expression of sympathy for someone convicted of treason is liable to land you in great danger. Nobody wants to hear about your bleeding heart. They just want to know whose side you're on.'

'Well, I'm not a traitor, if that's what you mean. But I do want to be sure that Madeha is alright. We were best friends for many years, and I can't just let her rot in jail without some reassurance that she's alright.'

'I suppose I understand that, but many people wouldn't.'

'Could you tell me anything about her situation?'

'She's in prison.'

'Where?'

'That's classified information, Loma. It's the sort of information I'm not at liberty to divulge.'

Loma began to wonder whether she had been right about Bilal. Perhaps he wasn't her savior? Perhaps he really was only in it for the sex? Perhaps she'd finally discovered one of his red lines?

'Of course,' continued Bilal, 'you have probably already guessed that she's at Abu Ghraib, and so it would be useless for me to deny it.'

Loma waited. Perhaps there was more.

'And if you were to guess that she'd been given a life sentence with no chance of parole, I could hardly argue with you. After all, that's the most likely outcome in such cases.'

'But not execution?'

'I couldn't comment on that. But if you had heard rumours that she was saved from execution solely due to her status as a mother of two children, then I would be powerless to deny such rumours. There are lots of rumours circulating in this city, and it's not my job to go around denying them all.'

'I see. Well, thank you for not attempting to comment on the rumours that I've heard.'

'You're most welcome.'

They sat in silence for some time, then Bilal started on the bread and cheese. Loma knew she should be eating too, but she was wound too tight. She poured another arak and took a gulp.

'Bilal, I know this is probably insane, but I need to visit Madeha.'

'Visit her?'

'Yes, just to check that she's alright.'

'It's impossible, I'm afraid.'

'Why? If you can put people in prison, why can't you arrange a prison visit?'

Loma could hear the anger in her voice now. It was the arak, dissolving her inhibitions.

'Well, I could arrange for you to visit her, but you'd be arrested the next day.'

'What for?'

'Conspiring, espionage, treason, plotting subversive acts – you name it.'

'But I just want to meet her. What's so wrong with that?'

'Everyone who visits Abu Ghraib is checked out. Your presence would be noticed, and questions would be asked. They'd wonder why the wife of a respectable diplomat was visiting a convicted traitor. They'd want to know why your husband had allowed such a thing. They'd wonder what he might be up to. And then they'd ask who had arranged the visit. I can't tell you how awkward that would be for everyone concerned, including myself.'

'But couldn't I go in disguise or something?'

Bilal laughed suddenly. Loma was shocked at his ability to switch between deadly seriousness and apparent hilarity.

'I'm not sure you're quite the person to be running around in disguises,' he said.

'But what about an unofficial meeting? Maybe in some other part of the prison? Surely they take bribes? I've heard of prison officers taking bribes. I refuse to believe that something couldn't be done. And anyway, I don't see what's so fucking wrong with visiting a friend in prison. I mean, all I want to do is check that she's okay. What's so fucking wrong with that?'

She drained her glass and poured another drink, knocking it back in one go. Bilal watched.

Suddenly, she felt herself dissolving into tears, just like last time. She put her hand up to cover her face as the tears rolled down. She sat there for a good minute as the feelings flooded out, wondering when they would stop.

Finally, Bilal spoke: 'Don't cry, Loma. You'll ruin everything, and it doesn't help. Don't cry.'

Loma expected him to come and sit on the sofa, placing his arms around her like he did before. But he didn't. Instead, he remained in his wooden chair, watching coolly, legs crossed, peanuts in hand. From his point of view, of course, Madeha was a traitor, a threat to national security. That made her a threat to the State, to the *Mukhabarat* – and ultimately also to him. In Bilal's book, any tears shed on behalf of such a woman were quite wasted.

Loma took out a handkerchief and blew her nose.

'I'm sorry. I wish I didn't cry all the time. It's just the pressure.'

'And the guilt?'

'Yes, I suppose so, the guilt too. The guilt more than anything.'

Bilal stood up and held out his hand.

'Come to bed now, and we'll talk about it later,' he said.

Loma took his hand and got to her feet. She was already drunk, and not quite steady on her feet. But it was just a short walk to the bedroom.

Abu Ghraib

Selma was awoken by two strong young men in suits. Bursting into the cell, they yanked her to her feet, shouting in her face.

'Get up! Time to go!'

'Get moving, you stupid bitch! We haven't got all day.'

She was dazed and confused, her head like cotton wool.

'What are you doing?' she said.

'Shut up and do what you're told!' said the shorter of the two men, slapping her hard round the face.

Selma slipped into her flip-flops, almost toppling over in the process. She was pushed into the brightly lit corridor, through a door and upstairs, then along another corridor and out into the harsh sunlight. They crossed a stony courtyard, which Selma recognized from the day of her arrival.

'Where are you taking me?'

'We've finished with you now. You're going home,' smiled the taller man.

'Home? I'm going home?'

'Yes, you're going to your new home: Abu Ghraib.'

The men burst out laughing, tightening their grip on Selma's arms as she came to a halt.

'Abu Ghraib? Why? What have I done?'

'If you don't know by now, I suppose you never will.'

There was more laughter as Selma was handed over to a uniformed prison guard who grabbed her by the wrists while another put a sack over her head. She was then dragged into the back of a waiting van. The doors slammed shut and the vehicle pulled away.

Selma felt dizzy and nauseous. Every time they turned a corner, she slid off her seat. The guard would heave her back into the sitting position, taking every opportunity to feel her breasts in the process. Selma was too sick and drowsy to object. She was only glad when the journey finally ended.

The doors were thrown open and she heard a woman's voice, harsh and gravelly, the product of many years of smoking and shouting: 'Not another whore!'

'Yes, I'm afraid so,' said the male guard. 'This one's a real bitch, so you'd better break her in.'

'It'll be a pleasure.'

The sack was ripped off, and Selma saw a squat woman in the uniform of a prison guard.

'Don't look at me, you bitch!' shouted the woman.

Selma was filled with rage. She took a step forward and spat in the woman's face.

Immediately, she received a blow to the back of the head. Falling to the floor, she was kicked and beaten all over. She curled up into a ball, doing her best to protect her face. Even so, she got a boot in the mouth.

When the beating was over, the female guard bent down and spoke softly: 'I think we're going to have to take special care of you.'

Selma had heard many stories of the goings on inside the women's wing at Abu Ghraib, and none of them were pleasant. Beatings, torture and rape were all quite normal, as was prolonged solitary confinement. The sick were lucky if they received proper medical treatment, and inmates might go years without the chance of talking to a lawyer. Many women died while serving their sentences.

As she lay in the dirt, bleeding from the mouth, Selma resolved to control her temper until she had a better handle on things.

She was marched into a large building and through a series of metal doors, each of which was unlocked with a huge bunch of keys. She was handed a blanket, a towel and a blue cotton dress and then led to a dormitory with ten beds, five down each wall. Each bed was carefully made, with a grey blanket, some sheets and a grubby pillow. Several women sat on their beds, while the rest were down the far end, seated on the floor, playing a game of cards.

'This is your bed,' said the guard. 'Keep it clean and tidy. If you have any questions, ask the other inmates.'

The guard departed, sliding the iron bars shut and locking them in place.

Selma looked around at the olive-coloured walls, the cracked floor-tiles, the bare bulbs hanging from long wires overhead. She examined the woman sitting cross-legged on the next bed; she looked tired and haggard, her face lined, eyes puffy. Wisps of grey hair were escaping her black headscarf. She might be anywhere between 40 and 60 years old; it was hard to tell.

Selma began making her bed, a task she had rarely performed at home. However, she'd watched the maids often enough, taking the time to critique their technique. She put the pillow in its case and smoothed out the white cotton sheet. Finally, she sat on the edge of the bed and nursed her two broken fingers, still wrapped in their make-shift cast.

'What are you in here for?' said the woman.

'I have no idea.'

'You're not the only one. Half the people in here don't know their crime.'

'Well, I'm not a criminal. I know that much.'

'I was put in here for criticizing the government. I was upset because my son was killed in the war. I said some things I shouldn't have said. I just wanted someone to blame for my loss. I didn't have time to grieve properly before I was arrested. I've been here for two years now. I have no idea when I'm being released.'

Selma really wasn't interested in the woman's complaints. She was wondering how on earth she was going to pass the time for the next however many years.

'My name's Helana,' said the woman.

'Selma.'

'It's nice to meet you, Selma. Don't worry. We are in God's hands.'

'Well, I don't think much of his handling.'

Selma lay back on her bed and gazed at the ceiling. Moments later, a stocky middle-aged woman appeared at the foot of the bed. She was wearing cheap jewellery and several layers of make-up. Selma hadn't imagined they'd have access to make-up in prison. The woman was staring, arms crossed, chewing gum with her mouth open.

'What's this old crab doing here?' she said.

'She doesn't know,' said Helana.

'Probably a prostitute then, from the looks of it.'

The woman chewed her gum and stared Selma in the face. Helana was silent.

'Are you a whore, then?' insisted the woman. 'You look a bit old for a whore.'

Selma said nothing. She felt the anger surging through her body, but she was determined to avoid further trouble unless absolutely necessary. Added to which, her fingers were hurting like mad, and she wasn't sure how they'd hold up in a fight.

The woman was smiling now, apparently happy to have found a passive victim. She came round to the side of Selma's bed and towered over her. Selma tried to gauge her size, deciding that she couldn't be much more than five foot eight inches tall, perhaps less.

'My name's Zebedah,' she said. 'I'm charge here. So, when I tell you to do something, you fucking do it, okay?'

Selma lay perfectly still, arms behind her head. She looked into Zebedah's eyes but said nothing. She knew this would make her crazy, but she just couldn't bring herself to cow-tow – certainly not to a cheap whore from the lower classes.

'I said I'm in fucking charge, you bitch!' said the Zebedah, leaning forward and clipping Selma round the head.

Selma sprang off the bed and launched herself forward, grabbing Zebedah's blonde hair and yanking her to the floor. A sharp pain shot through her broken fingers as she did so, and she let out a scream, channelling her pain into fury.

Zebedah was screaming too, issuing curses and insults as they rolled around the floor, scratching and punching: 'You fucking bitch! You fucking bitch! I'm going to fucking kill you! You fucking whore!'

Selma felt the girl's nails digging into her face, and she replied with a punch to the nose. In a moment, Selma was on top, landing punch after punch, but Zebedah somehow wriggled onto her side and slipped away, grabbing Selma by the hair once more, and they fell against the iron bars, still scratching and punching.

Every time Selma landed a punch with her left hand, a shock of pain ran through her fingers, and finally, she resorted to fighting one-handed, wondering now if she might lose a fight for the first time in many years.

Suddenly, the bars slid open and a group of female guards poured in, separating the pair and dragging them into different corners, where they were beaten with batons. Then Selma was dragged from the room and down a long corridor.

In the distance, she heard Zebedah shouting at the top of her lungs: 'She fucking started it! That bitch started it! I'll fucking kill her! I'll fucking kill the bitch!'

Selma was thrown into a small, dark room and the door slammed shut. She lay on the floor as the guards kicked and beat her like never before. Very soon, she lost consciousness.

* * *

Selma's new cell was much like the one at the interrogation centre: small, with bare walls and a filthy floor, no bed, and a stinking hole in one corner. She lay in a huddle for hours, drifting in and out of consciousness. Every part of her body ached, and she didn't dare to move for fear that her bones were broken. Then, at some point, she awoke to find herself in a new position, apparently still able to move her arms and legs. Very slowly, she got to her hands and knees. She relieved herself over the hole and then crouched in the opposite corner, waiting for the next round of mistreatment.

She didn't have to wait long.

The door opened and several male guards rushed in, launching into a new round of beatings. After a minute, a mattress was brought in, and Selma was dragged onto it. The guards held her arms and legs, pinning her down and pulling her dress up around her waist. One of the men lay on top and forced himself inside. Selma started screaming, but a large hand was clamped over her mouth.

Once the first man had finished, another one got on top and had his turn. Everyone was laughing, making crude comments, asking if she was enjoying herself. Once all six guards had had their fun, they got to their feet, rolled up the mattress and departed.

Selma curled up in a ball and cried.

Her solitary confinement lasted over a week, and in that time, she was raped on a daily basis. Sometimes the men were different, but the mattress was always the same. She soon learned that resisting was pointless. It was much easier, she decided, to let them have their way and get it over with.

After all, she thought, *prostitutes do this every day. I must just imagine myself to be a prostitute. And then it won't matter. Anyway, it's just my body; they can't touch my mind.*

* * *

Finally, the day came when Selma was led back to the dormitory. She sat on her bed and examined her fingers. Strangely, despite the cuts and bruises all over her body, the fingers seemed to be much better. She removed the splint and bent them, making a fist. Yes, they were much better.

The other women were all down the far end, sitting in a huddle while someone told a story. It was Zebedah, detailing a brutal fight she'd had in her youth – a fight she had inevitably won. Some of the women looked at Selma but then looked away. Zebedha whispered something and everyone laughed.

Selma picked up her towel from the bed and walked casually down to the end of the room. Zebedah was still telling her story, apparently unconcerned by the return of Selma. It was a show of bravado, a sign that she feared no-one, least of all newbies who had spent the past ten days in solitary confinement.

Selma approached her enemy from behind, the towel in both hands. With a sudden movement, she wrapped it around Zebedah's head, smothering her face, and yanking her backwards onto the floor. Zebedah started screaming, lashing out blindly with her sharp nails. But Selma was too quick, sitting on her opponent and stuffing the towel into her mouth to silence the screams. Zebeda grabbed at the towel and tried to pull it away, but Selma took her head in both hands and slammed it against the floor, again and again: *thump, thump, thump.*

Dazed, Zebedah went momentarily limp, at which point Selma flipped her onto her front and grabbed her wrist, forcing her arm high up her back. She pushed so hard that the woman's shoulder finally gave way, dislocating with a sickening *crack.*

Zebedha screamed at the top of her lungs, but Selma reached round and forced the towel deeper into her mouth, muffling the sound. She then punched her victim in the belly over and over again, until Zebeda could no longer breathe, much less scream.

Selma stood up, retrieved her towel, and walked calmly back to her bed. She spread the towel carefully over her pillow and lay down, gazing quietly at the ceiling.

All the other women went back to their beds, as Zebedah finally found her breath and started to howl in pain.

The bars slid open and a team of guards rushed in, led by the stocky bitch who had given Selma her first beating.

'What's going on?' she demanded. 'What's wrong with Zebedha?'

'She was standing on her bed, and she fell off,' said one woman, casually turning the pages of a magazine.

'Is that right?' said the guard, looking around the room.

'Yes, that's right,' said another girl. 'She fell off the bed and hurt her shoulder.'

'Alright then,' said the guard. 'Get her to the infirmary.'

Zebedah was helped from the room, groaning in pain.

A minute passed in silence, and then a pretty young woman came and stood by Selma's bed.

'You did the right thing,' she said. 'We never liked Zebedah anyway.'

Another woman turned up.

'Yeah, you did the right thing. She needed to be put in her place.'

Soon the whole room was standing around Selma's bed, offering congratulations on her victory, praising her fighting skills. They said that Zebedha was a whore anyway, sleeping with the prison guards for money. She always cheated at cards too, they complained. One woman offered to give Selma foot a massage, saying that it was her speciality. Before her arrest, she explained, she had worked in all the best hotels.

Good, thought Selma, *now they know who's boss.*

* * *

The following week, Selma was in the yard with her cell-mates, taking her daily hour of exercise, when a strange, huddled figure came shuffling over. The woman's blue dress was unusually dirty, and she had scratches and bite marks on her arms and legs. Her hair was a mess: long, untidy and horribly greasy. She hung her head low, looking at the floor.

Selma was on the point of saying something nasty when the woman looked up.

It was Madeha – or a version of her.

Selma was shocked at the transformation. Gone was the pretty, youthful woman, with glowing skin and lots to say. This Madeha was ten years older, pale and gaunt, with dark rings around her eyes and a look of abject misery. Her mouth was turned down at the corners, as if she might burst into tears at any moment. Selma noticed more marks on her face, no doubt from beatings or torture.

'Hello, Selma,' whispered Madeha, eyes still fixed on the floor.

'Well, well, if it isn't Madeha! You're looking good, darling, I must say.'

'I don't feel too good.'

'No, I was joking. You look terrible.'

'Oh ...'

'I wondered if I might bump into you in this place. You made a rather dramatic exit and then we heard no more about you. Some people thought you were dead. But you seem to be still alive, just about.'

Madeha remained silent. She glanced over one shoulder, then the other, as if expecting an attack from behind.

'Come and sit by me,' said Selma. 'Tell me all your news.'

Madeha joined her on the bench. Selma offered her a cigarette.

'No, thanks. I couldn't.'

'Oh, you've given up smoking. That's very healthy of you.'

'I don't feel well.'

'No, well, that's not surprising. You look like they've given you a good beating, my dear. Did you get the full, five-star treatment, by any chance? Perhaps there's a baby on the way?'

Madeha buried her head in her hands and gasped.

Selma thought she might be about to scream, but thankfully she didn't. Instead, she returned her hands to her lap and sat perfectly still.

Selma took a drag on her cigarette, wondering where she might begin.

'Of course, you must feel pretty upset with Loma,' she began.

'What?'

'Loma. You must be pretty angry with her for what she did?'

'What do you mean?'

'Oh darling, don't be so coy. We all know what happened. You were arrested because she told her rotten husband, and then during the investigation she gave evidence against you.'

'No, I don't think ...'

'Of course, she did, my dear. Everyone knows what happened. She started to worry that she might be implicated in your little mess, and so she elaborated a little, just to show herself as a true patriot. She said you'd been plotting an attack on Uday Hussein with your terrorist friends, and that she'd forced you to confess. She said you had probably planned the whole thing in advance, and that's why you asked to visit London. She said you'd been in touch with that chap ... What was his name?'

'Munir.'

'Yes, you'd been in touch with Munir even while you were in Baghdad, and that was the reason for your trip to England. You were probably an important member of the terrorist cell. That's what Loma told them. She lied through her teeth to save her skin. Forget about friendship, darling. Once the shit hits the fan, it's everyone for herself.'

'Selma, are you really sure …?'

'Oh, yes, you can ask anyone. She's even been boasting about it. She got a letter of thanks from the President. Apparently, Riaz will be made an ambassador very soon. They're both as pleased as punch. I think it's disgusting, of course. After all, what sort of friend would do a thing like that?'

Madeha was silent. She lifted her head and looked at the sky. It was a bright and cloudless afternoon. High overhead, a pair of herons were flapping slowly along. They were heading north, following the river.

How wonderful, thought Madeha, *to be a bird, to fly freely and know nothing of humans and their sordid business.*

Selma took a deep drag on her cigarette and resumed her monologue.

'If you don't believe me, just ask yourself what she's done to help you. Has she sent you a letter? Has she been to visit? Has she found you a lawyer? No, I very much doubt it. She's washed her hands of you. So far as she's concerned, Madeha, you're dead.'

'I wish I *was* dead.'

'Surely not? You've got years ahead of you, my dear. You're still young. Of course, you'll spend them all behind bars, but that can't be helped, not now.'

'I really do wish I was dead.'

'I see you've got a few scratches on you. And are those bite marks? Have the men been playing rough? They can be beasts, can't they? Animals, that's what they are.'

Selma was pretty sure that Madeha had been raped, but she wanted to be sure. She wanted to locate the gaping wound and pour in some salt.

Before she could do so, however, Madeha got to her feet.

'I don't think you'll ever change, Selma,' she said.

'What on earth do you mean?'

'Even being in Abu Ghraib hasn't changed you.'

'Well, it hasn't beaten me, if that's what you mean. If anything, I'm stronger. It's sink-or-swim in here, and I'm not about to fucking drown. I'm a winner, not a quitter. And if I ever get out of here, I'll get my revenge on that fucking bitch. Don't you worry about that. I'll do it for the both of us.'

'There's really no need. I'm not interested in revenge.'

'Well, I'll do it for myself then,' said Selma, rising to her feet and stamping out her cigarette butt. 'You just lay down and die if you want to.'

A prison guard marched over, shouting at the two of them: 'What are you doing there? Keep moving. This is exercise time, not a lover's rendezvous. Or do you want to go back into solitary confinement? You'll get plenty of romance in there, girls.'

Selma flashed an insincere smile and walked away, leaving Madeha to limp along behind, tears in her eyes.

A romantic dinner

Tony was waiting at Heathrow, as promised, holding a sign with Loma's name on it.

'Welcome back, ma'am,' he said, taking her suitcase. 'Nice to see you again.'

'Hello, Tony. Nice to see you too.'

'I'm afraid you've arrived in time for a downpour.'

'Yes, I noticed it was raining. I'm not really surprised.'

'Well, an English summer is never long without rain. Otherwise we'd get bored.'

'Yes, I suppose so.'

Driving through the wet streets of London, Loma felt she was returning to square one. Despite all the frantic activity of the past two months, she'd really achieved very little. There has been a torrid love affair, of course, and Selma had been arrested. But there'd been no progress on contacting Madeha. If Bilal had had any luck in arranging a prison visit, he'd kept pretty quiet about it. And here was Loma, back in London, hurtling at full speed toward her domineering husband, rushing to obey his orders like some trembling slave. No doubt she would have to share his bed tonight, the very thought of which made her sick.

Yes, so much had happened, and yet nothing had changed. She was like a fly in a spider's web, buzzing and struggling, but ultimately doomed. She leaned her head against the cold window

and wished it was all over. Not just the struggle to help Madeha –
but everything.

Stepping through the front door, Loma found the house cold and
empty. The maid was nowhere to be seen. No fires had been lit,
and the radiators were turned off. Predictably, Riaz was at work.

'Where are the children?' she asked Tony.

'Out with friends, I think, ma'am. Your husband said they'd be
staying over at their house, if I remember rightly.'

Loma was shocked and hurt. Had nobody thought to provide a
welcome for her? No fires, no hot meal, no hugs from her loving
family?

'I'll take that, thank you,' she said, grabbing the suitcase and
heading up to her room.

She showered and threw on a track-suit, then lay on the bed,
reflecting on her so-called life. Whose idea was it for the boys to
be staying elsewhere? Perhaps Riaz had thought it up as some
sort of punishment? Perhaps the boys had objected and been
overruled? Were they really so grown up now that they didn't feel
the need to rush into their mother's arms after a long absence?

She gazed across the room at the rain-spattered window, at the
dark clouds and the branches of a tree that rocked with the wind.
She felt utterly alone in the world, just as she had two weeks
before, when she'd learned of Selma's arrest. Utterly alone and
largely unloved. There was Bilal, of course, but who could say

where that might lead? After all, with Riaz returning to Baghdad, the chances of continuing a love affair undetected seemed pretty slim. And who was to say that Bilal wasn't in it just for the sex? Perhaps the sense of romance was all on her side – the sad fantasies of a lonely housewife?

What she needed was a drink.

She went down to the living room and poured herself a large gin-and-tonic, knocked it back, then poured another. Standing by the drinks cabinet, she surveyed her various pictures and ornaments, all of which would have to be packed before departing for Baghdad. There was the paperweight from St Paul's Cathedral; there the miniature print of a painting by Turner; there the little marble bust of William Shakespeare.

And there was her ancient bronze statue of Ishtar, recently purchased from Museum Street. She reached out and touched it, running her fingers down the soft curves, from head to feet. She wondered whether she was real, this goddess, or just a myth.

More to the point, what would Ishtar have done in Loma's shoes? How would Ishtar have navigated such a desperate situation?

It was a ridiculous question, of course, because no self-respecting warrior goddess would

have gotten into such a situation in the first place. Loma collapsed on the sofa, switched on the TV and lit a cigarette. After all, if she couldn't come to terms with her life, she could at least try to block it out. Just as she was settling into an old movie, she heard the front door open.

'You're back then,' said Riaz, strolling into the living room, briefcase in hand.

'Yes, I'm back.'

'How was the flight?'

'Same as usual. I managed to sleep a little bit.'

'Good,' he said. 'I'm glad to have you home again.'

He leaned over and planted a kiss on her mouth. He was smiling, playing the role of the warm-hearted husband. Loma did her best to reciprocate, bending her lips into the shape of a smile, looking briefly into his dark eyes. She had been married to the man for 13 years, and yet she felt not one scrap of genuine affection.

Riaz wandered off into the kitchen, while Loma lit a fresh cigarette and stared at the television. Should she confront him over the lack of fires in the house? How about the absent children? Was there any point in starting a fight?

'We're going out for a meal tonight,' said Riaz, returning with a glass of white wine.

'A meal? Where?'

'I've booked a table for two at Claridge's.'

'Really?'

'Yes, I thought you might like a romantic dinner.'

'I'm a bit tired.'

'But I want to celebrate your return.'

Loma couldn't quite bring herself to look at him. Her idea of a romantic dinner these days was quaffing arak on Bilal's dusty sofa. That was something real, or at least pleasurable. The prospect of a posh meal at Claridge's with Riaz left her utterly cold.

'I've really missed you,' he said, taking a seat on the sofa.

'Yes, me too.'

He lay his big hand on her thigh and gave it a squeeze.

'The house has been pretty empty without you,' he continued.

'Where are the boys?'

'They're staying over at Salim's house tonight. They get along well with Salim's children.'

'Didn't they want to see me?'

'I don't know. I didn't ask them. They just said they were staying over. It's Friday night. They often stay there.'

'It would have been nice to see them.'

'Well, you'll see them tomorrow. Tonight is just for you and me – a romantic evening.'

He put his arm around her shoulders and pulled her close, engaging her in a soft, wet kiss. She responded as well as she could, eyes closed, counting the seconds until it was over.

'Well, I should probably change then,' she said at last, rising from the sofa.

'Yes, if you wish. Our table is for seven o'clock, so you have plenty of time.'

Loma took another shower. It was the only place where she could be alone with her thoughts. Just the day before, she had rehearsed a speech in which she demanded a divorce. She had made the argument that neither she nor Riaz were truly happy, that they would both be better off apart. There was no love in the marriage, no romance, and no trust. They owed it to themselves and each other to make a clean break and seek happiness elsewhere. They could make the change privately, without fuss, and share the task of child-rearing. After all, the boys were old enough now to understand such things, assuming they were explained with care. Her final version of the speech had seemed perfectly reasonable, and she had been planning to deliver it during her trip to London.

Now, out of the blue, Riaz was proposing a romantic dinner at Claridge's, lavishing her with affection and saying how much he'd missed her. He was like a different man – or rather, he was like the man she'd married 13 years ago. It was just a shame that he'd been such a bastard in the period in between.

As she towelled dry, she wondered whether he was planning to turn over a new leaf. Would this spurt of romantic sentiment last beyond the weekend? And if so, would she find her own romantic feelings rekindled? Could she ever love him again?

* * *

She was still pondering these questions as the waiter handed her a menu.

Riaz started explaining the various dishes, as if Loma had never heard of them before. He was affecting a French accent, and a very bad one too. Perhaps he had her confused with one of his young trollops?

'You may like the *salade niçoise* or the *salade au chevre*. Both are quite nice.'

'Yes, I know what they are.'

'You like salad, don't you?'

'Yes, of course I do.'

'There's the *filet de boeuf en croûte*. I think you'll like that. And the lobster, which is very good here.'

'Riaz, you don't have to explain the menu to me. I've eaten in nice restaurants before. And I speak French just as well as you, if you remember.'

'There's not need to snap, Loma. I'm trying to be helpful, that's all.'

'Well, I'd rather read it for myself, if you don't mind.'

In the end, Loma ordered the French onion soup, followed by a veal cutlet. While they waited, she tucked into the bread and butter, washed down with white wine. She certainly couldn't complain about the setting: the beautiful room, the candles, the soft piano music. If only she could believe in her husband's new-found romantic efforts, she might be able to relax.

She listened while he chatted about his job and all that had happened in her absence. He explained how he'd received news of the promotion, and all that he had to accomplish before leaving London. He would soon be one of Iraq's top people for foreign affairs, and he had some bold new ideas to put forward.

Loma commented from time to time, expressing her gladness at his good fortune, all the while conscious that it came courtesy of Madeha's suffering.

'Are you sure you're alright, my dear?' said Riaz, reaching across the table and laying his hand on hers.

'Yes, I'm fine. Just a bit tired from the flight.'

She withdrew her hand and prepared another slice of bread.

'You seem cold,' said Riaz. 'I was hoping for a romantic evening, but you don't seem to be in the mood. What's wrong?'

'Nothing's wrong. Like I said, I'm just tired.'

The waiter arrived with their starters, and Loma tucked into the soup, while Riaz took his first bite of *pâté de foie gras*.

'Well, there's clearly something wrong. You've been cold with me since you first arrived. I've gone to a lot of trouble to make you feel welcome, but you're treating me like a stranger.'

'Don't be silly, Riaz. I just have a lot on my mind.'

'Well, what do you have on your mind, exactly? Is it some sort of secret?'

'No, I'm just worried about my mother.'

'Your mother? What's up with her?'

'Nothing really. She's just getting old, that's all.'

'Don't be silly. That's nothing new. She hasn't suddenly aged in the space of a few weeks.'

There was another uncomfortable silence. Riaz was looking at his wife, who was studiously avoiding eye contact.

'Loma, there's clearly something wrong, and you're not telling me what it is. I'm getting a bit sick and tired of this.'

'Well, I can't help you there, I'm afraid.'

He reached out to touch her hand again, but she withdrew it quickly, in the process jogging her bowl of soup and knocking the spoon onto the tablecloth.

'Look what you've done!' said Riaz.

'That wasn't me. It's you trying to hold my hand all the time.'

'This has gone on long enough. I demand to know what's going on. There's something you're not telling me, and I demand an explanation.'

Riaz had raised his voice now, and Loma could see other diners looking over. She blushed and began cleaning up the soup. The waiter arrived, apparently concerned at the disturbance.

'Can I help, madam?' he said.

'I just spilled some soup, that's all.'

'Allow me ...' began the waiter, but Riaz interrupted.

'We're having a private conversation, if you don't mind.'

The waiter bowed and disappeared back to the kitchen. Loma continued with her soup, but Riaz had lost all interest in food.

'You tell me right now what's going on!' he said. 'I'm not an idiot, and I won't be treated like one. Something happened while you were in Baghdad, and I want to know what it was.'

'Nothing happened in Baghdad. What are you talking about?'

'I'm not an idiot!' shouted Riaz, slamming his hand down on the table.

Everyone was looking now, and Loma was blushing more than ever. The waiter appeared once more, hovering at a distance, a frown on his face.

'Riaz, stop making a scene,' hissed Loma. 'Everyone's looking at us.'

'I don't care if the whole world is looking at us. You will tell me what's wrong, or I'll wring it out of you.'

She looked at his red face and bulging eyes. It was the same expression he'd worn during their last argument, immediately after Madeha's arrest. He had threatened her with divorce, and she had begged him to go through with it. At which point he had threatened to beat her to death. Now, after a brief interlude, they were back to that same situation: she had displeased him, and he was furious. Perhaps he would threaten her again?

'Speak!' he shouted, banging the table again.

The waiter marched over: 'I'm sorry, sir, but we cannot have arguments in the restaurant. You are disturbing the other guests. I must ask you ...'

'Get away from me!' said Riaz, standing up and taking a step toward the waiter, who left the room in search of reinforcements.

'Riaz, please calm down. You've lost control. I have no idea what ...'

'Do you want me to beat it out of you?'

He was leaning across the table now, glaring into her face.

'Is that what it comes down to?' she said. 'Violence? Is that your solution?'

'Yes, violence, if necessary. I will not have my wife keeping secrets from me.'

'Well, you've kept secrets from me, haven't you? How many whores and mistresses have you had behind my back? How many years have I had to put up with your bullshit?'

'Shut up, you *stupid* woman!'

'I'll shut up when you give me a divorce. I've had enough of your lies and your threats, Riaz. You can give me a divorce and then I'll tell you anything you want. But I will not continue to share a bed with you for one more night. You disgust me ...'

'You would dare to threaten me with divorce?'

He picked up his glass of wine and threw it in Loma's face.

She screamed and got to her feet.

The waiter returned with the restaurant manager, who attempted to calm the situation.

'Please, sir,' he said, 'perhaps you could continue this discussion in more appropriate surroundings?'

Riaz ignored him completely, aiming his next question at his wife.

'Who is it?'

'Who is what?'

'Who are you fucking?'

'What on earth are you talking about?'

Loma wondered for a moment whether he had guessed about Bilal. It wasn't inconceivable that someone had seen them together. Or perhaps Bilal had been indiscrete, boasting about his conquest. One thing was for sure: if Riaz ever found out, he would almost certainly kill her. She looked at the cutlery on the table and wondered how she'd defend herself against a knife attack.

'Is it Ali?'

'Ali?'

'I've heard the rumours, you stupid bitch. Don't think I haven't heard the rumours. Everyone knows what's going on'

Loma started laughing, partly from relief. If Riaz was worried about Ali, then he really was barking up the wrong tree. She knew

Ali to be happily married, with three children, the youngest still in primary school. If he had any plans to rekindle his romance with Loma, he had kept very quiet about it.

Loma's laughter sent Riaz into a rage. He picked up a side-plate and threw it, hitting her square in the face. He then grabbed a fork and lunged at her. The restaurant staff held him back, while another waiter and a chef arrived on the scene. As they wrestled the fork from Riaz's hand, Loma slipped outside and began the long walk home.

* * *

Loma opened her eyes and wondered for a moment where she was. She didn't recognize the dark, wooden object in front of her. She shifted a little and looked around. Yes, it was a desk, the desk in her office, where she'd spent the night sleeping on the sofa. Judging by the light pouring through the window, she had slept right through. There were birds chirping and the sun was out. She sat up slowly, her head still heavy from last night's booze. She squinted at the clock; it was just gone nine o'clock.

If Riaz had come home last night, he had probably already showered and left the house. Of course, he might easily have spent the night in a hotel with one of his women. In any case,

Loma was glad that she'd locked the door, because his behaviour in the restaurant had been truly frightening.

She felt her lips, which had been cut by the flying plate. They were still sore, and she could feel the scabs forming already. She would have to take special care in applying her make-up for a while.

She stood up, straightened her clothes and went to the door, checking that it was still locked. She stood still for a minute, listening for movement in the house. Hearing nothing, she turned the key and stepped into the corridor, heading into the kitchen, barefoot.

There, to her horror, was Riaz. He was sitting at the breakfast table in his suit and tie. He looked horribly tired, but just about presentable.

'Good morning,' he said, quietly.

'Good morning.'

Loma watched him warily, wondering whether he might rush at her once more with a fork. But he simply picked up a slice of toast and began munching on it, apparently engrossed in the front page of the newspaper.

'There's coffee in the pot,' he said.

'Okay, thanks.'

Loma poured a cup of coffee and stirred in some sugar. She stood with it by the fridge, reasoning that if he did make any sudden movements, she could easily dash into her office.

'Aren't you late for work?' she said.

'No, I've already phoned in. My first meeting is at ten o'clock.'

'Okay.'

'Last night was unfortunate,' he said, putting down the newspaper.

'Yes, it was. Very unfortunate.'

'I'm willing to forgive and forget.'

'Well, I'm willing to forgive, Riaz, but I'm not sure I can forget.'

'What do you mean?' he said, turning to face her.

'How can we just continue after that, as if nothing happened?'

'Well, nothing did happen. It was just an argument. No big deal.'

'No big deal? You threw a plate in my face and threatened to stab me with a fork. How is that no big deal?'

'I lost my temper. You kept pushing and pushing, and I snapped. It's normal. I'm not super-human. I'm not a saint. I have my limits.'

'Yes, I and have my limits too. And we've gone way past them now. Last night, went way beyond what I'm willing to put up with. That's it.'

'What on earth are you talking about?'

'I'm not willing to go on like this. It's crazy. I'm not willing to be bullied and threatened any more. I'm not willing to be beaten and stabbed and hit and told what to do all the time. I've had enough, Riaz. I've really had enough.'

Loma was shocked at herself. It was as if someone else was speaking through her. As if some force of rebellion or independence were surging through her body and out of her mouth. She really didn't know where she was finding the courage to be so bold. She knew very well that saying such things might provoke another bout of rage on the part of Riaz, but somehow she didn't care. She'd had enough. This was the end.

Riaz was walking across the kitchen now, a scrap of toast still in one hand. Loma began backing up toward the door, wondering if she still had time to bolt for her office.

'Are you fucking serious?' he shouted. 'Are you still talking about divorce?'

'Yes, I am.'

'Are you out of your mind? I'll never allow you to divorce me. Don't you understand? You're the mother of my children, you're my wife. What on earth makes you think I'm going to let you go?'

'It's not a matter of letting me go, Riaz. The divorce laws have been changed, in case you didn't notice. I don't need your permission for a divorce. You assaulted me last night, and there are plenty of witnesses. I can get a divorce by going in front of a judge and showing my injuries. You can't stop me.'

'Well, I can kill you before you get to a judge. Or I can have you killed afterwards. Or I can have your mother killed or your sister raped. You have no idea what I'll do if you insult me by seeking a divorce. You really have no idea. Do you think I would allow myself to be shamed and insulted in that way? And after my promotion, do you think that would be acceptable? Do you think it would look nice for me to be promoted to an important job and then immediately divorced by my wife? What would people say?'

'I really don't care what would people say.'

'Well, I do. They'd say it's because my wife has been fucking her old boyfriend, Ali. Everyone says you're having an affair, and that would be the final proof. I'd never outlive the shame. Nor would your children. They'd turn their backs on you. Once they realized what a whore their mother is, they'd just turn their backs. Nobody wants a whore for a mother.'

Riaz was shouting now, his face red. Loma decided to try calming things down.

'I wouldn't divorce you, Riaz, unless you agreed to it. I'm not saying I would *ever* divorce you without your consent. But I think we should discuss our options, because this marriage is obviously not working. You're not happy, and I'm not happy, and it isn't good for the children.'

'What's good for the children is having a mother and father together, and a mother who stays at home and looks after them. So that's what you're going to do. That's *exactly* what you're going to do. There will be no divorce, and no more discussion.'

'Well, you can't just lock me up at home, Riaz. We're not savages.'

'Are you sure I can't? I think most people would understand if I brought you under control, bearing in mind that you've been fucking around. In fact, most people would understand if you suddenly disappeared. Such things happen all the time.'

Loma wondered for a moment whether he was really capable of following through on such a threat – having his wife kidnapped and murdered. She looked at the hatred in his face and decided that she couldn't rule it out entirely.

'Let's just be very clear about one thing,' said Riaz. 'Whatever happens, whether you live or you die, the boys will stay with me. Do you understand? You will *never* take my boys away. They will stay with me. Understand?'

Loma looked down and realized for the first time that Riaz wasn't only holding a scrap of toast. In his other hand was a knife. It was only a butter knife, but in the hands of a powerful man, it was a deadly weapon.

She slowly turned and walked back to the office, locking the door behind her.

A prison visit

Loma woke up crying. She had been having the same nightmare all week: Madeha was on the floor, covered in cuts and bruises following a torture session, and Selma was shouting, 'You're responsible for this, you bitch!'

The same terrible scene had been repeated every night since Loma's return to Baghdad, waking her in the dead of night, drenched in sweat. Even moving to her mother's house hadn't helped. Perhaps after the prison visit it would stop?

She rolled over and checked the time on the alarm clock. It was just gone 6am, which meant she had three hours before her appointment at Abu Ghraib. She would get up soon, give the boys their breakfast, and then head out. She had no idea what the day might bring, and she wanted to plant some happy memories, just in case.

She closed her eyes for a moment, wondering if she really had the strength to go through with this. The answer, as always, was simple: she really had no choice. It had to be done, like it or not, even at the risk of her own life. And ideally, it should be done while Riaz was still in London, because he absolutely must not find out.

Added to which, she could hardly go back to Bilal and say that she'd changed her mind. She had begged him for this opportunity, and perhaps against his better judgement, he had finally come through. Now the ball was in her court.

She looked around the room, which had hardly changed since her youth – the final days of Ali and the first days of Riaz. There was the old mahogany wardrobe, stuffed with clothes, most of them horribly out of date. There were the posters of Abba and Abdel Halim Hafez, cut from magazines and stuck to the walls. She recalled how she and Madeha had played at belly-dancing here, imitating Nagwa Fouad, then collapsing in laughter on the floor. How naïve she had been then, how lacking in awareness of life's dangers.

Reflecting that nostalgia would change nothing, she dragged herself from the bed and walked along the corridor to the bathroom. Her mother's bedroom door was open, and there she was, on the floor, murmuring prayers to God, asking for forgiveness and protection.

'Good morning, my dear.'

'Good morning, Mum.'

'Did you sleep well?'

'Yes, thanks, very well.'

By the time Loma had showered and dressed, her mother had served breakfast on the patio. There was strong tea, juice, bread, feta cheese, jam, cream and fried eggs.

The boys were also up and about, running around in their pyjamas, playing with toy tanks and aeroplanes. They seemed perfectly happy, quite unaware of the drama unfolding in the world of adults.

How wonderful it would be, thought Loma, *if they could stay this way.*

'Boys, come and have some breakfast,' she said.

The boys took their seats and began to fill their plates. Loma watched Walid as he cut up his bread, spreading feta on one piece and jam on another. He looked so tall and grown-up these days, so mature. Of course, she shouldn't be surprised, because he was a teenager now. Perhaps soon he'd start to feel embarrassed at having to hold his mother's hand in public or give her a goodbye kiss. Before long, he would get his first girlfriend and start planning a life of his own.

'Are you alright, Mum?' said Walid.

'Yes, I'm fine, my dear. I'm just a little tired, that's all. Now, eat your breakfast and then you can go and play in the garden. It's a lovely day.'

Before leaving the house, Loma told her boys how much she loved them. They hugged her warmly, just like they always had, and then dashed off into the garden to continue their game. Loma's mother was clearing away the breakfast things, humming some old tune.

Loma stood in the doorway, drinking in the scene, telling herself that if she never returned, her boys would be alright. There were two spacious houses at their disposal, with large gardens and no end of toys. They only had one grandparent now – the others having departed for the next world – but the old woman doted on them, taking every opportunity to offer love and praise. Riaz wasn't exactly a model father, but he would provide financially. The boys would be upset, of course, to learn of their mother's death – but they would bounce back.

* * *

As she sped westwards toward Abu Ghraib, Loma reviewed the instructions she'd received from Bilal. They seemed straightforward enough. If anything went wrong, it wouldn't be due to her own error, but the result of someone else's betrayal, sloppiness or change of heart. Of course, she had no control over such things, and so it was best not to think about it.

Even so, she couldn't help the intense feeling of dread as she wound down the window and introduced herself to the guards. They made a phone call and waved her through, directing her to a special parking spot. She thanked God that she wouldn't be joining the long and shabby line of people hoping to visit their loved ones behind bars, carrying parcels of food to supplement the meagre prison diet. They would be searched and abused and subjected to long waits, some of them turned away with bad news.

Loma was shown into an office, where she was greeted by a short man in a military-style uniform. He looked older and scruffier than Loma had imagined. Was this really the deputy warden of the women's prison?

There was no invitation to take a seat, nor the offer of a cup of tea. Instead, the man simply welcomed her to the facility and held out his hand. Loma gave him the envelope, and he nodded to the guards. Before she knew it, she was walking down a flight of stairs and along a bare corridor with flickering neon lights. A guard unlocked a door and Loma stepped inside.

There before her was a bare metal table and two chairs, on one of which sat a hunched figure, head hung low. Her face was hidden by a mass of long, greasy hair. Her blue dress was grubby, and her arms bore numerous cuts and bruises.

Loma stood still, frozen to the spot, waiting. Her heart was beating hard with fear.

The woman looked up. It was clearly Madeha, but not as Loma remembered her. The face was thin and drawn, the eyes lifeless and sunken, ringed with grey. There was a large bruise on one cheek-bone, and a general impression of abject misery.

Loma moved forward and took a seat, placing the brown-paper parcel on the table.

'I've brought you some things,' she said.

Madeha looked at the parcel but didn't move.

Loma undid the string and revealed a pink bath towel, some scented soap and a bottle of shampoo. Also, a box of chocolates, some stuffed dates, a novel and some magazines. She waited for Madeha to comment, but there was silence.

'I wasn't sure what you'd need, so I just put a few things together.'

Madeha closed her eyes.

'I'm sorry I haven't been to visit before now,' continued Loma. 'I didn't know where you were. It's been very difficult finding you.'

'You needn't bother to explain.'

'But I think I should. I want to. I couldn't ask Riaz for help, nor anybody working with him. He'd be furious if they knew I was here. I've had to arrange it through other channels.'

Madeha uttered a cynical laugh. 'So, you've made a special effort to find me?'

'Yes, of course I have. I couldn't just forget about you and leave you to rot in prison.'

'Have you arranged for my release then?'

'No, I haven't. It's very difficult, Madeha. I'm not even supposed to be here.'

Loma looked over her shoulder at the guard, who was standing by the open door. She then looked back at Madeha, examining the injuries to her arms. So, it was true: she was being tortured. The nightmares hadn't been misleading.

She reached out and took hold of Madeha's hand, but Madeha withdrew it, crossing her arms, stony-faced. Loma felt like crying, but she knew she had to keep it together.

'Listen, I need to explain something to you,' she said.

'This should be good.'

'Madeha, I did try to protect you. I argued with Riaz about turning you in. I said we should just deal with it ourselves. But he wouldn't listen. He insisted on having you arrested, and ...'

'And what? And you had to go along with him?'

Madeha issued another cynical laugh and shook her head.

'Yes, I had to go along with him. He threatened to kill me.'

'Riaz has often threatened to kill you, Loma, but he's never done it. What's so different about this time? Why couldn't you stand up to him?'

'It wouldn't have made any difference. Once the *Mukhabarat* were involved, I didn't really have any choice.'

'So, you had to rat on me? Is that it?'

'I didn't *rat* on you, Madeha. I just told them what you'd told me. But I said that you'd been manipulated. I explained that you'd been blackmailed and ...'

'And they listened very carefully, gave you a big pat on the back, and then threw me in jail.'

Loma didn't know what else to say. Madeha's summary wasn't so far from the truth. She had given the authorities her version of the story, and she had indeed been complimented on her loyalty to the system. Riaz had got his promotion too. Why was she making excuses for herself?

'Well, having ratted on me, I can quite understand that you feel guilty, Loma, and it's very nice of you to come and visit me. Thanks for the dates. I think you can go now.'

'Madeha, please don't be angry with me. It wasn't my fault. You put yourself in this situation. I didn't tell you to go off sleeping with Munir, did I?'

'No, you didn't. And I didn't ask you to betray me to the *Mukhabarat*.'

'I didn't betray you. I had no choice in the matter. It was Riaz. Munir sent him the photos and he just went ballistic. I tried to reason with him, but he wouldn't listen. As always, he just did what he thought best.'

'Yes, I know. He's a very important person, and now he's an ambassador. Well, he's done very well for himself out of it. So, I suppose I should be glad about that.'

'He's not an ambassador. What are you talking about?'

'I thought he'd been promoted.'

'Not to ambassador. Who told you that?'

Madeha was silent. She sat with her arms crossed, looking at the scratched table-top.

Loma continued: 'Who told you that Riaz had been promoted?'

'Well, I'm not the only person in here who was once among your circle of friends.'

'Are you talking about Selma?'

Loma was shocked. Just the sound of the woman's name filled her with fear.

'Yes, she's in here. She says you ratted on her too. It seems you have a habit of putting people behind bars.'

'What has she been saying?'

'Just the truth, which is that you saved yourself by giving evidence against me. You said I was part of some huge terrorist network, apparently, and that I'd been plotting for years. They must have been very impressed with you.'

'Madeha, it's not true. I didn't say anything like that. I just said ...'

The guard walked over and stood by the table.

'You've got two minutes left,' he said.

'Well, go away then and let us talk for two minutes,' said Loma.

The guard rapped the table gently with his baton and walked away.

Loma was dismayed. She had hoped that this visit might help to heal the rift between them, but apparently Selma had made that task so much more difficult.

She reached across the table and took Madeha's hands, unfolding her crossed arms. Looking into her eyes, she spoke calmly and deliberately: 'Listen, please believe me. I never betrayed you. Whatever Selma said, she was telling lies. You know her. She'll do anything to cause people pain and upset. She wants to come between us. I would never betray you. You just have to trust me on that.'

Madeha was staring mournfully at Loma, her eyes brimming with tears.

Loma continued: 'Who do you believe? Selma or me?'

After a pause, Madeha shook her head, tears running down her cheeks.

'Do you know what they did to me?' she said.

'No, honey, I don't.'

'If you knew what they did to me in here …'

'What did they do to you, honey?'

Madeha opened her mouth to speak, then closed it again.

The guard came over to the table. 'Time's up now. The visit's over,' he said.

Loma grasped her friend's hands more tightly.

'Listen, Madeha, you've got to believe me. I never meant to cause you any harm. I'm sorry that you're in here, and I hope you can forgive me. I'm going to do my best to get you out, okay? I'm going to get a lawyer or something, and I'm going to get you out.'

'I don't think I can hold on much longer.'

'You have to hold on. You have to be strong.'

'I really don't think I can.'

The guard put his hand on Loma's arm, urging her to stand up: 'Time's up. Let's go.'

Both women were crying now. Loma leaned across the table, enfolding Madeha in her arms, despite the protestations of the guard.

'I'm sorry,' she said. 'I'm so sorry.'

Madeha put her mouth by Loma's ear, as if she were about to whisper something, but no words came out.

Moments later, Loma was being led from the room and back along the dark corridor. She heard Madeha's voice, complaining loudly at something. Then a metal door slammed shut, and the voice was silenced.

Friends in high places

Malaka ran her hand over the fabric of the sofa. It was expensive stuff, stylish but durable, of traditional design but with a chic modern twist. The sofa had probably been made to order, reflecting the fine tastes and high standards of the customer – a man of some importance in Iraq's intelligence apparatus. Not only was the sofa stylish, but also fabulously comfortable, the sort of furniture on which one could happily make love for hours.

She scanned the living room. The décor was impeccable: Persian rugs, lacquer tables, porcelain lamps and original paintings on the walls. A mahogany bookcase boasted dozens of volumes, many of them leather-bound antiques. Music oozed from hidden speakers, and the lights were on low in anticipation of dusk. If this was Hisham's little bolt-hole, Malaka wondered what his family home must look like.

She could hear him mixing the drinks in the kitchen, pouring and stirring and adding ice. Finally, he entered the living room, handing a glass to Malaka, complete with a little red umbrella and a slice of lime.

'Let me know if it's too strong,' he said, 'and I'll add some more soda.'

'I very much doubt it'll be too strong.' She took a sip: 'Wonderful, just right.'

Hisham took a seat in a nearby armchair, sipping at his own cocktail. As he did so, he discretely checked his wrist-watch. Malaka's visit was important to him, of course, but there were only so many hours in a day. The main event was due in half an hour.

He was quite bald on top, his shiny pate edged with neatly cropped grey hair. His moustache was likewise neat, his face regular, verging on handsome. Indeed, if Malaka had been the marrying type, Hisham would have been on her shortlist. Assuming, of course, that he was willing to forego the younger flesh and devote himself entirely to one woman – which seemed highly unlikely.

And one could hardly expect him to be a highly attentive husband. His work was more than a little demanding. In the past two years, he'd been promoted to a new agency tasked with overseeing the work of the other branches of the *Mukhabarat*. He now spent his days monitoring their performance and watching for signs of disloyalty. No doubt this meant long and irregular hours, not to mention high stress levels.

Malaka had first met Hisham many years before, when he was still a lieutenant. She had been sent to provide for his sexual needs, which she'd done willingly. He was business-like but also energetic and brimming with appreciation. Later on, he'd risen to captain, and then to major, by which time, she'd gone into

•

business for herself. Then it was her turn to send out the young flesh. The last she'd heard, he'd been promoted to colonel. She had no idea of his rank now, but she was fairly confident that he was the most powerful of her spooky contacts. Certainly, he towered above the annoying little shits that she dealt with on a weekly basis, those bone-headed runts who gave her orders and demanded results.

Yes, if anybody could help Malaka with her present problem, it was Hisham.

'Thank you so much for agreeing to this little meeting,' she said.

'Not at all, my dear. The pleasure is all mine.'

'Well, thank you anyway. I know you're horribly busy.'

'Cigarette?' he said, opening an old ivory box on the coffee table.

'I have my menthols, thank you.'

'How's business?'

'Oh, not so bad. Booming, actually. I've filled the staffing gaps I was talking about. There are some lovely young things coming through now.'

'Yes, I just adore Colette.'

'Yes, there's Colette, of course. And some beautiful girls from the south who arrived last week. I'll introduce you some time. Very charming to look at.'

'You're really too kind.'

'It's no trouble at all. You're very firmly on my VIP list, and that means VIP service.'

'I'm glad to hear it.'

Malaka grabbed the big glass lighter from the coffee table and lit her menthol cigarette. She drew in a lung-full and let it out, pondering her next line. She was rarely nervous, but this afternoon she was very much on edge. Hisham watched her with cool, intelligent eyes.

'So, to what do I owe the pleasure of your company today?' he said.

'Well, I'm really following up on my message of last week. I believe Colette handed you a note on my behalf?'

'Your note concerning Selma?'

'That's right.'

'Yes, I have some information for you. I've looked into the matter and discovered one or two details of interest.'

'Wonderful, thank you so much.'

'Selma has been sentenced to 15 years in prison, and she'll most likely spend that at Abu Ghraib. There's very little chance of her being released early.'

'Good God! That's a very long sentence.'

'Yes, but she might easily have been given more.'

'What was she convicted of exactly?'

'Gosh, a whole list of things: blackmail, assault, issuing death threats, conspiring against the state. I forget the details, but the list is long.'

'And what about an appeal?'

'Oh, that's quite out of the question. She was tried by a security court. The decision is final.'

'But I can't believe it. She's never done any of those things, so far as I'm aware.'

'Perhaps not, but there are witnesses who swear otherwise.'

'What witnesses? Who has been telling tales?'

Hisham tipped his head back and laughed. Malaka could see the fillings in his teeth.

'I'm afraid I can't tell you that,' he said. 'Such information is highly confidential.'

'Yes, of course. I'm sorry.'

Malaka stirred her cocktail and took a large gulp. She had to be very careful how she approached this topic. She didn't want to land in Abu Ghraib herself.

The music came to an end, and Hisham walked over to the record player. He removed the LP and replaced it with another, setting the stylus down with great care. After some crackling, the voice of Nazem al-Ghazali started up, backed by his orchestra of traditional instruments.

'Something from my era,' said Hisham.

'There's nobody better.'

Hisham took a seat on the sofa next to Malaka and picked up a handful of peanuts. He popped a few into his mouth and began crunching.

'You seem to be pretty fond of this Selma?' he said. 'Is she a very close friend?'

It was Malaka's turn to laugh. 'I wouldn't call her a friend exactly.'

'Then why are you so concerned for her welfare?'

'It's more a matter of practicalities. She's a very useful part of my network. As you know, I assist several of your colleagues with their work, and that requires me to maintain a large network of informants. It has taken me many years to build that network. I pride myself on being able to source all sorts of information, and at times to influence outcomes.'

'And Selma is an important part of that?'

'Yes, very important. She has long been an acquaintance of mine, although hardly a friend. In fact, we've often been more enemies than anything else. But just recently I managed to win her over to my side. She's done some very important work for me, and I anticipate her doing more in the same line. It would be a shame to throw all of that away for the sake of some trifling allegations, particularly if they turn out to be false.'

'Oh, I'm not sure the allegations are entirely false. There are witnesses, after all.'

'Yes, well, she's hardly an angel. But all the same, I can think of several people who might wish to stitch her up for the sake of revenge. She has quite a few enemies. Some of them are bored housewives with nothing better to do than spread false accusations. It's sickening.'

Hisham tipped his cigarette ash and sipped his drink. He wasn't a man to speak unless he had something particular to say. Malaka thought it best not to interrupt his thoughts. He picked up another handful of peanuts and continued crunching.

Finally, he spoke: 'Has she achieved anything of particular significance since she started working for you?'

'Well, she's been pretty useful in checking up on this American diplomat, Jerry Cole.'

'How so?'

'She's been able to apply pressure to his lover, Zelfa.'

'Oh, I see. That's Selma, is it?'

'Yes, and she's been very useful. There's no telling when I might need her again.'

'Well, she won't be needed on that job again. That's all over.'

'What's over?'

'The American. That operation is finished now.'

'Is it really?'

'Yes, his days are very much numbered.'

'Oh, I didn't know that.'

'Your handlers haven't been keeping you very well informed, have they?'

'No, I'm afraid not.'

Malaka felt a sudden flash of anger. When they needed something, they were all over her, showering her with praise and pouring the booze. But when she wanted just a little favour in return, a little tit-bit of information, they dried up. One minute she was a queen, a highly-valued asset in the field, a woman of great power of experience – and the next minute, she was an old whore whose phone calls were not worth returning.

'I'm not really the right person to be asking about this, you know,' said Hisham.

'Yes, I know.'

'You ought to go through your handlers wherever possible.'

'Well, I've tried that, of course, but I'm getting nowhere.'

Hisham sucked a lump of ice into his mouth and crunched it to pieces. As he did so, he gazed at a painting on the wall, apparently lost in thought. It showed an ancient temple in the desert, the stone blocks crumbling amid a sea of sand.

'Of course,' he said at last, 'if it's considered in the interests of national security, a convicted prisoner might be released for operational purposes. One would need some sort of assurance that she'd be put to good use, ideally on an active operation. And she'd have to stay out of trouble; one false move and she'd be back behind bars, possibly for life.'

'I don't see that as being a problem. I have any number of little jobs lined up for her.'

'Well then, perhaps that's the way forward. If you can think of something concrete for Selma to be doing, I'll make some enquiries on your behalf.'

'That would be wonderful. Thank you so much, Hisham.'

'Have a good think about it and get back to me after the weekend.'

'I certainly will.'

Malaka heaved a huge sigh and drained her glass. She could feel the tension leaving her body. She stubbed out her cigarette and lit a new one.

Hisham was smiling as he watched her. He had always admired Malaka's fighting spirit. She seemed like a cat, all sleek and sensuous but with sharp claws always at the ready. Right now, as they sat side by side on the sofa, he felt himself growing aroused. He knew from experience that she was an expert between the sheets. He still recalled their early sexual encounters, when she was still young and fresh. He knew every inch of her body. He glanced at his watch, wondering if there might be time for a little action in the bedroom before Colette arrived.

Malaka guessed his thoughts. She wasn't really averse to the idea, but it would be a shame to spoil his appetite.

'I should probably be going,' she said. 'But to show you my appreciation, tonight's entertainment is on the house.'

'Oh, that's so very kind of you.'

'Not at all. It's the least I can do.'

She walked to the front door. Standing on the threshold, she turned and squeezed his hand.

'Of course,' she said, 'I probably owe you a personal favour at some point, if that would please you at all.'

'That would be very lovely, my dear. I look forward to it.'

'You're most welcome.'

As Malaka stepped onto the street, Colette was climbing out of a car. She looked stunning in her little black, sequinned dress, her fur stole and pearl necklace.

'Give him the full works tonight,' said Malaka. 'Take him to Paradise and back.'

'Yes, Madam Malaka.'

Clutching at straws

Loma hadn't stopped all morning. First, there had been the gardener with his grandson, visiting early to mow the lawn and put in some new, summery flowers. Then a team of painters had turned up to decorate the living room, shifting all the furniture to the middle and covering it with sheets. Then Sadah had started on the bedrooms, stripping the beds, putting mattresses out to air, sweeping behind cupboards. Sadah's cousin had turned up too, going to work in the kitchen, scrubbing out the oven with wire wool.

At first, Loma had attempted to help – or at least to supervise – but finding that everyone knew their job perfectly well, she had decided to start her own project in the study. She wanted to get the place spotless before Riaz returned on Monday. She returned books to their shelves, threw out old magazines, emptied the bins, and took the rugs outside to be beaten. Finally, just before noon, she collapsed in a chair on the patio, covered in dust and feeling just a little dizzy.

Work was good, she told herself. There was nothing to be gained from thinking all the time, particularly when there was no obvious solution in sight. If there was some way to get Madeha released from jail, the answer would make itself known in due course. Gnawing away at the problem would help nobody. The same was true of her marriage. Stressing about it helped nobody; if it was going to fall apart, then it would do so in its own time. For now, she was determined to be a dutiful wife; cleaning the house from top to bottom was a good start.

It had been nearly two weeks since her visit to Abu Ghraib, and the memories were fading. At first, she'd been horrified, unable to sleep. But now it seemed almost dreamlike, as if it had never happened. She would have to do something for Madeha eventually, of course, but not just yet. She could only cope with one thing at a time.

She closed her eyes and thought of her boys. They were still at their grandmother's house, apparently quite content, playing their usual boyish games and shunning homework. The summer holidays were to be enjoyed, and they were certainly doing that. Once more, Loma wondered how they'd cope if she were suddenly to die – or to disappear. And the same conclusion presented itself: they would be sad, but not heartbroken. They would have as good a chance at happiness as any other kids of their generation.

How nice it would be, she thought, *just to drift away and never return.*

'Madam,' said a voice from behind, 'you haven't opened your mail.'

It was Sadah, standing there in her grubby housecoat, a sheaf of envelopes in her hand.

'Thank you, Sadah. I'll look at them now.'

'Would you like a drink?'

'Lemonade please, lots of ice.'

'Right away.'

Loma spread the letters on the table and began to open them, one by one. There were a few bills and an invitation to a fashion show. Also, a note from a cousin, inviting her to a wedding. She hadn't heard from that particular cousin for years, but no doubt news of Riaz's promotion had reached every twig on the family tree.

Finally, hidden within a newspaper, was a small blue envelope bearing untidy handwriting. Loma's heart leapt. She recognized the handwriting as Madeha's, despite the obvious deterioration in style. Normally, Madeha's script was neat and elegant, leaning gently to the right. Now it was scruffy and disjointed, barely legible in places.

Loma tore it open and began to read:

Dear Loma,

I would like to thank you for coming to visit me. It was very kind of you to take the time, and I'm so glad I got to see you again. It's horrible that you had to visit this place. I hope you never have to make the trip again. People like you should never visit places like this.

I have been thinking about everything you said, and I want to give my response.

There is so much to say, and I really don't have the energy to go into everything. But I want to say that I forgive you. It doesn't matter what you did or didn't do. And I don't think I'll ever know for sure anyway. But that's not the point. The point is that I forgive you.

We were always the best of friends. And that can never be changed. That's our history and the past can't be undone.

Anyway, it was my own stupidity that got me into trouble. I should be apologising for all the problems I've caused you. I hope you can forgive me too.

As for my life now, I really don't know what to say. So much has happened to me in here, and I can't begin to describe it. I never imagined that human beings could behave like monsters, but they can. And they enjoy it too. You have no idea what they've done to me, Loma. I don't even want to talk about it, not even to you.

So, I think it would be best if we draw a line and say goodbye. I would rather remember our friendship as it used to be. Dragging you into my life now would just ruin everything. So please don't visit me again. And please don't write to me or try contact me in any way.

Please try to understand.

I'm being moved soon anyway, and I won't be coming back to this
place. I sometimes wish I could fly away like a bird, but of course
that's not possible. I have to be more practical.
I wish you a happy life, Loma, and lots of luck. You deserve it.
Love,
Madeha

Just as Loma finished the letter, Sadah turned up with the
lemonade.

'Here you are, madam. That should cool you down.'

'Thank you,' said Loma, folding the letter and slipping it into her
pocket.

She discretely wiped away her tears and sipped her drink. Sadah
stood watching for a while and then walked away. She knew when
to leave well alone.

* * *

Minutes later, Loma was in her car, driving through the streets at
high speed. She stopped by the usual phone box and dialled a
number.

'Hello,' said Bilal.

'Bilal, it's me, Loma.'

'Yes, I guessed it might be.'

'I have to speak to you, urgently.'

'Well, I'm a bit busy at the moment. I'm driving.'

'Yes, but what about tonight?'

'I can't meet you tonight. I'm out of Baghdad. What's the problem?'

'Is Madeha being moved to a new prison?'

'How would I know?'

'What do you mean? Of course you would know. You put her in prison, didn't you?'

'Loma, I don't follow her case on a daily basis. I'm busy with my own work. I have a lot on my plate.'

'I got a letter from her, saying she's being moved. Where would they be moving her to?'

'Loma, I can't talk now. This will have to wait. I'll call you when I'm back in Baghdad, okay?'

'Bilal, don't hang up. I'm frantic. I can't just sit around waiting. I'm worried about …'

'Look, I'm going to have to go. This will have to wait. I'll call you soon.'

'Bilal, wait!'

The line went dead, and Loma stared at the receiver, open-mouthed. She had a terrible pain in her chest, as if she'd been stabbed through the heart. She felt sick and weak at the knees. She was sweating, her hands trembling. Had Bilal really just hung up on her in a moment of crisis? Had her saviour, the man she'd come to rely on, really brushed her off like some annoying stranger?

She walked back to the car and began driving again, heading automatically for Adhamiya. She felt like she'd been shoved out of an aeroplane without a parachute. She was in free-fall, with no prospect of a happy landing. And her instructor was still in the plane.

She tried to recall the content of Madeha's letter, but all she could remember was the line about being moved somewhere else. Where was she being moved to? What other prisons might house women convicted of offences against national security? She drew a blank, more conscious than ever of her utter helplessness in the face of the security state and its machinations.

Then an idea flashed into her mind: Zelfa was well connected. Or rather, her daughter was. Everyone knew that Nada attended parties with Uday Hussein and his close circle of friends. Perhaps she could ask a few questions? Perhaps she could even pull some strings?

* * *

Loma parked outside Zelfa's house and took a moment to compose herself. She had no idea what she was doing to say, but

480

she had to get the ball rolling somehow. She lit a cigarette and sat smoking for a while, hoping to calm her nerves. Finally, she got out and rang the doorbell.

There was no answer.

She peered through a window and saw the lights on in the living room. There was a huge mess: plates, glasses and bottles on the coffee table; magazines and records on the floor; bins and ashtrays overflowing; blankets on the sofa. Zelfa had never been particularly tidy, but this was going to extremes.

Loma rang the bell again and waited. Getting no reply, she walked around to the side of the house and tried the gate into the back garden. It was open, and she walked through, calling Zelfa's name. The garden was empty, but the patio doors were open, and Loma stepped into the house.

The kitchen was a mess too. It looked like Zelfa had thrown several parties, one after the other, without bothering to clean up.

'Hello! Zelfa?' she shouted. 'Is anyone home?'

There was a bump upstairs and then silence.

Loma climbed the stairs and knocked on the door to the master bedroom.

'Zelfa, are you in there?'

'Come in.'

Loma stepped inside and found Zelfa sitting crossed-legged on the bed, surrounded by shoe boxes, the contents of which had been tipped onto the bedsheets. There was a little doll in the shape of a man, crafted from white cotton, with buttons for its eyes. There was a little-girl's doll too, made of plastic and wearing a white wedding dress. There was a bowl of flower-heads from the garden, several bottles of perfume, and ribbons of every colour. There were strings of prayer beads, and scraps of paper with strange symbols scrawled on them. A candle was burning on the bed-side table, right next to an open bottle of Martini Bianco.

'What are you doing?' said Loma.

Zelfa looked at her in shock, unable to speak. She picked up the telephone receiver, which was cradled in her lap, and spoke into it: 'Listen, Crista, I've got to go. I'll call you back later.'

Zelfa hung up and started returning the dolls and associated paraphernalia to their shoeboxes. Loma took a seat in a nearby chair, watching in amazement. She'd heard of Zelfa's infatuation with witchcraft, but she never thought she'd witness the casting of a spell. The shoeboxes were shoved under the bed, and Zelfa returned to her cross-legged position. She reached for the bottle of Martini and drank deeply.

'Are you alright?' ventured Loma.

'I'm fine, thanks.'

'You don't look alright.'

Zelfa sniffed and blew her nose.

'I've just got a cold, that's all.'

'What's all that stuff in the boxes?'

'It's nothing.'

'It looks like Voodoo.'

'Well, it's not. It's just some dolls I'm making.'

'If you're sticking pins into dolls, don't forget Riaz, will you?'

Zelfa smiled, remembering that Loma had always had a good sense of humour. She'd always been among the kind and reasonable people – and they were rare.

'I wasn't sticking needles into anyone. I was just trying … I was trying …'

Zelfa collapsed sideways on the bed, dissolving in tears. Loma rushed over and put an arm around her.

'He's gone!' said Zelfa.

'Who's gone?'

'Jerry. They put him on a plane and he just went. He didn't even say goodbye.'

'Where's he gone to?'

'Back to America. He's been deported.'

'Deported? Why? What's he done?'

Zelfa didn't reply. She just put her face in her hands and sobbed. Loma waited in silence, occasionally handing over a fresh batch of tissues.

'Well, you'll probably see him again.'

'No, I won't.'

'Why not?'

'If he wanted to see me again, he'd have said goodbye. But he just disappeared. I only found out because Crista's uncle works at the airport. Jerry was told last week that he'd be leaving Iraq, and he didn't even phone me.'

'Maybe you missed his call?'

'I've been alone in the house all week, waiting, and he never phoned. He could have put a note through the letter box, but he didn't.'

'Did you go to his house?'

'No, I never went there. He said it was dangerous.'

'Well, maybe he wanted to get in touch but wasn't allowed. I'm sure the US Embassy has rules about that sort of thing. I know our embassy in London does. Diplomats aren't allowed to just phone people when they want to, especially when there's a diplomatic incident. Maybe he'll get in touch when he's back in American and the dust has settled.'

'Do you think so?'

'Yes, it's possible. The important thing is not to fall apart. Despair really doesn't help at all. I know, because I've tried it many times.'

Zelfa laughed and sat up, blowing her nose once more.

'You're very kind, Loma. I really do need a friend at the moment. I'm going mad.'

'That's okay. Let's go downstairs and get some coffee. You'll feel better.'

'Okay.'

In the kitchen, Zelfa sat at the breakfast bar while Loma set to work. She piled the dirty cups and plates in the sink, washed a few essentials, and finally got the coffee on the stove. As she stared into the blue gas flame, she wondered whether it would be wrong to ask about Nada's high-end connections. Her own concerns about Madeha seemed suddenly far less urgent. Perhaps it could wait another day or two. At the very least, she should wait until Zelfa had sobered up.

Just as she was pouring the coffee, there was a loud screech outside, as if a car had come to an abrupt halt. There were voices and car doors slamming.

'What was that?' said Loma.

'Probably someone hit a dog. They drive like crazy down this road sometimes.'

'I'll go and see.'

Loma left the house and walked through the front garden. Just as she reached the gate, a black Mercedes sped away. Loma watched it reach the end of the road and vanish around a corner. She stepped into the street, half expecting to find a dead dog.

Instead, she found a young woman lying in a heap, as if dumped from a vehicle. She lay face-down on the asphalt, quite still. She was totally naked and smeared in blood.

Loma looked left and right, then up at the surrounding houses. A face was visible at an upstairs window; then it disappeared and the curtains were pulled shut. Further down the street, a woman was standing at her garden gate; she shook her head and went back inside.

Loma bent down and gently rolled the body over.

It was Nada.

Her face was soaked in blood, her nose broken, lips split open. Her eyes were puffy and swollen, like those of a boxer on the losing end of a twelve-round title fight. There was blood everywhere, but the worst of it was down her legs. There were also burn marks from cigarettes. At first, she seemed to be dead, but then she opened her mouth and tried to speak.

Suddenly, Loma was aware of screaming. It wasn't Nada, but Zelfa, who had apparently come out to see the commotion for herself. She stood in the street staring at Nada, screaming at the top of her lungs, hands clenched into fists.

'She's alive,' said Loma. 'She's not dead, she's alive.'

Zelfa dropped to her knees and gathered Nada into her arms, shouting her name and calling for God's mercy. More people had now appeared at windows, and one man had walked to his garden gate. He was watching closely, apparently concerned. Under normal circumstances, the street would have been filled with neighbours – and even strangers – willing to help. But everyone knew what the black Mercedes meant, and they didn't want to get involved.

'Come on,' said Loma, 'let's get her inside.'

She grabbed Nada under the arms, while Zelfa took the ankles, and they carried her into the house. She was lifted onto the sofa and wrapped in a blanket. Zelfa stroked her hair and whispered soothing words. Loma went to phone for a doctor.

She returned two minutes later with a bowl of warm water and a clean flannel.

'I've spoken with my gynaecologist,' she said. 'He'll be here in ten minutes with an ambulance. He'll take her to his private clinic and check her over. He's a great surgeon.'

'Okay, thanks.'

'I'll pay for everything.'

'You don't have to do that.'

'No, I want to. It's the least I can do.'

Zelfa dabbed gently at her daughter's face, cleaning away the worse of the blood. Loma prayed silently that the internal injuries would not prove to be fatal. She watched mother and daughter, reflecting on the vulnerability of these two lambs in a world of wolves.

Whatever friendships Nada had nurtured in high circles were clearly at an end. She had served a purpose for a time, and now the party was over. The sins of the mother had been visited upon the daughter: two birds with one stone.

Nada had been groaning in pain, but now she seemed to be sleeping, soothed by her mother's loving presence. Zelfa planted a kiss on her daughter's forehead and looked up.

'This is my punishment, Loma.'

'Punishment for what?'

'For being happy.'

Loma wanted to say it was nonsense, but she understood perfectly.

Condolences

Riaz was looking very serious this morning as he stood before the long bedroom mirror. He was putting the finishing touches to his tie and picking little specks from his new grey suit. He adjusted his cuffs, admiring the gold cufflinks, a memento of London.

'Give me a brush, will you?' he said.

Loma picked up the clothes-brush and ran it over the shoulders, then down the back and the lapels. The problem, so far as she could see, was dandruff, but she didn't want to say so. On such an important morning, with so much at stake, Riaz might fly into a rage.

'There you go,' she said. 'You look fine.'

'Just fine?'

'You look very smart, Riaz. I'm sure you'll be the best-dressed man in the room.'

'The President may be there.'

'Well, not the best dressed then, but certainly very smart.'

Looking into the mirror once more, Riaz seemed to spy something in the distance. He turned around, eyes pinned on the little bronze statue on the dressing table.

'What's that doing here?'

'What?'

'That bloody statue.'

'Ishtar? I brought her back on the plane.'

'Well, that's very stupid of you. It's an antique, looted from Iraq by some British collector. You can't just carry such objects around without the proper papers. It should be handed over to the National Museum of Iraq.'

'Well, perhaps I'll do that at some point. But for now, it's on my dressing table.'

'It's inappropriate, Loma.'

'Well, it's gives me inspiration.'

Riaz frowned, clearly agitated.

'We shall discuss this some other time.'

'As you wish.'

He looked down at his shiny black shoes and clicked them together.

'Alright, I'm off,' he said, walking from the room.

There was no goodbye kiss, nor any promise to be home in time for dinner. Such pleasantries were ancient history. Indeed, as Loma listened to her husband clomping down the stairs and slamming the front door, she was simply glad that he was gone – out of her life for another day.

She stood at the bedroom window and watched him climb into the back of his official car. The driver got behind the wheel and the vehicle moved away. Was it going to be like this for the rest of her life? Was she really expected to just *cope*?

She moved over to the dressing table and ran her fingers over the little statue, starting at the head and moving down, over the prominent breasts and the curvaceous hips, down the slender legs to the big, square base. Just touching the thing sent a tingle through Loma's body. Perhaps she ought to have been an archaeologist? If only she hadn't married ...

She opened a draw and pulled out a pad of writing paper. Flicking through the leaves, she found Madeha's letter, still in its envelope. She would reply today, no matter what it took, no matter how torturous the process.

She grabbed the statue and wandered down to the kitchen.

'Good morning, Sadah.'

'Good morning, madam. Would you like some more coffee?'

'Tea please, Sadah. I'll be in the garden.'

'Yes, of course.'

Loma took a seat at a little table under a fig tree. The gardener had placed it there over the weekend, saying it would give madam a secluded place in which to read and write. The old man seemed to know her better than her own husband.

She read the letter again. She'd been through it dozens of times, but she still couldn't decide on a suitable reply. On the one hand, she wanted to say that she completely understood Madeha's wishes for a fresh start, and she would respect her wishes, as any true friend would. On the other hand, she wanted to rebel against such a notion, to insist on the importance of their friendship, saying that such a close bond was worth more than life itself, and that they should never give up on that.

She wanted to promise to obtain Madeha's freedom, or at least to strive to accomplish it. At the same time, she didn't want to make promises that she couldn't deliver on. When Madeha had been so honest, so brave in the face of harsh realities, was it right to indulge in false hope?

At the very least, Loma wanted to know where her friend was being moved to. What was this new prison? Where was it located?

Loma opened the notepad at a fresh page. Picking up the pen, she gazed at the flowers as they nodded in the fresh breeze. Ishtar stood on the table before her, no doubt certain of the way forward. If only the little goddess could speak!

Before she could put pen to paper, Sadah turned up with the tea on a little tray.

'Your tea, madam.'

'Thank you.'

'Your mother has telephoned.'

'What did she want?'

'She said to pass on her condolences regarding Madeha.'

'Condolences?'

'Yes, that's what she said.'

'Condolences for what?'

Loma got to her feet, spilling the tea across the writing pad.

'She didn't say any more than that, madam. She said that if you wanted to talk about it, she would be at home.'

* * *

Loma came to a screeching halt outside her mother's house. She grabbed her handbag and the little bronze statue and marched up to the front door. It was her sister who answered, and she looked deathly pale.

'Where are the boys?' said Loma.

'They're at the club with Sulaf and her kids. Why?'

'Where's mother?'

'In the kitchen.'

Loma found her mother hard at work, filleting a large fish. She had blood on her hands and down her apron.

'Loma, darling. Did you get my message?' she said.

'Yes, I did. But what are you talking about? Condolences for what?'

The mother looked shocked. She tried to speak but failed, looking to her younger daughter for help.

'Come and sit down,' said Huda.

'No, just tell me now. What's this all about? Has something happened to Madeha?'

'Come into the living room,' insisted the little sister.

Loma wandered into the living room and collapsed on the sofa. She suspected the very worst. She felt sick and dizzy, her body flooded with pain, hands and feet suddenly cold. She closed her eyes and braced for calamity.

Huda sat down on the sofa and took her hand gently.

'We thought you knew already,' she said.

'Knew what?'

'About Madeha.'

'Yes, but what about her? What about Madeha?'

Loma looked into Huda's face and saw tears welling up.

'She's dead.'

'Dead? How? What do you mean? How can she be dead? She's in prison.'

'Yes, but she committed suicide.'

'That's nonsense. She'd never do that.'

'She hanged herself.'

'Who told you that?'

Huda looked at her mother, who was standing in the middle of the living room, covered in fish blood.

'Selma told us this morning,' she said.

'How could Selma tell you anything? She's in prison. They're both in prison. This must be a joke. Someone's playing a trick on you.'

'No, she's not in prison,' continued the mother. 'She came here this morning to offer her condolences. She said you probably knew about it already, so she just wanted to say how sorry she was. She said that if you needed someone to talk to, she would be there for you.'

Loma jumped to her feet, yanking her hand free from Huda's grasp.

'What are you talking about? Selma can't be out of prison. She's been sentenced to 15 years behind bars. It must have been someone else.'

'How can it have been someone else?' said Huda. 'We saw her with her own eyes. She came in and had a cup of tea.'

'You gave that bitch a cup of tea after she killed Madeha? What's wrong with you people? What on earth is *wrong* with you?'

Loma was shouting now, and both her mother and sister were afraid. They'd seen her losing it before, and they didn't want to see it again.

'Calm down,' said Huda, taking hold of her hand.

'Don't touch me!' shouted Loma, racing from the room.

Upstairs, she took out her little black book and dialled Bilal's car-phone.

'Hello,' said Bilal.

'Bilal, it's you. Thank God!'

'Of course it's me. Who did you expect?'

'I need to speak to you.'

'This isn't the best time, Loma. I'm driving. I've got an appointment in Rashid Street. We can meet there this evening, if you like.'

'No, I need to speak to you now. It's an emergency.'

'Everything's an emergency, Loma. My whole life is emergencies. That's what I do for a living. You'll just have to wait in line.'

'Bilal, listen to me, for fuck's sake! Has Selma been released from prison?'

'Loma, I really can't ...'

'Has she been released?'

'Yes.'

'What? How is that even possible?'

'I can't discuss it now. We can't talk about these things on the phone. Where are you calling from anyway?'

'She claims that something has happened to Madeha. Is it true?'

Loma waited for a reply but there was none, just the sound of the city: car horns, people shouting, the wind blowing through an open window.

'Bilal, are you there?'

'Yes, I'm here. Let's talk about Madeha this evening. I'll see you at 7pm, as usual.'

'No, I need to know! Tell me now!'

'Yes, it's true.'

'What's true?'

'I was planning to tell you that as well, but I've been really busy since ...'

Loma screamed and dropped the receiver. She clutched her head and threw herself onto the bed. She buried her head in the pillow and screamed some more.

The door opened, and Huda stood watching, afraid to enter. Loma launched herself across the room, slamming the door in her sister's face.

'Get out!' she screamed. 'Get out! Get out!'

She sat on the bed, sobbing.

After a while she heard a tiny voice wafting up from the telephone receiver on the floor. Loma lifted it to her ear.

'Listen to me,' said Bilal. 'I know you're upset, and I'm really sorry this has happened, but don't do anything stupid. Just stay calm and we'll talk about it this evening. I'll explain everything. Just don't do anything stupid. Loma, can you hear me? Hello?'

Loma slammed the phone down.

Birthday bash

Anybody watching Loma would have seen an attractive middle-aged woman emerging from a villa, marching briskly along the pavement and turning into her neighbour's front garden. It was hardly an unusual sight in Sabah Street, aside perhaps from the speed with which the ground was covered.

For Loma, however, the short journey to Selma's house was far from normal. For one thing, the fear was gone. As far back as she could remember, she had been afraid of something: getting bad grades at school, failing to find a boyfriend, losing her boyfriend, aborting her unborn child, marrying in haste, being trapped in a loveless marriage, having her sordid past revealed for public examination, and suffering the wrath of Riaz in return.

She had been afraid of Selma's every move, whether it be a new round of malicious gossip, a deliberate public humiliation or a physical confrontation. Her fear of Selma had caused her sleepless nights, anxiety attacks, emotional exhaustion. It has pushed her to the point of conspiring with security officials to have someone locked up in Abu Ghraib on false charges. The fear had ruled her life – and ruined it.

Now, after so many years, the fear was gone.

In its place was a sense of controlled aggression, a total commitment to the task of confronting her mortal enemy and exacting revenge, regardless of the dangers involved. Loma would exact revenge for all the torment she'd experienced over the years, for the manipulation, intimidation and downright cruelty. More importantly, she would avenge the murder of her best friend. Because Loma was quite sure that Selma had pushed Madeha to suicide, whispering in her ear at every opportunity. Such an act of evil could not go unpunished – and Loma had become the vector of justice.

She felt simultaneously calm and exhilarated, focussed and fully charged, like a power cable on the point of completing its deadly circuit. She didn't so much walk around to Selma's house as glide, as if she were some goddess walking on air. Nothing and nobody could stop her.

Standing outside Selma's house, she rang the bell, then immediately started pounding on the door. She stood back and yelled at the top of her voice: 'Selma! Selma, you fucking bitch! Come out here! Selma! Come out here now, you fucking whore! Selma!'

Loma wondered for a moment how she had become so foul-mouthed. Once upon a time, she had hated swearing, but these days it seemed to be second nature. She felt simultaneously empowered and repulsed – as if she were two people, the stronger and more vicious personality having taken control.

She looked through the living-room window but found the place empty, the lights off. There was no movement at the upstairs windows, the shutters closed.

She walked around to the side gate but found it locked. She banged and kicked and shouted some more: 'Selma! Selma!'

Back around the front of the house, she stood among the flower pots and picked up a rock. She was on the point of lobbing it through the living-room window when she heard something. It was music, mingled with voices, chatting and laughing. It sounded like a garden party, and it was coming from Malaka's place.

Loma dropped the rock and marched further along the street, turning into Malaka's front garden. Two waiters were standing there in dinner jackets and bow-ties, sharing a sneaky cigarette. They hid the fag and smiled nervously, but Loma ignored them, stepping through the front door into the house.

There was indeed a party taking place – the sort of casual affair where guests wander between house and garden, sipping drinks and grazing at the luncheon buffet. Jazz music played softly in the background.

She headed through the living room, scanning the faces as she went. Out on the patio, she stopped to survey the garden. There were at least fifty guests, complete with the usual buffet tables, free bar and waiters with silver trays. It was a beautiful summer's day, the sun high in a wide blue sky. The garden was in full bloom.

Then she spotted them: Malaka and Selma, standing at the centre of a huddle by the water feature. The fountain was working at full throttle, sending a plume of water high into the air. A little brown bird was drinking from the rock pool below.

As Loma strode across the lawn, the little group around Selma seemed to be laughing at a joke. A man in a white suit was gesticulating, apparently elaborating on a punch-line. But Selma wasn't paying any attention – because she had spotted Loma.

Their eyes locked at 30 metres, like cold-blooded gun-slingers in the Wild West, triggers on fingers. Everything else melted away: the party, the people, the music. All that mattered was the storm of violence that was about to break.

As Loma closed the gap, however, she realized that she had no definite plan of action. She had been hell-bent on revenge, and that much hadn't changed – but she hadn't reckoned on an audience of fifty highly-civilized, law-abiding citizens at a summer garden party. As more and more heads turned her way, some of them frowning, Loma began to doubt her current mission. Was she really intending to kill Selma in broad daylight? If so, how exactly did she plan to go about it?

I should at least have brought a gun, she reflected.

Before she could get within striking distance, Malaka intervened, stepping boldly forward with a conspicuous display of affection.

She grabbed Loma by the shoulders and planted two big kisses on her cheeks.

'Mwa! Mwa! Loma, you absolute darling! I'm so *very* glad that you could make it. I was worried that you might be too busy, what with your husband's return. Of course, it wouldn't be a party without you. I must get you a drink right away.'

Loma hadn't heard a word. She was still looking at Selma, who was looking straight back at her, a placid smile on her lips. The bitch seemed entirely unperturbed, totally innocent. Butter wouldn't melt in her mouth.

Malaka continued: 'Oh, and you've brought me a birthday present! How wonderful! A birthday really isn't complete without a work of art. And you have such divine taste in decorations, Loma. I can always rely on you where matters of style are concerned.'

Loma looked down and realized that she was clutching the statue of Ishtar in her left hand. She didn't recall having brought it with her, but she clearly had – because there it was, grasped tightly in her slender fingers.

There was a brief silence, during which all eyes were on the newcomer with the bronze statue, and then Malaka burst into action once more.

'Come with me darling,' she said, putting a firm arm around Loma's shoulders. 'I know exactly where I'll put that statue. It can go into my study. I've just had it redecorated. It's all terracotta now. I think an ancient *object d'art* would look wonderful on a shelf.'

Loma found herself being walked firmly back toward the house. Behind her, the man in the white suit had resumed his humorous anecdote. Selma was laughing at full volume.

'It's quite stunning,' continued Malaka. 'Wherever did you get it? No, don't tell me. You got it in London, didn't you?'

'Yes, I did.'

'Well, I'm a great fan of antiquities. That's another thing we have in common.'

Before she knew it, Loma was standing in Malaka's study.

'Just wait here, my darling, and I'll get you a drink. What will you have?'

'Erm ... I don't ...'

'You look like you need a gin and tonic. Wait there, my dear. Help yourself to a cigarette if you wish. They're on the desk.'

Malaka disappeared, click-clacking down the hallway to the kitchen.

Loma set the statue down on the desk and slowly released her grip. She'd been clutching the thing so tightly that there were deep indentations in her flesh. She curled and uncurled her fingers, waiting for the circulation to return.

She looked around the room, which had indeed been painted terracotta. She had never imagined Malaka to have a study, much less rows of antique books and *objects d'art* on mahogany bookshelves. The woman put a lot of energy into seeming classy and civilized, but it was all show. She was a housemaid-turned-whore, and no amount of interior design could disguise the fact. Her enthusiasm for the little bronze statue was no doubt fake, just like everything else.

Of course, she was a successful business-woman now, and that meant a certain amount of administration. If nothing else, she needed somewhere to shuffle papers. The desk was littered with the usual paraphernalia: stacks of bills and receipts, unopened letters, newspapers, a pot of pens, a steel ruler, a stapler, a bone-handled letter-opener – shiny and pointed.

Loma reached for the little mother-of-pearl box and took out a cigarette, sparking up with the large brass lighter. She took a long drag and closed her eyes.

This was madness; she knew it was madness. Yes, she was justified in being upset, but that was no reason to launch on a murder spree. What on earth was she thinking? Maybe she should just chat with Malaka for a while, knock back the drink and disappear? That would certainly be the sensible option. Anger was reasonable; murder was not. It was criminal, insane. And she was neither a killer nor a lunatic.

She looked at the little bronze goddess and wondered whether she should indeed hand it over to Malaka? Maybe it was cursed? Maybe she would calm down once it was gone?

'I'm so sorry to keep you waiting,' said Malaka, sweeping into the room. 'Here's your drink. It's a double. I thought you might need a stiff one.'

'Thanks very much,' said Loma, gulping half the glass.

'You do seem a little bit wound up, my dear. Is everything alright?'

'Oh, yes. I'm fine. Just a little tired.'

'Tired?'

'And stressed. It's been a frantic week.'

'Yes, I can quite imagine.'

Malaka was surveying Loma with her usual close attention, those dark, beady eyes searching for clues. Perhaps she had already guessed Loma's murderous intentions? If so, she had done well to avert calamity. Perhaps, at some point in the distant future, Loma would thank this old whore for saving her from disaster?

The next moment, Loma was hit with a terrible realization. The way things were going, any such future would also involve Selma, because the woman seemed impervious to harm. She had been sentenced to 15 years behind bars, and yet here she was on the outside, swanning around at birthday parties like she'd never been away. She was looking good too, strong and confident. Prison had apparently been good to her.

Loma's eyes locked with Malaka's for a moment, and she couldn't help wondering what role the woman had had in securing Selma's release. Were they really such a tight team these days? If so, could Loma ever defeat one without eliminating the other?

'It really is a lovely piece,' said Malaka, looking at the statue. 'I suppose it's authentic?'

'Oh, yes, I think so. I got it from a little shop by the British Museum. They sell all sorts of little objects. I have a certificate to go with it.'

'Well, that's wonderful. I would like to have the certificate too.'

'Yes, I'll bring it round.'

'Now, where shall I put it?' said Malaka, turning to survey her shelves.

Loma knocked back the rest of her drink, the ice jangling in the glass.

'Oh, you've finished already,' said the hostess. 'You *are* a thirsty girl. I'll get you a fresh one. Don't move a muscle.'

Malaka headed back to the kitchen, and Loma decided that now was her chance to disappear. She had experienced a moment of madness and had a lucky escape. Now it was time to go home. Just at that precise moment, Selma appeared in the doorway, looking elegant in her white silk dress with padded shoulders and a plunging neck-line. Her hair was shorter than usual, cut into a stylish bob, dyed blonde from a bottle.

'I thought I might find you in here,' she said.

Loma froze.

Selma walked slowly across the room, glass in hand, that same placid smile on her lips.

'I didn't know you'd been invited to Malaka's birthday party,' she said.

'I wasn't invited.'

'So, you just thought you'd drop by?'

'Something like that.'

'Well, it's good that you did, because I wanted a little chat with you.'

'Really?'

'Yes, I want to say how sorry I am about Madeha. I know you two were close. It's always tough, losing a good friend.'

Loma looked at the doorway. With just a few steps, she could be out of there. All she had to do was ignore Selma and start walking. Why was that so difficult?

'Of course, it must be doubly tough on you,' continued Selma.

'Why?'

'Well, because you're largely responsible for Madeha being in prison in the first place. You must already be feeling guilty about that. And then she goes and commits suicide … Well, it must be crippling for you. I really can't begin to imagine what you're going through.'

Selma was still smiling as she took a sip of wine.

'I'm actually not concerned for my own feelings, Selma. It's Madeha who suffered the most. And I believe you played a big role in that.'

'Well, you may think what you like, my dear, but the fact is that some people are just not cut out for prison. Now, take me, for example. I thrived in Abu Ghraib. It was difficult, of course, but everything they threw at me just made me stronger. That's because I'm basically a strong and resilient person. Madeha, on the other hand, was a weak person. She was weak before she went in, and she got weaker by the day. It was pretty inevitable that she'd break at some point. It's just the natural order of things: sink or swim. Madeha was a weak-minded individual, so she sank like a stone. It's sad, of course, but hardly worth losing sleep over.'

With this final remark, Selma's smile spread into a grin.

'You're sick,' said Loma. 'You're really just sick and evil. You should have been drowned at birth. I think you're probably possessed by Satan or something. There's no other explanation.'

Selma laughed.

'Well, I may be possessed, my dear, but I'm not pathetic. Unlike you, clinging to your memories of darling Ali, all the while spreading your legs for that fat, ugly husband of yours. You're pathetic, Loma, just like your dead friend. Weak, that's what you are. A weak-minded little coward with no friends. Nobody likes you, Loma, so you crash people's birthday parties, bearing stupid little gifts …'

Selma lifted the statue of Ishtar from the desk, but Loma snatched it away.

'Don't you dare touch this statue!' she said.

Loma was gripping it firmly, like before, only now she held it more like a hammer, ready to strike with the heavy square base. Selma, recognizing the fighting posture, grabbed the bone-handled letter-opener. Taking a step back in her white stilettoes, she pointed the knife at Loma's face.

For a brief moment, they froze – then all hell broke loose.

It was Loma who swung first, bringing the statue round in a wide arc and just clipping the tip of Selma's nose. Selma stepped back and then lunged forward with a slashing movement of her own, ripping through Loma's blue blouse and just scratching her left breast.

Loma swung the statue in a broad arc again, this time with a back-handed motion, much like a tennis champion at Wimbledon. Selma dodged the blow, then darted forward once more, aiming the blade and Loma's eyes. As she did so, however, the heel on her left stiletto snapped.

Seeing her opportunity, Loma brought the statue's square base down on Selma's head, right in the middle, two inches above the hair-line. Selma closed her eyes and screwed up her face, and Loma thought she might collapse.

Instead, she somehow found her balance and lunged forward, the knife raised high overhead, poised for a killing blow.

Loma toppled back in terror, tripping over a little coffee table and landing with a bump on the Persian rug.

So, this is how it all ends, she thought.

Suddenly, there was a white flash and a loud bang – like a car back-firing.

Selma jerked like a puppet on strings, stopped for a brief moment in mid-air, then slumped forward, falling like a sack of potatoes next to Loma. Her eyes were wide open, staring at her mortal enemy. She seemed to be in great pain, but the expression faded as the eyelids slowly closed.

Loma lay still, wondering what on earth had happened. She thought that Selma might rouse herself and continue the fight, but she didn't. Instead, she lay perfectly still, like a sleeping beauty, blood soaking into her white silk gown.

Then a new figure appeared, standing over the body. It was Bilal, looking stressed and sweaty, gun in hand.

Like a bird

Loma watched as the chauffeur-driven car disappeared up the road. Riaz wouldn't be back before dinner time. With Sadah visiting relatives in the south, she was alone in the house. This was her window of opportunity.

She stripped and stepped into the shower, washing carefully from top to toe. The bruises were still sore, as was her cracked rib. Her swollen face was particularly sensitive.

Towelling dry, she stood before the bathroom mirror and gazed at her reflection. During the course of their long marriage, Riaz had slapped her on several occasions. It had been his way of punctuating the end of a heated discussion, asserting his refusal to back down. Before last week, however, he had never punched his wife in the face. Nor had he spat at her, kicked her on the floor, or gripped her neck so hard that she passed out.

A week after the assault, Loma was left with a black eye, slowly turning to brown. She had feared a broken nose, but she was saved that indignity. The split lip was healing too. She thanked God that she had not lost any teeth.

She recalled his comments at the time: 'I'm letting you live because I haven't made the necessary preparations for your death, and people would ask questions. But be warned, if you embarrass me again, I'll finish you completely. Have no doubts about that.'

Riaz certainly had been embarrassed by the events at Malaka's birthday party. The official story was that Selma – a convicted criminal – had launched a vicious and unprovoked assault on Loma. Seeing the wife of an important Ba'ath Party official in mortal danger, Bilal – who just happened to be present – had swung into action, neutralizing the danger. The assailant had been seriously wounded but was expected to pull through. Bearing in mind her previous convictions, Selma was now facing life behind bars, if not execution. That was assuming, of course, that government psychiatrists didn't commit her to a lunatic asylum. Bilal had been officially commended for his presence of mind, although he insisted that he was simply doing his duty. All week, Riaz and Loma had been receiving flowers and messages of sympathy from on high.

Riaz had accepted the condolences with good grace. However, he had a number of urgent questions for his wife. Why had he not been informed of Selma's incarceration in Abu Ghraib and Loma's part in it? Who had secured Selma's conditional release, and if it was Malaka, why was she still going about her daily business, apparently immune to criticism? How was it that Bilal just happened to be at Malaka's birthday party, when they barely knew each other? Was Loma having an affair with the man? What else was going on in Loma's life that she had neglected to tell her husband about?

Loma had tried to answer the questions, but she was apparently less than convincing, and so Riaz had decided to beat it out of her. In a sense, she had been glad when the fists started flying, because it seemed to distract from the questions. She was pretty sure that, had Riaz learned of her infidelity, he would have killed her on the spot. In the end, he seemed content to leave her broken and bloody on the floor, the message well and truly delivered.

Snapping back to the present, Loma headed into the bedroom, dressing in jeans, t-shirt and trainers – her preferred travel attire. Then she took two suitcases down from the big wardrobe and put them on the bed. Slowly and methodically, she filled them with all the clothing she might need for a new life in a cold climate. In went her woolly jumpers, her hats, gloves and scarves, also her rain mac and English umbrella.

Opening a draw, she took out an old photo album and began flicking through the pages. There were her boys at various stages of growth, there was her dear departed father, her beloved mother and sister. And there, tucked away at the back, an old photo of herself and Madeha as teenagers, sitting by the pool with wet hair. Loma planted a loving kiss on her dead friend, then buried the whole lot in amongst the jumpers.

Her diaries went in too, along with a little book of poems, and her one remaining love letter from Ali. She paused to read it, savouring the youthful optimism, the bold expressions of love. How naïve she had been – how short-sighted. And yet, there was no denying that the feelings were real. She'd never felt anything to match it, and probably never would.

Putting the letter down, Loma opened her little black book and stopped at a number with no name. Sitting on the bed, she dialled and waited.

'Hello.'

'Hello Ali, it's me.'

In the ensuing pause, Loma could hear voices in the background. Children were playing and a woman – presumably their mother – was advising caution. A television was also on, cartoons blaring out.

'Ali?'

'Yes, sorry. I'm just a little surprised to hear your voice.'

'It's been a long time.'

'Yes, it has.'

There was another pause, during which Loma heard a dog barking and a child squealing with delight. The mother once more advised caution.

'The children seem to be doing well.'

'Yes, they're full of beans, as usual. How are your boys?'

'Full of beans too. There's no stopping them.'

'I know the feeling. Once the new school term starts, we'll get some peace at last.'

'That's right. Listen, Ali, I phoned for a reason.'

'I thought you might have done.'

'I'm going away.'

'On holiday?'

'Not exactly. I can't explain just now, but I want to say something before I go.'

Loma could hear him breathing into the receiver. She recalled his face as a teenager, young and handsome, suntanned, with three days of stubble. How she'd love him then.

'I'm going away,' she continued, 'but I just want to say, before I go … Gosh this sounds pretty strange, I know, but I wanted to say that I forgive you. Which sounds awful, because you probably don't think you've done anything wrong … which you haven't, in a way. But even so, I was very upset about the way we broke up, and … well, I suppose I resented you for years because of it. The whole thing seemed so unfair.'

'I know. I'm sorry.'

'What?'

'I said I'm sorry. I know that you suffered a lot, Loma. And I know that I was a bastard. I should have done things very different, but … well, I was young and stupid, very stupid.'

'Yes, well, we were both young and stupid, I suppose.'

Ali laughed weakly. Loma could imagine his expression, that self-deprecating smile of his.

'Anyway, I don't want to rake the whole thing over,' she continued, trying to hide the quiver in her voice. 'I just wanted to say that I don't hold any grudges, and I wish you a long and happy life. Your happiness is important to me.'

'Same here, Loma. I wish you a long and happy life. And I really am sorry.'

'I know you are.'

The other woman's voice grew louder, and Loma could hear her asking who was on the phone. Ali told her it was an old friend.

'Listen,' he said, returning to Loma, 'I've got to go now. But thank you for your message. And I wish you a happy journey.'

'You too.'

Loma hung up and bit her lip, doing her best to hold back the tears. She'd done enough crying for one year. In fact, she'd spent much of the past week crying about her boys, who she might not see again for several years. She'd cried herself to exhaustion, and now it was over. This morning she had to be strong.

She got to her feet again and finished her packing: in went the jewellery box, make-up bag and hair-drier. Finally, she reached into a draw and took out a brown envelope stuffed with bank notes of various currencies. This she hid among the sanitary towels. Last but not least, she checked her passport, with its brand-new visa, dropping it into her handbag.

Loma took one last look around, committing the scene to memory. She gazed through the window at the birds, flitting from tree to tree. They were so innocent, following their instincts, chirping madly in a language all their own.

She recalled Madeha's comment about wishing she could just fly away, like a bird. In a sense, that's what she'd done. People said that suicide was the coward's way out, but Loma didn't think so. It took a certain amount of courage to take that final step into the unknown, to embark upon that mysterious journey.

Loma dragged the luggage down to the car. Starting the engine, she began to roll out of the drive, then suddenly slammed on the breaks.

She dashed back into the house. A minute later, she was behind the wheel again, key in the ignition. On the passenger seat beside her was Ishtar – goddess of love and war.

Now she was ready.

Printed in Great Britain
by Amazon